TIME OUT

Marita van der Vyver

Translated by Mari Weeks

Tafelberg

Nessun maggior dolore
Che ricordarsi del tempo felice
Nella miseria.
Dante Alighieri ("Inferno")

There is a town in France called Lunel,
but the one in this novel is the product of
the writer's imagination – as are all the characters.

ILLUSIONS

1

Do you still dream? Are there any dreams left where you are now? That's what I wondered when I awoke this morning.

It was the cold that awoke me, before dawn, pitch dark outside, bitterly cold inside. I lay awake for an hour or two waiting for the first signs of light. At daybreak I went to stand at the window with a blanket round my shoulders watching the trees skate over the frozen ground. Sometimes in the early mornings the trees appear to move. Such a strange dream landscape. This morning some were cloaked in white blossom, skaters wearing white fur. Yesterday morning heavy trails of mist hung over the landscape turning the skating trees into swirling ghosts.

Are you sometimes bothered by ghosts? Little ghosts, surely, like the struggling lemon tree in our front garden. Do they talk to you? Or do they simply stare at you with eyes of innocence and desolation? You are a woman who did the undo-able. How does one do that? That is what I'm trying to understand.

I, who would give everything, my husband, my family, my home, my country, if I could undo that óne deed. Wrench one day out of my life. Not even a whole day, I wouldn't be that presumptuous, I'm not asking for miracles, only for an hour. If I could erase óne hour. Like pressing the key on the computer. *Delete.* Woosh, gone. *Are you sure you want to . . .* Yes! Of course I want a miracle!

It's supposed to be spring. The kitchen calendar announces it, after all it's the second week in March, but out there nature

9

seems to have difficulty reading the message. Only a few fruit trees have cracked the code. Exploding overnight in bright white and pink blossom. The poplars still shiver naked and meagre in the cold. The pale plane trees wait leaflessly for better days. The vineyards look as vulnerable as old men without clothes, bent by the winter, knobbly arthritic bodies, row upon row upon row. No blessed glimmering of green in those resigned rows. The olive trees on the hill behind the house do have leaves, but of course they're never really green. Gnarled forms with silver-grey crowns. Olive trees are born old.

These are the things I've noticed since we've been here.

Trees, clouds, the direction of the wind. Easier to look out, to observe nature, than to face the hurricane inside me. André thinks I see nothing, thinks I stare out blindly because I'm afraid to look into his eyes, but I see much more than during the last month in South Africa. Granted, that last month I could see but was blind, could hear but was deaf, could speak but was mute. Could still feel though. Not with my fingers, they had fallen off, all ten of them. Couldn't even caress my husband's cheek. With my heart is what I mean.

How much heaviness can a heart actually bear? How much shock, sorrow, anger, love can be loaded onto such a fragile organ before it breaks down? Myriam, I wonder how much yóur heart weighs these days.

What I have also noticed, since we arrived here last week, is dust and rubble. André hasn't even really started breaking and building – he's still collecting material, preparing his tools, buying bags of cement every day, piles of floor tiles, nuts and bolts and planks and pipes – and already I wonder how I'm going to survive in a house that's being torn down and rebuilt around me. How I'm going to live with all this dust.

Restoration, my architect-husband calls it.

"It won't be so bad, Hester," he tried to reassure me last

night in bed. (Bed! Mattress on the floor. That's what it is.) "It will keep us busy. At night we'll be too exhausted to grieve."

Speak for yourself, husband of mine. The more exhausted I become, the easier the flow of tears. As it is I've been weeping for weeks. I'm tired of my sorrowful face in the mirror in the morning, fed up with my drooping shoulders and my shuffling old-woman steps, sick of my listless voice. I've had it with crying. And here I go again. Tears dripping onto the kitchen table. *With dull heavy thuds like bullets in the dust. Oh the painful thought. Pack up the moon and dismantle the sun.* Poems don't comfort. Words become meaningless. Even silence is no comfort.

"Whose bright idea was it to come and live in this dump anyway?" my thirteen-year-old son asked the other day at this very table. While a fine cloud of dust drifted from the ceiling onto our plates. By now everything tastes of dust. Meat, greens, bread. Even after brushing my teeth at night, I lie in bed with a dusty tongue. On the mattress, I mean.

The "bright idea" started with me. Mea culpa. I'm the one who has always lived with one foot in France. The French teacher. But I refuse to take responsibility for "this dump". I'd have preferred a building with modern conveniences. Electrical wiring and heating in every room. Hot-water taps in the bathroom. "This dump" was my husband's idea. His Project for our Year in Provence.

That something you dream of for years can turn out such a nightmare.

And then I think of you, Myriam, who must also have dreamed of a new life waiting for you in France. And the nightmare that yóur dream became. Not even a particularly ambitious dream. You only wanted to get away from poverty and violence, have a solid roof over your head, food and clothing for you and your children, a more promising future

11

for all of you. Now you have a solid roof over your head. Exceptionally solid. You get fed every day. They've even given you clothes. But you have lost your children, and with that your innocence, your freedom, probably also your soul.

I feel touched by you, I'm not sure why, maybe only because you're also a woman of Africa. Because you're also caught up in a European nightmare. You cling to me, with fierce dirty black hands, ever since I heard about you last week on the radio. Yesterday I even went to buy a newspaper, for the first time in weeks, because I wanted to read more about you. Not that I learnt much.

Your name is Myriam. Myriam Soro from the Democratic Republic of Congo. Young – unbelievably young! – with black holes where your eyes should be. No emotion on your smooth face. Silent as the grave. As all the mass graves in Africa. Incomprehensible to the French legal system. An incomprehensible savage. Not Rousseau's noble savage. Not you.

Think of Myriam, I say to myself. Think of Myriam Soro and count your blessings, Hester Human. I may be sitting in a hovel, sleeping on the floor and choking in the dust as I drink my morning coffee, I may not be able to have a hot bath at night, but I can walk out of here if I want to. Of course I can. No bars to stop me. If only I could raise my sorrowful body out of this chair, I could take a few steps to the front door, stroke the wilted branches of the little lemon tree, hear the blue wooden gate in the high wall click closed behind me, feel the cold air pinch my nostrils as I climb the hill, breathlessly past the rustling olive grove, past the deserted vineyards and the overfull cemetery, along the winding path to the top cherry orchard.

From there I can look out over the clay-tiled roofs of this stony village, the round tower of the former castle, the ruins of two other towers of the same castle, the rectangular church

12

tower with the clock that chimes every half hour. And beyond, over the whole outstretched valley, grey and bare so early in spring, but soon a verdant garden, splashed with green, purple and yellow – something to look forward to! isn't it? – with silver flashes of the river in the distance. Other villages all over the valley, more tiled roofs, more castle towers, more, more, more.

In Europe there is always more, it seems to me. In Africa, never enough.

From there I'd be able to look out and count my blessings. If only I could lift my body out of this chair.

My daughter is standing in the kitchen doorway looking at me. Reddish-blonde curls tangled as always, cheeks rosier than usual, as if she has been running about outside. Come in, I want to say to her, come in out of the cold, my love.

"Mommy, why do you cry all the time?"

I don't trust my voice to answer her. Just open my arms to bring her closer, to gather the almost six-year-old body onto my lap. She is no longer plump and soft as a teddy bear. She has more bumps and angles now. My baby who is no longer a baby.

She shakes her head with a sly smile. "First stop crying. Then I'll come and sit on your lap."

Which of course starts me bawling all over again.

⤞⤝

André tries to gauge Hester's frame of mind by studying the slump of her shoulders, the droop of her neck, the distance from her forehead to the kitchen table. As a weatherman studies the wind and clouds, so he studies his wife's body these days to predict her moods. Mostly rainy. Sometimes thunder and lightning, but more often just a disconsolate drizzle. Wet

13

and cold, that's what his once sunny wife has become over the past few weeks. Wet and cold with clouds in her grey eyes. At least, that is the front that he observes. He can only surmise about the scattered storms in her interior.

But today her forehead is a fraction higher, her neck not quite as listlessly bent as yesterday. Yesterday was a low point. Literally and figuratively. Her nose almost floated in her coffee. This morning there is at least a suggestion of tension in that slender neck. Muscles straining to resist gravity. A miracle of engineering ingenuity here before him. That a bridge can look so fragile and yet be so strong. That is how he felt the first time he stood before the Pont du Gard near Nîmes. Quite disconcerted.

Perhaps he should suggest that they drive in that direction once again to look at the antique aquaduct, like long ago, before they had children. Perhaps it will remind her of happier times. Lift the clouds in her eyes for a few moments.

That's all he can hope for.

Take it one day at a time, the therapist in Cape Town suggested. Live from day to day. Since arriving in France, he has found that even a day is too much to handle. Too many emotions bottled up. After a few hours everything becomes too heavy, like a mat soaking in a bath; you can't lift it out to hang it outside, you don't know how you'll ever get it dry again. Since they've been here, he has lived from moment to moment. A few moments of clarity in Hester's eyes, a shadow of a smile at the corners of her mouth, then he feels as though he's achieved something.

From moment to moment. It makes you look at the world differently. Never before has he been so aware of the transitoriness of everything around him. Blink and it's vanished. Blink, over. Blink, gone.

Just another reason to visit the Pont du Gard. It has been

14

there for two thousand years. The opposite of impermanence. Not eternal, no, sooner or later the whole thing will probably collapse, but still, exceptionally durable. Look, Hester, he would like to say, not éverything is futile, is it? Not everything always crumbles to dust. Not immediately.

His involuntary sigh makes her look up from her cup of cold coffee. He quickly draws his lips into something that feels like a smile. Not that it matters much what he does with his facial muscles. Her clouded eyes look right through him.

"I'm going to the market," he says. "Don't you feel like coming?"

She pretends to consider it for a moment. Shakes her head as if truly regretful.

"Not this morning," she says. "There are still a few things . . . things I have to do here."

Like what? he wants to ask. Count your tears?

"I still haven't finished unpacking my suitcase," is her excuse.

"But you can do that this afternoon. Come on, come with me. We'll get something nice for supper. What do you feel like?"

Wrong question. His wife doesn't feel like anything. She can no longer be enticed with food. Look how thin she has become. Look how lank her hair is. Look how rough her hands are on the coffee cup.

"You choose something," she says.

"I was thinking of some fresh fish. What do you say?"

His wife says nothing. Just nods like an obedient child. Looks back at her rough hands.

André feels his throat constricting, as if she has clasped those hands around his neck. As if she wants to strangle him slowly, very slowly. He can't reproach her for her rough hands, her oily hair and her dirty cardigan. It's an incredible struggle to stay clean in this house, to wash your hair and your body in a plastic basin, with water that has to be heated

15

on a gas stove. And the icy air dries you out from top to toe like a piece of biltong. Emile's skin is so dry that it has split round his thumbnails. André noticed the small superficial cuts when he dropped the child off at the bus stop this morning. Emile didn't complain – like his mother he is also talking less and less – but he picked his school bag up exceedingly carefully. Thumbs sticking straight out in the air. At that moment André had felt the same grip on his neck as now, watching the child's mother.

"Anything else we need?" he prods again. "Vegetables? Cheese?"

She shrugs and waves in the direction of the food cupboard.

"I don't think so. You have a look."

He has already looked. Made his list long before. Was only trying to get a reaction, a suggestion, a request from his wife, proof that she still has a will of her own.

Not today.

"Right. Then I'll be off. Won't be long."

What is he dóing to his family? This is the question he tortures himself with daily. As if they haven't all suffered enough.

"André," says his wife as he reaches the front door, her voice preoccupied as though she is talking to her coffee cup. "I'm sorry. About everything."

He stands still for a moment, frowning, his hand on the doorknob. As he closes the door behind him he wonders whether he hasn't just imagined hearing her voice.

That's what happens when you live from moment to moment. He walks past the dead and neglected plants in the front garden. Your memory becomes very short. Clicks open the blue wooden gate. You don't just live from moment to moment. You also forget from moment to moment.

⌒⌒

16

Now you've dug a hole for yourself, Hester Human. If you still haven't unpacked your suitcase when André returns from the morning market, he'll give you that disappointed look again. As if you're a teenager who simply refuses to listen to well-meant parental advice.

As if I've become Emile, I sometimes think.

All my thirteen-year-old son tries to do, is to melt into the thick stone walls of this house. To be as little trouble as possible to anyone. The mother causes enough trouble under this roof. The mother is a Problem Case, demanding everyone's attention. There simply isn't room for the unpredictable moods of a normal teenager.

Just occasionally, a flickering. "Whose bright idea was this?" Sulky. Rebellious. Fed up. "This dump". But then he looks at me, the Problem Case, and his boy's face changes instantly to an adult mask, a blend of guilt and remorse and powerlessness, all equally unsuccessfully suppressed. And then without another word he will eat his dusty food.

My child to whom I can offer no comfort.

The other one sits on the wooden floor under the window. The light shines through her hair, colouring her curls pink. Strawberry blonde is what this shade is called. Strawberries and cream. My berry-love.

Like me, she is looking at the large red suitcase lying open on the bedroom floor. Bedroom? Have I ever actually slépt in this room? Probably last year when we spent a few days squatting in the house, when it was all still a big adventure. If we had only known. My bed is a mattress, my wardrobe a suitcase. My heart is in the sea, my child on the moon. Low on the ground I've been living since last week. Mean as a snake. Touch me and you're dead. Mother Snake. The grandmother of all fallen angels.

Clothes spill out of the suitcase like sponge rubber from a

torn cushion. Sweaters, scarves, socks in many colours, bras and tiny lace panties, mostly black, T-shirts, jeans, slacks, a few summer dresses. Can't believe that it will ever again be warm enough to wear a sleeveless dress.

André's case has long been unpacked, his clothes in a tidy pile on temporary shelves rigged up in the corner, three hangers with shirts and trousers on a hook behind the door. Even Emile's case is unpacked. André helped him the other day. Offered to help me too. As I said. As if I were an untidy teenager needing a firm parental hand. I fended him off. I will get round to it. Patience, husband, patience. He gave me that withering look. Branding me with his disappointment.

In my daughter's eyes I read something else. Curiosity as to how I'm going to clear up this mess. Pleased that the tables are turned this time? In Cape Town I was always nagging her to tidy up her toys.

What will happen if you have to get up to wee in the night? You could break your leg falling over those toys in the dark!

I never fall over my toys, Mommy. I know where everything is.

Well, I don't. If you call me in the night I could come a real cropper on this floor.

You won't fall, Mommy. I'll tell you where to step.

Don't argue, Manon. I'm waiting for you to tidy it all away.

But tomorrow I want to play some more. Then I'll have to unpack it all again.

To silence her, I'd then say: Tomorrow is the day-after-tomorrow's yesterday. Now you have to put everything away.

Tomorrow is the day-after-tomorrow's yesterday.

I pull everything hugger-mugger out of the suitcase and throw it in heaps on the mattress. Now the room is even more of a mess than before. But the case is empty. Mission accomplished.

"But Mommy, you're cheating now!" Manon exclaims.

"Says who?" I hold out my hand to her. "Let's go and put the case in the storeroom."

She gets up reluctantly.

"Will you tell me the story of the house again?"

"Again?" I pretend surprise.

"Again," she laughs. "Again and again."

"Long long ago, in a far country," I begin, while struggling down the steep staircase with the case that feels like a small-ish coffin in my hands. An empty red coffin for a child. She follows, subdued. With stories, I could always get her to do anything. "A rather tumbledown house, hundreds of years old, that had stood empty for a long time. Neglected and lonely, like a lost dog that no one wants to adopt, that's how the house looked. And then one day a man and a woman passed by and they could see beyond the outer neglect, right into the heart of the house . . ."

By this time we've reached the first floor where the children's bedrooms are next to one another off a narrow passage. The bathroom, if you could call it that, is opposite: a vast cold space, probably also a bedroom once, with an old-fashioned bath on claw feet, a dripping tap and a rather ancient bidet. A tail-bath, I explained to Manon. A bath for your bottom, giggled Emile – last year, when he still giggled.

No toilet. That is in a dark little room hidden behind the kitchen, next to the storeroom. André grumbled that he would never understand the French's anal obsession. After all, wasn't it more important to have a toilet – an easily accessible, clean and convenient place to pee! – than to be washing your behind all the time?

Maybe the French just like peeing outside, teased Emile. Like you, Dad.

Not in the middle of the night at minus three degrees,

rejoined André. Then he wants a toilet. As close as possible to his bed.

"And then they decided to adopt the house," says Manon alongside me. By now she knows the story by heart. "To change the sad house into a happy house."

"They knew it wouldn't be easy," I continue as we take a wider staircase to the ground floor. "They knew it would take hard work, lots of sweat and stamina."

They didn't know how many tears it would cost. There were so many things that they didn't know.

"But they were full of courage and plans," Manon prompts when she sees the desperation flickering in my eyes. These days she recognises that little flame, often before I myself am aware of it, and immediately begins quenching for all she is worth. Keeping her voice cheerful, laughing too loudly, pulling faces, anything to prevent a conflagration. "Weren't they, Mommy?"

We walk through the kitchen and the large black hole which will hopefully one day become the living room, past the hidden toilet, to the storeroom. There is no window here, only a square opening high in one wall with bars in front, no pane to keep the wind out, no sunbeams ever penetrating here. This is the shady side of the house. The coldest, darkest room in a cold, dark house. The freezer room, Emile calls it. Our own walk-in refrigerator. Like at a butcher's. Or a morgue.

"Go on, go on," begs Manon. "Tell about all the plans."

I dump the red suitcase there and turn round quickly. Close the door firmly behind me. Forget about it. Don't look back, don't look forward. Just stay with this moment. My daughter blurs in front of my eyes.

"Another day," I say to her.

Now I can't see her at all. I'm bawling again.

⌇⌇

Emile stares through the window of the bus at the blue mountains in the distance. Some of the peaks still have snow on them. He wonders if it will ever melt.

Spring is here, oh spring is here, Life is skittles, life is beer. As his mother always sings. Used to sing. Other years, other springtimes. He can't remember when he last heard her sing.

Spring! Bah! Just another story they spun him. Just look what the cold does to his fingers. Full of cracks like crackle glaze on porcelain. Too sore to write properly at school. Now his father comes with the bright idea that he should wear gloves like a bloody girl. Hell no, forget that, he told his father, he'd rather have chapped fingers.

The vineyards flashing past the window are bare and brown. The villages through which the bus passes seem just as bare and brown. A few stone cottages clinging to a hill like flies on a turd. A church, a café, a square with leafless trees where old men sit on park benches. Sometimes a few playing with iron balls in the feeble winter sun. Nothing else ever happens in such a village, of that he is certain.

More bare vineyards.

Whose bright idea was it anyway? His mother's of course. Since he can remember, she was always going on about "a year in the French countryside". His father's too, because his father always slipstreams his mother's ideas, like a bike behind a lorry. His father could never say no to his mother.

An elderly woman next to him touches his arm and asks him something. He shrugs and dulls his eyes.

"*Parle pas francais,*" he mumbles.

She glares at him suspiciously. Printed scarf tied under her chin, a few stringy grey hairs hanging out, face like a potato. She looks like an illustration in one of his sister's nursery books. The witch in the woods. The man-eater's mother. The devil's grandmother. She points to his watch. He holds his wrist close to her face so that she can see the time for herself. Thanks, says the old witch.

He can't blame her for looking at him askance. He doesn't look like a tourist, he looks like a French kid going home from school. He's sitting next to her with a heavy rucksack of books on his lap. And then he tells her he doesn't speak French.

He does speak a little French – enough to tell someone the time, anyway – his mother saw to that before they came here. Francophile. That's what she calls herself. He struggled to remember the word until he realised that it's almost like "paedophile", which everyone knows these days. "Phile" means to like something. To be mad about something. His mother has always been mad about France. She even studied for a while in Paris when she was young. After that she taught French at a high school in Cape Town and taught her own children French songs and rhymes. *Petit doigt, es-tu là? Me voilà.* He can count, *un deux trois*, name the parts of his body, *la tête la main le pied,* the days of the week, *lundi mardi mercredi.* But a few nursery rhymes and a mouthful of French words don't equip him to suddenly start going to school in French!

His father had pleaded and flattered and threatened, but he had dug in his heels. It was bad enough that they dragged him to another country against his will. There was no way they'd get him to go to a French school, he told his father, except by dragging him by the hair to class and tying him to a desk with thick ropes.

Don't tempt me, his father growled.

In the end he was enrolled in an international school in Avignon, where all subjects were taught in English – except of course French, which he hates with a resentful passion. He feels as if he is becoming the opposite of a francophile – what would that be? – just because the language is being forced

22

down his throat all day. That certainly isn't what his mother wanted.

But then, well, his mother.

The school costs a pile of money and his father complains that as it is they don't have enough money for this year in a foreign country. Everything they inherited has to go into the house. But that isn't his problem. He thinks his father is stupid to pour all of his inheritance into a dump of a house in a country village. He could at least have used some of it to build a swimming pool at their Cape Town house.

The other problem with the school in Avignon is that he has to spend two hours each day in a bus. And not even a school bus. The school bus that the other children in their village catch in the mornings only goes to the nearest French high school. No, it's an ordinary bus, this one, full of sullen grown-ups and crying babies, stopping at every little town to drop off or pick up passengers. Among the passengers there are always a few old ladies with headscarves and potato faces.

More bloody vineyards.

"It's only a year, son," his father had consoled him every morning last week, while they waited in the car at the bus stop. "You won't believe how quickly it will pass."

"Only a year! That's forever, Dad. My pals won't even recognise me any more when we go home!"

"That's possible. At the rate you're growing now, in a year's time you'll be about a head taller with a deep voice and a wild beard."

He didn't even smile at his father's little joke.

"You could have left me in Cape Town. I said right from the start I'd rather go to boarding school than come here."

"We'd have missed you too much."

"No, you wouldn't," Emile said scornfully. "It's 'only' a year, you know."

23

His father glanced down, fiddled with the radio controls till he found a station with classical music, and looked up with pleading eyes.

"If things had been different, we might have done it. But not now. Not after everything that happened."

Everything that happened. That's what everyone says every time they want to talk about that terrible day. Or don't want to.

Especially don't want to.

"We need you, son," his father said. "Your mother needs you very much."

"Mom doesn't even see me! Mom is somewhere else, on another bloody planet!"

His father turned up the piano music. His mother believes his father is addicted to music like other people are to chocolate, but Emile is beginning to suspect that it's more than an addiction. It's also a kind of wall that he builds around himself. Every time they get to "everything that happened" his father gets down behind that wall.

They saw the bus coming from a long way away, through an avenue of bare plane trees, behind the *boulangerie* and the *boucherie* and the *épicerie*. More French words that his mother had taught him. Bakery. Butchery. Grocer's shop. Right away his father straightened up behind the wheel. He couldn't wait for Emile to get out of the car.

It's a strain for both of them, this chatting in the mornings in the car, even though it's the only chance they still get to talk. When his mother is present, they only open and close their mouths. Sounds come out, words come out, but no meaning: Pass the salt, please. The radio says it will be warmer tomorrow. I can't find a clean pair of socks. I need a compass for maths.

As soon as it's warmer and stays light a little later in the

24

afternoons, says his father, then Emile can ride to the bus stop on his bike. It's less than three kilometers from their house in the village of Lunel to the bus stop in the next town, and most of it level road. Wouldn't it be better if Emile could do his own thing in the afternoons, says his father, if he didn't have to come straight home in the afternoons after the bus dropped him? If for instance he wanted to go to a friend or such.

What friend? wonders Emile. The children at the international school all live closer to Avignon. And he can't make friends with the children of Lunel if he doesn't go to the same school as them. He takes the bus early in the morning and only returns home in the evening. But maybe a bike is not such a bad idea, he thinks, then at least he doesn't have to sit and argue with his father every morning.

"You must be patient with your mother," his father had said that morning, moments before the bus stopped. The other passengers were already waiting on the square. A fat woman with a baby, a man with a beard, two old ladies. Of course. He'll never get away from old ladies. "It's the worst thing that has ever happened to her."

"It's the worst thing that has ever happened to any of us," Emile said. "She isn't the only one who's having a hard time."

His father turned the music up louder, filling the stuffy interior of the car with piano notes crashing like thunder and wind instruments flashing like lightning, a whole storm of sound pouring over them.

"She's a mother," he sighed.

And you're a father, Emile wanted to exclaim. I'm a brother! But his father looked so miserable that he kept quiet. Just said goodbye abruptly and slammed the door hard behind him.

The bus is travelling through another bare, brown village. With a last suspicious glance at him, the potato face beside him begins to shuffle slowly to the door. A limp basket hangs on one arm. A baguette and a bunch of leeks stick out of the top. When the bus stops, she climbs down the step grunting and groaning.

Emile stares at her through the window. She puts the basket on the ground, pulls her coat collar up round her neck, tightens the headscarf under her chin. Probably feeling the cold, poor thing. On an impulse he waves at her. To his amazement she waves back, just before the bus pulls away.

Can you believe it. He managed to make friends with someone. An old lady in a headscarf.

☙❧

"Good news," says André at the table, after he'd cleared his throat to get everyone's attention. "The plumber is coming next week. Then we'll be able to lay the pipes to the bathroom – and at the same time also to the upper floor for the smaller bathroom that we'll build later – and install the geyser. Hot-water taps, an outlet pipe for the washing machine, all those things. That should make our lives a little easier."

Pleased, he sits back in his chair waiting for a reaction from someone. The children say nothing, just chew unenthusiastically on the fresh salmon and little red potatoes that he bought at the market this morning. He steamed the salmon so that it is soft and juicy and rosy as twilight on our blue plates. He dripped melted butter and sprinkled fennel seeds on the potatoes. He sees that we eat well in this house. He sees to everything in this house.

"I'm pleased to hear that," I say.

"Just as well I started telephoning from Cape Town to find someone otherwise we'd have waited for wééks."

"What would we have done without you?" I ask.

It sounds sarcastic. I hadn't meant it like that. I really don't

26

know how we would survive without him. He is the one who sees that the children get to school, who does the housekeeping, who shops and cooks. All the traditional women's tasks I leave in my husband's capable hands. So that I can grieve undisturbed. I do help a little with the dishes and the laundry, though. It comforts me to scour a saucepan, to scrub dirty jeans and socks, till my knuckles are raw and my arms heavy as lead. Probably a sort of self-punishment. Once the plumber has been, we'll be able to use the washing machine and the dishwasher. What will I do then to torture my body?

You know all about that, Myriam. No court can punish a mother the way she can punish herself. No prison can confine your feeling of guilt or your miserable longing. There are no bars strong enough, no chains heavy enough, no hole deep enough.

I wish I could talk to you. Or just sit with you. Hold your hand. All day long I write letters to you in my head. You're the only person with whom I've really communicated this past week. You and my daughter. All other people feel unreachable, as if I'm looking at them through one-way glass, no way to make contact.

"I thought we might as well start with the bathroom." André puts a piece of salmon and a bit of potato on his fork, chews with concentration before he continues. "If we can just clean our clothes and ourselves on a daily basis, the house may feel less like a labour camp."

He breaks my heart. He tries so hard to cheer us up. To generate a little enthusiasm for his Project

"Will there be a toilet in the bathroom?" asks Emile. "Or do we have to go on peeing in the bidet at night?"

"Of course there'll be a toilet," André assures him. "It is one of the most urgent needs in this house. A place where the most urgent needs can be met."

Still making jokes, playing with words, giving our miserable gathering a semblance of normality. My urgent needs have nothing to do with the body, husband of mine. It's my soul that is in urgent need. No word game can change us into a happy family.

"We're going to buy the toilet next week," he tells Emile. "Mom and I. The toilet, the basin, the taps and so on. I'll rent a truck, then we can buy beds and cupboards for the bedrooms at the same time. At that second-hand shop where I was the other day."

Now he looks at me at the other end of the table, over the bunch of tulips that separates us. The flowers he also brought from the market this morning: Look, Hes, the tulips are out. Spring is here.

I suspect the flowers were grown in a hothouse, but I didn't want to contradict him.

He tries so hard.

"They have the best selection I've seen in this area," he says to me. "And the prices are very reasonable. I'm sure we'll find something we like."

We're sitting at a small round table. If we each stretched our arms, we would be able to touch hands over the tulips. Even so, it feels as though I'm sitting on the moon, looking down at him.

"Are you going too, Mommy?" Manon asks, surprised. "With Daddy to the shops?"

"Your dad insists," I mumble.

"Sorry, I didn't hear that," says André, fork stopped in the air.

"No, nothing," I say and fill my mouth with fish.

As if I care a hoot what the toilet I sit on looks like! As if a nice bed at night will make me sleep any better. Earthbound things, that's what I think of furniture and tulips and salmon, of all my husband's pathetic efforts to draw me back.

28

Once upon a time things like that probably were important to me. I suppose I had an aesthetic inclination. Wouldn't really manage without, being married to an architect. It's his job, after all, to design attractive spaces where people can live comfortably. We liked surrounding ourselves with beautiful things, not necessarily luxury items, but utilitarian things that were cleverly designed and well made. We always had fresh flowers in our house and good food on the table.

We were never wealthy, my husband was too philanthropic for that. He wasn't keen on glamorous commissions, he was more interested in planning more modest buildings for more modest people, structures that would make a real difference to the lives of the users. Community centres and nursery schools, clinics and low-cost housing. The only really selfish thing he ever did in his career was to take this year off to create a holiday home for his family. And even that he did more for his wife than for himself. Still, we've always had enough money to make our little corner of the earth aesthetically pleasing.

Now it just doesn't seem important to me. I've been living on the moon for weeks now, my child and I, from where I look down on all this inexplicable mundane scrambling.

꩜

At least since last weekend it's been a bit warmer outside. A little spark in the air, as if spring is winking at nature, caressing the ground, teasing the plants and provoking both man and beast with vague promises. Here she comes. There she goes. Flirt.

And considerably warmer in the house. The electrician followed hot on the heels of the plumber. My excellent husband's excellent arrangements. Applause, please. While André was helping the plumber to lay the pipes to the bathrooms, the one that already exists and the one that still has to be created, the electrician and his helper installed power points in all the rooms. For the past three nights we've slept next to electric heaters.

And tonight, barring a catastrophe, I shall be able to soak in a hot bath for the first time in more than three weeks. André and the plumber are still having a last look at the pipes, turning on the taps, testing the water pressure. But basically the bath is ready to be inaugurated. Well, not quite an inauguration. It's an ancient bath on claw feet that had been used for decades, probably in another home before it landed up in this improvised bathroom. It's stained brown on the inside, its enamel is chipped and who knows how many naked bodies have lain in it. When we happened on this neglected house last year during our holiday in France, we did consider buying a new bath, but we both prefer old things to new. André decided rather to restore the old bath – although it isn't one of the most "urgent needs" on his list. As long as we have hot water, he reckons, we can use the old stained and chipped object for the time being.

I have my own reasons for wanting to keep the bath. I have a memory of a smooth soapy, wriggly child's body in the bath, eyes shut tight, soap suds in the hair, a giggling mouth. *Mother's child, Mother's tousle-haired child.*

Last year after we'd decided to buy the house, we camped in the place for a few days. Sleeping bags, torches and candles, meals on a little portable gas stove. Or a braaivleis fire outside. It was summertime, it was fun, we were all excited about the adventure that lay ahead.

André wanted to feel how the house breathes, as he put it, before he tackled his restoration project. He believes in showing respect for the past of any old building that you want to change. You have to know why the front door was placed here and not there, why the windows look out this way, why the fireplace was built in that particular corner, where the sun shines in at what hour, from which quarter the wind mostly blows, what the rain sounds like on the roof, whether it pelts down or sighs. My architect-husband believes that our fore-fathers knew what they were doing. Just look at the Roman bridges around here, the Romanesque churches, the medieval castles that stand to this day. Even the simplest farmhouse is practical and perfectly planned. The thickness of the stone walls that always remain cool in summer and yet conserve the warmth of the sun for the dark winter months ahead. The angle of the roofs, steep enough for rainwater to run off easily, flat enough for the clay tiles to cling to. The blind northern facades, no unnecessary openings for the relentless mistral wind to blow through. All these things my husband explained to me.

But to holiday in a derelict country house in summer is not the same as coming to live in the same house at the end of a long winter. In summer you can manage without hot water and heating, hang your clothes outside to dry in the sun, eat under the stars at night. We were not prepared for the cold, the dark, the dust, the cooped-up feeling that has gripped us in the past three weeks. It no longer feels like an adventure. It feels like deprivation.

Never have I looked forward to a hot bath so much.

Sleeping on a bed for the past few nights, next to a heater, has admittedly made a difference to my state of mind. I hadn't thought it would. I hadn't thought that anything could inter-rupt my tears for long enough to allow me to walk out of the front door on my own. But yesterday I got up from the kitchen table, got up out of my rags and my filth, in a manner of speaking, and walked to the top cherry orchard on the hill. The orchard looked like a mass wedding, hundreds of brides in

31

lacy white waiting for their bridegrooms. I buried my nose in a branch of blossom and thought of Tchekov. Of his cherry orchard. Of the quiet despair of his characters.

My husband was right. Isn't he always? The body is a mindless pet. Keep it clean and healthy, give it food and warmth and a comfortable place to sleep, that's all it really wants. The body isn't bothered with the soul. The body doesn't feel anything for metaphysical questions and spiritual pain. The body has its own needs, is wholly selfish, and in extreme circumstances can drive one to the most unthinkable deeds.

Speaking of the unthinkable. Nothing more in the papers about Myriam Soro. Everyone seems to have forgotten about her and her appalling story – at least until she has to appear in court in a few months.

In the meantime other ghastly stories are told daily, in the newspaper, over the radio, on TV. Last week when my husband bought the beds, he also bought a second-hand TV set. An ugly little grey monster that immediately disturbed the peace in our home. The argument went that it would help him and Emile to improve their French. The real reason, I suspect, is that it gives us all something to do in the evenings – besides staring accusingly at one another. Now we don't look at one another, we all look at the TV screen in the kitchen. In the corner above the refrigerator, that's where the little monster has made its temporary nest.

I suppose I can't say the peace has been disturbed, because peace has never really reigned in this house. Rather a sort of dull resignation brought on by a sorrow too great to absorb, a voluntary withdrawal from the outside world. Now the outside world has irrupted – on that screen above the refrigerator – with the violence of a fist breaking through a cardboard wall. The biggest news of the past week, the biggest horror for European TV channels, is the bombs on the trains in Madrid. Several bombs exploding in quick succession on different trains in the Spanish capital. Terrorism striking at the heart of Europe. Of course it wasn't the first time. It will certainly not be the last.

And yet this is a new kind of terrorism. Muslim fanaticism and Arab short-sightedness against Christian hypocrisy and Western arrogance. It's Crusader against Moor, my husband alleges, a return to the Dark Ages. A threat to everyone who believes in tolerance and brotherly love, my husband says with despair in his voice. He becomes very upset in front of the TV, even though he battles to understand the language, or maybe precisely because he battles to understand the language. One more frustration.

Tolerance?

Brotherly love?

Not much of thát to be seen on TV.

Last night – to take our minds off the train bombings in Madrid – we watched a documentary programme about the genocide in Rwanda. You could say from the frying pan into the fire. Three months of insane human slaughter that started exactly a decade ago this month. Men, women, children, old people and babies, teachers and illiterates, nuns and prostitutes, the crippled and the sick, all murdered, without exception. Many Europeans still fail to come to terms with this bloodbath, rather like a parent who cannot understand that his children could turn against one another, that one brother could murder another. Of course it's paternalistic, but where have you ever heard of an unpaternalistic coloniser?

So last night while I washed the dishes, the French television served up genocide. A gruesome dessert to round off a silent meal. People who had somehow miraculously survived took turns to tell what had happened to them. The blood, the axes, the terror, the screams, the smells, the rotting corpses, the bones that are still being dug up. Piles of skeletal remains

33

of friends and family. Mothers who lost all their children. It was too much for me. I kept my eyes fixed on the dishwater, cloudy as thin soup, oily. Unfortunately I couldn't close my ears to the onslaught of the voices. For my husband and my son it worked the other way round. Their French isn't good enough to understand the voices, but their eyes told them all they wanted to know. More than anybody wants to know.

Manon wasn't there. Thank heaven. Manon was sleeping safely in her bed on the moon.

Later, while brushing my teeth, I heard muffled sobs coming from Emile's room. It knocked my legs from under me. I wanted to go to him, to comfort him, press his face against my breast, but I sat down on the bathroom floor with the toothbrush sticking out of my mouth like a thermometer. Toothpaste foaming on my lips. Mad dog. Bitch that can't even comfort her own pup. By the time I regained the use of my legs, it was quiet in his room. I put my ear to the door. Even called his name softly. No sound.

At breakfast this morning his face was closed again. *No entry. Stay away. Private property.* I wondered if I had only imagined that I heard him cry last night.

Why would that programme have upset him so much? When you think of all that he has experienced recently without shedding a tear. At first I thought he was still suffering from shock, the tears would surely come. But it's been two months already.

Granted, he never was one to cry. Sometimes his eyes fill with tears of anger or frustration or such, but I honestly can't remember when last he really sobbed. He's like you, Myriam. He keeps a lid on his face. The train bombings in Madrid didn't even lift that lid a crack. I had thought they would, we are after all in Europe now, not that far from Madrid. At least much closer than to Rwanda!

No, he was never one to cry. That's what I've been telling myself for the past two months. But now I need to ask myself whether he has perhaps not been smothering his sobs in his pillow every night.

Inauguration of the bath. I lie here soaking like a rusk in a mug of coffee. No, let's be more romantic. Cleopatra luxuriating in milk? Probably more what my husband had in mind.

He has put a dozen candles in empty wine bottles on the floor, lit a rose-scented incense stick, stirred a few drops of aromatherapy oil into the water, put a cassette of chamber music in the portable player. Piano and cello. Something that Schumann composed for Clara. The love of a man for his wife. My husband did everything, short of taking my clothes off for me. And had I asked him, he would have done that too.

He told me to close my eyes before leading me into the bathroom. When I opened my eyes and saw the Victorian bathtub surrounded by flickering candles, it made me think of an altar. What would the sacrifice be, I wondered fleetingly. Usually it is something like the naked body of a young virgin. I'm sorry, husband of mine, it's been a long time since I've been young and virginal.

I also wondered, involuntarily, what he hoped to achieve with such a sacrifice. Which gods he wanted to appease.

He must have seen doubt in my eyes. I saw disappointment in his. Nothing he does is good enough for his inconsolable wife.

"Thank you," I said. "It's going to be wonderful."

"Would you like me to wash your back?"

I wouldn't. I cannot endure his touch. Not on my bare skin. Not on the parts usually covered with clothes. I long for his embrace, I want him to enfold me in his arms, but in a fatherly way, comforting, chaste. And he longs for something more than chastity.

"I'll call you when I'm ready," I said and pulled my sweater over my head. "I first want to lie a while."

Alone. It didn't need saying. He turned and walked away, hurt.

Now I'm trying to gather enough courage to call him.

I can't keep him from my body indefinitely. Sooner or later I'll simply have to close my eyes, allow him to do what he must do, even pretend to enjoy it. But I am so afraid.

That first week, while the news was still sinking in, we fell upon each other at night like wild animals. As if we wanted to tear each other apart with our teeth and hands. Unbearable anger, unbearable sorrow, unbearable lust, all boiling together in the same witches' cauldron, a poisonous brew. *Fucking against the dying of the light.* Every time ended in tears. That's what we were looking for. The end justifying the means. Not post-coital melancholy, oh no, something far more dramatic. Sobs that struck our defenceless bodies like earthquakes. To cling to each other, to smear each other with snot and tears and sweat and spittle and semen and blood, to infect each other with a grief that is too great to be borne alone.

Till one night I just knew it had to end. My body had become too fragile for such turbulence. Every time he touched my breasts, I thought of my child. I began to feel guilty about carrying on like this under such circumstances and began shrinking from his hands. Made excuses every time he approached. After a week or two he stopped making overtures. At night he wandered like a stranger in his own house and fell asleep in front of the TV. In the morning I would find his long body on the sofa, curled up in impossible, tortured positions. Possibly his way of self-punishment.

In this house we share a bed again. Perhaps only because we don't have a sofa here, not even a living room, only the black hole next to the kitchen. We lie curved into each other's backs, protecting each other against the cold, chaste as children.

Only sometimes he still looks at me with the longing eyes of a dog.

"André!" I call with a rough voice. "Do you still want to wash my back?"

He opens the door carefully, hesitates outside the ring of candles, inclines his head to listen to the cello. His eyes instantly film over. I envy him this ability to lose himself in music, to be absorbed into it, like sugar in coffee. I suspect this is all that has carried him through the recent weeks. Music. I don't have that, the transformation, the dissolution. No matter how breathtaking a composition is, something in me remains outside of all sound.

Yearning for silence.

I look at the flickering shadows on the wall while I soap the cloth. Then I hold it out to him. My sacrifice, my offering. I give you my bare back. He kneels next to the bath as if to pray.

I arch my back, drop my head onto my drawn-up knees, close my eyes when he begins to rub the washcloth over my shoulders with small circular movements.

"Tomorrow it will be ten weeks," he says when he reaches the small of my back.

"I know," I say without opening my eyes.

He drops the cloth in the bathwater to rinse it and presses it against my neck so that a thin stream runs down my spine. I can't prevent the gooseflesh on my arms.

"Will it ever be the same again?" I ask, my head still on my knees. "Will we ever again be really happy?"

"It will never be as it was," he answers while his fingers begin to massage my shoulders. *Oh the shoe that I see. The times that were will never again be.* His thumbs press so hard against my knotted muscles that I can't help groaning. "Am I hurting you?"

"It has to hurt or it won't do any good."

"We can't have the past back," he says. "But we can be happy again. We will be happy again."

When, I want to ask. One day when we're eighty?

"I need your body, Hester. How long must I still wait?"

I gave him my back. I should have known it wouldn't be enough. I turn my head towards him, put my hand behind his neck to draw his face closer, kiss him on his forehead.

"Come and get into the bath with me," I say. "Behind me, with your legs on either side so that I can lean against your chest."

As we always used to bath at home.

He looks so grateful that I glance away quickly. What's a body between an old married couple like us? Such a trivial gift. Can't even call it an offering. And yet he's smiling as though I'm offering him the Milky Way.

⌒⌒

"Do you see what I see?" Emile asks Nathalie just after they've walked out of the school gate. He stands still in amazement, his eyes fixed on a wet patch on the tarmac by his feet. "Look, it's a map of Africa!"

"Wow," says Nathalie in her nasal English. "You sure have a lot of imagination."

Not imagination, he thinks, just longing. The dark black patch against the lighter surface looks like the outline of Africa. Like an elongated, warped heart. The left hand bulge larger than the rounding on the right. The strange sharp rhino horn shape sticking out on the right. He puts the toe of his trainer on the bottom point.

"That's where I come from," pointing with his foot. "And you?"

Nathalie gives him a sidelong glance.

"I'm from here," she says.

"Where?"

"Hére," she says impatiently. "I was born in France."

"Oh."

Then she starts to laugh. She is very pretty when she laughs. The whitest teeth imaginable.

"Do you think all black people come from Africa?"

"No," he says curtly. "I come from Africa and I'm not black."

He hurries on, so offended that he no longer wants to talk to her. She is the first kid in this international school that he has tried to befriend. Because she is also from Africa. Because he thought she was also from Africa. Because he thought she would understand how it feels.

She catches up quickly, her voice coaxing.

"My mom and dad are from Africa," she explains. "My mom from Ethiopia and my dad from Ivory Coast. Mom speaks English and Dad French. I grew up speaking both. I was born here, okay, but I started school in America. When we came back here, my mother decided it would be best to continue my schooling in English. First in Paris and now here. And I promise you, now you know more about me than anyone else at school!"

"Sounds as if you've moved around a lot," he says a little uncomfortably.

"All the time," she sighs. "My dad is a sculptor. He can work anywhere in the world. My mom lectures in psychology. She can't work everywhere, but she'll follow him to the ends

39

of the earth. I guess that's what they call love. They probably have nomadic blood in their veins. You know, all those African tribes that never stop moving."

"And you? Do you also feel 'nomadic'?"

Funny word, he thinks. A European girl would have talked about gypsy blood.

"I don't know. I liked America. And I like France. Of course. But I'm not sure if I liked Africa. We lived in Ivory Coast for a while." Every time she smiles her whole face seems to change into a massive mouth. All you see are white teeth. "I told you we never stop moving! But Africa felt strange to me. I mean, there was lots I liked, but I felt like a tourist the whole time."

He inspects her surreptitiously. In her red Nike trainers, jeans flapping loosely round her legs and black hooded zipper jacket, she looks like any other French schoolgirl. But she moves differently. Her legs are longer, her strides bigger – she has no difficulty keeping up with him like most girls walking beside him do – and yet there is nothing ungainly about her movements. Nothing unfeminine, as his grandmother would say. She is the tallest girl in the class, even a fraction taller than he. Or rather, she is slightly shorter up to her shoulders, but then she has this incredible giraffe-neck that lifts her above everyone else. That's what she reminds him of, he realises. A giraffe. Her legs, her neck, the swaying gait, even her large black eyes and long lashes. An animal of Africa. No matter what she says.

"Do you know that they have about sixty different languages in Ivory Coast?" she asks.

"Wow," he says. "And I thought my country's eleven official languages were quite something."

"My dad says they're dialects rather than languages. I wouldn't know, they all sound Greek to me. Do you speak an African language?"

"Yes. My home language is Afrikaans."

"What does that sound like?"

"A little like Dutch."

"Dutch?"

"But there are lots of words from other languages," he tries to explain. "I think it was the Malay slaves that first started talking it. From Malaysia," he adds when he sees her puzzlement. "An island somewhere in the East. Next to Indonesia?"

"So it's a mixture of Dutch and some or other Eastern language?" She looks at him sceptically. "But then how come you call it an African language?"

"It is African," he says, suddenly heated, "because it started in Africa! That's why it's called 'Afrikaans'."

"Okay, okay. I believe you."

She holds her palms up as if to ward him off. Dusky pink palms against the black of her jacket, the milk chocolate of her cheeks, the tight black curls on her head, glistening with something like gel or oil. He feels foolish. It's as though he's loaded with landmines. The slightest touch can make him explode. One queer look, one wrong word, and he starts to tremble inside. His father says it's only hormones, totally normal for his age, but it doesn't feel normal to him. It feels lethally dangerous. If all these landmines were to go off at the same time, he'd blow himself and everyone round him off the face of the earth.

"Say something to me in Afrikaans," Nathalie placates him with another dazzling smile. "Just so I can hear what it sounds like."

He hesitates, but decides to risk it anyway.

"*Jy is baie mooi*," he says in his mother tongue, every word slowly and clearly.

"What does it mean?"

"I'll tell you one day. When I know you better." He clears his throat to hide his embarrassment. Suddenly he sounds just like his father. "This is where I turn off to catch the bus. See you tomorrow?"

He walks swiftly down a small cobbled street, gasping a little at his own daring. *Jy is baie mooi.* You are very pretty. For the first time in weeks his body feels light and empty as if the whole lot of landmines have miraculously disappeared, as if he has shaken a heavy blanket off his shoulders. He never knew that guilt could be such an unbearable burden.

André still studies his wife's body. Her shoulders still droop, but at least no longer over the kitchen table all day. Her feet still drag, but at least not only over the floor of the house. This past week she has regularly ventured through the front door. Perhaps only because the weather is improving daily. It's difficult to stay indoors all day, however dark one's mood, when the sun is shining in a cloudless blue sky.

He doesn't care what the reason is. He is a desperate doctor searching for signs of improvement in his patient. It doesn't matter how she gets better – through modern science or witch doctors or blind faith – as long as she gets well again.

He just wants to hear his wife laugh again.

After almost a month in this house she is at last showing a little interest in their restoration project. Although "interest" is a little exaggerated. For the past week she has been helping him with the bathroom walls. Scraping off old layers of paint and filling holes, treating the surface against damp, applying the protective undercoat, and finally the new layers of paint. But she works like a prisoner in a Nazi concentration camp. Not because she wishes to, but because she has to. *Arbeit macht frei.* For hours on end, seemingly tireless, but without a grain of enthusiasm.

Except for the day before yesterday when she had the paint for the walls mixed. "*Non, non, non,*" she gesticulated at the bewildered young man, her voice brusque, almost rude. "*Le couleur du sang. Vieux sang.*" The colour of old blood. That's what Hester wants on their bathroom walls.

André had in mind a dark terracotta, a sort of burnt orange, maybe with subtle undertones of red. Definitely not a blood red. And yet he was so relieved to hear the sudden passion in Hester's voice – even over something as trivial as a tin of paint – that he didn't try to stop her.

"Are you sure?" he asked when she finally nodded approval. The young man operating the paint mixer sighed like someone who had barely managed to avoid a fatal accident. "Aren't we going to feel like Jonah trapped in the belly of a whale?"

"Not a belly," said Hester. "More like a womb."

"The womb of a whale?"

"Forget the whale, André! A bath is a way of returning to the womb, isn't it? The water, the warmth, the safety . . ."

"If you say so, Hester."

So here they are actually turning their bathroom into a womb.

They paint with their backs to each other, she on the floor, he high up a ladder. She paints with slow even strokes. Like a robot, he thinks while he watches her from the ladder. She is wearing old tracksuit trousers and a jumper covered in splashes of red-brown paint. She looks like someone injured in a terrorist attack, clothes spattered with blood, one of the victims of the recent train bombs in Madrid. An impression supported by her dazed manner, the slightly delayed movements of someone suffering from shock. Even her dark hair is spattered with bloodied spots. From the top of the ladder he can see the unmistakable glimmer of grey hair at the crown of her head.

He wonders if he should remind her that her hair is due for colouring. It's the sort of innocent remark that these days can drive her to tears. Sometimes it feels as if anything he says to her drives her to tears. As if his very presence makes her want to cry without ever stopping.

"I must admit it looks better than I thought it would," he says carefully, soothingly. "What colour did you have in mind for our bedroom?"

She doesn't answer right away.

"White," she says after a few more slow brush strokes.

"White?"

"Pure and innocent," she nods. "Chaste. Such an old-fashioned word, isn't it? 'Chaste'."

His wife wants a chaste bedroom. A chaste man in her chaste bed. A pure and innocent relationship. His legs suddenly feel so weak that he almost loses his balance on the ladder. He had hoped that the few times they had recently made love, would awaken something in her. Reawaken. It was once there after all, not so long ago. Now he knows that he was trying to deceive himself. Hester does what she does because she must and not because she wants to. Hester does everything, from eating to making love, in the same mechanical manner in which she is now painting that wall.

"I thought we could go for a picnic somewhere this weekend," he suggests after they've worked in silence for a while. "A family outing. Now that it's warmer."

"A family outing," Hester repeats in a flat voice.

We aren't a family any more, André. That is the reproach he hears beneath her words. We're a little shipwrecked group in a bobbing lifeboat. One unexpected wave and we could capsize.

"How about the Pont du Gard? We haven't been there for ages."

"Shouldn't we first finish the bathroom walls?"

"We didn't come here just to work all the time, Hester."

"Why did we come here?" Her voice is so low that at first he thinks he hasn't heard correctly. But then she repeats her question. "Why are we here, André?"

He climbs slowly down the ladder, sits on the edge of the bath, looks at his wife's back in dismay.

"Hester. When my father died last year, we could have used the inheritance for anything. An imported sports car, a luxury world cruise, a trust fund for the children. We decided to buy this house. To take a year off to renovate it. Because it's a good investment. Because we would be able to rent it out to tourists. But above all because you wanted to do it. As long as I've known you, you've dreamed of a year in the French countryside. We wouldn't have been able to do it without that inheritance. And now . . ."

He sighs, spreads his hands helplessly in front of him, stares at the red-brown paint spots on his palms.

"Maybe you should have opted for the imported sports car."

He is afraid to answer her. Afraid that the lump in his throat will burst open in a cry of impatience. He fixes on the back of her head while trying to curb his frustration.

"I don't want a sports car, Hester. I want this house. This year together with you. I thought this is what we both wanted."

"It is what I wanted all my life," agrees Hester, all the while painting with mechanical strokes. "But now, I don't know, it feels as if I'm no longer alive. There is nothing I want anymore. Except for the one thing I can never have again."

⌒⌒

It's the most pathetic picnic imaginable. Nothing wrong with the place or the weather or the fare on the tartan blanket. André has provided an attractive selection of breads and

45

cheeses and patés and salad. André always provides for every-thing. A bottle of wine with real glasses. Stainless steel cut-lery, china plates. My aesthetic husband detests eating from plastic or paper. The sky above is endlessly blue. The sun casts a beneficent warmth, like a wood fire in winter, nothing un-pleasant or overdone about the heat. Some of the trees around us are still bare, but most have begun to put out fine green buds. The river gleams next to us, the classical aquaduct forms a magnificent frame behind us. Arch upon arch upon arch, row after row after row, next to and above one another. When I saw it for the first time many years ago, it took my breath away.

Now it just makes me sad.

Pont du Gard.

Déjeuner sur l'herbe. André takes a photo using the auto-matic button on his camera. Point, press and run to his place on the tartan blanket. Among the bread and cheese, his back-side almost in the paté dish. *Sad family with Roman bridge in background.* If the photo had to have a title, like a painting, it would be something like that.

It's a perfect spring day, the surroundings are beautiful, the food looks delicious – but we remain a sad, sorrowful family.

André draws his lips into a smile for the photo. He doesn't usually smile for the camera. His is the sort of face that looks better when serious. Narrow and angular, high cheekbones, high nose bridge, dark eyes. Hair pitch black when we met. Wild curls like a pirate. These days he wears his grey-black hair shaved short. Many men do, it's supposed to be fashionable, but few men have a strong enough face to get away with so little hair. My husband has. A face that could have been chis-elled from granite, gigantic against a cliff on Mount Rushmore. And yet today that stone face grins like a court jester, proba-bly to compensate for the miserable faces of his family.

46

I also try to smile, but my lips feel glued to my gums.

Emile doesn't even try. Stares surlily at the camera, baseball cap back-to-front, red earphones in his ears, minuscule music machine hanging like a medal round his neck. Some or other rebellious rapper spitting out phrases full of swear words. Don't know if they should be called "singers". They don't sing, says Emile, they perform to the beat of the music. Luckily I don't hear the words of the performance, only the dull boom near my son's ears. Too much bass, as usual. He sits with his sharp knees pulled up under his chin, his legs too long and too thin for the rest of his body, his hands and feet hopelessly too big. This last year he has become clumsy, keeps knocking glasses over, bumping into doorways, as if he's growing so fast that he doesn't always know where his extremities end.

Somewhere in that knobbly body, somewhere behind that sullen face, my gentle, dark-haired boy is hiding. If only I had the strength to look, I would find him. Be able to pull him to me for a few moments.

But all my strength is going into my daughter. To keep her with me. To stop her from also becoming unreachable. She is sitting next to me on the picnic blanket. The sun shines in her light eyes so that she puckers them protectively. *Ouistiti,* she says, as I taught her last year. The French equivalent of "cheese" for the camera. But her lips don't fold open round the word. Her mouth remains a rosebud, pink and closed, a bloom picked too soon.

After the photo André stretches out on the blanket and gazes dreamily at the bridge behind me.

"Two things I can never tire of looking at," he sighs. "That bridge and my wife's face."

The wife under discussion quickly turns her face away. Looks out over the shimmering river, the groups of people admiring the bridge from all angles, amazed that there are so many tourists so early in the season. Uncomfortable with her husband's uninvited flattery.

"Emile, why don't you take those things out of your ears and look round," says André loudly and with gestures, as if talking to a deaf person.

"I don't need my ears to see, Dad," says Emile, dutifully looking around him.

"But you need your ears to hear. Listen to the birds!"

Emile removes the earphones and listens in a bored way to the twittering birds in the trees around us. No cursing lyrics, no booming bass notes, clearly not nearly as exciting as Eminem or 50 Cent.

André turns onto his back, clasps his hands under his head, closes his eyes to listen more acutely. That's how he likes to listen to his beloved classical music, Mahler symphonies or Schubert lieder, stretched out on his back on the floor, his eyes closed in total concentration. In the first years of our relationship my insides used to lurch with desire whenever he did that. Something about this position, the vulnerability of his long body, the ecstasy on his narrow face, used to drive me mad with lust. Now I look at him without any desire at all, only nostalgia for what was, melancholy for what we have become.

After a while his chest begins to rise and fall rhythmically. The birds have sung him to sleep. Emile has already put the red buttons back in his ears and stares unseeingly in front of him with his lips moving silently. Like a creature from another planet, he looks at me. *Take me to your leader.*

"I'm going to walk to the water," I announce.

No reaction from my sleeping husband or my deaf son. Only Manon who jumps up immediately, her eyes so bright, so happy, so blue, that my heart nearly stops beating. *Mother's child, Mother's tousle-haired child. Running free and running wild.*

"Can I come with you, Mommy?"

"Of course," I say and hold my hand out for her.

But she skips past my hand. She runs to the water with the sun like flames in her hair. All I can do is to stumble blindly after her.

2

"Guess what I found at the market today," says André as he walks in at the front door.

I hear the excitement in his voice, in the kitchen where I'm emptying the dishwasher. He puts the basket on the round table and takes out something. Carefully, as if it's a newborn babe, he shows it to me. On my husband's paint-spattered hands lie two bundles of asparagus, perfectly formed with their little dark green heads and light green legs.

"April is asparagus month," he says. "You always say the first ones are the best, don't you?"

With a lump in my throat I look at my husband's gift.

"The children don't eat asparagus," I say.

André frowns with irritation.

"If Emile doesn't want to eat it, that's his problem. He can get himself a cheese sandwich. I bought them for yóu, Hester."

And what about Manon, I wonder.

But I don't want to irritate my husband any further, so I accept the gift with a grateful nod, resisting the temptation to make a modest curtsy, and walk over to the refrigerator to store them.

"You really should come to the market with me sometime," says André. "All the spring fruit and vegetables are coming in now. Every week there is more to choose from. I even saw strawberries today, would you believe? Imported from somewhere I suppose, but any day now we should be getting the local ones. My mouth waters at the mere thought of those big sweet ones from Carpentras."

50

He clearly wants mine to water too. But my mouth remains bone dry, a little dusty as usual, while I carry on unpacking the dishes.

"Hester." His voice has that pleading tone. I wish I could block my ears, but I have a glass bowl in my hands. "Last year you were mad about the weekly markets. You wanted to go to a different one each morning."

Last year was last year, husband dear. *Oh the shoe that I see. The times that were will never again be.*

"I have another surprise for you," he says behind me.

He never gives up, does he?

I turn to the table, my eyes on the basket, and wait meekly for the next offering to be taken from it.

"No, it's not something I found at the market," he smiles. "Habib says he has a sister who can come and help you in the house once or twice a week. With cleaning and ironing and so on."

I look at him, startled. Habib is a young man of Moroccan descent who appeared a few days ago after we'd pinned up a notice in the local *épicerie*. Now that the womb-like bathroom is practically finished, André wants to tackle the breaking and building of the living room in earnest. For that he needs a handyman, one with more muscles and skill than his wife. More cheerfulness too. After Habib had helped him the day before yesterday to lay tiles on the bathroom floor, André said he did work a little slowly but he grinned and whistled all the while. If he'd worked faster but with a sullen face, André probably wouldn't have taken him on. We have enough long faces in this house.

But I don't need more people round me. It's bad enough keeping up appearances in front of my family. Not to roar out my pain like a lion. Now there is a stranger as well who watches me with foreign eyes, my sad mouth, my heavy

51

silences, the muttering way I have of talking to myself. The handyman has probably already decided I should be in an institution, that's why he wants to bring his sister along. It must be clear to him that I'm too unstable to care for myself and my family.

"It's not necessary," I say with more vehemence than I've heard in my voice for a long time. "What's there to clean anyway? We use only two of the rooms – the kitchen and the bathroom – and once you start working in the living room, the kitchen is in any case going to be covered in dust all the time. The bedrooms are where we sleep at night, that's all. There's nothing but a bed and a wardrobe in each room. All you could do there is sweep the floor. And even if you swept twenty times a day, it would still be covered in dust. Until we've varnished the floors and painted the walls and patched the holes in the ceilings, it's a complete waste of time to clean up properly!"

"Maybe she could help you with the laundry?" My angry monologue has caught my husband so unawares that he actually staggers back a step or two. "Or the dishes?"

"I have a machine for the laundry. And a machine for the dishes."

"But not yet a machine for ironing." He produces this like a trump card.

"What is there that needs ironing? You and I wear old clothes full of paint spots. The children don't wear school uniforms as they did in South Africa. Emile would have a fit if I tried to iron his frayed jeans! Do you want your underpants and socks ironed?"

He turns away from me silently and lights the gas stove to boil water for tea. I know I ought to apologise for my sharpness. He meant so well. As always. He wanted to help me.

"Maybe later, when the living room is finished, when the

place no longer looks like a building site," I try to make peace behind his back. "Maybe then we'll need someone to help?"

He refuses to look at me, simply stares at the flame under the kettle with folded arms and stiff shoulders. Come in out of the cold, my love, I want to say to him. I will show you where to step. But I can't get the words past my stiff lips. Together we listen as the water in the kettle starts to sing.

Dear Myriam. No, I haven't forgotten you yet. In my head I write letters to you all the time. While I paint walls, while I wander with my husband through hardware stores or flea markets, while we're selecting towel rails or mirrors. At least one letter a day.

The bathroom is finished. The walls are painted brown-red, the rough ceiling beams are stained a light warm brown, almost the same shade as the clay tiles that my husband and Habib have laid on the floor, the Victorian bath is restored to its former glory. Looking splendid, cream-coloured, spotless, shiny. There are smaller clay tiles on the walls above the bath and the basin. Below the basin there is a raw wooden cabinet that André found at a flea market last Sunday. Above the basin there is another flea-market find, a large mirror with an antique wooden frame.

Only the finishing touches left to do. A few towel rails, a lampshade for the bare globe on the ceiling, a cupboard to be built by a carpenter to house the washing machine and the tumble dryer. André's idea of course. The machines spoil the rustic effect that he is trying to create.

How worldly this must all sound to you. Even I sometimes want to shake my husband by the shoulders, ask if it really matters what the stupid lampshade in the bathroom looks like.

Most of the time I want to shake my own shoulders. It was I who started all of this with my silly dream of living in another country. All I can do now is to help make the house liveable so that I can go back to where I belong.

I write to you every day, but I have to wait for your court case before I can see you again. I wonder if your face is still such an empty mask. If the months behind bars, away from your children, far from everyone and everything familiar, have left scars by now. If you have lost weight. No, probably not, you were already as thin as a shadow. You come from a land of war and poverty. The food they give you in prison is in all likelihood more than you're used to. And what's more, you can eat everything on your plate, you don't have to keep the greater portion for your children. Your children are no longer hungry. Now isn't that a comforting thought? Or what am I saying?

How would I know, Myriam? My children have never gone hungry. Everything that has happened to you and your children is so far outside my experience that I have to dig deep in my imagination to make sense of it. The only thing that I truly understand – with my insides rather than my head – is that you are a mother. A mother is always a mother, no matter what becomes of her children. And that you are from Africa. That your scalp yearns for the blistering heat of the African sun, that the soles of your feet long for dry dust, that your lips thirst for fresh rain water. God, Myriam, I never knew that one could carry a whole continent around in one's body!

Always thought I was born in the wrong place. Wrong colour, wrong continent. Somewhere someone made a mistake. Stuffed the wrong address into the stork's beak. Hey, look here, I'm white! That's what I've wanted to shout since I was little. This sun is burning holes in my skin! Take me away.

Now my husband has taken me away. And now I realise

that my heart stayed behind. My heart was cremated and scattered over the sea near Cape Point. In its place I find a continent in the shape of Africa. Knock, knock. Who's there?

Africa.

I had to come and grieve in Europe to begin to understand this.

⌢⌢

April isn't only the month of the asparagus, it's apparently also the month of wind. The mistral has been blowing for more than a week now. André puts down his head and lifts his shoulders high to forge ahead over the square. Like a bull, he thinks, vaguely amused, a bull with a baguette tucked under its front paw.

He has just bought bread at the *boulangerie* and butter at the *épicerie* next door. He chooses a short cut across the square, directly in the teeth of the raging wind, at an angle to the café where a few of the older men are already having their first drink of the day while perusing the sports pages of the newspaper. In front of him, at the northern end of the square, is a little municipal office and a modest monument to the locals fallen in the two world wars, an obelisk of pale stone with a long list of names chiselled on two sides. *Enfants de Lunel. Morts pour la France.*

Why did only children die in this town? Emile wanted to know when they came here last year to buy the house. Where had all the grown-ups gone? Hester had to explain that *enfants* doesn't always literally mean "children", that it can be another word for citizens or inhabitants. Like the words of the French national anthem, she said and started humming the Marseillaise: *Allons, enfants de la patrie* . . . Children of the fatherland.

Those were the days when Hester was still Hester. Always the teacher, always eager to clear up what's unclear, to resolve misunderstandings, to spread knowledge like balm on children's souls. Now her whole life has become a misunderstanding. No balm for that.

In the centre of the square is a fountain with water gushing from the mouth of an antique stone monster. There are four of these strange stone creatures looking to the four cardinal points, like fierce guards protecting the precious fountain water from enemy attack. It's not clear whether they started out as images of actual animals or of mythological creatures. The stone has been worn so smooth over the centuries, by wind and rain and the touch of generations of villagers fetching their daily drinking water, that the faces have become unidentifiable. The only facial remains are vague indications of eyes, ears, nostrils. And of course the gaping mouths, like the one from which a surprisingly strong stream of water is spouting today.

It was next to these stone monsters that André had noticed his son amongst a group of laughing teenagers last night. At first he thought his eyes were deceiving him in the twilight. As far as he knew, Emile was in his room at home. As far as he knew, Emile didn't know any of the village children. Emile was always complaining that his French wasn't good enough for him to make friends with anyone. And yet, when the boy next to the fountain threw his lean body back as he laughed, André was no longer in any doubt. He knows that jerky movement only too well, so full of false bravado, enough to break a father's heart. That's what his son has always done when he feels more self-conscious than usual.

André's first feeling was of confused joy. When last had he heard his son laugh? But there was something in the communal gaiety that bothered him, a mocking sound, something forced that he couldn't quite put his finger on. Suddenly he didn't want Emile to see him. He kept to the dark side of the square and slipped past his son like the proverbial thief in the night.

When he looked back over his shoulder, the laughing teenagers all seemed to him a good deal older than Emile. Fifteen, sixteen, maybe even seventeen years old. Three boys and two girls, though one of the girls might have been a boy. It was getting harder to tell these days. Or maybe just another sign that he had become undeniably middle-aged. After all, in his youth boys and girls had also looked alike – long hair, loose clothes, lots of chains and bracelets and rings – but he had never had trouble distinguishing the sexes. His hormones had always led him in the right direction.

André also noticed that at least two of the teenagers on the square were smoking. The ends of their cigarettes glowed like dragons' eyes in the twilight. Behind them the stone monsters were only just visible.

He walked home with heavy steps.

He has always been a pragmatic man. He is not one to meet trouble halfway. But if something frightens him he tries to catch the fear and look it in the face, tries to tame it, as it were. He asks himself whether he's worried that his thirteen-year-old son smokes on the sly. Yes, of course, but he knows that his anxiety lies far deeper. Is he afraid that the teenagers' cigarettes are filled with something stronger than tobacco? Yes, that too, although he suspects this is a foolish fear. Surely the children wouldn't smoke marijuana like that, openly on the town square. Or would they?

His heart beats faster, as though fear itself has bared its fangs at him.

Maybe he's upset simply because Emile hasn't told him that he has made friends with this group of teenagers. He thought they didn't have secrets from each other. But it's still not the heart of ~~his~~ fear. Basically he is afraid that the child has become so lonely that he will make friends with anyone, even children with whom in normal circumstances he'd have nothing in common, teenagers too old and too experienced for him. Adolescents who smoke and drink and do who knows what else. And Emile, even though he is as tall as some sixteen-year-olds, is still wet behind the ears. Just thirteen, his body still smooth and undeveloped, his voice not yet broken. His hormones are beginning to bother him, he is definitely more moody than before, but in his heart and body he is a mere child.

Or is he?

Of course, thinks André, lowering his head even more like a rugby player preparing to scrum. He regularly showers with his son. He would surely have noticed if the child's body had started changing!

Well, he used to shower regularly with his son. In the derelict stone house in Lunel there isn't a shower. And during the last few weeks before they left South Africa, Emile kept to himself. In that time they all kept to themselves, didn't they? Each like a dog in a corner licking its wounds.

He suddenly realises he can't remember when last he saw his child naked.

In the Christmas holiday? *Four months ago?*

It is as if a tap starts dripping in his chest. Ice cold water running slowly over his heart. The very thought that he could be losing his son too is enough to turn his whole body into a block of ice.

The school vacation started yesterday. Spring vacation it's called, although it feels as though this furious wind has blown the spring right away. Perhaps during the holiday he can somehow involve Emile in the restoration of the living room. Not scraping paint off walls or window frames, that would be far too boring. Action, that's what the child needs. Perhaps Emile can help him to demolish the inside wall with the hired compressed-air drill. After all, at that age breaking down always sounds more fun than building up.

He swerves right to take on the last steep incline up to the grey-blue garden gate. The wind isn't as dreadful in this little side street. The row of houses to the left of him forms a barrier to the north. The houses are all deserted, the shutters closed and the gardens neglected. In the summer when the owners from all over France and further into Europe – some even from America and the East – arrive for their holidays, Lunel becomes a busy, sociable, cosmopolitan little town. That was what the Human family experienced when they bought their derelict house the previous summer. The estate agent did warn them that it could get very quiet out of season. Exactly what we're looking for, Hester said. They never dreamed that it could get this quiet. That some of the streets could become so eerily empty. That you would feel as if you were walking through a cemetery every time you went to buy bread.

Yet another thing they hadn't been prepared for. The list grows daily.

If only the wind would die down.

Just the other day he read something in a British newspaper about a "Mistral room", a chamber in a home for terminally ill children that looks like an ordinary children's room, full of bright colours and soft toys, but much colder than any other room. The temperature is maintained at eight degrees Celsius, because this is where the children are kept after their death, sometimes for days, so that parents and siblings can take their leave slowly, unhurriedly. The architect in André was immediately stimulated by the practical as well as the humanistic aspect of such a chamber. The father in him was deeply moved by the image of a dead child in a cool room full of toys.

59

The room is named for the Provençal wind because you can feel the wind, as you can a dead child's presence, but not see it. That was the explanation André read in the newspaper – although the same can actually be said of all winds. Surely there can't be a special connection between the mistral and dead children, André speculates as he pauses for a moment at the garden gate to get his breath back.

Or can there?

It's a wind that blows in multiples of three, Habib explained yesterday, in his strange mixture of French and broken English peppered with Arabic phrases and delivered with an astonishing variety of gestures and facial expressions. Once it's blown for three days on end, you can prepare for nine days of wind. And if it's blown for nine days (Habib bent his left thumb back and waved his other fingers dramatically in front of André's face), you might as well start preparing for *twenty-seven* windy days. André wished Habib would rather use his hands for the task he was being paid for – to take a chisel to the stone wall and remove the layers of old paint and plaster – but he finds the young man's company so entertaining that he can't bring himself to be strict with him. It's a relief having such a voluble, carefree handyman. So different from Hester.

At first they had difficulty communicating. Habib's English is even poorer than André's French. Habib's home language is Arabic, of which André doesn't understand a single word – and Habib obviously doesn't understand André's Afrikaans. For the first few days Hester had to interpret all the time, but they soon had a mouthful of basic phrases and devised a specially demonstrative sign language between them. Now they mostly manage without Hester.

This morning, however, Habib is not expected. André closes the garden gate behind him and walks heavily into his quiet

60

house. On Saturdays and Sundays he is at the mercy of his silent wife and his evasive son.

If only the wind would die down, he might stop thinking of dead children.

Emile sits on his bed playing Gameboy when his father pushes open the door after a tentative knock.

"May I come in?"

Before Emile can answer, André is already in the room. He looks around, his mouth slightly open, like an old-time explorer lost in an exotic jungle. His amazement baffles his son. The room is as bare as all the other rooms in the house. A second-hand bed, a second-hand wardrobe, a little patterned mat in front of the bed. Next to the bed, on a low bookshelf that his father hammered together the other day, there are a few CDs and computer games, a magazine for surfers, three science fiction books, a brown apple stalk, a banana peel and an assortment of sweet papers. On the opposite wall Emile has put up a poster of Eminem and a map of Africa. The cork board that his father hung above his bed for pinning up photos and postcards and papers looks as deserted as a moon landscape. In the bottom left hand corner is a postcard of Table Mountain and a photo of Emile and Manon taken last year at Euro Disney outside Paris. Nothing more.

"I see you're beginning to make yourself at home." His father rubs his hands nervously while looking at the insolent expression on Eminem's face. "Where did you get the map?"

"Bought it in Avignon."

"Hmm. It's good to remember where one comes from."

Emile glares at his father. He doesn't need a map on a wall to remind him that he doesn't belong hére. He bought the map because he wanted to know exactly where Ivory Coast is, where Nathalie's father was born. And Ethiopia, where her mother comes from. And Rwanda, after watching that shocking programme on TV the other night. He'd realised that he knew precious little about the continent he was born in. On a map of Europe he would know most countries, except perhaps for the new little ones in the east, Lithonia, Latonia, Letuania, whatever. But when he looks at an African map, he is lost. Egypt at the top and his own country right at the bottom. That was about all he knew until the other day.

"Anything you still need?" asks his father. "I mean for the time being, till we do this room over."

"A table," says Emile. "Or a desk or something I can do my homework on."

"Where have you been doing your homework till now?" asks his father with a surprised frown.

"In the bus, most of the time."

"Not to be recommended for neat handwriting, is it?" His father sits on the foot of his bed, his eyes still roving through the room. "And yours was never very neat to begin with. Never mind, mine neither. Your mother always says it's only boring people who have the time to develop a neat handwriting. You know your mother and her sweeping statements."

Emile lifts his thumbs off the purple Gameboy set and waits with suppressed impatience for his father to say what he has to say. He most certainly didn't come here to discuss the family's handwriting.

"I see you've made friends with a few. . . older children in the village," says his father.

"When did you see that?"

"Oh, I've noticed you in the square a few times now."

"I wouldn't call them friends exactly," says Emile defensively. "I hang out with them because there's no one else to hang out with."

"You mean no one nearer your age?"

"They aren't that much older than me. Anyway, since when do I need permission to talk to older children?"

"No one says you should ask permission," says his father soothingly. "It's just, well, I noticed that some of them smoke. And you know that I . . ."

"So that's what you're stressing about!" interrupts Emile, his voice high with indignation. "Don't worry, Dad, you've been brainwashing me for so many years about how hard it was for you to give up that I've never for a moment wanted to start. You did a good job."

"Pleased to hear it," his father smiles with his eyes on the map of Africa again.

The capital of Ivory Coast, Emile read on the internet, is Ya-mous-sou-kro. Yamoussoukro. The sort of word that a year ago he would immediately have shared with his mother: Just listen, Mom, doesn't it sound lovely? And she would have smiled as though he was giving her a gift: Oh, it's so nice in Yamoussoukro. Do you remember the picture book of the little tiger and the little bear? As if he'd ever forget, all the books that she read to them at night, to him and his little sister. Even long after he was too old for bedtime stories, he'd secretly listen along with his sister, pretending not to. Right to the end, till the last night before the silence descended on their house.

"But it isn't only the smoking that bothers me," his father muddles on. "I'd prefer you to . . . hang out with children of your own age."

"Me too, Dad," sighs Emile. "Just show me where they're hiding."

For a while his father sits motionless, listening to the wind

63

tugging at the shutters in front of the windows. The sliver of night sky showing between the half-open shutters is black as pitch. No moon tonight. In Ivory Coast, Emile also read on the internet, there is a civil war going on. More than half the population cannot read or write and most people don't live beyond the age of 46. His father is 48, Emile calculated. If they lived in Ivory Coast, his father would be dead. He wonders how old Nathalie's father is.

"And even if there were children of my age in this village," says Emile with a shrug, "they'd probably also smoke. Here in the French countryside everyone between twelve and eighty smokes. Or haven't you noticed?"

"Also true," mutters his father. "Well, I should probably be pleased that your French has improved so much that you can start making friends. With whoever. Do they understand a little English?"

"We manage. I teach them English words and they teach me French words."

"Pleased to hear it," his father says again.

His father wouldn't be so pleased to hear that it's mainly swear words being exchanged. These French teenagers have an unbelievable interest in the foulest depths of the English language. It's like exchanging marbles. Each time he sees them, he has to pull a few more rude words out of his little bag. In exchange for "fucking hell" and "motherfucker" and "suck my dick," they've offered him *putain* and *nic ta mere* and *suce ma bite*. His supply of swear words will soon be exhausted. Then they'll probably lose interest in him.

"We've never actually had the father-son talk, have we?" says his father with an embarrassed little cough.

"Isn't that what we're doing now?"

"No, I mean, you know, about 'the birds and the bees'." His father tries a mocking smile, but his eyes look so anxious that

64

it falls flat. "About how boys' bodies change when they become men and so on."

"We don't have to talk about it," Emile stops him. "I've known it all for ages."

"Oh." His father sighs, probably with relief. "How come?"

"Well, after all, Mom's been giving me these books from when I was small. *Mommy laid an egg* and *What's happening to me?* Books like that."

"Mommy laid an egg?"

"A funny book about how babies are made. Manon was also mad about it." He watches his father's Adam's apple bulging out and disappearing again as he swallows. "And then you see everything else in movies and on TV, don't you?"

"Unlike when I was your age," André nods. "I had to guess about most things."

"And the older kids also talk, you know, Dad." He keeps his voice cool, not bothered.

"The older kids here on the square?"

"No, I mean in Cape Town. My pals' older brothers and so on."

"So you know about wet dreams and all those things?"

"Yip."

"And there's nothing you want to ask me?"

Won't you just leave me alone? That's what he'd like to ask. But he just shakes his head, determined to put this uncomfortable conversation behind them as soon as possible so that he can go on with his electronic game.

"And do you know how girls' bodies work?"

"Sort of." Now he is the one to fix his eyes on the map of Africa. Ethiopia lies in the East, in the horn of the rhino; the capital is Addis Ababa and the flag is green, yellow and red like the crowns and tams the Rastas in Cape Town wear over their dreadlocks. Maybe Nathalie's mother was also a Rasta in

65

her younger days. Smoking weed and listening to reggae. Maybe even now. Imagine that. "I only wish someone would explain to me how their heads work."

"I'm afraid I can't help you with that," grins André and clumsily ruffles Emile's hair. "That's something I've been wondering about for more than forty years."

In Ethiopia things look even worse than in Ivory Coast. Sixty percent of the population is illiterate and life expectancy is barely 42 years. If they lived in Ethiopia, both his father and mother would be dead by now. But at least there's no war going on there. Not at present.

In Rwanda, which also has a green, yellow and red flag, life expectancy is even lower. Forty years, that's how long you can hope to live there. He didn't mean to learn these ghastly statistics off by heart. They simply stuck there, maybe because they had shocked him so, and now he can't forget them. If only the conjugation of French verbs would stick like that!

In April 1994 about a million Rwandans were murdered in barely two weeks. He was three years old, in April 1994, when his own country got a democratic government for the first time. In this democratic country of his, he also read last week on the internet, more than twenty percent of the population has AIDS. That means one out of every five people you see in the street, in a soccer stadium, in a crowd. His heart felt so constricted that he got up from the school computer and fled blindly out of the room, supposedly to the toilet, but really only to breathe. This was worse than any thriller that he had ever read, all these ghastly facts about the continent where he was born, where he had always lived, to which he wanted to return.

"Well then, I'll be saying good night for now." His father got up from the bed, suddenly in a hurry. "Don't stay up too late, now."

"I'm on holiday, Dad."

"Even so. Growing boys need to get enough sleep."

André takes a last look over the room. In the second before he turns back to the door, he no longer looks like an explorer in a jungle, more like a frightened child lost in a forest. Emile quickly looks down at the Gameboy screen. It's not his problem. Nothing he can do about it.

It is purely for Manon's sake that I decided to care for the black kitten.

On the first windless day in three weeks, we go together up to the top cherry orchard, where the white bridal veils have by this time all blown away. The blossoms lie strewn like a thick layer of confetti under the trees. The branches are full of new green leaves and the first buds of tiny fruit. Next month we'll be eating cherries, I promise my daughter. May is the month of cherries.

"In April we eat asparagus," she says in a sing-song voice while marching like a tin soldier down the hill, her red T-shirt a flamboyant splash in the floating pale green landscape. "And in May many, many cherries. How does the rest of the rhyme go?"

"No, how should I know? You're the one who made it up."

"What comes after May?"

"June."

"And what do we eat in June?"

"Strawberries. Melons and strawberries after the many, many cherries. And in July, peaches and figs and raspberries." We laugh at my silly rhyming. I lift my head to the blue sky and feel a kind of stubborn joy rise in me. In spite of everything. "In August . . . let's see . . . apricots and blackberries? In September mushrooms – and then October looms! With sweet oranges!"

If poetry can't comfort, corny ditties might.

"Look," says Manon as we walk past the cemetery. "Look at the kitten, Mommy!"

Next to the wrought-iron gate, in front of the high stone wall of the churchyard lies something that looks like a ball of downy black wool. Dead, I think at first. A little dead animal. But then the ball of wool moves. Sits up and stares at us with enormous yellow eyes.

"Now where would such a little thing come from?" I wonder aloud. "Must be from one of the farmhouses round here."

"No," says Manon breathlessly. "It's a dead person's kitten, Mommy. Why else would it be lying here next to the graves, all sad and sorrowful?"

"He doesn't look so sorrowful to me," I say defensively because I can see what's coming. She runs to the gate, and to my surprise the kitten doesn't scurry away. It jumps eagerly into her outstretched arms and starts a pitiful meowing. "Maybe he's just a little hungry."

"He must be frightfully hungry," says Manon while she presses it passionately to her. "Maybe his owner has been dead for weeks!"

"Manon, listen to me . . ."

"Never mind, kitty-cat, I'll look after you," she whispers and strokes it behind its ears until it stops meowing.

"No, Manon, we can't take him home. What if someone is looking for him? Let me see if he has a tattoo or a collar or something."

The instant I take the bundle from her, my resistance begins to melt away. Light as candyfloss the creature lies in my hands. Under the thick black pelt the body is thin, perhaps even emaciated. A male indeed, I notice. Barely a few months old. No sign of ownership to be found.

"If it was your kitten that got lost," I say to my daughter, "you wouldn't like it if someone else took him away."

"If I were dead," answers my daughter, "I would like it if someone else cared for my kitten."

"It isn't a dead person's cat, Manon," I say impatiently. "Maybe an abandoned cat. But we can't be sure of that. We can't just take him."

"But we can't just leave him here, Mommy!" she calls out when I put the little creature down. "He could die of hunger!"

Now I have two pairs of eyes pleading with me. My daughter's blue and full of tears, the cat's yellow and glistening. The joint assault makes my last bit of resistance crumble like dry clay.

"I'll tell you what we'll do. We'll go straight away to fetch him some food and bring it here. But we won't take him home with us."

I take her by the wrist and pull her reluctant body behind me while she keeps on glancing back over her shoulder. The kitten has reminded us both of the ginger cat that we had to leave at home when we came here. Her cat, Caramel – the same age as she, grown up with her – had to stay behind with her grandparents in Cape Town.

"Look, Mommy," she says after a few steps. "He's following us. He wants to come with us!"

"Be off," I hiss at the cat. "Scram!"

I stamp my foot on the ground and shoo him away with my arms. He stops, nervous, but the minute we carry on walking he follows us again at a safe distance, with small pattering steps.

I beg the cat: "Wait here for us. We'll bring you food. You can't come home with us. There's no room for you."

"He can sleep with me," Manon begs in her turn. "Please, Mommy, please. Just until we find out who he belongs to?"

"And how will we find that out?" I ask as we walk on, my steps already more resigned, with the ball of black wool rolling all the way behind us. "A notice in the cemetery for the dead to read?"

"I knew you'd say yes!" she calls out and throws her arms so tightly round my hips that I can't move another step.

"I haven't said yes yet," I mutter.

But I know the battle is lost. I will ask in the village, put up a notice in the supermarket, do my best to find the cat's owner. In the meantime I will take due care of him with the growing hope that no one will claim him. I don't ever again want to grow fond of something, anything, that I have to give up.

"I've given up too much," I say to my daughter.

But she no longer hears me. She has swept the cat up in her arms and is skipping ahead of me. Along the stone wall of the churchyard, past the first purple irises that have just started blooming by the road, past the vineyards stark and bare still waiting for leaves, past the stately silver-green olive grove in the distance, all the way home I follow the moving red splash of her T-shirt. Like a little light in the dark, that shirt flickers for me. Growing fainter, growing smaller, further and further away from me.

3

"Come in," André points the way. "*Entrez, entrez, entrez.*" As if he wants to compensate for his meagre French vocabulary by repeating the same word. "Let me introduce you to my wife. Hester! Where are you?"

He hears her footsteps on the floor above, in the spare room. This is where she licks her wounds these days, ever since the building operations in the living room drove her from the kitchen. He has found her there so many times, curled up on the bed, in broad daylight, with that damn cat in her arms.

"I'm coming," she says on the stair, her voice a little breathless and slightly guilty.

She appears in the inside kitchen door, frowns when she sees the stranger, passes her fingers through her hair. And suddenly André looks at his once attractive, well-groomed wife through the eyes of the stranger next to him. She was always slightly built and slim, but lately she has lost so much weight that she is beginning to look haggard. Her shortish dark hair is standing up uncombed, the grey at the crown of her head ever more noticeable, even a few grey hairs in her untidy fringe. The eyes under the fringe are hollow with grief, worn deep by guilt, sunken in their sockets like two empty caves. Her skin is as dull and lifeless as her eyes. Her mouth, formerly generous and smiling and often painted bright red, has become a thin colourless line. Is it possible that someone could undergo such a complete trans-

71

formation in four months? As though she is suffering from an incurable disease, thinks André. His wife's body is being consumed from within by incurable grief. And all he can do is stand by helplessly and watch her wither away. For every vague sign of improvement that he detects, probably only wishful thinking from his side, there are new symptoms of decline every week that he can't ignore.

"Hester." He is surprised by the crack in his own voice, coughs hastily, tries again. "Hester, this is Habib's sister that I told you about. Her name is Aïsha. Aïsha, this is Hester."

"I told you I didn't need her," Hester says curtly in Afrikaans, without a trace of her customary courtesy. She barely looks at the dark-haired girl next to André.

"I know, Hes, but I ran into her in the street, so I suggested she come with me so that you can at least meet. Just in case you may need her one day. She's prepared to do anything in the house, cleaning, ironing, cooking. Whatever. She needs the pocket money."

Hester shrugs as if to say that's not her problem. Aïsha's smile stretches ever more fixedly over her face, but it makes no impression on Hester. Then they both look down at Hester's feet, where the black kitten has appeared. The stiffness in Aïsha's expression vanishes instantly. She crouches to call the little creature to her softly and picks him up eagerly.

"Do you know the cat?" Hester asks in formal French, her eyes panicky.

"No, madame," answers Aïsha while the cat purrs in her arms. "But he's very cute. What's his name?"

A smile as fleeting as lightning flickers over Hester's face. Then she looks at Aïsha with her usual doleful expression. But now at least she takes in the young girl. She no longer stares right through her body to beyond the kitchen window.

"Fantôme," says Hester. "We found him in the cemetery. Are you still at school, Aïsha?"

"No, I finished last year, madame." She strokes the cat's head while talking, her voice so soft that Hester has to step closer to hear her. "I'm doing a part-time course this year so that one day I can go and work in a nursery school."

"So I take it you like children?"

Aïsha nods with a shy smile. "But in the meantime I'll do anything for pocket money, so if I can help madame in the house . . ."

"Call me Hester. Can I offer you a cup of tea?"

Aïsha timidly touches her long black hair.

"Madame surely has other things to do?"

"I assure you I have nothing else to do," says Hester and switches on the gas stove under the kettle. "Come and sit here at the table. And call me Hester, otherwise I definitely won't employ you."

André listens in amazement to the teasing undertone in his wife's voice. Like a faint echo from days long gone, it sounds to him.

"Thank you, a cup of tea will be nice," says Aïsha and pulls out a chair.

"Maybe I can pay you to come and drink tea with me once a week," muses Hester. "My French is getting very rusty."

"Madame's . . . your French is excellent," says Aïsha.

"Well, then, I'll leave you two on your own for now," André excuses himself. "I have work to do. *À bientôt,* Aïsha."

Until soon, he greets her. He suspects that they will see much more of this shy Moroccan girl. The sudden hunger that he noticed in Hester's eyes makes him slightly uneasy, almost as though he brought an unsuspecting victim to a cannibal's lair, but he doesn't allow himself to think any further along those lines. Any emotion, even a vague unease, is

73

surely better than the helplessness with which he'd looked at his wife's neglected appearance minutes before.

⮜⮞

"So what did you do the whole holiday?" Nathalie asks next to the school gate, where she's actually been waiting for him.

He grins gratefully. The whole day he's been watching her out of the corner of his eye, but she was surrounded by her girl friends most of the time. He wishes he could say that he was surrounded by his male friends, but he hasn't really made any yet. A stoutish, dense-ish British boy called Winston who trails after him everywhere, and a nerdy Dutch guy with whom he sometimes tries to talk Afrikaans, that's all. If it weren't for Nathalie he'd definitely have walked out of this school. Stolen his father's credit card to buy an air ticket back to South Africa. The only thing that keeps him here is the hope of walking with her to the bus stop some afternoons.

"I helped my dad to break down a wall," he says. "With a rented drill that makes a hell of a racket."

"Wow. That must have been cool."

He looks at her askance, not sure whether she's teasing or not.

"Well, it was the coolest thing I did the whole holiday. Which should give you an idea of how boring the rest was."

They walk side by side on the sidewalk in one of the many little alleys that snake through the heart of Avignon. For Emile the whole of the area within the medieval city wall is a maze where he still gets lost whenever he's on his own, but Nathalie knows even the narrowest lanes, the deserted alleys and the interesting dead ends, the canals and the age-old water mills in quiet side streets, the shady little squares that open up so unexpectedly when you turn a corner. Almost every day she

74

chooses a different route – which makes it even more difficult to find the right way when he's on his own – but he doesn't mind. It's a fantastic way to get to know the city.

Better still, it's a fantastic way to get to know Nathalie.

He can't even orient himself according to the sun, because by this time of the afternoon the sun has dipped behind the tall buildings on either side of them. Not skyscrapers, of course. This is Avignon, not New York. Most buildings are more than a century old and no higher than six storeys. Which is still higher than anything in a miserable little village like Lunel. And today he's actually thankful that the buildings are obstructing the sun, because it's the hottest day since he's been here and Nathalie's proximity is enough to make him sweaty under the arms even on a cool day.

"I didn't do anything to get excited about either," she says. "Like, you know, going to the movies a few times and trawling through the shops and for the rest just reading in my room."

"You're lucky to live in a town with movies and shops. Where I live, there's nothing but bloody vineyards."

"No friends?"

He shakes his head.

"And you don't have brothers or sisters?"

"No," he says, swallowing hard at the lie.

"Me neither. It's not nice, hey? I really miss a sister."

"Me too. I also miss a sister." His voice breaks so unexpectedly on the last word that Nathalie looks at him in surprise. He digs his hands deep into the pockets of his jeans and keeps his eyes fixed on the path. "I had a sister. But she's dead."

"I'm sorry . . . if I'd known . . ." stammers Nathalie.

"You couldn't have known," he says quickly. "I haven't told anyone at school. It's too difficult to talk about . . ."

For a while she walks in silence next to him. She keeps her

75

fingers in front of her mouth as though to stop any further foolish remarks.

"My father dragged me off to a therapist," says Emile when the silence becomes too heavy. "But I couldn't even talk to hér about it."

He wants to cry just thinking about those awful sessions in the stuffy consulting room. First all of them together, his stunned mother, his desperate father, and he, angry because he didn't want to be there, because he had nothing to say to them, because he couldn't remember what had happened. And Trudi the therapist, with her hook nose and her wild head of grey hair who eyed him all the time like a witch wanting to devour him, and who kept on and on at him, relentlessly asking questions, first in the presence of his parents and later on his own, as if she didn't believe him, as if she thought he was lying when he said he couldn't remember, when he protested that he'd forgotten everything that happened on that unforgettable day. The deeper he delved into his memory to arrive at that day, the bigger and blacker the hole around him got, until he couldn't see any blue sky above him, couldn't even breathe any more, until he stormed out of the room panic-stricken to gasp at the fresh air outside like someone who has nearly suffocated.

"When was this?" asks Nathalie.

"Not so long ago."

She stands still and takes his hand, which brings him to a stop too. He can't believe how cool her fingers feel on such a hot day. She looks at him solemnly, her eyes black like secrets you couldn't ever tell anyone. He turns his head away and stares over her shoulder at the display window of a boutique selling elegant ladies' clothing.

"I won't ask any more questions. Promise."

"She was shot dead," he says, keeping his eyes on the mannequin behind her shoulder. He hears her intake of breath. "The one moment she was standing next to me laughing. The next moment she was lying in a pool of blood in front of my feet. In between there is a sort of . . . darkness. Like when all the electricity in the house is suddenly knocked out by a storm. Or like a painting covered over with black paint. I can't get the black scraped off. Do you know what I mean?"

She stares at him, dumbfounded.

"Now I have to get going, otherwise I'll miss the bus," he says and turns on his heel and runs the whole way to the bus terminus outside the city wall.

Not that he really thinks he might miss the bus, rather because he wants to forget what he has just told Nathalie. It's easier when you're tired, when you're panting for breath, when your legs and arms are working so hard that your head isn't able to brood. Easier to forget everything you don't want to remember.

⤚⤚

My husband watches me all the time, as if I'm a prisoner and he my keeper. Of course this has been going on for months, but in the past week or two it's been getting worse by the day. Something in his scrutinising gaze has changed. The accusation has been replaced with distrust. Maybe it's just my imagination, maybe just another sign that I'm losing my mind, as he evidently thinks.

I can't imagine how it must feel for you to be so constantly watched, Myriam. And in your case by strangers, too. Without any possibility of escape. I at least have my escape routes, my hiding places, a few ways of rendering myself invisible. I can return to my metaphorical womb, bolt the door and fill the claw-foot bath with warm water and lie there floating for an hour or more. I had to insist on the bolt. André didn't think it a good idea. Like any dutiful warder he wants access to his prisoner, day and night, everywhere. To prevent her escaping or hurting herself.

Sometimes self-mutilation is the only escape route left, but I'm not thére yet. Whatever dark thoughts my husband might detect in my head, I still cling to what remains of my existence. Like Oedipus who refused to take his own life because that wouldn't have been punishment enough. Do you know the story of Oedipus? He chose to pluck his eyes out, rather than ending it all quickly, to wander sightless and homeless through the world, continuing to punish himself year after year. Come to think of it, in that newspaper picture I saw of you, you had no eyes either. Only two holes in your expressionless face.

As far as I'm concerned, there are still things I'd like to see and hear. Not many. But still.

I still talk to myself and to you and to my daughter. And of course to my new phantom cat. When my arms get so light and empty that it feels as if they're going to turn into wings, I grab Fantôme's woolly black body. He follows me everywhere, even when I go walking — something I do more often, now that I don't have the excuse of wind and cold keeping me captive indoors all day – but he always turns back when we're close to the cemetery. As if he's afraid I'll leave him there next to the graves where I found him.

My best refuge, after the bathroom, is the cherry orchard up the hill. I lie there on my back under the trees and wait for the small red fruit to ripen. They're almost ready for eating, but still not quite as black and sweet as I like them. Firm yet juicy, like a baby's heart in a cannibal's mouth. I wait patiently, my eyes usually closed, while the sun breaks through the leaves now and again and strokes my skin like a lascivious lover.

Sometimes I doze, then I have strange dreams about my daughter being in prison and you sitting at a kitchen table watching your tears drop into a coffee cup, and me looking down at both of you from above, as if I'm floating, as if I'm dead. Strange, but not disturbing. Apparently the idea of my own death no longer upsets me.

Sometimes I think of my silent, melancholy father and my mother who has tried for so many years to cheer him up. Why he should be melancholic, nobody knows, least of all himself. My mother suspects it has something to do with his own father's early death as a soldier in the Second World War. But then there are millions of children who lose parents in wars without becoming depressive adults. No, I suspect it's genetic, an inherent melancholy that came with his blue-grey eyes and his brown hair. I in turn inherited the eyes and hair, but thank heaven not the melancholy. Or so I always thought. I take more after my optimistic mother, a woman with an unshake-able belief in life and love and enough fresh fruit and vegetables every day.

And yet these last months I've become more and more like my father. Morose and taciturn. As if this melancholy is a virus that I've been carrying in me all my life, unsuspecting and naive, until a terrible crime destroyed my natural immunity.

And as always, I wonder about you, Myriam. Whether you feel as despairing as I do. Or is my kind of despair a Western concept, a fate reserved for well-to-do white women?

It's apparently a rather disappointing spring, according to the local people that my husband overhears in the mornings at the little supermarket. Temperatures a good bit lower than usual, they complain, which is the reason the cherries aren't ripe yet. Awkward winds blowing from a different direction every day. I don't complain about the weather. The numbing cold of those first few weeks froze my tongue. My body is thawing slowly like an iceberg, little by little, as I lie under the cherry trees.

When at last I pluck the first of those babies' hearts from the tree and stuff it into my greedy mouth, I will think of you, Myriam. Sweeter than sweet it will taste, sweet as the voices of dead children.

⌒⌒

"Who are you talking to, Hester?" André unexpectedly asks behind me.

I start with surprise, almost falling over backwards in the front garden where I'm sitting on my haunches planting lavender shrubs. It was he who bought these boxes full of plants this morning – all kinds of herbs for the clay pots in front of the kitchen window, lilac-blue hydrangeas for the shady patches, arums for the damp corner where the tap constantly drips, old-fashioned white rambling roses to train up the stone walls – but it is I who must get them to grow. You've got green fingers, Hes. My fingers haven't been green for a long time, I wanted to say to him, my fingers rotted and fell off. I can't even stroke your cheek, husband dear. But I knew he wouldn't listen. It's the keeper's latest plan to occupy his prisoner.

"To myself," I mumble.

"I'm worried about you." He squats next to me and waits for me to look at him, but I keep my eyes on the hole I'm digging in the earth. "You're drifting further and further away from me. From everyone around you."

"I'm not drifting André, I'm gardening. Isn't that what you wanted?"

"Isn't that what yóu wanted? I took your garden plan with me to the nursery, Hester, the plan you drew yourself last year.

80

What you wanted to plant where, the lavender, the climbers, the herbs in pots, the whole garden was your idea!"

It's true that I was rather excited about my garden-to-be when we bought the house last summer. There were remains of an earlier garden: the struggling little lemon tree near the gate, the gnarled trunk of an ancient wisteria that has just begun to bloom again by the front door, the white rambling roses against one of the side walls. And a row of rosemary bushes against the kitchen wall. The rest was all weeds.

A fantastic challenge, I thought last summer. Hours of drawing pictures and making plans. More climbers for the side walls, lavender in front of the living room windows, a whole variety of herbs in front of the kitchen window. Hydrangeas, irises, arum lilies, narcissi, everything in shades of lilac-blue and creamy white, with a dash of bright yellow here and there, some tulips, a row of freesias, a kind of miniature sunflower growing wild next to the road in this region, the gleaming lemons on the tree near the gate. That's if you can convince the lemon tree to ever bear fruit again, my husband admonished. Of course I can do it, I assured him. My fingers were green, my creative urge was stimulated, my enthusiasm endless. I could take on anything. Last year.

The times that were.

"You refuse to speak to me, Hester."

"What am I doing now?"

"You're asking silly rhetorical questions, that's what you're doing. You don't want to talk to me, you don't want to talk to a psychologist, you refuse to talk to anyone who might be able to help you. But you talk more and more to yourself. Or to the damn cat. Or to . . . whatever, I don't know, ghosts, shadows, hallucinations?"

"Do you think I'm going mad?" I ask as calmly as I can.

"No, I don't think you're mad, Hes, but I think you are suffering from a form of depression. And as a result of that, you sometimes . . . lose touch with reality."

I push a lavender plant into the hole I have just dug with the garden fork. Then I fill it up from the pile of soil next to it. I keep my movements slow, economical, deliberate. The scream that I feel welling up in me I suppress just as deliberately. Not a muscle twitches in my tense face.

"Precisely what do you mean when you say I 'lose touch' with reality?"

"Hester. Look at me. Please." He puts his hand on my chin and turns my face to him. Nothing forced in his touch. Carefully, as though my skin is an eggshell that can crack. I offer no resistance, only empty my eyes so that he won't read any false messages there. "I've heard a few times how you . . . " He's the first to look away. He shakes his head and asks in a dull voice: "May I ask who Myriam is?"

"Myriam?"

"Someone you write letters to. I haven't read them," he immediately assures me. "I was going through the kitchen drawers looking for scissors and came across this bundle of letters." I don't know whether I want to believe him. I press the soil down firmly with the garden fork and start digging the next hole. "Who is Myriam and why do you write to her?"

"What do you think, André?"

"I wish you would stop throwing everything I say back into my face with a damn question!"

For the first time in weeks I feel the sharp edge of his impatience.

"Sorry. It's a bad habit I picked up from Trudi the Therapist."

Now I've really infuriated him. He hates my negative attitude to Trudi and her therapy. For weeks it was a refrain in our house: She can help us, Hester. No one can help me, André.

"Whó is Myriam?" He passes his hand over his face, such an exhausted, despairing gesture that I wish I could give him a reassuring answer. "Is it the woman in the newspaper report?"

"Which newspaper report? Sorry. Another question."

'The press cutting I found in another drawer in the kitchen," he says slowly, almost threateningly, fixing his gaze on me. "Thát I did read. My French isn't good enough to understand it all. I do understand that she's in prison. On a murder charge?"

He takes my hand, forces me to drop the garden fork, and presses me gently down until I sit flat on the ground. His face is suddenly so close to mine that I want to back away in panic, but I take a deep breath and manage to keep looking at him motionlessly.

"Tell me about this woman, Hester."

His voice assumes the pleading tone that I have come to fear these last four months.

"Myriam is a young woman from the Democratic Republic of the Congo," I tell him. "Her husband's name is Joseph. They both wanted to get out of the Congo. Do you know that one of the bloodiest wars on earth has been raging there in the last decade? Two-and-half million dead in seven years. Happened to hear it on the radio the other day."

I don't look at my husband as I speak, keep my eyes on the lavender bush I've just planted, but I hear his rapid breathing next to my left ear. He must be more upset than he cares to show. I know more about the DRC than I care to show. Read up in a book about Africa that my son brought from his school library. But this is a story about a woman, not a country.

"Joseph could get a French passport because his father was a French citizen. Apparently came to France to work when Joseph was a little boy and never went back to his wife and children. So Joseph and Myriam saved all their money, sold everything they could sell, to buy a single air ticket to France. For Joseph. The idea was for him to get settled here, look for work and somewhere to live and all those things, then as soon as possible send her money so that she and the children could also come. The eldest girl was about a year old when Joseph left. And she was expecting the second."

Out of the corner of my eye I see that Fantôme has started playing with a pigeon feather under the lemon tree. His black coat shines in the sun as he rolls around on his back. I wish I could call him to me and hug him. I wish I could hug my husband while telling him about Myriam, then I won't have to see the incomprehension in his eyes.

"It seems Joseph had no luck finding work here in France. And didn't send word very often. I assume neither one of them can read and write very well, and remember there was a war going on, so one doesn't know if postal services were operating. In any event, all contact from his side stopped after about a year. He could have been dead, for all Myriam knew, but she refused to even think of such a possibility. He was her only hope of ever getting out of Africa, of leaving war and poverty and sickness and famine behind and trying to make a better life for her children in Europe."

"The official language in Myriam's native land is French and about half the population belong to the Catholic church, but it's not Europe, it's very far from Europe. The average life expectancy in Myriam's country of birth is 45 years. In France these days it's over 80 years. Apparently everyone in Europe will live to be 100 years old in the foreseeable future. The gap between Africa and Europe grows larger every day, in all spheres. Who can blame Myriam Soro that she was prepared to do anything to bridge this gap?

"When it became clear that no money for air tickets would be forthcoming, she realised that she would have to raise the money herself. She was young, she was attractive, she did what she could. She became a prostitute."

I hear a huskiness in my voice. I wonder if it is emotion, or simply the physical consequence of unused vocal chords, since I'm no longer used to speaking more than a few sentences at a time. At least not with other people, only to myself or with animals and trees and clouds and people that no one else can see, the way I did when I was small.

"In the meantime the war came to an end a year ago. Or came to a temporary halt. Did you know that in half the African countries where conflict ends, the warring starts again within five years?"

"Since when do you know so much about Africa?"

He doesn't mean it sarcastically. I can hear he's really amazed at what I'm telling him. All of it.

"Since coming to live in Europe," I answer. "Anyway, Myriam decided she had to use the cessation of hostilities to make her getaway. It was a question of now or never. So towards the end of last year she and her two little daughters – then three and four years old – flew to France to come and look for her husband. What she still had to do to get all the right papers, who she had to sleep with and who she had to bribe, no one will ever know."

My voice cracks unexpectedly. I keep quiet for a few moments and watch the cat, now bored with the feather, sniffing at the herb plants in the boxes. André sits with his head in his hands till I go on.

"Joseph had left the last address he'd given her a long time before. Also the one after, that she'd got from someone else. But she followed the trail, from address to address, all the way from Paris to Marseille. Searched for about three months before she finally tracked him down. Two hungry children with her all the time. I don't know how she kept them alive. Probably

85

prostitution again. When she finally reached Joseph, he wanted nothing to do with her or the children. He'd in the meantime married another woman, unlawfully of course, and didn't want the new wife to know that he was already married. He had a son by her, of whom he was very proud. And then . . . well . . . the end of the story you probably read in the newspaper report?"

"Then she murdered the two daughters?"

I hear the horror in my husband's voice. It gives me the courage to turn my head and look him in the eye.

"She smothered them with a pillow while they were sleeping. Then she gave herself up to the police. She did what she could, André, once again. The only thing left for her to do."

"To kill her children?"

Now my husband is the one who looks as though he wants to back off. To flinch from my empty gaze, from my incomprehensible words, from the stranger that I have become to him. I look down at my hands lying in my lap, pale as dead flesh.

"She couldn't keep them alive in France, except through prostitution, and she obviously couldn't see herself carrying on with that. She had no money to fly back to Africa – and how could she in any case take them back to everything she'd wanted to take them away from? Even if another war didn't break out in her country, everyone would still suffer the aftermath of the previous one for years to come. So she couldn't go back and she couldn't stay. What should she have done?"

André shakes his head repeatedly.

"How do you know all this?" he asks at last, frowning.

"I read the dry facts of the story in the newspaper."

"And the rest?"

"You're an architect, André. When you study the plans of

86

a house, something that to other people would simply look like lines on paper, you see a three-dimensional building, don't you?"

"You've lost me, Hester."

No, I want to say, it's you who have lost me. Along with your daughter.

"When I read the bones of the story in the newspaper, the rest became clear to me." Now I really sound insane. Can't blame my husband that he thinks I've lost my bearings. "I understand this woman, André. I understand why she did what she did."

"No, listen, Hester, I can understand that you have empathy with her because she lost her children. But there are after all thousands of people who lose their children. This woman murdered her children. She herself caused their deaths."

"We all cause our children's deaths. Simply by bringing them into the world."

"You're only saying that because you're depressed," he says, clicking his tongue disconsolately.

"No, I'm saying it because it's a terrible truth that only recently dawned on me. For all I know it's our greatest responsibility as parents. To help them die."

"To help them live, I prefer to call it."

"Of course. And when you see a half empty bottle of wine, you prefer to call it half full. That's how you are."

꩜

It's hard to believe that his wife has become so pessimistic, thinks André as he watches her through the dusty kitchen window. She is sitting in the front garden again, ostensibly planting herbs in clay pots, but mostly staring unseeingly in front of her. He's been standing right in front of her, only a pane of dirty glass separating them, for at least ten minutes, but she remains totally unaware of him. His cup of tea has long grown cold in his hands. Not that it matters. His throat feels so constricted that he wouldn't be able to drink it anyway.

Hester always had the kind of nature that could be described as sunny. An ability (which sometimes irritated him, he now has to admit shamefacedly) to see a silver lining round every dark cloud. Even to invent one if she couldn't spot it. The eternal optimism of a born pedagogue, he used to tease her. And you, she would reply, what about you? Don't think you fool me with your pretended pessimism!

"You wouldn't have become an architect if you hadn't believed that you could somehow make the world a better place to live in. That's what I call optimism."

"I'm in it for the money," he grinned.

"What money? That you're hiding where?" She looked around in mock surprise. This was in their bedroom in Cape Town. A Sunday morning they spent in bed drinking coffee and reading the papers. Hester's hair stood uncombed all over her head and the stretched shoulder straps of her nightdress hung slack over her bare arms. In the soft light of the late summer's morning she was irresistibly beautiful to him. "If you were doing it for the money, you'd be designing mansions for millionaires, not community centres for townships."

"It's a compromise. I do it to make money while at the same time soothing my conscience."

"You do it because you're an optimist and an idealist and a good Samaritan. And that's why after all these years I'm still in love with you."

She leaned over and planted a kiss on his unshaven cheek. He pressed her into the crook of his arm and sniffed at her hair like a hungry hound and wondered if the children would leave them alone for long enough for him to draw her down to him on the bed.

"No, Hes," he said with his nose in her hair, "you know my motto: Everything will turn out right in the end – but along the way everything that can possibly go wrong, will go wrong. That's what two decades in the building industry has taught me."

"Aha! You see?" She clapped triumphantly on his chest. "That's what's called pessimistic optimism!"

And now the pessimistic optimist stands in his dusty house in France longing for the wife that lay laughing in bed beside him on that Sunday morning. The sorrowful woman out there is someone he doesn't know, an intruder with whom he doesn't want to live any longer, a substitute that he wants to grab by the shoulders and chase away. So that Hester can return.

Every now and then she looks at a spot next to her, with a sliver of a smile that gives him cold shivers, and mutters a few words into the air. He can't hear what she's saying. But he knows to whom she is talking.

He forces himself to take a few sips of the cold tea before he throws open the window. It's such a brutal gesture that Hester's head starts up in fright. A wave of pity, tenderness, love rises up in him, but he holds his breath and waits for the wave to recede. The time has come to drive the ghosts from this house.

"*She isn't here, Hes,*" he says softly, but urgently. "She's never again going to be here. She can't hear you, she can't answer you, she's been dead for four months. Do you hear what I say, Hes? Manon was shot on the thirteenth of January this year in a shop on the corner of our street."

She closes her eyes tight and presses her hands over her

89

ears while her upper body begins to jerk as though to vomit. But all that comes out of her mouth is a high, keening, inhuman sound, like a blaring siren. Like the sound of the ambulance that sweltering afternoon in their leafy street in Cape Town.

DREAMS

4

Of course I know my daughter is dead. When I speak to her, when I hear her laughing excitedly like a bleating goat, when I see the rosy sheen of her hair in the sunlight, then I know that she now exists only in my memory. I also know that my memory is all that I have to hold on to. I'm hanging over a precipice and clinging with all my might to the very last straw. Even if it's an imaginary straw, it doesn't matter, it works for me. Beggars can't be choosers.

I have become a beggar. I rummage around in my memory as though it's a rubbish bin that will yield up something useful, a memory that can be recycled like a bottle, a conversation that can be pored over like an old newspaper, or simply a forgotten gesture that can feed my terrible hunger. I go to bed at night with hands outstretched like a supplicant. Not clasped in prayer, no, with cupped hands I go to meet my dreams. Alms, scraps, that's what I'm asking. Every time Manon appears in a dream, I weep with gratitude.

These last few days I've been trying very hard, for the sake of my husband and my son, to behave more like a normal person. Though I'm not sure what "normal behaviour" constitutes in these circumstances There is nothing "normal" about the death of a child. The violent death of my five-year-old daughter is the most abnormal, senseless, obscene thing that has ever happened to me. Surely it's abnormal to try to act normal!

And yet I do it because I know it is what they expect of

me. *Come in out of the cold, my love. I'll show you where to step.*

I smile with my husband because of the beautiful living room he and Habib have built for us. Because of the large stone fireplace that they have restored, the clay tiles that they have laid on the floor, the lovely slabs of white stone around the doorways that they have uncovered under many layers of plaster. Even at their unexpected little discoveries like the doorknobs of glowing copper that had been hidden under layers of paint for decades, even over that I rejoice with my husband. I look with pride at the formerly dark little back room, now modernised with a shiny new toilet and walls plastered white and a few bookshelves and a basket for magazines, a cosy little library. Truly a place to take one's ease.

And I grumble good-naturedly about my kitchen becoming the next battlefield in my husband's triumphal march through the house. This last week we've been having our meals in the garden, where the lavender plants are beginning to bush impressively, or in the dining corner of the spacious living room where the round kitchen table has found a temporary home. The kitchen is out of bounds while André and his helper install wooden cupboards and lay tiles. This means cooking on a portable gas stove or heating instant meals in a microwave oven – both appliances also temporarily lodged in the living room – or having barbecues outside. Or else we eat cold food, much easier after all, olives and patés and salads, picnic food, bread and ham and cheese, fresh fruit and raw vegetables, summer food. Luckily by this time it's warm enough to be eating cold food. No, actually nothing to do with luck, that's how my husband planned it. As soon as summer starts, as soon as we can eat out of doors comfortably, he'd said from the beginning, we'd tackle the kitchen. Once our "most urgent needs" like hot water and working toilets and reliable electricity had been satisfied.

According to my husband we've now dealt with our most urgent needs.

My most urgent need still remains outside his reach, beyond his competence, but on the whole I manage to keep that from him.

As I say, I'm behaving more like a normal person. During the day, in any case, as long as they're watching me. At night it's a different story. *Oh the red patchwork blanket. The sorrow and tears when the candle is snuffed.*

I can't forbid my daughter the house. Show me a mother who can do that. I keep her near me all the time, in my shadow, under my wide red summer dress, next to my heart. Shh, I say, don't cry, my love. Don't let them hear you. But at night, when everyone is asleep, she tiptoes barefoot through the house, from room to room, from bed to bed, to slip into our dreams.

At first I thought it was only I who dreamed about her all the time – at least three times a week since I started concealing her in the daytime – but I now suspect that she appears almost as frequently in her father's and her brother's dreams.

When last week I awoke with wet cheeks once again, André was sitting up in bed next to me, his dark eyes questioning me. My first reaction was a wave of irritation. Am I now being watched even in my sleep?

But then he sighed and said: "I've also had another long dream about her."

I remained lying on my back, wiped my cheeks and stared at the ceiling.

"What did you dream?" I asked after a few moments, without looking at him.

"We were on a beach. Clifton, I think, but not quite. Clifton mixed with Hermanus. Or some other place. There was a river mouth at the beach. And the sea water was hot. Not warm like the Mediterranean Sea, hot like a bath, steaming. You and Emile were building a sand castle that looked like the Notre Dame in Paris. Incredibly impressive. Emile was about five years old. Manon too. In the dream they were the same age. Like twins. Manon walked into the steaming water with me, hand in hand. I swear I could feel her hand, Hester."

His voice cracked like glass. I knew that if I looked into his eyes at that moment, it would be like looking into a shattered mirror. I would see all kinds of phantoms behind the cracks.

"And then?"

"We walked in deeper and deeper and she held my hand ever more tightly. She was a little anxious, but not frightened. Laughing all the while. That husky giggly laugh of hers. I looked back to the beach and saw that the Notre Dame had grown much bigger than you and Emile. You were standing under one of the towers, looking up at a gargoyle, and I was suddenly afraid that the tower would collapse and that you'd both be buried under tons of sand, so I dropped Manon's hand to wave at you to stand aside. And when I looked back at the water, Manon was gone. The steam had become a bank of dense fog, I couldn't believe it, I could barely see my hand in front of my face. I dived under the water and desperately searched around me, but even underwater everything was misty, and when I came up again, the water was beginning to form blocks of ice. And then I woke up. Frozen from top to toe."

I felt him shudder and took his hand, my eyes still fixed on the ceiling.

"That's how most of my dreams about her end," he said. "Suddenly she's just gone. In a car, in a supermarket, in the sea, wherever."

That isn't a dream, dearest husband. It actually happened. Suddenly she was just gone. One particularly hot summer's day she went with her brother to the corner shop to buy ice cream – and never came home again.

"I don't have dreams of terror," I confessed. "I have no more fear left. Not about her. All my worst nightmares have been realised. I have dreams of consolation instead. Ordinary everyday scenes where we do things together."

"Then why do you cry when you wake up?"

"Because she's gone when I wake up."

After this conversation I decided to ask Emile if he also dreams about her. It wasn't easy. I no longer know how to talk to my son. It's as if we're standing on two high cliffs opposite each other with an unbridgeable abyss between us into which all our words drop like stones. Maybe all mothers feel like this when their cute little boys change into uncommunicative adolescents. But in our case the abyss has grown wider because of Manon's death.

He was there when it happened – and I wasn't. That's what it amounts to.

He feels guilty that he couldn't defend her. And I feel guilty because I wasn't there to protect her. And he suspects that somewhere in my darkest depths, I blame him because he couldn't protect her.

I don't know if it is true. I'd rather not think about it. There are jagged holes in a mother's heart that can't bear the light of self-examination.

Therefore I started by asking about his schoolwork. One morning in the temporary kitchen that we had rigged up in the living room, while I was warming a cup of cold coffee in the microwave.

"Dad says you're doing better all the time at maths. As I've told you before, it must be a talent you got from him, because for me maths has always been torture. But if I can help with any of the other subjects . . . How're you coping with the French verbs?"

My sudden interest caught him so unawares that he froze. For a moment the knife with which he was spreading Nutella on a slice of bread dangled motionless in his right hand. Then he hunched his shoulders, those bony boy shoulders that sometimes look as fragile as porcelain cups, and said: "Okay."

Cul-de-sac. The abyss between us yawned wider than ever. I looked down and felt giddy.

"Since when do you eat bread and chocolate for breakfast?" I joked. "A boy your age needs a plate of porridge to see him through the day, doesn't he?"

Since when do you give a damn about what I eat in the mornings? That's the accusation I read in his glance. I deserved it, I know.

"We're in France, Mom. Where would I find *porridge*?"

"I can buy you oats if you like. Or something like Weet-bix?"

"If you like, Mom," he answered.

Another cul-de-sac. It was clear that the breakfast route wouldn't get us any further than the schoolwork route. Time to stop beating about the bush, I decided with my heart in my mouth. Jump like a trapeze artiste. Stretch out your hands and hope your son catches you.

"I dreamed about Manon again last night," I said.

Apparently unmoved, he carried on spreading his bread, glued two slices together and took a large bite. No attempt to catch me. I had to make a desperate somersault in the air to break my fall.

"Your dad says that every time he dreams of her it ends in a nightmare. He says it's got so bad that he's afraid to go to

98

sleep at night. With me it's the opposite. My dreams are mostly so pleasant that I don't want to wake up. And yours?"

He looked distrustfully at me. "I can't remember my dreams."

"Never?"

"Just about never." He took another huge bite of the bread and thought for a moment. "A few nights ago I dreamt of a girl in my class. That one was OK."

"A pretty girl?" Another pathetic attempt to keep it light.

"Uh-huh."

He stuffed the last of the bread into his mouth, picked up his rucksack, ready to go to school. His T-shirt hung like a sack on his thin body. His wide trouser legs were frayed at the bottom and trampled by his dirty trainers. I know it's the fashion amongst teenagers to look as if they've stolen a destitute giant's clothes, but my eyes suddenly stung with tears that I didn't want to shed. The kind of tears I hadn't shed in months, tears of tenderness rather than loss.

"Bye," he said, without looking round, and walked out of the front door.

I listened to the sound of his bicycle wheels over the gravel in the front garden, to the gate clicking closed behind him, to the silence descending on me, slowly, like mist. It felt like a welcome embrace. Safe in the arms of silence.

⌒⌒

As usual André takes a short cut across the village square, grateful for the shade of the plane trees on this hot day. He stops, surprised to see Hester standing in the middle of the square, next to the fountain where there is not a sliver of shade, only the stone beasts shining almost blindingly white in the merciless light. She's talking to a little girl of about eight, leaning forward eagerly to hear the child better, her whole attitude one of intense attention. The sun glistens on her brown hair (the grey sheen has disappeared this last week; surely, he thinks, a sign of improvement?) and sparkles in the clear spring water gushing from the mouth of one of the stone figures. The splashing of the water makes him long for a cold beer, but Hester seems oblivious of the heat, unaware of anything but the child with her.

He lengthens his stride to hear what they're talking about in such earnest. Then, suddenly afraid his wife will stop talking if she sees him, he consciously slows down. A few of the patrons sitting outside the café under the coloured umbrellas that have mushroomed here in the past week, watch his uneven progress over the square. Inquisitive, amused, perhaps only bored, all of them strangers, tourists and holiday-makers who arrived along with the early heat wave. He tucks the newspaper and baguette he has just bought tightly under his arm, self-conscious in front of so many strange eyes. He wonders if they would take him for a resident of Lunel. In his sweaty T-shirt and dirty work trousers he probably looks like a local artisan, a builder or a plumber, perhaps even a farmer.

No, he decides, one glance should be enough to tell them that he, like them, doesn't really belong here. That he's just a visitor, a well-to-do foreigner playing at being a modest labourer, someone silly enough to imagine that he looks at home here. The little girl with Hester doesn't look as if she belongs either. He's noticed her before near the little primary school. He couldn't but notice her. She's the only black child in the village.

Odd that he's never seen any adult black inhabitants. Maybe her parents work a night shift, maybe her father's a truck driver or a commercial traveller seldom sleeping at home, maybe her mother's an invalid or handicapped. Or simply someone who doesn't like to leave home, a woman who doesn't make contact easily.

Like Hester these days.

The child is wearing a canary-yellow shirt and a short coloured skirt and a red rucksack that looks far too heavy for her thin back. Her legs are matchstick thin, her feet in sandals. But it's her hairstyle that strikes him most of all, at least a dozen short little pigtails, all fastened with shiny coloured balls. Like wearing a collection of marbles on her head.

". . . come and visit," he hears the child say when he leaves the shade of the plane trees to walk to the fountain. "But I'll first have to ask my mom."

"Of course." Hester greets him with a smile that could almost be described as broad. "Look, André, I've made friends with someone in the town. Her name's Aurore and she'll be eleven soon."

To him the child looks a lot younger than eleven. Not only because she's so small and thin; also in the way she studies him, head at an angle, with that openly curious gaze of a toddler. The way Manon often stared at strangers.

"Hello, Aurore. My name is André."

"This is my husband," Hester says to the child. "He's the one who draws so well."

"The architect?" Her voice is as clear as the marbles on her head. "Will you show me how to draw a house? I like drawing people, but I have trouble with houses."

"*My* difficulty is drawing people," says André.

"He will," Hester answers for him. "If you come and visit, he can show you."

"But now I must go home to eat. My mom will be waiting for me."

"*Á bientôt*, Aurore," says Hester and watches her thoughtfully as she runs across the square, the heavy red rucksack bobbing on the thin back. "There's something about that little body . . ."

She leaves the phrase hanging in the air like a wish.

"Makes one think of Manon, doesn't it?" says André carefully. "Is that why you invited her to come and visit?"

"She invited herself." Hester laughs unsteadily, her eyes less cloudy than usual. "She's unbelievably inquisitive. Like Manon. When she heard I was from Africa, there was no stopping her. Ten questions a minute."

"Has she been to Africa herself?" asks André as they start walking home together.

"She was born in Rwanda. But she can't remember anything, she was a baby when she came here. If she's ten now, it must have been at the time of the genocide."

Hester looks at the sheaf of dried-out flowers with their faded red-white-and-blue ribbon leaning against the war monument. For a moment it looks as if she'll stop, read the names on the monument, show some kind of respect, but then she shakes her head and walks on.

"You know, till now the whole tragedy between the Hutus and the Tutsis has been rather abstract for me," she muses as they turn into the narrow alley next to the little municipal building. "Horrendous but abstract. And now it suddenly feels . . . close."

"Are her parents also here in town?"

"I would guess that her whole family was murdered." The cobblestones lie baking in the pale glow of the sun that now hangs right above their heads, but she shivers as if she's cold and folds her arms across her chest. "I didn't want to ask too much. She preferred to talk about other things, as you'd expect. But it sounds as though she's been adopted by a French family."

"The mother that she talks about . . ."

102

"She wouldn't be able to remember her biological mother." Hester looks so upset that he places his arm clumsily over her shoulders. "And yet one can't help wondering what might have stuck in such a child's subconscious. Especially now that the slaughter is so constantly in the news again. Only this morning I heard someone on the radio, a young girl who survived by feigning death. A whole day and night of hiding under her mother's dead body. What do you think would go through Aurore's mind if she were to hear something like that?"

"I don't know if it's any comfort, but it won't stay in the news for long," sighs André and shows her the front page of the newspaper he has just bought. "There are new catastrophes hatching in Africa. Have you seen what's happening in Sudan? In Darfur?"

"I don't want to see it. I'm fed up with bad news out of Africa. Fed-the-hell-up with Africa, to tell you the truth. Isn't it better to stay here? Now that we're here anyway?"

He is so dumbfounded that for a few moments he can't utter a word.

"To do what?" he asks in a hoarse voice.

"Start all over again?"

"But how would we live?"

"With a hell of a lot of pain," she says and grimaces. "Is there any other way?"

"Hester." He tries to keep his voice calm. "A month ago you couldn't wait to go back."

"Now I can." She walks up the hill so fast that he struggles to keep up. "The first few weeks were hell, André. But one can get used to anything, even hell. And it remains a relative concept. Now I'm beginning to wonder about the hell waiting in Cape Town. Where everything, every street and every tree, every piece of furniture in our house, every person that I know, will remind me of her."

"Wait, wait, Hester," he pants behind her. "What do you really want to get away from? The miseries of Africa? Or your own memories?"

"From everything," she says curtly. "From the whole damned catastrophe."

"No, you're confusing things," he persists. "You can't be angry with Africa – or with any city in Africa – because your child died there."

"Here in Europe you can send your child to a corner shop without being afraid that someone is going to be waiting for her with a gun."

Their voices echo between the stone buildings in the narrow street. Luckily no one can understand what they're saying, he comforts himself. Here in Europe.

"Here in Europe there are other things to be scared of," he protests and stops for breath, but she just shakes her head and pushes on, gasping by the time she reaches the garden gate. "Here you and your child can board a train and a bomb can explode under your seat. Or you get into an aircraft and it gets hijacked by a bunch of kamikaze terrorists. Or you can . . ."

She isn't listening to him any longer. She tugs impatiently at the stiff handle, shoulders the wooden gate open and disappears behind the high wall.

"One can't be safe anywhere anymore," says André to himself in the deserted street.

⌒⌒

And there, suddenly last night, you walked across our TV screen, Myriam. Your face a dark haunted house, no light burning, not even in your eyes. Your cheekbones sharp as barbed wire to ward off intruders. Your broad nose a solid

104

guard before the door of your silent mouth. Your fleshy lips under lock and key.

It was old file material, a glimpse of you being shepherded into a police vehicle when you were arrested a few months ago. A short item on the eight o'clock news announcing that your court case starts today in Marseille. The monster mother, as one of the sensational magazines called you. The Medea of Africa, according to *Le Monde*. I'm apparently not the only one whose imagination has been gripped by you. They predict that the courtroom will be packed. You are becoming a *cause célèbre*. Human rights organisations, feminist movements, anti-racism groups, immigrants from Africa, all of them suddenly want to speak on your behalf. Is that because you don't have anything to say yourself? A bunch of far-right Front Nationale supporters will be staging a demonstration outside the court. What you did – such an unthinkable "primitive" deed – is just more proof, according to them, that people like you don't belong here. Raise the drawbridge, barricade the gates, man the loopholes. The barbarians are coming.

I wonder what you think of all of this. I suspect that your face today in court will be even more closed than last night on TV. Mouth muzzled, shutters in front of the eyes, interior inaccessible.

Would you like me to talk about something else? Shall I tell you about the heatwave that hit us this past week? Temperatures of nearly forty degrees every day. In Africa it gets hotter, I know, but we're not in Africa and we didn't expect such heat so early in summer. Caught unawares again. Why can't we get our act together, as Emile asked the other night, rather down in the mouth. Why are we so constantly taken by surprise, swept off our feet? By the cold, by dust, by desolation, by the wind, the sun, the heat, the flies, the mosquitoes, the spiders, by everything around us? Probably because our feet aren't planted firmly on the ground, I could say. Because for months we've simply been bobbing through life, drifting on the surface, holding our breath from moment to moment, that's all. Too scared to look back, even more scared to look forward.

According to the weather report following the eight o'clock news, it should start cooling down tomorrow. Until then, we'll sweat and cover our heads and restrict our movements. As in Africa.

And yet every time I look around me, I know I'm far from Africa. The landscape has lost that delicate light-green sheen of early spring. Everything is now bright green, dark green, robust shades of green, growing unchecked, rampant – the vineyards, the orchards, the patchwork fields of vegetables on the outskirts of the village. The square slumbers all day in the shade of the plane trees; the fountain water shimmers in the fierce sunlight; wisteria hangs over doorways and hedges, also over our front door; white roses climb the stone walls, also up our stone wall. At midday the cobbled streets grow still and the shutters in front of the windows are closed. Then you hear nothing but the screech of the cicadas. Towards late afternoon the village comes to life again, friends gather under umbrellas outside the café, grey-haired men play *boules* next to the fountain, tourists cycle through avenues of plane trees.

This is what I dreamed of, Myriam. Such carefree summer scenes, so different from the cold and deprivation of our first weeks in this house. The smells and sounds and the extravagant variety of the overflowing morning markets. Yesterday I counted seven different kinds of lettuce at a single stall. Four kinds of tomato, three kinds of melon, strawberries and raspberries and the last boxes of black cherries for the season. And now that summer has spread its riches in front of me, I still feel as though I'm dreaming.

The icy cold of that first spell was less unreal. The ghostly desolation of the streets was a better match for my state of mind. Now I have to wear summer clothes, bare my legs and arms, but my heart remains frozen solid in sorrow.

And you, Myriam? Do you feel the heat in your cell? Or do they have air-conditioning in French prisons these days? Perhaps you've also become a frozen block of longing. An eternal icy continent. Antarctica.

Speaking of which, my son seems to have turned into an iceberg, a treacherous object drifting further and further away from the mother continent, showing only the tip of his emotions. Most of what he thinks and feels and experiences remains hidden. Underwater. I don't have the strength to try plumbing those depths with sonar. I keep silent, he keeps silent, we both keep silent together.

While my husband carries on furiously building our house. His igloo, I suppose I can call it, his only shelter from his wife's cold heart. With Habib whistling away at his side. The kitchen looks a lot better already, no longer quite like the scene of a recent bomb explosion. The wooden cupboards are in, the walls plastered and tiled, only the floor tiles still to be done. My husband has decided on a rustic look, the same as the bathroom. Rough dirty-white tiles for the walls, the untiled parts unevenly plastered, the lines of the trowel visible. Raw wooden cupboards stained in a Provençal shade of blue, the woodgrain showing through, everything deliberately old-fashioned and simple. A little too deliberate, I'd say, but I don't say anything. Fine wire netting in the cupboard doors so that the crockery and utensils are visible. Aesthetically satisfying, my husband reckons. Time-consuming, I reckon, because everything inside will have to be kept tidy, and these days that kind of aesthetic is rather low on my list of urgent needs.

I've become a slob. I neglect my body and I neglect my home. I'd like to neglect the garden too, but then my husband has decided the garden is Hester's Project. Therapy for the depression I apparently suffer from: getting things to grow, seeing new life take shape under my fingers. So I scratch in the soil all day long – that's when I'm not lying on a bed, grieving, with filthy fingernails – and leave the house in my husband's competent hands.

At least Habib's sweet-tempered sister comes once a week to vacuum and iron. There isn't nearly enough ironing for her. I brought only three summer dresses, my husband wears the same dirty work clothes every day, and my son is terrified that ironed jeans and T-shirts will make him look like a nerd. So every week I scrape together a pile of serviettes and pillow-slips – sometimes I deliberately crease the previous week's un-used laundry so that she'll have something other than vacu-uming to occupy her.

The vacuuming is a task that would have discouraged Sisyphus – there are decades, maybe even centuries, of dust under this roof – but Aïsha tackles it every week with a feroci-ty that amazes me. Damp from perspiration by the time she's made her way through all three floors, her dark hair sticking to her temples, her dusky cheeks rosy from the exertion. Most of the time I work with her, because I can't lie and grieve on the bed like a colonial madame while the vacuum cleaner drones through the house. I shake out mats and move furniture to look busy, but there are too few mats, too little furniture, too little of everything except dust and sorrow in this house.

When we have finished, we drink tea. That is the extent of my social life. One visitor per week. And yet certainly more active than yours, Myriam. I suspect your only visitors are those forced upon you, the lawyer and the psychologist and all the other professional advisers.

In the meantime, in Africa, far from us, the next catastrophe is hatching. As my husband puts it. Already hatched, it sounds to me when I read the newspapers. In Darfur, a western province of Sudan (an area about the size of France, I read) an ethnic slaughter has been going on for months. Another one. Yet again. Well, actually a civil war has been raging there for more than twenty years, claiming about two million victims, but most Westerners are blissfully unaware of this. I learnt about it only the other day. The only reason that Western leaders have now become slightly concerned about the situation is that Sudan is a source of oil. But it seems no one is concerned enough to prevent the next predictable disaster in Africa. *Chronicle of a genocide foretold*. That's what we're talking about here.

I'm not cynical, Myriam. I've lost my former hopefulness, that's all. Hope is a summer condition. I told you I've become winter, haven't I? Full of doubts about the world.

I doubt, for instance, whether I could say anything to give you courage for your hearing in court today. So I'd rather keep quiet like you.

Your silent supporter
Hester Human.

～～

"Did your sister look like you?" Nathalie asks out of the blue.

They are sitting together on a park bench, legs stretched out in the sun. He follows her gaze to where a bunch of noisy toddlers are playing on a jungle gym a little way from them.

"No," he answers. "She was always much more attractive than me."

"Maybe it's only you who think so."

"No, my mother and father thought so too." He pulls at a

109

piece of loose skin next to his thumbnail. It hurts, but less than it would to watch the shrill children playing. "She was beautiful from the moment she was born. Had a head of wild black hair that went lighter later on. Large blue eyes and a cute little nose. Everything about her was cute."

He swallows, embarrassed at his sentimental description, but he carries on talking just to keep her next to him. For the first time they're chatting outside of school, the first time he has no bus to catch, because they've been let off the last two periods. Madame Curnier, their fierce French teacher, was taken ill unexpectedly. He is so delighted to have the free time to spend with Nathalie that he almost manages to feel sorry for the old dragon of a teacher.

"And she was an easy baby. My mother always said so. Cried very little and slept a lot. I was the opposite. Apparently I yelled for hours and drove my mother demented. I looked like a tall, thin, weed when I was born. With big hands and big feet. More or less the way I still look," he smiles and feels his face redden.

"I like the way you look," she says. "Maybe I like tall thin weeds because I'm one myself."

He almost chokes with indignation.

"You don't know what you're talking about!"

She might be tall and slender, but she isn't clumsy and shy as he is. Everyone in the school likes her. She has no trouble speaking to the other kids. She can charm anyone with her smile. He still fails to understand why she has made friends with him.

"Of course I know," she says, suddenly serious, her eyes on a grey pigeon that has landed near her feet. "I know you feel different from the other kids in school. But you must have noticed that most of them look more like you than like me?"

He stares frowning at her legs, long bare chocolate legs,

and realises it's the first time he's seen her in a skirt. One of those buttoned denim skirts hanging low on her hips and coming to well below her knees when she's standing, but now it has fallen open over her thighs. Truly a day of firsts.

"Have you counted how many black kids there are in that school?" She lifts her chin and looks at him challengingly. "Most black people in this country can't afford to send their children to snobbish private schools."

"Same in my country," he says uncomfortably.

"In Paris it was different. There were loads of diplomats' children in the international school. Children of Africa, like you."

Children of Africa.

Then, unexpectedly, she asks: "Are you looking at my legs?"

"No. Well. I mean . . ."

"Why not? Don't you like my legs?"

She giggles at his confusion, sits up straight and closes up her skirt over her knees.

"*Jy't mooi bene*," he says in Afrikaans, to cover his confusion and regain the upper hand. *You've got lovely legs.*

She looks at him askance and turns her head away quickly, back towards the children on the jungle gym. One of them catches his attention, a little girl with a self-possessed air and a head of wild curls. Blonder than his sister was. Or maybe his sister was blonder than he remembers. What does he actually remember about his sister?

"Don't you feel like an ice cream?" asks Nathalie as though she feels his sudden anxiety.

"I don't have money on me."

"I'll buy you one. Come on."

She grabs his hand before he can offer any further resistance, pulls him up and leads him to the kiosk next to the toddlers' playground. A few mothers and minders sit at round tables under coloured umbrellas, chatting or paging through magazines or keeping an eye on the children. Only now does he notice that Nathalie is the only black person in the park.

It's funny, but he's never before thought of himself as a child of Africa. It's only since living in Europe that Africa has begun to mean anything to him. And yet, if any of the other people in the park were to look at him and Nathalie, they would see only one child of Africa – and it wouldn't be him.

⌒⌒

Hester sits outside next to the lavender bushes, her body in a pool of sunlight, the newspaper open on the table in front of her. The croissant that André brought her half an hour before, with the paper, lies untouched on the side plate. She has been staring for who knows how long at a photograph in the paper – the black-and-white one she had hidden in the kitchen drawer for a while – her body quite still and her face expressionless.

All that André sees, looking at the photograph, is a young girl – hardly older than twenty, he guesses – with a printed cloth on her head worn like a turban. Big eyes, high cheekbones, wide lips. Someone who in other circumstances would perhaps be called attractive, but in this picture she looks blunt as a block of wood. Completely closed off from the outside world. Autistic.

The way Hester sometimes looked in that first month after Manon's death.

The way she looks at this moment, he decides, watching her from the front door.

"What do they say about her?"

"She remains an enigma," Hester answers without looking up. "She hasn't spoken a word for weeks. The state prosecutor says she's keeping silent wilfully, simply to win sympathy. Her advocate says she's really become mute, a psychological condition caused by trauma and depression."

André carries his mug of tea a little closer and looks over her shoulder at the report on page 5. Not front-page news. Not enough people interested in the trial of a homeless black prostitute who murdered her own children. But yet quite a large heading: *Medée d'Afrique se mure dans le mutisme.* Medea of Africa encloses herself in a wall of muteness. Something like that.

"What do you think?"

"I think a woman's tongue wasn't made to describe the death of her children. I can understand that she became mute."

"A woman's hands were also not made to cause her children's death, don't you think?"

"She can't slice off her hands." Hester's tone is impatient. "What would she use? The plastic knife with which she's supposed to eat her food? But she can bite off her tongue. Metaphorically."

"Doesn't she realise that the advocate is trying to help her? How can he do anything for her if she refuses to talk to him?"

"You think too rationally, André," she sighs and lets her eyes slide over the report again. "The case probably won't last long. After all, she gave herself up to the police and told them what she'd done. They have it all in writing, a full confession, signed and everything. All the court has to do is to decide on her punishment. If there are extenuating or aggravating circumstances. Maybe she was temporarily insane. Not responsible for her actions. Whatever."

André carries on reading over her shoulder, slowly, with difficulty. In his three years of classes at the Alliance Française in Cape Town, he never encountered criminal court cases or complicated legal terms.

"So her advocate says she was a good mother who did everything within her power to give her children a better life," he paraphrases what he has gleaned. "But she was driven to a point where she thought it better for them to be dead than to go on living?"

Hester nods. "And the state prosecutor says that's rubbish, why didn't she kill herself as well if she was in such deep despair?"

"Well, why didn't she?"

"You're too rational, André!" Her tongue clicks with annoyance. "You sound like the damned prosecutor. He says she was a woman of loose morals, a prostitute and a chancer, clearly not a devoted mother, and to top it all, jealous of her husband's new woman. He says she killed the children to avenge herself on her husband."

"Well, she wás a prostitute, Hester." He swallows some tea while choosing his words carefully. "I just wonder if you aren't painting her a little too white. Maybe revenge was indeed a factor."

"I never said she's an angel, André. I just think it's a waste of time to look for reasons for what she did. It's an utterly senseless deed." Hester shakes her head angrily and lifts the paper to push the picture under his nose. "Look at her! Does this look like a jealous, vengeful woman?"

"It looks like a woman who shows no emotion."

"Because there's none left to show! Because she's déád as she stands there." She drops the paper onto the table again and gesticulates with the back of her hand. "I know what I'm talking about, André. I know how it feels to stop feeling anything."

"I don't know why you identify with her so, Hes." He hears panic rising in his voice. Every time his wife uses that despairing tone, he gets panicky. "There's a world of difference between a woman who loses her child and one who kills her child."

"No, it's only a difference of degree, André, and the outcome and effect are the same." He's looking at the back of her head, but he can hear she's close to tears. "I recognise those dead eyes of Myriam. I see them every morning when I look in the mirror to brush my teeth."

"Look at me, Hes," he pleads. "You will begin to feel again. But first you must agree to go on living."

"I don't know how," she says, her voice totally flat. "I don't know how to do it without her. I don't know how I will get through the rest of my life."

He turns and takes his mug back to the kitchen. He doesn't even know how they will see this year through. An incomplete family in an incomplete house, that's what they've become, an incomplete house in an unknown country.

The country of loss.

∽

Emile can't imagine how he will get through the summer vacation. In less than two weeks the school will close for more than two months. That means two months without his best friend.

His only friend.

Most afternoons they walk a short way to the point where he turns off to catch his bus. Some days they even sit together at the same table over the lunch break in the school's self-service dining room. Her girl friends don't really like this – they tease her all the time for spending so much time with a loser like him – but fortunately she doesn't pay much attention to them. And he still doesn't have male friends to tease him, so he's only too pleased when she makes for the empty chair next to him with her tray. He always keeps that chair free. Just in case.

The bus rumbles past another village hanging sleepily against a hill in the late afternoon sun. Now that summer is really here, the villages along the bus route look a lot less brown and stark. The stone walls glow in the sun and the clay tiles on the roofs take on an orange lustre. The trees along the streets and squares have turned into a sea of green. And there are definitely more people about than in winter. But it remains a rather dull area, far from the excitement of a city, dreadfully far from Cape Town.

He still longs for Cape Town, every single day, for the salty smell of the sea and the clouds that tumble over the mountain, for his talkative grandmother and his silent grandfather and his sister's cat that stayed behind, and of course for all his pals. Although he sometimes wonders whether by next year he might not miss Nathalie as much as he now misses Pietman and Dylan and Zakes. In Cape Town he didn't really have any friends who were girls. Zakes and the others would find it very funny if they were to hear that his best friend – his only friend – is a long-legged girl who reminds him of a giraffe.

He glares at the old woman who has taken the seat next to him. She smiles at him, her teeth as yellow and uneven as pips on a mealie cob, her eyes two black prunes, her cheeks dried peaches. The old ladies on the bus are not quite what they were in winter either. The sun has made them all thaw a little. They smile more easily, chat more, their coloured dresses look a lot more cheerful than the black overcoats they previously wore. This makes it even more difficult to keep them at a distance. Some of the regular passengers have even started greeting him by name. *Ah, Emile, ça va?* The other day one of them stuffed a plastic bag of toffees into his hand! As if they all knew that his surly face was just a mask to keep them at bay.

Unfortunately their gaily coloured dresses also show more of their awful old-woman bodies than he cares to see. He wonders if his mother will also look like this one day. Swollen ankles, blue varicose veins snaking all over their calves, brown spots on the backs of their wrinkled hands. No, his mother has always been attractive, she looks after herself, uses skin creams on her body and wears hats to protect her face against the summer sun. Or that's what she used to do. Since they've been in France, she's apparently lost interest in looking decent in old age. To be absolutely honest, it doesn't look as if she wants to reach old age. If she doesn't stop grieving over Manon, she's going to fade away right in front of their eyes.

Evaporate like a rainbow, he thinks some days.

Sometimes when they're at table she regards him in such a strange way, with an almost cruel set to her mouth, and then he wonders if she isn't wishing that he'd rather been the one to die. It's such an unbearable thought that he always suppresses it immediately. Unbidden, the brutal words of a childhood rhyme come to him. *Wring his neck, dump him in the ditch.* Staring in boredom at the vineyards moving past the window, he can't help wondering again. *Stomp on his head, then he'll be dead.* Another of those nursery songs his mother used to sing, a lifetime ago, before she became so silent that for hours on end nothing but a sigh escapes her mouth. He knows his mother loved Manon more than she loved him. He has always known this.

Siembamba. Mama's little baby.

His mother had dreamt of having a daughter for years before Manon finally arrived. He was too young to remember much, but he does remember that there were copious tears. More than once they told him he was to have a brother or sister – and then, just as his mother's tummy started making

117

a cute little bump, everything fell flat again like a cake in an oven. Then there were tears again, visits to hospitals, half-knitted baby clothes hidden in the darkest corners of his mother's wardrobe. By the time his mother expected Manon, they were too afraid to tell him anything. For months he knew nothing, just thought his mother was getting rather stout.

The day Manon was born, his mother and father looked happier than he'd ever seen them. It was a wet cold day in the middle of the Cape winter, but to him it felt as if a great big sun was hanging over her hospital bed. That's how he drew the scene the following day. His mother's brown hair wild about her head and a wide toothy smile on her face and a baby in her arms looking like a gift wrapped in pink paper. His father with his chest out like a pouter pigeon presiding next to her bed. And he was there too, the eight-year-old boy leaning over the bed with a teddy bear in his hands, like one of the Three Wise Men with his offering for the babe in the stable. Instead of the shining star leading the kings to the stable, he had drawn an enormous round sun with long yellow rays above his mother's bed.

His mother kept the picture for years. Maybe she still has it in that box in which she stored her best souvenirs of Manon, the box they left with his grandparents, along with the cat. Or maybe she threw it away with all the broken toys and torn colouring books and odd socks that she got rid of in the last week before their departure.

That week, while she cleared out Manon's room for the people who would be renting their house, it was as if she was emptying herself little by little, as if everything in her was leaking out like dirty bathwater. She no longer wanted to come to France, she didn't want to do anything any more, but the air tickets had been bought, the house rented out, everything arranged long ago for this "dream year" in Provence. On the last day she delivered a load of Manon's dolls to a home for street children. By that time her eyes were as empty and lifeless as the plastic eyes of the dolls in her arms.

Emile presses his forehead against the bus window so that the old lady next to him shouldn't see that he suddenly wants to cry, and concentrates as hard as he can on an olive grove glittering all silver in the sun. A row of wild fig trees close to the road. More bloody vineyards.

He concedes that he was sometimes jealous of his sister. Everyone's attention was always on the cute new baby, no one heard him when he asked for something or looked if he wanted to show them something. There were indeed times he wished she hadn't been born, that everything could stay the way it had been before she came, just his mother, his father and him.

Just the three of them.

Now it is just the three of them, here in France, as before she arrived. He screws up his eyes to hold back his unbidden tears.

Other days again he wished his little sister had been a boy, a little brother with whom he could wrestle and play rugby and do rough boy things. If she'd been a boy she wouldn't have been quite so special to everyone. She would have been just another one like him, almost exactly like him, just slightly different.

But he could never really bluff himself. Even if Manon had been a boy, she would have been totally different from him. She would always have smiled more and slept better and fed more easily than he did.

A dream baby, as his mother used to say. A dream of a child. Now they've awoken, he and his mother and his father, just the three of them.

119

5

Twenty years behind bars. That's the sentence the judge passed on you today. Two decades before you'll be free again.

This morning I almost got into my car to drive to Marseille. I knew it would be the last chance I'd ever get to see you in the flesh, in the court, in the dock, and I wanted to see you, whatever it took. It was my husband – my practical, reasonable husband – who convinced me that it was a crazy idea.

"The courtroom was full every day, Hes. Today it'll be at its worst. There's no way you'll get in. You won't be able to see her. Forget about her now."

Forget about her now?

"It'll be okay if I don't get in," I protested, rather feebly, because I knew he was right. As usual. "I just want to be close to her. Even if I have to stand waiting outside the court all day."

"In this heat? With all those dreadful Neo-Nazis?"

"It's not only Neo-Nazis who are demonstrating outside the court. There are feminist groups and human rights organisations and . . ."

He interrupted me impatiently. "That stubble-haired feminist we saw on TV last night sounds almost as insane as the stubble-haired racists she's demonstrating against."

The woman who took up your cause on TV last night did indeed sound as if she'd lost her common sense along with her hair. According to her you did what you did because you hate men. Simple as that. Because no woman from the patriarchal culture of Africa can but hate men. You were therefore not to blame for what you did, it was the fault of men. All men.

Oh, no, not so, my husband muttered, he doesn't even know you, he refuses to bear your guilt.

It's people like her who have turned your hearing into a media circus. They've hijacked the whole affair to get publicity for their own causes, the feminists and the racists and the chauvinists and the nationalists and all the other *ex-ists*, as André calls them. Previously, he was also one of them, an idealist who wanted to change the world. Now the world is no longer his home, now he only wants to change his own house. Break down walls and lay floor tiles.

The reason I want to be there, I told my husband, had nothing to do with any -isms.

"What about voyeurism?"

I was so shocked by the question that my jaw dropped.

I shook my head and said it was too difficult to try explaining in a few words. Or perhaps it's so simple that I'm afraid my husband won't believe me. Because I'm also a mother. Because I'm also grieving over a child. Because my heart is also simultaneously pulled in two directions, away from Africa and back to Africa. Because I recognise enough of myself in this woman to forgive her everything, even the deeds that I don't understand? Or is it especially the deeds that I don't understand? As Flaubert said of Emma Bovary – perhaps that is what I should've answered my husband – Myriam Soro is me?

⌒⌒

"Twenty years." André shrugs and raises his eyebrows in a resigned gesture. "I suppose it could have been worse."

"There are people who think it shóuld have been worse,"

says Hester. "They say she'll never serve out the full twenty years; even the most dangerous criminals get out sooner these days, so if she's released after ten or fifteen years she won't even be forty. Not too old to have more children."

André is standing next to a portable barbecue, cooking sausages over the coals while watching Hester lay the table in the courtyard. She sets three plates, three knives and three forks. For Daddy Bear, Mommy Bear and Baby Bear, she used to tell Emile. After Manon's birth she started laying a fourth place for Goldilocks. It's nearly six months since Goldilocks disappeared, but sometimes she'll still absent-mindedly lay a fourth place.

"Surely they don't think she'd murder her children again?"

"There are people who believe she's a monster. If they could, they'd have cut out her womb. Although it's apparently not that unusual for mothers to murder their children. I read the other day that there are only two kinds of crime that women commit as frequently as men. One is ordinary shoplifting. The other is murdering their children."

Hester stands handling the third plate like a blind person while her voice drops to a mumble. "Of all the women on death row in the USA, nearly a quarter are there for murdering their children."

André steps back quickly and blinks his eyes against a cloud of smoke that has suddenly changed direction. Now that the court case is over, he's been hoping that Hester will at last begin to forget this unknown woman. It seems as if once again he has been an optimistic idiot.

Now it sounds as though Hester has started doing research on women who have murdered their children.

What's next, he wonders as he watches her from behind his smoke screen. Her jeans hang so loosely on her hips that she has to hitch them up with a belt. Her breasts, never very big, have shrunk away. Two little bumps under the T-shirt, like a twelve-year-old wearing her first bra. Come back to me, Hester, he wants to shout.

"Well, maybe this Myriam will think of starting all over again after her release one day," he tries to console her. "To marry again, have children, whatever."

"She'll first have to learn to talk again."

"Twenty years is long enough to learn to talk all over again."

"If you have something to say," mumbles Hester staring blankly at the glowing coals.

Her face and arms have acquired a summery colour. She always used to wear a hat to protect her face from the sun, but these days she wanders about hatless, sometimes for hours, on the hill outside the village, her skin as exposed as her psyche. The transformation of Hester Human continues. Will anything remain of the mother of his children? Child. Singular.

"Today there was some sort of altercation between Habib and Aïsha," she murmurs when he turns the grid for the last time. "She was ironing here in the kitchen when he suddenly burst in and started scolding her."

"But he wasn't supposed to come to work today. I told him I'd be away all day buying building material."

"He must have misunderstood you. You know, with all the languages you talk between you."

"*Try* to talk," he says with a self-mocking smile. "What was the argument about?"

"It wasn't really an argument. More like scolding. Habib scolding and Aïsha looking ashamed and guilty. All in Arabic, of course, so I couldn't understand a word."

"It's hard to imagine Habib scolding anyone."

Habib is short and stocky with the soulful brown eyes of a cow – and the placid nature of a cow. That is more or less how

123

André summed him up. Habib does all his handiwork at a slightly retarded pace, not exactly a young man bursting with energy, not the sharpest knife in the drawer, but reliable and imperturbable.

"That's why I was so astonished," says Hester. "I could hardly believe my ears when I heard this angry voice down below in the kitchen. When I walked in, he stopped immediately – he must have thought I wasn't home – but he didn't greet me in his usual friendly way. Just gave me a dirty look and left."

"And Aïsha? Didn't she tell you what it was about?"

"She seemed very upset but wouldn't say."

"Probably some family quarrel that has nothing to do with us."

"I thought he was a nice young man," Hester says thoughtfully. "Do you think it's possible that we've completely misjudged him?"

"No, hang on, Hester, we can't judge if we don't know the background," André warns as he takes the grid off the coals. "The sausages are ready. You can call the children."

Children. There he goes again. He wonders how long still before it really sinks in that only one child remains. Before they stop laying an unnecessary place at the table, using unnecessary plurals when they talk. He glances apologetically at his wife, but she is staring at the coals as if she hasn't even heard him.

"Doesn't matter whát the background is. It's not an excuse to speak so . . . contemptuously to his sister," says Hester and turns toward the front door to call Emile. "What upset me most was that she allows him to do it."

"Hes," sighs André. "Don't interfere. These are other people's problems."

We have enough problems of our own, he wants to add.

124

But it's also possible that his wife is grasping at other people's problems precisely to try to forget her own.

⮐

"I'd like to go to Avignon for a day," Emile announces when they're eating outside again. "To go and visit one of my friends."

"The friend who phoned this morning?" his father asks eagerly.

He nods and stuffs his mouth full of marinated chicken so that he doesn't have to go on talking. One could have sworn it was Nelson Mandela on the line. Okay, it's not as if anyone in this house is exactly overwhelmed by calls – it was actually the first time the phone had rung since school closed a week before – but still. His father needn't sound so pathetically grateful that *someone* finally wants to talk to his son.

"I'll take you. I have to go to Avignon at some stage anyway to get a few things for the house."

"It's not necessary." Emile tries to discourage the idea, his mouth still full. "I can go by bus."

"Not at all, it's easier by car."

"I want to go by bus, Dad."

His father gives him a funny look. Hurt?

"I'd prefer to drop you there, Emile. Then I can meet the child's parents at the same time. You can come back by bus, if you like."

"They're decent people, Dad. You don't have to go and check them out."

His father smiles and cuts his potato with the precision of a biology teacher dissecting a dead frog. Emile remembers how Nathalie shuddered the other day when they had to cut open frogs in class. He didn't know that a skin as dark as hers could go so grey.

125

"It's not that I don't trust you, Emile. It's just that . . . one can never be too careful."

And look where being careful brought you! Emile slices up his potato without looking at his father again. Your daughter was shot dead when she went to buy ice cream at the corner shop. Slice, slice, shred, shred, smaller and smaller, quite ridiculous, as if he can take his sudden anger out on the potato. Nothing you can do about it. Angrily mashes the little pieces with his fork. Fuck all. When he finally brings the mashed potato to his mouth, it tastes like medicine.

"They're decent people who live in a decent house and earn decent money. I don't know how much they earn, but I can try to find out if it will make you feel any better, Dad."

"Emile!" His mother looks at him, shocked. It is the first word she has uttered since they began eating. "You know that's not what your father meant."

"I don't know whát Dad means," he says, amazed that he's managed to break through his mother's aura of absent-mindedness. "What's the good of meeting someone's parents like that? To chat to them for five minutes? What can you discover in such a short time?"

"Whether they have good manners," says his father unperturbed.

"And what good will that do you? Perhaps they're serial killers with very good manners!"

"Perhaps," agrees his father, chewing calmly before he resumes. "But it's all you can do as a parent. You can't hire a private detective every time your child makes a new friend."

"What's the child's name?" asks his mother.

"Nathalie."

"A girl?" He hears her trying to hide the surprise in her voice.

"A black girl," he says, deliberately, to surprise her even further.

"From Africa?" To his disappointment she sounds more interested than surprised.

"That's what I thought at first, but she's actually more European than I am. Anyway, is it okay if I go and visit her the day after tomorrow? You can drop me if you like, Dad."

"Of course it's all right," says his father and takes a quick sip of wine.

"The day after tomorrow?" asks his mother with her hand in front of her mouth.

He nods and carries on eating. He doesn't want to talk about the day after tomorrow. Another reason he's so very glad that Nathalie telephoned. It allows him a chance to get away from the day after tomorrow.

⊂≈

"You know what the date is the day after tomorrow, don't you?" says André later that night as they lie in bed pretending to read.

"Hmm," says Hester without looking up from the French décor magazine she's paging through.

"She would be turning six." He stares at a do-it-yourself catalogue, a whole page full of pictures of different ladders, without really seeing anything. "It's going to be a difficult day."

"Every day is a difficult day," says Hester.

Maybe he is making it more difficult by talking about it. He turns the page in the catalogue. Electric drills. All the photographs look slightly out of focus, as though the drills are wreathed in mist. He can't concentrate hard enough to make the images sharp.

"You've always been bad at remembering significant dates," his wife says, her tone faintly accusing. "You often forget our wedding date."

127

"Blame it on my sexist upbringing." He keeps his voice light, skating on the surface, afraid of breaking the ice. Terrified of the depths lurking beneath his wife's words. "It was always my mother's duty to remind my father of birthdays and such things. All he could remember was the date of the next Broederbond meeting."

Hester doesn't smile at his joke. No one in this house smiles at his jokes any more.

"I rather hoped you might forget this date as well," she says.

"Would it have been easier for you? If I'd forgotten?"

"No, I'd probably have resented it. Pitied myself even more than usual. I don't know how you stand it with me!"

"Sometimes I also wonder."

Another joke that doesn't work. He wishes he could pull her down under his arm, rub his nose through her hair, make her laugh as before. He stretches out his hand to touch her head, but at the same instant she leans forward to drop the magazine with a dull thud on her side of the bed and his hand is left hovering like a big brown moth in mid-air above her shoulder.

"Maybe we should pretend we've forgotten," he suggests. "Treat it like any other day."

She stares through the open window in the opposite wall. It's a sultry evening, not a breeze stirring, the air heavy and black as a shroud. The crescent moon's shiny sliver looks like a keyhole in an unimaginably huge door.

"No," she says abstractedly. "I feel that I ought to . . . I suppose 'celebrate' isn't the right word. Commemorate? Maybe I should bake a cake. Have a kind of party."

"Isn't that a little macabre?"

"I don't mean a cake with six candles! I'm only looking for something to keep me busy. If I bake a cake and invite someone over for a slice. . . "

128

"Who would you invite?"

"That's the problem. I can't think of anyone besides Aïsha and Aurore. Aïsha has classes on Mondays, so she won't be able to come, and Aurore's mother doesn't want her to come and visit me."

He looks at her inquiringly.

"Quite understandable," she says with a frustrated frown. "She doesn't know us from a bar of soap. If a complete stranger had suddenly invited Manon to come and play at her house, I'd probably also have refused."

"But can't you go and meet the mother? Invite her with the child?"

"It gets harder and harder to meet people. To deal with the questions. To give the right answers. Children are easier, they ask fewer predictable questions, but the adults . . . 'How many children do you have?' What should I say when someone asks me that? What do yóu answer?"

"One." His voice fades. "I know. It feels like a betrayal."

"It ís a betrayal. Every time you say that, you betray the other one. We brought two children into this world, you and I, we will always have two children."

"But if you say 'two', you have to explain that one of them isn't alive any more. And that makes people uncomfortable, or it spoils the atmosphere, or it leads to further questions and explanations. And you don't always feel up to explaining."

"Exactly what I mean. It's easier not to meet people."

She turns her back to him and settles down with her hand over her mouth, one leg drawn up, the way she usually falls asleep. He admires the outline of the bent leg under the thin white cotton throw.

"But you can't become a recluse, Hes."

"Says who."

Her voice sounds sleepy already. Probably exaggerated.

129

Afraid that he'll roll over to her, that she'll have to fold that seductive leg over his demanding body, have to pretend that she can still enjoy anything on earth. He slaps the catalogue shut and switches off the bedside lamp. He feels like a wrestler losing the most important fight of his life, pinned down by his opponent, all the breath squeezed out of his chest. In the dark he slides his arm over her side, carefully, until his palm rests against her stomach. Against the T-shirt that covers her stomach. The skin underneath the fabric he dares not touch.

"Hes," he whispers in the dark, his mouth against her neck. "If it hadn't been so difficult to fall pregnant with Manon . . ." His voice gets lost in her hair. If only it weren't so difficult. "If we hadn't struggled so much before, wouldn't you like to have another child?"

It is an issue he has been wrestling with for months. He doubts whether he'd be prepared to take on that battle again. They are that much older, almost too old, that much more vulnerable. But just suppose she should want to? Mightn't that be the miracle they need to release them from this hell?

She doesn't answer. Her breathing is relaxed and regular. Minutes later, when he is also falling asleep, he hears her voice from very far away. Floating as if in a dream, and yet heavy with tears.

"Let's not waste time with futile questions, my love," she says.

When he wakes the next morning, he decides that it must have been a dream. He can't remember when last she called him "my love".

⌒⌒

The apartment is on the top floor of an old-fashioned five-storey building that immediately impresses his architect father.

One of those typical buildings you see in photos of Parisian boulevards. Long narrow windows with wrought-iron railings on miniature balconies. Elegant without being ostentatious. A wide staircase and a tiny elevator down in the entrance hall with a trellis door that opens like a concertina.

His father chooses the elevator, which proceeds so falteringly to the top that the stairs would definitely have been the faster option. Emile drums his fingers on his thigh, uncomfortable at being trapped in this oppressive space with his father, impatient to see Nathalie again. Naturally also impatient to be rid of his father, who walks to the front door with him like a redundant bodyguard, waiting next to him after he's rung the bell. They wait a long time. When the door opens at last, Emile feels about six years old, quite shrivelled with embarrassment and nervousness.

"Hi," says Nathalie in her American accent, smiling widely and kissing his father on the cheek as if she has known him for years. "Come in. Come and meet my mom and dad."

He is amazed all over again at how easily she communicates with other people, how at ease she is in her dark skin, how effortlessly she controls her long arms and legs without ever banging into things by accident. So different from him. They follow her to the kitchen, a super-modern room full of stainless steel surfaces – unexpected in such an old building – where her parents are busy cooking. Nathalie's mother takes Emile's breath away, his father's also, he suspects, because she's even taller and more giraffe-like than Nathalie. She wears simple loose trousers and a loose overshirt under a grubby butcher's apron, with such self-confidence you'd swear that grubby aprons had overnight become the latest fad from Paris. He stares in fascination at her feet in flat sandals. One thin brown toe is decorated with a silver ring.

"Hello," she says holding out a long slender hand, first to

Emile and then to his father, with the same irresistible smile as her daughter's. "My name is Naomi."

And he'd thought dope-head and Rasta gear.

"And I'm Laurent," says the bearded giant behind her. His shoulders are so broad that Emile's father, who is himself fairly tall, looks quite puny next to him.

"I don't know what you're preparing," his father says after he has also introduced himself, "but it smells fantastic."

"*Bouillabaisse*," says Naomi. "That's why the kitchen looks like a battlefield. We've invited a few friends for supper."

"Lucky friends."

"Do you like *bouillabaisse?*" asks Laurent. "Then you must come and eat with us next time!"

"Be warned." says Naomi. "It's a sort of test of friendship. If you can eat three bowls of Laurent's fish soup, you've won his loyalty for life. But if you can't even manage the first one . . ."

"It's the outer darkness for you!" Laurent roars with a voice like thunder.

Emile has to admit he's relieved that both of them speak English – Naomi with a British accent, Laurent with a heavy French drawl – otherwise he and his father would have had to bring on their poor French. On the other hand, if his father had had to speak French, he'd have looked less at home in this gleaming modern kitchen. Would definitely not have accepted Naomi's offer of a cup of espresso so eagerly. And all Emile really wants is for his father to leave as soon as possible.

"What fish are you using?" His father moves closer to the stove. "May I take a look?"

"Of course," says Laurent. "Sounds as if you cook yourself?"

"I like experimenting in the kitchen," his father replies with false modesty.

"Now they're going to exchange recipes and talk about sauces for hours," Nathalie mutters under her breath to Emile.

"Dad, didn't you have to get a lot of things for the house?" Emile hints, frowning heavily.

"Oh, that can wait. First I have to play detective here," says his father, his smile getting broader all the time. "Every *bouillabaisse* has a secret ingredient that the cook will never divulge."

"Ah!" Laurent's laugh starts with a rumble somewhere in his stomach, like a volcano deep inside a mountain, before erupting tremendously from his mouth. "The white man is cleverer than he looks!"

Nathalie pulls a face, rolls her eyes and gestures with her head for Emile to follow her. She takes him down a long passage to her room, which to his surprise is almost as untidy as his. Shoes and magazines lie all over the floor, books and clothes on the bed, CDs and scrunched up pieces of paper on the desk.

"They seem to be getting on well," says Nathalie as she casually brushes more clothes and books from her bed onto the floor. "Must be the Africa connection."

Not quite sure – as so often – whether she is teasing or serious, he merely shrugs and walks over to the window. It is actually a glass door leading onto one of those ridiculously small balconies that his father admired from the street.

"So what would you like to do?" She's sitting on the edge of the bed looking expectantly at him. He pushes his hands deeper into his pockets and stares at the pedestrians in the street below. "Listen to music? Watch a DVD? Play a computer game? Discuss the meaning of life?" she adds, giggling nervously.

"Maybe we could go for a walk?" he suggests.

That's what they're used to. It's what they do every day

after school. He isn't sure he could sit and talk to her here in her untidy room. It feels too . . . private. As though they suddenly have to behave like grown-ups.

"Cool." She jumps up so readily that he realises she's just as keen as he is to escape from the room. "The festival has just begun, so the streets are really lively."

"Festival?"

"The arts festival they have here every summer," she says over her shoulder, already on her way out. "Lots of actors and musicians perform in the streets or go about in funny costumes handing out pamphlets to advertise their shows. It's brilliant. You'll see."

In the kitchen their fathers are talking recipes, just as Nathalie predicted. They greet as they pass and close the front door behind them with relief.

"I'll race you to the bottom!" she calls out laughing and chases him down the staircase instead of waiting for the slow elevator.

They reach the street so out of breath and weak with laughter that they have to hold on to one another to remain steady. And suddenly everything feels like it always did. No more pressure to be anything but pals.

Much later, after wandering through many streets and talking at length about school, the teachers and their classmates, after watching a performance of modern dancing on the Place d'Horloge and laughing uproariously at a Chinese comedian's acrobatic turns in front of the Palais des Papes, Emile says out of the blue: "Today is my sister's birthday."

As if he has waited all day long to tell someone.

She stops in her tracks, startled.

"She would have been six today." He can't believe how calm his voice is. He was sure he'd start crying if he talked about this. But suddenly, for the first time this year, he wánts to talk about his sister. "Last year we celebrated her birthday here in France. It was soon after we bought the house in Lunel. A real dump, wish you could have seen it. The water and electricity had been cut off, there was no furniture, we lived like squatters. Sleeping on the floor and eating outside."

"Sounds like fun."

"It was. My sister was mad about it. The evening of her birthday we lit candles outside, must have been about a hundred candles, so that she could blow then out one by one. Because we couldn't bake her a birthday cake, my mother said, because there was no oven or electricity. Every time she blew all the candles out, my father would light them again. Then she'd run from candle to candle to blow each one out again. I think it was the best birthday present we ever gave her."

Nathalie takes his hand, maybe just to make sure they don't lose each other in the crowd. They're on their way back from the large square in front of the Pope's palace in the direction of the Place d'Horloge, but there are so many people milling round them that they can't really move, and so much noise that it gets harder all the time to hear each other. For about a minute they're pushed this way and that by the crowd, their bodies almost uncomfortably close to each other, while Nathalie clings ever more tightly to his hand. His fingers are starting to lose all feeling by the time she is finally able to break free of the crush and pull him into a narrow side street.

"Wow." He wipes his sweaty forehead. "I'm not used to so many people any more! Do you think I've become a country bumpkin?"

"Oh no, crowds like this make me claustrophobic too. And I'm *definitely* not a country bumpkin." She's still holding his hand, though it's not strictly necessary any longer. She gazes at the ground uncomfortably. "Thanks for telling me. About your little sister. I can't imagine how you must miss her."

He doesn't know what to say. They walk past the back door of a restaurant where a mangy ginger cat is sniffing at a row of rubbish bins. The cat reminds him of Caramel who had to stay behind in Cape Town.

"There are so many things that remind me of her. Some days it feels as if absolutely everything reminds me of her. But I'm glad I didn't stay at home today. I mean that I can be here with you. When I saw my mother's face this morning . . ."

"Did you and your dad leave her at home alone?"

He hears a faint reproach in her voice.

"My dad tried to persuade her to come with us, but she didn't want to. She reminds me of an elephant, you know. They say elephants break away from the herd when they feel their time for dying is close. That's how she's behaving. As though she doesn't want to be part of the herd any more."

Their footsteps resound in the sunless alley. He is terribly aware of her cool palm against his, her slender fingers flexed through his.

"My dad and I are still sort of in the herd. We do what's expected of us. I mean, my dad might be standing there in your kitchen making jokes, but I bet you he really wants to tear the hair from his head in sorrow. And I'm here walking round Avignon with you, even though I really want to lie somewhere in the dark and just howl. But my mother doesn't care any more what anyone expects of her. Not even me or my dad."

She turns her head towards him and all of a sudden her mouth is so close to him that he wishes he could kiss her right here, in an unsavoury alley in Avignon. But then they arrive in a wider street again and the moment has passed. They blink at the bright sunlight, the noisy traffic, the rowdy pedestrians around them.

"Can I come over to visit you sometime in the vacation?" she asks a few paces further on.

"There's nothing to do," he warns her. "It's a really dull little town. And our house, with my mother grieving all day long . . . it's about as cheerful as a haunted house."

"I rather like haunted houses," she says earnestly.

"Well, if you really want to . . ."

"Not if you don't want me to."

"Of course I want you to," he assures her, amazed that she can't see how much he wants it. "Just say when!"

She rewards him with a smile that would make even a haunted house feel like a cheerful place.

⁀⁀

Today she is all around me, all the time, no way of shaking her off. Not that I would want to. Not today. We're alone at home, she and I and the cat. My phantom child and my phantom cat.

In our shiny new kitchen (yes, finished, thanks be to the gods, my husband and Habib) she is pasting scraps of paper on the stove, the refrigerator, the blue Provençal cupboard doors, the baskets hanging on hooks along the wall, the round wooden table in the middle of the terracotta tile floor, even on the enamel milk jug in which I arranged six yellow rosebuds. Doesn't a yellow ribbon signify something like "I'm waiting for you?" Yellow ribbons welcoming soldiers and prisoners home? I wonder if yellow rosebuds impart the same message.

And yet I wasn't thinking of any special message when I picked them early this morning. They were just suddenly there when I walked out of the front door. Exactly half a dozen butter-yellow buds on a single bush, six roses for a sixth birthday, as if I'd ordered them. Inexplicable. I could've sworn there were only four yesterday.

On every scrap of paper, my daughter draws a picture or writes a few letters, some upside down or back to front, to represent a particular object. Stove, table, milk jug. Etcetera. The idea is that I should stick the right paper on the right object. It's a game we played constantly last year, after she'd discovered that certain letters stood for certain sounds, and – better still – that a specific sequence of letters could form a specific word. She was endlessly excited about the endless possibilities of letters. I had found an ally, I imagined, someone who would share my passion for words. For poetry, for lyrics, for foreign languages, even for nonsense rhymes and silly songs. *Mother's child, Mother's tousle-haired child. Oh the red patchwork blanket. Rock-a-bye baby in the tree top.*

On other days, though, she wanted nothing to do with words. Then it was all action, movement, hopping and skipping, raw emotion, tears and giggles and yells, a wordless tragi-comedy like an old black-and-white movie, Chaplin or Keaton or such. If she hád to talk, she'd make sounds like a duck, babbling gibberish. As if to warn me not to depend too much on language for communication.

After her death I learned that there are emotions that can't be expressed in language.

And yet today I need my daughter's words. Talk to me, my love – how many times has André not whispered this to me? At night in the dark refuge of our bed. But I can't talk, the bed doesn't offer enough safety, the dark smothers me, the stars feel too far away. I can't talk to my husband, especially not about our daughter.

She is here with me, she plays at my feet while I maunder around our so-called rustic kitchen, putting away a clean glass here in the wire-netting cupboard, hanging up a white cotton cloth there, anything to occupy my searching hands. But it's becoming harder to hear her voice. Like a lunatic waiting for the voice of an angel, I wait for the words of my child. I wonder if I'm losing my mind. Where do the scraps of paper sticking to the stove and the table come from? I put my hand out to the yellow roses, crumple the piece of paper stuck to the milk jug, assure myself I'm not dreaming.

I don't believe in ghosts. I know I'm awake. There hás to be some explanation.

Except for this unbearable longing.

I flee from the kitchen, up the stairs to my daughter's room, which my husband now wants to turn into a guest room. For me it is almost unthinkable that we will ever again receive guests. It's a totally impersonal room, a narrow single bed, a low bedside cabinet, a wardrobe in the corner on the bare pine floor, nothing that reminds me of her. Only the idea that it would have been her room if she had come here with us this year.

So different from her room in Cape Town, her bed with the shocking-pink fairy cover, her crayon drawings on the walls, her picture books on the bookshelf, her dolls on a red rocking chair, her transparent fairy wings and her magic wand and her ghost's sheet in a purple dressing-up chest, her gaily striped mat on the floor. Her fragrance that pervades the pillows, hides in the folds of the red curtains, hangs in the corners of the ceiling. Even after I'd packed away her clothes and her toys and her books, after I'd washed the bedclothes and torn the drawings from the walls, after I'd done everything in my power to change her room into an impersonal space – for the sake of the strangers who would be renting our house this year – I could still feel her presence between the four walls.

Or else it was an absence so strong that it became a presence. As when you take a picture off the wall after many years and the outline remains visible, a square where the paint is darker than the rest of the wall. That's what happened to that

139

room in Cape Town. It has always been Manon's room, it is still Manon's room, it will always be Manon's room. A sanctum of recollections, holy with memories.

Actually the whole house became a sort of altar for a dead child, a temple filled with reliquaries, every room a cave of desolation. Behind every door a ghostly voice whispering her name. Manon. Manon. Manon.

More and more I wonder if I'll be able to go back.

Every morning when I wake up, I'll wait in vain for her to come and crawl in next to me in bed with her sleepy eyes and her scarecrow hair. When we eat breakfast in the kitchen, I'll miss her drawings against the fridge and look for her bowl of chocolate cornflakes on the table. When we watch TV in the sitting room, I'll feel her empty place on the worn old couch. When we sit round the dining-room table at night, there'll be too many chairs and too few bodies. When I want to drown my sorrow in the bath, I'll wonder what became of her yellow plastic ducks and the row of naked dolls on the edge of the bath.

Everywhere in and around the house she will be present.

The old oak tree in the garden is where she liked to play school, her back to the rough trunk and a collection of teddy bears in an obedient circle around her. In autumn she and her 'pupils' used to watch in wonder as the squirrels flew from branch to branch. *Look, Mommy, they're giving a circus performance for us!* In winter that tree was her base camp, the headquarters of a large-scale operation to feed hungry birds. Initially the bowls of dry seed were meant for the fairies, but she soon discovered that, unlike the greedy birds, fairies tended not to eat much.

I'll never again be able to look at that tree without missing her.

What does one do with this longing? Even if I were to chop

down the tree, dig up the garden, blow up the whole house with dynamite, there would still be a hole left to remind me of my daughter. That square of darker paint.

The tree, the garden, the house, the street, the entire neighbourhood. The pavement in front of the house is where she grazed her knees on her first pair of roller skates. The neglected double-storey house a little way down the street is apparently the home of a powerful magician, so she told me in great confidence, who turns disobedient children into squirrels. But then you should have been a squirrel long ago, I teased. The shop on the corner is where she and her brother often went to buy bread and milk. And ice cream, on the hottest day of last summer.

It would be so much easier to stay on here, to continue my semi-existence in a foreign country, this protective trance I've been in for months now, rather than to return and be wrenched awake against my will.

An extreme reaction, my pragmatic husband reckons: Don't throw the baby out with the bathwater, Hester. Oops, his eyes apologise. Inappropriate saying. I've already lost the baby. I might as well throw out the bathwater, the baby's toys, the bath too, of course, why not the whole bathroom? Why not the whole damned house?

I flee further, out of this impersonal future guest room, higher up the steep staircase to my own room on the top floor. Fantôme patters after me and tries to catch my flapping sandals with his forepaws. Manon giggles at the cat's antics, that exuberant and slightly husky giggle of a five-year-old. Six, today. But she still refuses to talk to me.

And I yearn ceaselessly for her words. I want to feel the exact pressure of her voice against my ears, hear the suggestion of a lisp round the 's', listen for that imperceptible hesitation before she rolls an 'r'.

141

Talk to me, my love.

I throw the shutters wide open so that a wave of bright light comes spilling into the twilight room. The cat immediately forgets about my feet and paws the air playfully, trying to catch the motes of dust dancing in the streaming light. My daughter has become invisible in the almost blinding sheen on everything, but I hear her laughing nearby.

I stand by the window and look out over the clay roof tiles lower down the street, the landscape of young green vineyards further away, the forested hillsides and hazy mountains on the horizon. *And though the mountains lie so blue.* The sun hangs like a scourge high in the sky. Another hellishly hot summer's day in the south of France. The shrill screech of cicadas drowns out all other sounds, a veritable wave of sound to match the light wave streaming in at the window, until I feel as if I'm drifting. *Her words remain with me so true.*

Will they remain with me? For how long still? How long before I won't even remember her voice?

Bouts of panic shoot through my body like hiccups. I grab the shutters and shut out the brilliant light and the deafening sound, watch the walls and the furniture slowly melt away in the twilight again. In the merciful silence I hear the pitter-patter of the cat's paws on the wooden floor. I sink onto the bed without even kicking off my sandals, close my eyes thankfully and wait for the grace of sleep.

After six months I still don't know how to stay awake without her. How to get through the long empty days. Sleep is all that helps.

Rock-a-bye baby in the tree top, I sing to my daughter as I doze off, *when the wind blows, the cradle will rock.* Are my ears playing tricks on me? *When the bough breaks, the cradle will fall . . .* I hold my breath. No, it is not my imagination. I recognise her voice, its clarity and warmth, like sunshine in the dusky room.

My daughter is singing with me.

"I brought you something," says André when he comes back from Avignon, pecking me on the cheek. "A little token."

Because of our child's birthday? No, nothing to do with that, he's probably forgotten that again. More likely something like a sweet melon from Cavaillon or a bag of blushing apricots from the orchards near Nyons, the kind of seasonal offering that he often finds at a morning market or a delicatessen. Not that I don't appreciate it. It's just so terribly predictable, almost always something edible, a pathetic attempt to reawaken the former Hester. Hester the hedonist. Hester the gourmand. Now thére was a woman who could appreciate fine food!

What's become of that woman?

Sometimes by chance I catch a glimpse of my naked body in the bathroom mirror with the antique frame, the only largish mirror in the house, and I must admit it frightens me to death. It's not only my shoulders that hang. Everything hangs nowadays, my breasts, my buttocks, the slack skin of my stomach. As if my skeleton has shrunk while my skin has stretched. An empty, somewhat creased brown paper bag, that's what I think of when I see myself. I still have enough vanity to know I should do something about it, that's why every day I nibble dutifully at the food my husband cooks for me. But it seems that my taste buds no longer function. I find it hard to differentiate between sweet and sour and bitter. Everything has a slightly salty taste. Like tears.

Even the batter I've just mixed in a china bowl, the batter meant for my daughter's birthday cake, has a tearful taste.

André puts a flat rectangular paper packet on the kitchen

143

table. Clearly not a melon or apricots. I try to think of rectangular food. A slab of chocolate? I wipe my floury hands on my dress – because I forgot to put on an apron, because it's months since I've baked anything – and take a small handmade book from the parcel. A midnight-blue cover with silver stars painted on it, a hundred empty pages of heavy cream-coloured paper.

"For your dreams," my husband informs me with a self-satisfied smile. "Remember, we spoke the other day about a dream journal? That it would be a good idea to write down your dreams as soon as you wake up?"

I feel like dropping the book in the mixing bowl. Sticking it in the oven like a cake. If it became edible, like his other gifts, it would at least serve a purpose.

It was he who decided it would be a good idea for me to write down my dreams about Manon. A form of therapy, a way of making sense of my subconscious. I have no desire to go scratching around in my subconscious. It's the only place where I can communicate uninhibitedly with my daughter. Leave her there, that's how I feel, it's better to see her in my dreams than not see her anywhere at all. Ask Persephone's mother. Terrible if your child has to spend half the year in the dark, but anything is better than losing her for ever. Ask any mother.

And yet I know my husband means well, as always.

He knows that I could never resist a beautiful book. He knows that I'll keep the book next to my bed, first only to look at it, to admire the silver stars against the midnight blue background, then to smell and touch it, sniffing the odour of handmade paper, feeling the texture of the pages under my fingers, trying to resist the whole sensual package. But he also knows that at some stage, sooner or later, I will succumb. Start to explore the virginal paper with my pen. Sooner or later.

Sooner rather than later in this case. The book hadn't been next to my bed for a week when I awoke at six o'clock one Sunday morning with the memory of a dream as fresh as a newly baked loaf of bread. I couldn't stop myself from writing it down any more than you could stop yourself taking a bite out of a loaf warm from the oven.

The fact that my husband wasn't in bed next to me might have made it easier.

I've been sleeping in Manon's room for the past week because my husband has started breaking down the outside wall of the main bedroom, to make a small balcony on the roof. At first he wanted to carry our double bed down to Manon's room (which he refuses to call anything but "the spare room" or "the guest room") but the staircase is so narrow that the whole bed would have had to be taken apart. So I suggested (with guilty relief, I confess) that we rather leave the bed where it is and each sleep on our own somewhere else in the house.

"Shall I carry an extra mattress to the spare room?" he asked, casually, as if my answer didn't really matter. "Or do you prefer . . . ?"

"Oh no, don't bother, it's far too much trouble," I answered just as unconcerned. "One of us can use the studio couch in the living room. It's only for a month or so, isn't it?"

"As you wish," he said without meeting my eye.

Soon after this I heard him whistling cheerfully on the stairs. I reflected that it was perhaps a relief for him too to be sleeping on his own for a while. Or maybe Habib's whistling had become infectious. Maybe my husband whistles, as Habib does for all I know, because it's easier than talking.

It's only temporary, I comfort myself. A month or so.

The first dream in my book is as follows:

145

18 July
Walking somewhere in nature with a whole crowd of friends
and family. Griet, Sonja, Adriaan, Philip, some of whom I
haven't seen for years, some already dead, some with their
children. Manon is there, my mother too. I'm picking up toys
that lie strewn all along the path like rubbish. Manon is
dressed far too warmly, perspires and gasps and struggles, and
I persuade her with great difficulty to go behind a tree and take
off some of her clothes. We leave her in a kind of hut in a
forest because she wants to write something. Or draw? We're
on our way to a game reserve, says Mom, all of us. I want to
know if the wild animals won't tear us apart. Manon comes
running and announces proudly: "It's two years since I last
wrote and I made only two spelling mistakes!"

Two days later I record another dream, just as disjointed as the
previous one, and this time without Manon. Or any other
acquaintances.

20 July
Roaming alone through an enormous house with dozens of
empty rooms. Hotel? Looking for something but can't remem-
ber what. Then suddenly I'm behind the wheel of a car. Have
to drive to Johannesburg, but don't know the way. Hide the
car behind a pillar(?) and get out to look for a road sign with
directions, but find nothing. A stranger leans up against me
and tries to press a piece of paper in my hand. Maybe he
wants to help, but I don't trust him, start panicking, pull
away – and wake with a start, my heart hammering in my
chest.

And this afternoon, while lying on the bed in broad daylight,
perspiring, not really aware that I'd dozed off, there was

another dream that felt as intense as if it had really happened. No, more intense. Reality is getting vaguer all the time.

21 July
My large red coffin of a suitcase is packed to go off some-where. Bunch of friends lying on a double bed, chatting. I stand next to them with closed eyes, but nevertheless "see" them. Hannes and Griet and about a dozen others. Manon calls me from somewhere in the house. I follow her voice, walking past a living room where Emile drops a glass. "That's the third thing you've broken today!" I reprimand him. It isn't our house, I say, don't touch anything else. But he ignores me and stretches his arm out to touch the ceiling (how does he manage that? very low ceiling? very long arm?) and a whole lump of plaster falls out. Big hole left. I start crying hysteri-cally: "Now look what you've done!" Hannes comes to say I must fetch my suitcase, we're going to leave. I'm frantically searching for a pair of socks, feeling around on the floor next to the red suitcase. Open your eyes, someone says to me, then you might find them. Open your eyes, I repeat to myself, over and over. I concentrate all my will-power to achieve this. The moment I open my eyes, I see there's no hole in the ceiling. I'm lying in Manon's room, here in France, wrenched awake by the effort of opening my eyes.

Don't ask me why I write down these absurd scenes or what I hope to learn from doing so. Maybe I'm doing it to please my husband. A sort of consolation prize because I no longer want to sleep beside him. I keep my body to myself, but I offer you my dreams. How's that for a deal?

⁓

147

Myriam, Myriam, Myriam. I mutter your name like a mantra while I ramble through the sleeping village on moonlight nights. All the houses are full of people, merry holidaymakers, noisy tourists, children playing in the cobbled streets and adults laughing outside till late. Too many strange eyes watching me during the day, so I limit my wanderings to the dark hours when the town at last becomes silent. Not that there is much darkness or silence at this time of year. The sun only sets after nine at night, followed by a very long twilight in which music and voices spill out of open windows and over garden walls, while holidaymakers eat and drink and visit, on patios and verandas and in front of the restaurant on the square. Shrill children chase one another round the fountain, older boys try out daring skateboard tricks, older girls drape themselves over the wooden benches like merchandise in a shop window. Most people only retire after midnight.

Then at last I leave my fortress, a vampire climbing out of a coffin, to wander through the deserted streets. A few cats cross my path, a few dogs bark behind high walls, but there are no people to be seen anywhere. No one to watch me. Then I mutter your name and wonder what you are doing in your cell, wonder what it feels like to know that you can never wander outside, not even late at night.

If the moon is very bright, I leave the village streets behind me and walk up the hill, through the vineyards and past the olive grove – the leaves more silver than ever in the moon-light – past the rough stone wall of the cemetery, through the top cherry orchard, the last stretch a winding footpath that even at full moon can be treacherously dark, up to the iron cross on the summit of the hill. There I feel close to the stars, as if I merely need to stretch out my arm to pluck them like cherries from a tree, as if I can stuff these strange shining fruits into my mouth, feeding myself with stars instead of food. There I lean with my back against the pedestal of the cross and admire the landscape beneath me, a shining purplish veil over everything, so different from daytime when everything is cordoned off in light and shadow, blinding white flashes and sharp black splinters, painful to the naked eye.

Besides, during the day it's too hot to wander about outside. The heat keeps me captive behind closed shutters. In the early morning and evening, I potter in the garden, performing the chores that my keeper has assigned me, but for the rest I stay indoors. Only come out for lunch under the great square umbrella of unbleached calico, mostly just bread and salad and lots of water. I must admit the heat is sometimes a convenient excuse, a false explanation for my depressive listlessness, for the hours that I lie and dream in a darkened room. Some days André and Emile go to cool off in a public swimming pool or the river. Sometimes they try to drag me along, but I simply can't manage to behave like a carefree holidaymaker. I've become a creature of darkness and silence, a mole or an owl, a female Nosferatu.

It's becoming more incomprehensible to me by the day how anyone on earth can still behave in a carefree way. We don't live in a carefree world, we live on a planet full of pain. In Africa, at any rate, pain is the daily bread. The pain of hunger, the pain of sickness, the pain of war. As you will know, Myriam. Strange, the more I struggle to get away from that terrible continent, the harder I try to convince myself that I can be happier in Europe, the more I entangle myself in this net of pain. It becomes more difficult by the day to read the newspaper, listen to the radio, watch TV news.

The tragedy in Darfur remains hovering about the edges of the news, never quite the main event, but always somewhere in the background. Nagging, like a guilty conscience. In the newspaper *Libération* I recently read the testimony of one

Khadija, 35 years old and three months pregnant after she'd been continuously raped for ten days by four of the Janjaweed soldiers who occupied her village.

I am married, but my husband has been working in another country for two years. He doesn't know yet what happened here. I will tell him the truth. It will be a Janjaweed child, but yet I cannot reject and forsake this baby. He will be my baby. When he is grown up, he can decide whether he wants to stay with my people or be an Arab. If he prefers to be an Arab, I will let him go to them. If he decides to be one of us, he can stay with us.

But yet I cannot reject and forsake this baby.

Ever since I read that sentence, I've been pondering the strange paths on which motherhood can lead one. On one path you have someone like Khadija who is prepared to bring up the enemy's child – even though she may one day have to give him back to the enemy – simply because he has come forth from her body. On another path, in a completely different direction, you have a Myriam Soro who loved her children so much that she couldn't let them live any longer. And somewhere at a crossroads between them, completely lost, you have one Hester Human who gave up her child against her will and has no idea which direction to take.

Nor even if it is still possible to continue the journey.

Sometimes my husband walks with me through the dark village at night. Not often. Not at ease doing it. A romantic gesture, is how he thinks of it, a moonlight stroll with his beloved. An attempt to unfreeze his frozen wife. But I remain as cold as a corpse, and he is still a creature more at home in light and heat. The sun of logic and rationality warms my husband's soul.

He wants to know, for instance, why I don't write you a real letter. A letter in an envelope, he means, not these scrambled words in my head or on a piece of paper hidden in a kitchen drawer. An envelope with an address and a postage stamp, something I can drop into the yellow post box on the square.

"Send it to the prison in Marseille," he urged a few nights ago as we rambled through the sleeping town, the slip-on sandals on our feet flapping on the cobblestones, loud as slaps in the silence. "It can't be that difficult to get the address?"

The way I know him, he'll soon bring me the address, just as he brought the dream book the other day. The envelope and postage stamp too, so that I'll have no excuse to put it off any longer. His kind of love stops at nothing.

"I won't know what to write," I protested. "And in any case I can't write it in French!"

"Write what you can in French, Hes, and the rest in whatever language you want to. It doesn't really matter, she probably won't even read it."

"Well then what's the point of writing to her if she's not going to read it!"

"To get it out of your system. To get her out of your system."

As if I can drop everything that I think and feel about you into a post box. Off you go, sender unknown. Now you're no longer my problem, now you're the post office's problem.

"On the other hand, one never knows," André said soothingly when he saw my face in the yellow cast of the streetlight. "Maybe she'll read it after all. She could always ask someone to translate it. Maybe it will mean something to her?"

"She won't ask anyone anything. She doesn't talk, remember."

"How do you know that she hasn't in the meantime started speaking again?"

Good question.

"Believe me," I said to my husband, my voice sharp with irritation. "She's still mute."

I want you to be mute, I realised with horror. The eternally silent, always suffering victim. After all, this is the image of you that I have been constructing for weeks now.

Forgive me, Myriam. Perhaps that's why I whisper your name all the time. I'm seeking absolution, deliverance.

¥

On the way home from the bakery, a baguette clutched under his elbow as every morning, he sees Aïsha a little way ahead in the steep street. He doesn't recognise her immediately, doesn't realise that she's heading for the same blue garden gate, because her long black hair is covered with an olive green cloth that from the back makes her look like an old woman. It's almost as if the headscarf affects the way she walks, as if she moves more slowly and laboriously than usual. It's only when she reaches the gate, and glances round her quickly without seeing him in the shade of the houses further down the street, that he realises who it is. She pulls off the scarf and stuffs it into the pocket of her wide summer dress.

Her strange behaviour makes him stop instinctively and shrink even further into the shadow as she hastily slips in at the gate. He waits a while before crossing the street and pushing open the gate. It's better this way, he decides, without really knowing why it's better, better that she doesn't know he's seen her.

He walks through the garden, deep in thought, looking absent-mindedly at the bushes of lavender, the lilac-blue hydrangeas in the shady spots, the three arum lilies with their huge dark green leaves next to the dripping tap, the small white rambling roses that aren't really rambling yet though they do decorate the stone wall, an abundant shrub with yellow roses near the wisteria next to the front door. All exactly as Hester planned it last year. Different varieties of parsley and basil and mint growing as profusely as weeds in the clay pots in front of the kitchen window, also coriander, wild garlic, rosemary, marjoram, thyme, oregano and a few herbs that he can't name yet. Hester has clearly not lost her green fingers, even though her gardening has become a duty rather than a delight.

Just another former joy that has changed into a boring responsibility. Gardening, eating, reading, conversing, love-making, the list is growing all the time. Even breathing has become a sort of obligation, something that she continues to do merely to please her husband and her son. From the rest of her family, from her friends in South Africa, she has cut herself off completely.

He encounters them in the kitchen, Aïsha with a purring Fantôme in her arms, Hester's hungry eyes devouring the young girl and the cat. It's because she has no other social contact that Aïsha's weekly visit has taken on such excessive importance. *Se mure dans le mutisme.* Like that woman in the prison in Marseille. At least Hester still talks – when she wants to – but mostly she builds a wall of silence and sorrow around her. Her only company in this town, besides a nineteen-year-old Moroccan girl who comes once a week to iron a few pillow cases, is a ten-year-old girl from Rwanda whom she sometimes happens to see in the square. She doesn't answer letters or e-mails from family and friends, she never phones anyone and when, occasionally, a concerned friend calls from South Africa, she presses the telephone into her husband's hands with panic in her eyes: You talk. I don't know what to say. Say I'm okay.

Well, now, how shall I say, André says in a tone of forced

geniality. Yes, it's going a little better, but she needs time. But thanks for calling anyway. She appreciates it. It's just, you know, she's not ready to chat. Thanks. Yes. I'll tell her. Okay. She says she's okay . . .

The friend usually doesn't phone again. Quite understandable. It costs a fortune to ring from so far, just to listen to the false assurances of a spouse at his wits' end.

She says she's okay.

"Emile and I are cycling to the river," he says to his wife.

"Isn't Habib coming today?" she asks.

They talk Afrikaans, but Aïsha looks up from the cat in her arms at the sound of her brother's name.

"No, I told you that from now on he's coming only three times a week." Immediately irritated that once again she hasn't listened. It's bad enough living with a woman who constantly acts mute. It drives him demented when she seems to be deaf as well. "It's summertime, Hester, I don't know if you've noticed, but everyone round us is holidaying. I told you that from now on I'd be working on the balcony only every second day so that I can spend more time with Emile. And Habib can probably also do with a break. He's not used to doing such hard physical work five days a week."

Aïsha lets the cat jump down and hurries to the storeroom to fetch the vacuum cleaner. She seems more upset than Hester, who merely looks at him with folded arms.

"Have you had words with Habib?" she wants to know.

"Why would I have had words with him?" he asks bewildered.

"I just wondered." She shrugs and starts putting away clean dishes next to the sink. "He seems to be behaving oddly these days."

Aïsha too, he wants to say, but thinks better of it.

"I haven't noticed. Where's Emile?"

154

"On his bed," she sighs. "Glued to his earphones and his Gameboy."

"Why don't you come to the river with us?" he asks on the spur of the moment. "Take the car, then you can bring us a picnic basket?"

"Not today, André. I have to help Aïsha in the house."

"You don't háve to, Hester, she can manage on her own."

"You and Emile also." She drops a handful of knives with a clatter into a drawer, her back stiff and tense. "I would only be a spoilsport."

He turns away and walks to his son's room with legs that feel as heavy as cement. How on earth will he manage to pedal that bicycle all the way to the river?

My husband's latest Project – apart from the balcony he's building next to the bedroom – is to get me to write. Dreams, letters, e-mail messages, doesn't matter whát, just as long as I keep on writing and describing and jotting things down. We now have an internet connection and he's brought a small laptop computer to Manon's room. Like an offering he lay it on the bed, only the incense was missing: For you, my wife.

As a rain gauge collects water from the sky, this little machine is supposed to collect my words. My dreams, my fears, my longings. To measure my state of mind. Dangerous thunderstorms or dismal drizzle or protracted drought.

I follow the line of least resistance. Concerning the dreams at any rate. I'm even beginning to get used to lying very still in bed in the mornings, trying to catch an elusive dream like a fish. Perhaps I should regard it as a form of meditation – which can surely not be a bad thing – though I still doubt the therapeutic value of the process. Many mornings I can't

155

remember anything, just a tantalising flash of a scene behind a dark windowpane, a spot that itches but can't be scratched. The harder I try to reach that place, the shorter my arm becomes. *I waited for you the whole night long. And when I fell asleep it felt all wrong.* Sometimes I remember nothing but that my daughter appeared for a moment or two in the dream.

And what I do remember is generally disconnected and inexplicable, like scraps of a torn letter that I can't decipher.

For example:

23 July

Swimming pool, 2 dogs fall in. One is my brother Stef's woolly mongrel, the other pedigreed and unknown. I jump into the water to save them. Then I look for dry clothes in a bookshop(?) and knock a few shelves over by accident. Start crying and run away in fright. Thunderstorm raging outside. Ride a bike home, very far, soaking wet. Suddenly the bike becomes a car, but the inside of the car is as wet as the outside. Pools of water on the floor, over the pedals, up to my ankles. My brother and Manon sit on the back seat. Before I can see if they're also wet, I wake up.

Or this one:

26 July

Mom and Dad are getting dressed to go out. I'm still a child in their house, but Manon is standing next to me, just a few years younger than me. Mom chooses a costume from a dressing-up box, a magnificent embroidered African kaftan, and Manon claps her hands admiringly. Then Mom puts on a massive pair of platform sandals that make her look like a disco queen from the seventies, and steps on my left foot. I yell, but she doesn't hear, with the platform soles her head is too high, almost as

156

high as the ceiling, or otherwise I have shrunk. When I wake up, the whole of my left leg is numb. From the other leg lying on top of it?

I don't tell my husband about these bizarre dreams. The book lies next to the bed in Manon's room, he can read it if he wants to. But he avoids "the spare room" like a leper colony. Afraid of our daughter's ghost, or of me and my dreams, or maybe only of his own suppressed emotions. I wonder if we'll ever share a bed again. Could the building operations in our bedroom be the excuse we both needed to escape each other's bodies?

The only thing that shocks me about this thought is the fact that it doesn't shock me. It upsets me in a vague way, at a distance, as if it concerned someone else's relationship. More or less how I'd feel if my friend Griet were to tell me that she and her husband no longer sleep together.

To Myriam I haven't written, not a real letter, I can't go there yet. But since my husband keeps nagging me not to lose "contact" with "reality" (whatever that might mean), I wrote to my mother this week. A fairly honest letter, uncheerful, because cheerfulness is quite beyond me, but with my despair wrapped carefully in cotton wool. Hidden behind wistful words about the seasons passing and the people I miss. Wistfulness is so much more digestible than despair. Also looks better on paper. Fewer exclamation marks. *Oh the cup with the hole. There's a smile on my lips but a sob in my soul.*

I don't want my mother to realise how deep the hole is that I've fallen into. What would she be able to do about it in any case? She's much too far away to throw me a lifeline. And yet I also know there are things that you can't hide from your mother. I imagine she knows exactly how dark it is in this particular pit, that's why she phones so seldom.

157

After all, she's lived with a depressive husband for decades. But she writes regularly.

The apple tree in the back yard has produced exactly a dozen apples. All really strange shapes. One gigantic round one that Dad ate last week. He said it was tart, but nice. Some were oval and some square and there were even some rectangular ones! Caramel's favourite spot is on the low wall near the apple tree. He misses you all, but he's plump and healthy.

Meaningless bits of news about apples and cats. What the heart is full of, the tongue will sometimes *not* speak of.

My dear mother desperately wants to believe that melancholia is a male condition. Because my father suffers from it, because my younger brother has shown signs of it since adolescence. My mother thinks women are simply too practical for lasting pessimism. Along with the motherly instinct comes a sort of instinct for optimism – otherwise the human race would have died out long ago.

What about Myriam Soro, I wonder, or all the other women who murder their children or commit suicide while their children are still small? What happened to their instincts? Freaks, my mother would probably answer, freaks and exceptions. Sometimes my mother is so intensely cheerful that I wonder if she's not secretly struggling against depression. Oh, no, Hes, she would say if I were to enquire: I don't have time for such nonsense. That's your father's territory.

And my father is too melancholic to talk about his melancholia.

Therefore it remains a murky subject for me.

I also sent a lame round-robin letter to a few friends via the internet. It's summer, the sun is shining, the lavender is blooming, the house is slowly but surely beginning to look more like a house and less like a building site, and for the rest we are hanging in there, hope you are too. Leave me alone for heaven's sake so that I can drown in my own tears. No, I didn't add the last sentence. But it was the message I tried to convey between the lines.

And yet André looked so pleased and proud of my attempt to make "contact" that I wanted to grab him by the shoulders and shake him. It's not going any better, my dear husband! The bottle is still half empty, not half full. Come and stand here next to me, come and look through my eyes, then you'll see what I mean. And it's not filling up, let's not fool ourselves, it's very, very gradually emptying.

⁀⁀

She's behaving like a bad actress in a third-rate soapie, André decides as he watches his wife. She insisted on baking a milk tart, and he let her be because it would keep her busy while they waited for their guests to arrive, but now he wishes he'd rather bought a tart at the *patisserie*. She's just taken the pan out of the oven and is staring at it as if it's a mutilated human body instead of a burnt tart.

A slightly burnt tart.

"I'm not used to this oven!" she wails. "I should have baked a few other things first to practise!"

"You baked a cake the other day," he reminds her.

"Which was also a miserable flop!"

"Come on, Hester, don't exaggerate. We all had some of it."

"One slice each. I dumped the rest in the rubbish bin." There was nothing wrong with the cake, he would like to tell her, except for the whole concept of a cake to commemorate a dead child's birthday. The mere idea was enough to give one indigestion. Every bite stuck in his throat like a hard lump. "I'm afraid I'll have to throw away this one as well."

"No, wait, Hester." He stops her because she's already on

159

her way to the rubbish bin in the corner, takes the pan out of her hands and puts it on the table. "The crust is a little browner than usual. So what? Looks like a tart with a tan," he adds jokingly.

"No it's burnt, André, totally and irredeemably burnt!"

He casts a glance at the wall clock. Their guests should be here any minute now. The last thing he needs now is for his wife to fall apart over a damn milk tart.

"Hester," he says after taking a deep breath. "It doesn't mátter. You can scrape the burnt bits off if you want to. But even if it were a total flop, even if you'd made it with rotten eggs and sour milk, then it would still not matter. The people are coming to have coffee. We don't have to fééd them. Do you hear me?"

It doesn't look as if she has. She stares at the tart on the table with her hand clasped melodramatically over her mouth.

"You're carrying on as if you have to exhibit the thing at an agricultural show. Laurent and Naomi have probably never in their lives tasted a traditional South African milk tart. They don't know how it's supposed to taste. They won't even realise that it's burnt."

She sinks down next to the table and shakes her head in dismay.

"I'm sorry. It is so long since we've had guests . . ."

He knew that the invitation would upset her, but he didn't know it would be this bad. It happened spontaneously, before he'd had a chance to think about it. Emile had mentioned that Nathalie's parents were coming to drop her here over the weekend, so André suggested that they invite the family for a meal.

Emile immediately protested volubly.

"Why don't you invite your own friends for a meal! Leave my friends' parents out of it!"

160

What friends, André could have asked his son. But at that moment he saw his wife's stricken expression and decided rather to invite them for a cup of coffee only. Thank God, he thinks now. If Hester gets this flustered over a less-than-perfect tart, he can't imagine her handling the stress of a full meal.

"It's the least we can do after they've driven this distance," he said to Emile.

"They're not coming all this way only to drop her, Dad," his son retorted. "They have other things to do in the area, okay? They have a *life*."

André decided to ignore the sarcasm. "I also want your mother to meet them," he said easily. "I think she'll like them."

He no longer thinks so, but it's too late to do anything about that.

The irony is that Hester used to be the social partner in this relationship. Hester had a circle of friends as wide as nature's bounty. André was quite happy with two or three bosom buddies – and even those he didn't see all that regularly. He was happiest under his own roof, with his wife and children under his wing. My old homebird, gallus domesticus, Hester used to tease.

"What's your favourite car, Dad?" Emile had asked years before.

"That's got to be Jack O'Homebody's Model T," Hester had answered banteringly.

In his twenties, before he got to know her, he used to go out fairly regularly. Well, that's what one did when one was young. You went out looking for someone to grow old with. After he and Hester had set up home, he applied himself to growing old. With dedication, one could almost say with un- seemly haste. Lying on the carpet listening to classical music while she read, telling the children bedtime stories with her,

161

staying in bed on Sunday mornings to drink coffee and eat croissants and page through the papers.

With Hester by his side, he had no need of a crowd of friends. She was the person with whom he could talk most easily and laugh most readily. His better half in all senses of the words: Everything he needed to feel complete and whole.

Now Hester isn't whole any more, just a sombre shadow of the woman she was, and every day he almost physically feels the void that she has left. For the first time since he has known her, he looks for excuses to get away from her. For the first time he needs other people more than he needs her.

He hears the creak of the garden gate. The next moment Emile rushes down the stairs and whooshes through the kitchen like an express train. "They're here!" he calls over his shoulder. "Is the coffee ready?" Almost as hyped-up as his mother. It's clear that no one in the family is used to guests anymore.

Hester's hand trembles in his as he leads her outside.

And there are the three smiling guests in the courtyard. The tall slender woman, as strikingly beautiful as he remembers her, with a coloured turban on her head; the massive bearded bear of a man in a white T-shirt next to her; the pretty teen daughter with her short curly hair gleaming with gel. A fine example of a prosperous black nuclear family.

And opposite them the white nuclear family. The tall thin man with the dirty fingernails of a labourer (he tried that morning to scrub his nails, but after all these months of building he seems to have a permanent layer of dust, cement and dirt on his skin); the thin woman with the absent gaze of a blind person, deep lines of grief etched round her mouth; the teen son with his clumsy neither-fish-nor-fowl body, carrying his anger like a time bomb inside him. And the lost family member whose absence hangs over them like a cloud. Surely anyone can see it. Any stranger looking at this picture would notice straight away that something was missing.

The youngest child is erased, so hastily and untidily that the outlines are still vaguely visible.

"Shall we sit out here under the umbrella?" asks André after greetings and introductions have been done. He is using the forced convivial tone he uses when trying to reassure his wife's concerned friends on the telephone. "Such lovely sunny weather!"

"As long as you remember to show us what you've done in the house," Naomi says.

"It's more a case of what we still plan to do. It's a long way from being finished. But okay, let's do the guided tour before we drink anything."

"You do the tour," Hester whispers, breathless in her nervousness, "then I'll get on with the coffee. Or would anyone prefer tea?"

"Oh, no, coffee is just what we need to wake us up properly." Laurent's deep voice sounds even louder than usual, perhaps just in contrast with Hester's tense whisper. "We had an unplanned late night. Friends who pitched up unexpectedly, and it turned into quite a party. You know how it happens."

No, Hester no longer knows how it happens. Her laugh is uneven, quite unconvincing. But a laugh is a laugh, says André to himself while he leads the guests to the front door. Every time his sad wife laughs, an unquenchable hopefulness wells up in him.

"And you two?" Hester asks the children who are looking uncertainly at one another. "Want to have coffee with us? Or cold drinks?"

"It's okay, Mom," says Emile, "we'll help ourselves to cold drinks in the kitchen. I want to show Nathalie the town. The little there is to show."

"Can't be that bad," laughs Nathalie

"Want to bet?" asks Emile and disappears with her into the house.

As Laurent and Naomi admire the pale stone slabs surrounding the living room doors, André looks through one of the windows at Hester who has been left alone outside. She's standing with her head bowed, finger at her lips, quite still. Like Lot's wife turned to stone. The one who wasn't able to put the past behind her. He wonders if she's forgotten that she's supposed to be making coffee for their guests. He lifts his hand to knock on the window, to bring her back to the present, but then turns away quickly to conduct the guests through the rest of the house. At some time or other, he tries to convince himself, the stone woman out there will become human again. He must just be patient.

⌒⌒

"Why are they staring at us like that?" asks Nathalie, fidgeting uncomfortably beside him on the wooden bench.

Emile glares at the group of older teenagers leaning against the edge of the fountain. Every now and again one of them makes a low remark that evokes jeering laughter from the others. He can't hear what they're saying, but their body language is challenging and aggressive.

"Oh, just ignore them," he mutters. "They're a bunch of country bumpkins. They don't know any better."

"Do you know them?"

"In a village like this everyone knows everyone else," he answers with a sour taste in his mouth. "Except my mother who makes a point of not getting to know anyone."

He had led her through the few narrow streets of the town to the square, where they sat down on the wooden bench because the fountain was already occupied by the older teen-agers. The usual gang, Jason and his hangers-on, except that today there are no girls with them. Maybe that's why they're being so unexpectedly aggressive. His common sense tells him to take Nathalie away from here, to get going before there's any trouble, but he also doesn't want the boys to think he's afraid and running away from them.

"Are they always so . . . like they're spoiling for a fight?"

"No, in the beginning they were quite friendly. But all they really wanted was for me to teach them English swear words. When I couldn't think of any more, they lost interest in me."

She widens her eyes and laughs disbelievingly.

"I can't say I miss their company. And at least I also got something out of the deal. In a few weeks I learnt enough French swear words to understand any French rap song."

"Like what?" she asks moving closer to him. "Will you teach me a few?"

He feels a dreadful flush spreading from his neck over his cheeks. It isn't the first time he wishes he had Nathalie's dark skin. It can't always be wonderful to be black, but at least you don't blush all the time.

"That's not necessary. You speak French well enough."

"But I don't swear well enough." She stares glumly at her red Nike sports shoes. "My parents are só bourgeois. As you probably noticed. And like totally overprotective because I'm an only child. We've never lived in a rough neighbourhood, I've never had rough friends, my life is really unbelievably boring!"

"Well, you're welcome to come and live in the rough coun-tryside," he grins. "That crowd next to the fountain will teach you more than you want to know."

At that moment another burst of laughter comes from the fountain, almost as if they'd understood his words.

165

"Let's go," mumbles Nathalie. "They're looking right through my clothes."

He wants to say they're just not used to seeing such a pretty girl here on the square. But then he would blush again, so he keeps it to himself and they both get up. Jason's mocking laugh follows them all the way to the other side of the café veranda.

Emile feels his heart thumping uncontrollably in his chest. One day, one of these fine days, everything is going to erupt, everything that's been suppressed this past year. But not to-day. Please, just not today, he says to himself. It's the last time he'll see Nathalie before she leaves for a holiday in Spain, the last time he'll be able to talk to her before the new school year begins in September.

"So is your suitcase packed?" he asks as they cross the street.

"Not yet," she answers, "but I can't wait. We're going to the same beach as last year, so hopefully I'll see some of my pals from last year again. That way you're in the swing of things straight away, you know, like you don't have to waste time making the contacts. There are parties every night, every-where. It's brilliant."

She could have been decent enough to add that she would miss him. Even if it wasn't true. Just to be nice.

"And you?" she asks when she notices his hangdog expres-sion. "Aren't you going away at all?"

"We're away already. I mean we're in France, not at home in Cape Town."

"Yes, but you go to school here and your dad works on the house all the time, so it isn't actually a holiday, is it?"

"No. It definitely doesn't feel like a holiday. But we can't go away. My dad wants to finish the work on the house before winter sets in. And my mother, well, after all, you can see she's not exactly in a holiday mood."

166

They walk past the bakery, where as usual the aroma of fresh bread and confectionery hangs heavily in the air. A few of the townspeople nod in a friendly way at him and stare curiously at Nathalie. He ignores them all and walks on, dragging his feet.

"I actually thought it would be worse," says Nathalie lost in thought. "Your mom. You know. The way you described her, I thought she'd be half dead."

"But she is half dead!" he cries indignantly. "If you'd known her before, you would also think so. That sad woman you've just met isn't my mother!"

He shakes his head vigorously and increases his stride, but he'd forgotten how long her legs are. She keeps up with him step for step, till after a while he stops, out of breath.

"Sorry, I didn't mean to be rude, it's just . . ." He avoids her questioning eyes, deliberately looking past her head, staring through a haze at the stone village up the hillside. "I just don't know what the hell became of my mother."

6

⁓⁓

"I'm worried about Emile," confesses André on one of their nocturnal wanderings through the empty streets of Lunel.

It's full moon, the sky cloudless, the stone walls round them bathed in an unusually bright light. A silver twilight rather than a black darkness. Tonight there's no need for the yellowish streetlights to light their way. That's probably why Hester is walking faster than usual, without answering him, without any sign that she's heard him. He wonders if he should repeat his statement. No, maybe better to talk about something else. These days Hester only hears what she wants to hear.

Then she surprises him by reacting after all. A single word, more of a sigh than a question.

"Why?"

"He's spending far too much time on his own. It can't be good for him to brood so much. He still hasn't made a single friend of his own age in the village. Not even among the holidaymakers. And there áre some of his age among them, even some English-speakers, I hear them in the streets."

"One can understand his not feeling like making friends," says Hester in her abstracted manner.

His wife is the one who really concerns him, the one who spends far too much time brooding on her own, but he knows there is no point in talking to her about it. The coffee drinking with Nathalie's parents turned out not too badly – the anxiety-inducing milk tart even elicited a few compliments –

168

but after that, she retired even more deeply into her shell for days. With his wife, André has to admit, he's at his wits' end.

For his son he can perhaps still do something.

"Last month he did at least see Nathalie now and again. Or spoke to her on the phone. Now that she's in Spain, he watches TV all day long. I'm amazed that he hasn't put roots down in that settee. Or grown into those earphones that he wears on his head night and day. Even when I make him come out on the bike with me he keeps on those damn earphones."

"Hmm," says Hester.

"It's as if he deliberately shuts out the outside world. *Don't talk to me: I can't hear you.* And just to be quite sure that everyone gets the message, he pulls that baseball cap so low over his forehead that nobody can see his eyes!"

She doesn't need earphones or baseball caps to cut out the outside world. Her bare arm brushes accidentally against his, a touch that shoots through him like an electric shock, but apparently has no effect on her. Hester who doesn't hear, Hester who doesn't talk, Hester who doesn't feel.

"I try my best to do father-son things with him. But even if I were the best father on this earth – which clearly I'm not – it would still be better for him to have a pal of his own age, don't you think?"

He's startled when an owl suddenly calls near to them. The unearthly sound seems to be coming from the roof of a ruin, one of the age-old houses in the town not yet bought and restored by tourists. It's a comforting thought that there are still places where owls can shelter, even now in summer with the town full to bursting.

"What about the crowd that always hang about around the fountain? Didn't he make friends with them?"

He looks at her, surprised that she is even aware of the layabouts who gather there.

"They're too old for him," he says. "I warned him that they can be a bad influence."

Now it's her turn to look surprised.

"Then you can't complain that he doesn't have friends, can you?"

"I'm not complaining, Hester," he says, annoyed. "I'm worried about the child, as any normal parent would be!"

A swift intake of breath next to him, but she says nothing. Nothing but their footsteps on the cobblestones, a cricket calling from a dark garden, frogs croaking in the distance.

"And I'm not a normal parent any more," she remarks after a while.

"I didn't say that," he parries.

"I'm saying so. It's true. I no longer know how a normal parent behaves. I try my best, but nothing feels right. I can't look at Emile without seeing the empty space next to him where Manon ought to be. All I can do to protect myself – or maybe to protect him from me – is to look away."

"It's not Emile's fault that Manon isn't here any more," he mutters under his breath.

"I know!" Her cry echoes in the silent street, shockingly loud between the high stone walls. "Of course I know that, André, but it doesn't make it any easier to accept that hole next to him!"

"And when you look at me?" he asks, his heart hammering.

She doesn't answer immediately.

"That's perhaps even more difficult," she admits after a few seconds. "You look like her. You have her mouth and her cheeks and her chin, the whole lower half of her face."

"You have her eyes. And her hands."

"See what I mean? We can't look at each other without seeing our dead child. No wonder we'd rather look away."

They walk some distance in silence. Without looking at each other.

170

"Let's go to bed," he says at last, as calmly as he can.

She in their dead child's empty bed and he on the studio couch in the living room. He wonders if they will ever again fall asleep cosily against one another, like two spoons in a drawer. It's starting to seem ever more unlikely.

~~

Three days later Emile stumbles into the house crying, his nose bloody and his shirt torn. André, cutting up cucumbers for a cold soup in the kitchen, is so shocked by the blood and tears on his son's face that he can hardly utter a word.

"What . . . what is . . . what happened?" he stammers.

"Nothing." It's clear that Emile wants to push past him without further explanation. André automatically puts out his hand to stop the child. Emile pulls away, but stops after all. "Nothing to do with you, Dad!"

"Of course it has something to do with me if my son comes home in this condition." His voice is shaking with alarm, but he tries his best to keep the tone firm and fatherly. "Did you fight with someone?"

"Yes," answers Emile curtly and wipes his nose with his hand, leaving a streak of slimy blood behind.

"Who with?"

Emile looks disgustedly at the blood on the back of his hand. André grabs him by his bony shoulders. "Who with, Emile?" he insists.

"Doesn't matter, Dad." Under his hands his son's shoulders shake with a suppressed sob.

"Clean up your nose." André thrusts a roll of kitchen paper in the child's hands and waits for him to wipe off the worst of the blood and snot. Then he asks for the third time, with all the patience he can muster: "Who did you fight with, Emile?"

171

"Jason."

"Who is Jason?" But before Emile can answer, André suddenly knows. "One of those louts on the square?"

Who else, he wonders with a kind of resignation.

Emile nods and shuffles uncomfortably.

"But can't he pick on someone his own age?" André asks angrily.

"I hit him first."

"What for?" The red eyes, tearful cheeks, the shuddering shoulders in the torn T-shirt, the whole pathetic picture makes it difficult to keep his voice severe. Pity and tenderness threaten to break through. "If you're going to behave like a hooligan, then you can at least pick on someone your size."

"Hooligans don't fight with fists, Dad. They use knives."

"So I should be glad that you haven't come home with a knife wound?" he asks sarcastically. "What did this Jason do to make you so mad?"

"They were looking for trouble. They were all going for me."

"Emile, I did warn you that they . . ."

"I know you warned me!" Emile shouts and rushes past his father.

Half way up the stairs he runs into his mother. The angrily raised voices in the kitchen must have flushed her from her hiding place in the spare room.

"What's happened to you?" she asks in alarm.

"Leave me alone. I had a fight with someone."

"But you're not a fighter, Emile!" André, standing rigid in the kitchen, recognises his own confusion in Hester's shocked exclamation.

"Leave me alone, Mom. Don't try to hold me nów!" Emile shouts and storms up the rest of the way. Seconds later Hester appears in the door of the kitchen, her mouth trembling.

172

"No, I don't know what's going on either," says André. "We'll have to wait till he calms down before we can ask him anything more."

"He isn't a fighter," she says, dismayed, and subsides slowly into a chair. "He's never been a fighter. . . "

⤴⤵

When the knock on his door comes, he expects his father. To his surprise it's his mother standing in the door with a bowl of cold cucumber soup and a few slices of bread on a tray. He was too upset to eat with them, but by now he's so hungry that even the cold soup – that he normally can't stand – looks like a feast.

"Thanks," he mumbles, taking the tray from her.

She sits down on the bed next to him. Far enough away so their bodies don't touch, but nevertheless closer to him than she's been in months. He tucks into the soup greedily and tries to ignore her enquiring look.

"What was the fight about?" she asks at last when he picks up the second slice of bread. "What made you so angry that you wanted to hit someone?"

Had it been his father sitting next to him, it would have been easy to put him off the scent with a brusque reply. He's become used to evading his father's well-intentioned questions, whether about wet dreams or fist fights. But with his mother it's been so long since she's shown any interest in him, so long since she's really tried to talk to him, that his rebelliousness promptly starts to dissolve. All that remains is a miserable gratitude. That she still cares after all.

"They mocked me about Nathalie. They saw us together the other day when they were here."

"And that made you so mad you had to attack them?" his mother asks in disbelief.

173

"They said ugly things about her, Mom."

"Like what?"

"That she's a *salope*. A slut. A black slut. They wanted to know if it's true that black girls . . . I can't tell you this, Mom."

He feels the indignation welling up inside him all over again, the blind rage that for the first time in his life made him aim a fist at another guy's face. If he'd hesitated for a second, he'd have remembered that Jason was a few years older than he – besides being surrounded by his gang. If he'd thought for just that second, he'd have realised he stood no chance, but he was too angry to be scared. He wanted to smash in Jason's smug face, that's all.

"They're a bunch of racists, Mom. Just like all those racists at home that you and Dad are always going on about. In Cape Town I also have black pals, but no one has ever insulted me about them!"

His mother takes his hand cautiously, as if it's a plate that she's warmed in the oven, something that could burn her.

"Racism is unfortunately a worldwide phenomenon," she says. "Like small-mindedness and coarseness."

He allows her to fold her fingers over his and is amazed at how small her hand has become since he last felt it.

"I didn't expect it here. You always went on about how wonderful France is. I haven't seen anything wonderful here. I can't wait to go home."

"What about Nathalie?"

"Nathalie is the only good thing that's happened to me since I've been here. If it wasn't for her, I'd most probably by now have . . . done something terrible."

The sudden alarm in his mother's grey eyes makes him feel a little better.

"Aren't you going to miss her when you go back?"

"For sure. But she's all that I'll miss. Here I miss hundreds of things and people every day!"

174

"I'm so sorry, Emile," she sighs. "I shouldn't have brought you here. If I'd known . . ."

The next moment her eyes are brimming with tears. He looks away quickly, determined not to feel sorry for her.

"I should have come on my own."

"What do you mean, Mom?" His voice cracks with astonishment. "Left me and Dad at home?"

"That would have been better."

"But what would you have done on your own all the time?"

"What I do now," she answers as if to herself.

"Grieve?"

She nods absently. "But without bothering the two of you."

He wants to demur, to assure her that she doesn't really bother them, but the words sound false even before he can say them aloud.

"How long would you have wanted to be on your own?" he asks curtly.

"I don't know." She withdraws her hand from his and pats him soothingly on the knee. "As long as it would take to become human again?"

Two days after Emile arrived home with a bloody nose, Aïsha walks into the kitchen with a swollen purplish bruise on her cheek. Slipped on a smooth floor, she explains, and fell against the corner of a table. But the lie slips out far too slick and practised.

I look at her with a sceptical sideways glance. She lifts her chin and meets my gaze as if daring me not to believe her. I hide my concern and suggest that we have the weekly cup of tea straight away. Before she starts on the vacuuming or ironing, I say, because I feel the need to talk to someone. She looks a little cornered, but agrees. What else can she do? I'm her employer.

Her friend too, I'd like to think, but in her eyes probably only a friendly employer.

While the tea water boils, I tell her about my son's fist fight and of the insulting remarks that gave rise to it.

"I'm not surprised," she says and lifts Fantôme onto her lap. Her long black hair hangs like curtains on either side of her face as she strokes the cat. "I know that Jason. We were at school together. He was always a troublemaker."

"But such blatant racism? Does it happen to you as well sometimes? Here in this village?"

She looks up with an oblique smile and something like disbelief in her dark eyes. It strikes me again how pretty she is – in a quiet, almost old-fashioned way – without any awareness of her own beauty. Even with the shocking purple bruise on her dusky cheek.

"Most people are nice to me because I grew up here. Because my family has lived here a long time. But that doesn't mean they *like* Arabs."

She says it without resentment, as if it's simply a fact that she accepted long ago. I bring the lavender-blue teapot and cups to the table and sit next to her, waiting for her to carry on talking, but she just strokes the cat's back.

"Tell me about Morocco. I know nothing about your country."

"And I know nothing about yours."

"You first."

"Morocco is a wondrously beautiful country." It sounds like a sentence from an old-style guidebook: *A wondrously beautiful country*. But she says it without a hint of mockery. "All that most Europeans ever want to see is Casablanca and Marrakech. They don't know what they're missing. The coun-

176

tryside is beautiful. My family comes from the south, near the desert."

"Would you want to live there again? Rather than here?"

She shakes her head, deep in thought. "No. I've changed too much."

"But you surely don't want to live in this little town for the rest of your life?"

"I'd have liked to live in a big city like Paris," she says softly. "But I think I'll be living here for the rest of my life."

"In Lunel?"

"In this area." I look at her with such incomprehension that she explains somewhat reluctantly. "My brothers wouldn't allow me to go away. My family will find me a husband living nearby. Probably a creepy old widower."

Again that oblique smile that makes me hope for a minute that she's teasing me. But then she blinks quickly and hides her mouth behind the teacup.

"And if you refused to marry a creepy widower? If you went off to Paris?"

"It doesn't work like that, Hester." Suddenly she sounds the older of us two – perhaps because she so seldom addresses me by name. As if I'm the young girl needing to be helped out of my naive gullibility. "I'm a decent Muslim girl. I listen to my elder brothers."

"To Habib?"

"He's the eldest in the house. There are two others who are already married. They also live round here."

'What about your father?"

"He's old and sick. Habib is the master of our house. Even my mother is scared of him."

Scáred of him? Scáred of Habib? I remember the time he swore at her here in the kitchen, but I still have difficulty re- conciling that harsh rude voice with my husband's whistling,

177

joking helper. I convinced myself that it was a once-off family crisis having nothing to do with me.

"If I don't listen to him . . ." says Aïsha and brushes across her cheek with feigned nonchalance.

"Was it him?" She keeps her eyes fixed on the rough wood grain of the table as though she doesn't want to see my bewilderment. "Did he hit you?"

Perhaps it's the shock in my voice that at last makes her cry.

"He didn't hit me," she says as tears begin to run down her cheeks. "Pushed me around. Maybe harder than he meant to. That's when I fell against the table."

"But why, Aïsha?"

"He wants me to wear the headscarf all the time. Cover my head as a decent Muslim girl should." For the first time I hear sarcasm and rebellion in her soft voice. "I'm not used to it. I've always dressed like the French girls around me. Only worn the headscarf occasionally to keep my mother happy."

"Is that what the swearing in the kitchen was about?" I ask, stunned. "The time you were ironing . . ."

She nods and wipes away the tears that are still running down her cheeks with the back of her hand, touches the bruise too hard and winces at the pain.

"He wasn't supposed to be here. He'd come to fetch something he'd forgotten. Or that's what he said. I don't know, maybe he just wanted to catch me out. I make sure I wear the headscarf every time I leave our front door, just to keep him quiet, but mostly I take it off as soon as I'm far enough away from the house."

I can't believe that I was so obtuse. He had been pointing at her head – I suddenly recall it clearly – but I'd taken it to mean something like: use your common sense. Or: what's happened to your brain?

178

"How long has this been going on?"

"Really only the last few weeks. Previously he didn't care. But now the government wants to prohibit headscarves in schools and in the public services . . . so the whole issue has become important to him." She rummages in the pocket of her kaftan, brings out a crumpled scarf and blows her nose in it. "At least something it can be used for," she mumbles with false bravado.

"I got the impression he was changing."

"The whole world is changing." She gives me that almost-pitying look of a much older woman again. "I asked him if he feels so strongly about it, why doesn't he wear a headscarf? He didn't find it funny. That's when he . . . when I hurt my cheek."

I have no idea what to say to her. To hell with your brother? Don't listen to him, lead your own life, run off to Paris, come and live here with me? I can only look at her helplessly.

"But I can understand why he's acting so strangely," she says after a while. "I don't approve, I think he's completely stupid, but I can understand it. He's always tried very hard to be French. Not Moroccan. But the French have always sort of looked right through him, without noticing him. And now with Al Qaeda, and all the bombs going off everywhere, now they really notice him, for the first time. Now they look at him – for the first time – with something like fear in their eyes. Maybe even with hate."

She carries the cups to the sink and carries on with her back to me.

"I think he's realised that no matter how hard he tries, to the French around him he will always be an Arab first. Never a 'real' Frenchman. So now he probably wants to be a 'real' Arab?"

I look at her hair lying smooth against her back, shining in

179

the sunlight. Nothing makes sense to me. I thought I was coming to the land of freedom, equality and fraternity. Brotherhood – or sisterhood, why not? What I have found, thus far, is distrust, racism and chauvinism. My son gets involved for the first time in his life in a fist fight simply because he made friends with a black girl. My friend – my only friend here, even though she doesn't even know that – is assaulted by her brother because she wants to dress like any other French girl. My other potential friend, the ten-year-old Aurore, runs away from me these days because her mother apparently thinks I'm a paedophile or a pervert.

Of all the bitter pills that I have had to swallow this year, this disillusionment is perhaps the worst. One doesn't realise how bitter it tastes, because the doses are so small. But after six months the aftertaste stays on the tongue permanently.

〰️

No, it can't be true, decides André, discreetly watching his employee. They are standing close together in the cramped bathroom, tiling the wall. There is a heavy smell of perspiration in the air. Habib is breathing hard and wipes his damp face often with the back of his hand.

Je ne veux pas travailler . . . he hums through his teeth, a silly pop song, to amuse or tease André. I don't want to work – that's more or less what the words are saying – I just want to lie on my bed and smoke. André pretends not to hear. At first it amused him that Habib sang this every time he was tired or bored, but it has long since ceased to be funny.

He steals another covert glance at Habib's sweaty face, the soft plump cheeks, the soft brown eyes, the sort of chin that's usually described as weak, small and round and inconspicuous. How can it be possible that this mild, lazy sort of fellow can be a tyrant towards his sister? A dreadful chauvinist according to what Hester recounted last night, perhaps even a religious fanatic in the making. No, André speculates, Hester must have misunderstood. Aïsha must have exaggerated. Habib is as harmless as a cow.

"What do young people like you do in a town like this in their free time?" he asks pensively.

Habib looks surprised, which immediately makes him feel guilty. They've been working side by side for months. It's the sort of thing he should have asked long ago. But as they still struggle to communicate in a common language, they don't really chat when working. Habib whistles or sings along with the radio, sometimes makes a feeble joke, tells him something about the weather or about one of the townspeople. André listens and gives instructions in broken French.

"Oh, they smoke and drink and dance," says Habib. "Or they race around in motor cars and watch TV and surf the internet and play soccer. Much the same as young people everywhere."

"And you? What do you do? Play soccer? Or any other sport?"

"I like soccer. Marseille is my club. Zidane is my hero. But I don't play myself. I hunt."

"Hunt?"

Habib nods, puts the tile he was holding down on the cupboard, and lifts his arms to aim an imaginary gun at André, making sure André understands.

"What do you hunt?"

"Anything that moves," grins Habib.

"To eat?"

"No, just for sport."

André wonders if his helper is stringing him along and grimaces unhappily.

181

"Hares and birds and so on." Habib wipes his glistening face. "I give them to other people to eat. Sometimes sell them for pocket money. But really I do it because I like shooting. I should probably have been a soldier."

He looks embarrassed, suddenly almost ashamed.

"Why aren't you?" asks André with a reluctant sort of compassion.

"No, you have to be superfit to be a soldier. I don't like the running and the exercising. Only the shooting." Habib stands back a pace to admire their handiwork, folds his arms, satisfied, and starts humming again. "*Je ne veux pas travailler . . .*"

"Okay, okay, I get the message," says a resigned André. "It's almost lunchtime. We can stop now."

Impossible, he decides while wiping his sweaty forehead with a dirty handkerchief, impossible that Habib could be a threat to anyone. He is simply too slack to become a fanatic. About anything.

※

When I fled from the blistering heat to Manon's room this afternoon, I found the dream journal on the bedside table, neatly closed, whereas I was convinced I'd left it open on the bed this morning. I'd wanted to read through all the confused dreams to look for a pattern, some direction, some or other vague indication of where my subconscious was leading me. Halfway through I'd given up, because as usual I couldn't make head or tail of it. But I remembered that I had left the book open, with the lovely midnight blue spine turned up, because I wanted to go on reading later on.

Would my husband have crept into the room secretly to page through the book? Or could he have been looking for something in the room, noticed the book by chance and been tempted to look in it? In all probability read only a sentence or two. His conscience wouldn't have allowed him to go any further. Eternally decent.

It's not that I want to hide my confused dreams from him. I would just have preferred him to ask before looking. No, that's not true. If he'd asked, I'd probably have refused. I've become a miser, I hoard thoughts and emotions and dreams, keep them all to myself, sharing nothing. A centipede, curled up against the outside world, tightly coiled round my own inner world. Songololo, a Zulu centipede.

And yet, every now and again I make an effort to escape the spiral. Last week I even bought a kind of guide at the morning market. A wilted paperback I found on a table of second-hand books, to help me to understand my dreams. A complete waste of time and money. The subjects one is supposed to dream about, are divided alphabetically, each with a prophetic explanation. I say "supposed" because I never dream about eagles and bees and frogs, I dream about people (especially my daughter) and about places. Houses, shops, swimming pools. Nothing about those in the wilted little book.

The subjects I dream about regularly – that I'm on a journey somewhere, on foot or on a bike or in a car, that I struggle to get my case packed, am not ready for the trip, don't know the way, that I'm looking for something, that I lose my way – can all be explained fairly literally. I find myself in a foreign country, I am not ready for the experience, I feel lost in my own life, I am looking for meaning. I don't need a book to explain that to me.

13 August
My friend Griet stands gambling in something that looks like a telephone booth. I'm in the booth next to her, not gambling, just looking at her through the glass. Then I rush out to show

someone a photo of my daughter, but I only have photos show-
ing parts of her: a bright yellow jersey, a bare knee with a
sticking plaster on it, purple trainers with loose shoelaces; not
a single photo of her face.

If you dream of winning when you gamble, it means that you will lose something valuable. So the paperback book tells me. Nothing about a friend who gambles. Besides, she didn't win or lose, only gambled. Nothing about telephones or telephone booths. Nothing about photos. But, yes, well, once again I don't need a guide book to tell me that I would give anything on earth to see my daughter's face just once again.

I waited for you the whole night long.

I threw the silly little book into the kitchen garbage. Maybe my husband will find it there, amongst the damp coffee grinds and bits of hard baguette, when next he takes out the black garbage bag. Maybe it will help him to understand my dreams next time he digs around in my subconscious without permission.

☙

Myriam, I sent you a postcard today. A real postcard with a picture of a roaring maned lion (to remind you of Africa) and an address (the women's prison in Marseille) and a postage stamp, small and red like a speck of blood against the white paper. The postcard is one of a pile that we brought with us to France, lovely photos of white beaches and high mountains and wild animals, to show people where we come from. Which people? You may well ask.

Aïsha is the only person to whom I've shown some of these pictures.

Would love to show Aurore as well, but haven't seen her for weeks. As it's holiday time I can't pretend to bump into her in the square in the afternoons. I miss those thin brown legs, the bobbing red rucksack, the coloured glass balls in her hair, the complicated plaits that sometimes cross her head like paths in a maze.

She remains a fascinating puzzle to me. She doesn't hesitate to ask me about anything under the sun, but if I want to ask any questions, I have to be very careful not to step into all kinds of dark holes. About her murdered biological family in Rwanda she doesn't want to talk, surely understandably. But about her father here in France she won't talk either, simply pretends not to hear when I wonder aloud about him. Even about her French mother she is frustratingly vague.

I tried in roundabout ways, and without success, to find out why her mother is so distrustful of me. At first I wondered if she had perhaps spied on me from a distance, decided I look unstable or dangerous. Even secretly conceded that she could have a point. With my untidy hair and my staring eyes and muttering lips, I probably don't inspire confidence. After half a year I've hardly spoken to a soul in the village – and here out of the blue I invite a ten-year-old-girl to my home. Enough to make any parent suspicious.

Later I began to suspect that the woman's lack of trust wasn't aimed at me personally. That she was paranoid because she's had a traumatic experience with a paedophile or a molester or a violent person. Or perhaps poor Aurore has experienced some such trauma?

By now I have been living here long enough to think that the woman is neither paranoid nor even very neurotic. She is this way simply because she lives in Europe. The continent of distrust, especially when it comes to children. In every police station, in even the smallest town, there are posters full of photos of children who have disappeared without trace. Did you also notice that, Myriam? I suppose not. The day you

185

walked into a police station to declare that you'd killed your children, you wouldn't have looked at posters of other children. Such touching, rather fuzzy black-and-white snaps, row upon row of lost children, enough to break any parent's heart. For children who've been missing a long time, there's also a computer-generated image of how they are likely to look by this time, five or ten years on.

What strikes me whenever I see them is that most of the missing are girls – and that most of these girls disappeared between the ages of nine and eleven.

If I were Aurore's mother, I wouldn't let her out of my sight for a moment.

That's how I've come to think these days.

Today I don't take my favourite path up the hill. It's far too humid to tackle such a steep slope. The sun is beginning to set, the clouds in the west are already a spectacular pink, but the countryside still hangs like half-dead prey in the claws of the vicious heat. Today I take a level path leading out of the town in the opposite direction, between vineyards and a few sunflower fields, towards the river. The sunflowers are starting to dry out, the heavy yellow heads snapped on the high stalks, an undeniable sign that the summer is coming to an end. The green vineyards are studded with bunches of black grapes that will soon be harvested. Another sign of the transitory. Nothing can last for ever, I say to myself.

Nothing, not even my heartache.

I brush away the damp hair clinging to my temples – suspect there is heavy weather on the way, otherwise it wouldn't be so humid so late in the day – and pick a bunch of grapes hanging right next to the path. Just for a little moisture in my mouth. Hold the first grape for a moment like a marble on my tongue, before I bite into it. The fruit has been baked lukewarm by the sun, the flesh sweet and juicy, but the skin stays

186

tough and bitter in my mouth. I know this is a region of wine grapes, not table grapes, and yet I'm disappointed whenever I taste them. The tongue, like the heart, doesn't like listening to reason.

So much I'd like to ask you, Myriam. So much to tell you. So little room on a postcard.

Mothers who murder their children, I read on my husband's laptop computer, are usually regarded as insane rather than criminal. They are sent to institutions rather than prisons because of the general perception that children "belong" to a mother. After all it isn't a crime to damage your own property, although you would probably have to be insane to damage the property if it's really valuable.

And then there are the insights into how these murders are committed. Seldom at a distance, with a firearm, like most "ordinary" murders. Nearly always from very close by, with the mother's own hands. The children are smothered, drowned, poisoned. Caressing hands with a fatal touch. Sometimes shaken, hit, thrown. Corporal punishment, one could almost say, that gets out of hand.

And when the murdering mothers get rid of the bodies, it is as if they want to force them back into the womb. The bodies get wrapped in plastic or cloths, hidden underwater, buried with the mother's own hands – usually near the home, sometimes even in the home. While "ordinary" murderers often go to a lot of trouble to take their victims as far as possible from the house before they get rid of them.

All these behaviour patterns apparently confirm that for women like you, Myriam, their unthinkable deeds are identified with their own bodies. With an unimaginable kind of love. Maternal love?

I try to imagine how you did it. What the pillow looked like. How you held it. How long you held it against each one's face.

187

Longer for the older one, less time for the younger? Did they struggle desperately or just go limp? What did your eyes look at while you were doing it? Or were your eyes then already like two empty caverns?

Too much to ask. Too much to tell.

I would have liked to write to you about my wintry heart that still refuses to thaw, while everyone around me is holidaying noisily. I would have liked to ask about your heart, what remains of it, and your dreams, if you still have dreams, and about your daily life. What do you do, I wonder, when the longing for your daughters becomes too great?

Too little space on a postcard.

And yet a postcard was the only option. If you put a message in a bottle and throw it into the sea, you keep it short. You don't write an autobiography, you try to make contact with someone somewhere, even though your common sense cautions you that it is a fatuous undertaking. That is what the lion postcard was, Myriam. An unlikely message in a bottle. A terribly vague hope for contact.

I simply wrote my name and address, said I come from South Africa and was spending a year in France with my husband and my son, added that your story touched me and that I frequently think of you. That's all. Nothing about my daughter. Nothing about your daughters. Some words are too weighty for a postcard.

I don't expect an answer. I would just like you to know about me. As I know about you.

I carry on walking, ever more slowly, my body ever more damp in the unusual humidity, the air so heavy round me that it feels as if I'm labouring through water. Even the twittering of the birds in the trees by the river has become faint, like sounds that reach one underwater. Vineyards drift past me slowly, poplars as slender as seaweed, too slender to offer any

188

shade, the yellow flash of the sunflower field like an exotic coral reef in the distance. The more oppressive the air against my body, the lighter my head feels. I wonder what would happen if I fainted now, how long I'd lie here next to the road before someone discovered me, what the townspeople would say about it in the mornings when they gossip in the bakery.

A lush bramble hedge full of plump berries brings me out of my watery daydream, back to earth and my physical needs. The blackberries suddenly look so irresistible that I jump the hedge like someone who has gone hungry for weeks. As fast as I can pick the juicy black fruit, I stuff them into my mouth. The thorns wound my hands when I strip the branches, but I hardly notice. I cannot remember that blackberries have ever tasted so sublime. Black clouds melting on my tongue. Sweeter than innocence.

To tell the truth, I can't remember when last anything tasted like that to me. Like a hymn, a praise song, an ode. Is it possible that my taste buds have started functioning again at last? Resurrected by a bush of wild berries? Didn't God appear to Moses in a burning bramble bush?

Earnestly contemplating the mystical qualities of brambles, I start back to my husband and son. Only now I notice the bloody streaks on the backs of my hands. My mouth winces in pain, but at the same time wants to smile, because for a change I'm feeling something, even if it is pain.

MEMORIES

7

I haven't brought a photograph album with me, just stuffed a few photos of my daughter into an envelope in my handbag. Have never looked at them since getting here, mainly because I hardly ever use that large black handbag. Handbags are for going out, for dressing up and going out, something I seldom do these days. It was easy to keep the thing zipped up, the whole mess of pens and paper tissues and peppermints and documents that make up the contents of any woman's handbag, to hide it all in darkness and seal it tightly.

Very much like a coffin.

I allowed the envelope to sink to the bottom gradually, hidden under lipsticks, hair clasps and notebooks. Perhaps secretly hoped it would all decompose, like a corpse, if it could be buried for long enough. That one day I would find only a handful of dust at the bottom.

But this morning, while I was supposed to be sweeping the floor in Emile's room, I stood gazing for a long time at the photograph of him and Manon on the pinboard above his bed. The one taken last year in front of the gates of Euro Disney near Paris. The pinboard has for a while now not been as pathetically empty as in those first few weeks, the whole room looks less like a deserted country station, more like a place where a young boy is living. There is also a photo of him and Nathalie and another child on a school outing, one of his grandmother with Caramel in her arms, postcards that friends and family have sent from Cape Town. Quite a few posters on

193

the wall as well, basketball players, surfers, Eminem and other pop stars whose names I don't know.

But it's the photo of him and Manon that intrigued me. I looked at it as I would look at a photo of someone else's children, surprised at how they've grown, how much the boy is beginning to look like his father, how much the little blonde girl reminds one of both her dark-haired parents. The father's mouth and the mother's eyes.

The boy looks as though he wants to hide behind his sister, his glance guarded and his smile a little distrustful, clearly not at ease in front of a camera. The little girl poses like a princess, a silly cap with large Mickey Mouse ears like a crown on her head, royal self-confidence in her whole demeanour. She's wearing a red summer frock with an ice cream stain on the chest, arms and legs bronzed from three weeks of holiday sun, coloured sandals on the little feet.

I'd like to get in touch with their parents, that's what I felt in front of that pinboard. To let them know how the brother's timidity and the sister's charm beguile me. Tell them they can be proud of two such obviously intelligent, healthy, attractive children.

I would like to have such children myself.

I don't know how long I stared at the photo, with my hands and my chin resting on the broomstick, but when I eventually turned away, it was as if I'd come out of a kind of trance. I dropped the broom then and there and went looking for my big black handbag. The search became progressively more frenetic, till I found it under the double bed in the main bedroom.

The bed is still covered in plastic to protect it from the dust and rubble while my husband installs a small bathroom in the corner of the room. The balcony has been done, the bathroom nearly done, after which the cracks in the ceiling will be filled in, the peeling walls painted, the wooden floor sanded and

194

varnished. Less than a month's work, my husband thinks, then we'll be back in our bedroom again.

I hold onto my heart. How will I ever lie at ease in that bed again? Surrounded by my husband's limbs. Besieged by his breath in my ear. Like a fort invaded by the enemy, that's how my body will feel.

I dug out the black handbag – under the plastic, under the bed, right at the back in the darkest corner. *In the dark, dark, house there was a dark, dark room.* Do you remember Manon? *In the dark, dark room there was a dark, dark box.* Right at the bottom in the darkest part of the dark handbag, my fingers found the creased envelope. In the envelope I found the photos. Not decomposed. Perfectly preserved like the bodies of those early explorers in Antarctica.

I took the photos to the kitchen table and studied them one by one while I drank a cup of coffee.

In the first one a woman with a huge belly is sitting on a settee, her arms spread like wings round her husband and her son on either side of her. The little boy is about seven years old, with a wide gap-toothed grin and dark shining eyes, his head leaning against his mother's balloon of a stomach, as if he's listening to a joke being told by his unborn sister. The man's head is slightly turned away from the camera, his glance admiringly focused on his wife, conspicuously proud of her and her large tummy and whatever is going on inside it.

In the following photos a newborn baby suckles, a plump infant smiles in her father's arms, a little girl with coppery curls blows out three candles on a cake while her ten-year-old brother looks away shyly from the camera.

What I find fascinating when I compare the photos, is the continuous metamorphosis that children undergo in their early years. In the first photo the little girl is a chrysalis, safely spun into a cocoon, an invisible promise of future joy. In the second she has just emerged from the cocoon, her wings still folded, her feelers not yet reaching for the world. Then in front of your eyes she changes into a lovely butterfly, while her brother starts spinning himself into pre-adolescent privacy.

In the last photo the whole family is together again, all four on an armchair in front of a decorated Christmas tree. The woman sits in the middle of the chair with the four-year-old girl on her lap, the husband and the eleven-year-old boy balanced on either side on the armrests. The sister is laughing exuberantly at the silly face that the brother is making for the camera; the father is grinning anxiously because he's sliding off the armrest; the mother is trying to retain her dignity among the clowns around her, without much success.

That's how my husband finds me, submerged in these memories, the photographs spread open next to my coffee cup. He says nothing, just pulls up a chair and picks up the photos carefully, something like wonderment on his face.

"Where do these come from?"

"The bottom of my handbag."

"I also brought a few photos," he confesses. "Keep them in my wallet."

"How often do you look at them?" I ask.

"In the beginning I had to force myself. Now it's easier. I suppose one builds up a certain resistance to pain."

His hands are pale with dust. Crumbs of white paint are stuck in his hair like tiny snowflakes. He's actually only come to get a glass of water, but it's clear that for the time being he's forgotten about the building work on the top floor. I listen to Habib banging away with a hammer on wood, with a repetitive and irritating tac-tac-tac, while my husband takes his time over the photographs.

"But to come upon other photos so unexpectedly . . ." He rubs his cheek as if to wipe away invisible tears. A line of white dust remains around the stubble on his chin. "It's hard, seeing us so happy. So without any . . . premonition of mortality."

"I suppose that's what's meant by the innocence of paradise."

"Hmm." He stares at the last photo with a deep frown between his eyebrows. "And once you've lost that innocence, you can't ever get it back, can you? From now on, we'll always know that there's disaster waiting in the wings."

I'm suddenly so moved that I can say nothing.

André throws down the photos and grabs my hand, his voice pleading. "But that makes life just that much more precious, don't you think, Hes?"

I wish I could nod agreement.

But it would be a lie. Life no longer feels precious to me. It is something that I must get through, without my child, that's all.

∽∽

On the first day of the academic year Nathalie is not at school. When he calls her cellphone that evening to find out if she's sick, a canned voice tells him that the client on that number is not available. When, at his wits' end, he phones her home to speak to her mother or father, there's no reply.

On the second day she's absent again. By break he decides there's only one thing to do: he'll have to ask her hard-baked girl friends if they know what's happened to her. It takes all his courage to break through the giggling cordon of adolescent female hormones. Lola, the most stuck-up of the lot, looks at him as if he were a half-dead mouse dragged in by a cat and deposited in front of her feet. He can't understand how she manages it. She's easily a head shorter than he, but she creates the impression that she's looking down at him.

197

"Don't yóu know?" asks Lola.

"Don't I know what?" he squeaks, like a mouse.

"We thought she might have let you know. As you're such thick friends."

"Let me know what?"

"Come on Lola, You're pinching sweets from a baby," says the blonde one, Bianca, chewing gum with a bored expression. "Stop tormenting him."

"Wonder what Nats sees in him?" giggles the third member of the girl-gang, an anorexic little Asian girl with a silver ring in her right eyebrow.

Wonder what she sees in all of you, he thinks, but manages to keep his mouth shut. Just glares defiantly at them and wishes he could stop the blush that's spreading from his neck to his hairline like a red ink stain.

"No, we don't know what's up with her either," says the gum-chewing Bianca. He turns to her in such dismay that she adds, a fraction less aggressively than before: "Don't stop breathing, bro'. Something probably happened to keep them in Spain. If it was serious, someone would have let the school know."

"But what could have happened?"

"How the fuck should I know?" says Bianca impatiently. "Maybe they missed their flight. Maybe the Spanish airport crews are on strike. Your guess is as good as mine."

"They didn't fly. They drove."

"See? You obviously know more than we do," says Bianca and waves her hand in the air to drive him away like an insect bothering her.

As he walks away fast, he hears the anorexic Lee giggle behind his back. "Maybe she picked up a Spanish boyfriend who persuaded her to spend the rest of her life in Spain?"

On the third day Nathalie shows up at last.

He notices her immediately on the school grounds, her long neck rising above her girl friends, but they form such a laughing, shrill wall around her that he can't get close to her. In the classroom she greets him – nothing friendlier than she greets all the others – and explains to all and sundry that her father had a gastric upset and was too sick to drive back. "Probably ate too much paella, says my mother. Luckily he's all right now," she adds and smiles her beaming white smile.

What had he actually been afraid of? Emile wonders. Why does he suddenly feel quite shaky with relief? It's as if these days he's standing on a mat that's going to be pulled from under him at any moment. As if he's waiting all the time for that tug that will throw him off balance. He doesn't know when it will come, just knows that it must come, some time or other, as sure as death. He wonders if this is what is called pessimism. Or is it just how it feels to be growing up?

After that there's no chance to speak to her again until break. But break comes and goes without any overture from her side. She sits on a bench gossiping with Bianca and company, doesn't even look up when he strolls past them a few times, almost close enough to step on their toes.

Over the midday meal he keeps the chair next to him free, hopefully, mumbling a curt apology when Winston, the British fatty, tries to claim it. Feels a bit of remorse when Winston turns and slouches off with sloping shoulders, but not quite enough to call him back. All through lunch, the empty place mocks him. He doesn't hear the chattering of the other pupils or the clatter of cutlery, just stares glumly at the golden crumbs round the piece of frozen fish in his plate.

Friday is fish day in French schools, Nathalie has explained to him, because the Roman Catholics are supposed to have a meatless day on Fridays. Even in international schools like this one, pupils get a tasteless piece of defrosted fish every

199

Friday. He tries looking over his shoulder surreptitiously, to catch her eye without any of her friends noticing, but her full attention is with Lola and her gossip.

"He's so not right for her!" cries Lola indignantly. "And she won't admit it. She tells everyone he's actually cool. I mean really!"

He had even imagined that she would miss him when he had to return to Cape Town in a few months' time. He'd thought that they would keep contact, talk on the internet, send SMSs, the kind of thing you do when someone you're fond of is far away. Now it looks as if she's already forgotten about his existence. All it took was a month in Spain.

He leaves the tasteless fish in his plate and flees from the noisy dining room. Outside in the playground he gasps for breath, as if his lungs are not working well, as if he's breathing water instead of air. Just like the times he ran from Trudi the Therapist's rooms. Though with Trudi, at least, he had an excuse. He was "traumatised", as she put it, he couldn't control his emotions. Now, surely, he should be able to?

What's happening to him now, he tries to convince himself, is surely nothing in comparison with the day his little sister was shot dead in front of his eyes. Nathalie's unexpected cold shoulder can't in any way be compared to Manon's lifeless body on the floor of the shop. The shocking bloodstain on her chest, the melting pink ice cream on the floor next to her, the slightly surprised expression round her mouth. No. He still can't risk remembering. Nathalie is something quite different, he says to himself, as he angrily brushes over his eyes to stop even the slightest hint of tears. Nathalie is nothing.

Well, then, why does he feel as if he's suddenly become nothing as well? As if he's been wiped off the face of the earth, just because she doesn't want to look at him. He throws his head back, opens his mouth wide to force as much air as possible deep into his lungs, to make sure he still is alive.

Behind the clay-tile roof of the stately old school building, heavy steel-grey clouds are looming. Chances are that he'll get home sopping wet today. That would suit his mood, he decides, a dangerous thunderstorm with wild lightning and ferocious gusts of wind and sluicing rain.

$\sim\sim$

André stands on his new roof balcony and looks out over the gleaming landscape under low bruise-blue clouds. He stands there like a nobleman of old in his castle tower, proud of what he has wrought, afraid that he might lose it all in an instant. As if at any moment he might be attacked by an invisible enemy. He doesn't know where the enemy is hiding, he doesn't even know whát the enemy is, he only knows some calamity is imminent.

Perhaps it's just the threatening thunderstorm that makes him feel so ill at ease.

Everywhere in the vineyards below him are the bent backs of workers moving in groups, harvesting the heavy bunches. There's an urgency in their movements that's apparent even from a distance, a scrambling and hurrying to get as many baskets full of grapes onto the waiting tractor trailers before the rain sets in. He assumes that they are paid by the basket, rather than by the hour, to prevent shirking. They are mostly seasonal workers from poorer countries in Europe and from North Africa, who come every year to help with the harvest. At night they meander tiredly through the streets of the town, talk to one another in foreign languages and splash their sweaty faces in the fountain on the square – to the consternation of the baker, the café owner and the other respected burghers of the town.

André keeps to himself when the locals gossip, partly because his French isn't good enough to gossip along, partly because he really doesn't care what the workers get up to with the water in the fountain. For centuries it has been guarded by the four stone monsters on the square. It will hardly get infected overnight by a few dusty Spanish gypsies or Eastern European contract workers.

According to Habib it's the same every year. The low grumbling about the barbarian invaders, the strange foods that they eat, the unintelligible languages they speak.

"And what about the foreign tourists who come every summer?" André wanted to know. "After all they also eat strange food and speak foreign languages?"

Habib raised his eyebrows meaningfully and André looked away shaking his head. He knows from experience, after all, that tourists are received with open arms, that tourists don't have to wash their faces in the fountain because they stay in convenient houses with hot water, or in neat caravan parks with modern ablution facilities, so-called civilised places, in any case.

"Everyone knows the town needs tourists," Habib grumbled, "and so also the vineyards and the wine that lure them here, and so also the workers who pick the grapes the wine is made from. But no one wants to know where the workers sleep or wash or shit or piss. Just as long as it's not on the square."

Habib grinned as usual, but an unaccustomed bitterness in his voice prevented André from pursuing the subject. He finds that he treats his helper more cautiously since Hester told him about the bruise on Aïsha's cheek. The ugly purple mark disappeared long ago, but it has left a sort of scar on Hester's conscience. Probably on his as well, André has to admit. And yet, Habib behaves no differently from before. The same cheer-

202

ful, whistling façade. André would rather not know what lies behind the façade. He needs a helper to finish the work on the house before winter arrives. That's all that matters to him.

He had hoped that the summer months would allow enough time to paint the woodwork on the outside of the house, but in the end it was more important to spend extra time with his son. After the fisticuffs on the square, Emile looked even more lost than before, as if he had given up the thought of ever making friends in the village. Worse yet, as if he'd become afraid of leaving the house. Almost the way his mother had been in the beginning.

His primary job, André is beginning to think these days, is to keep his family together. To try to break through his wife and his son's self-imposed isolation. Otherwise this whole drawn-out restoration project of his will in any case have no sense any more.

In the meantime, the shabby peeling pale-blue paint on the shutters has become part of the charm of the old stone house for him. He doesn't want the place to look too tidy and spotless, just respectable enough to be rented out to tourists at a reasonable price. To pay for his family's next holiday in France.

That is, if he still has a family by the next holiday.

He turns back to the glass door of the bedroom and looks absent-mindedly at the little bathroom that he and the whistling handyman have installed. The Gaudi-like mosaic pattern that he himself laid on the floor of the shower cubicle, the washbasin that looks like a stylish serving bowl of blue glass, the taps like slender silver sculptures, the lovely Art Nouveau frame round the mirror. Hester had asked whether they could have just óne room that wasn't quite so rustic. So he created this little private art gallery for her. She said she liked it – but in the same tone of voice as "Please pass the salt".

In the bedroom, he ducks under the steel scaffold that he uses to paint the ceiling. As Habib isn't working today, the portable radio on the stand is for a change tuned to a classical music station. Tomorrow he'll have to put up with Habib's banal pop music again, only groaning now and again when the lyrics sound particularly ludicrous. And Habib, who in any case doesn't understand the mostly American words, will grin conspiratorially.

André has realised that his worker, like many young people of Arab origin, harbours complex, mixed feelings about America. They hate the patriotic, arrogant America of Bush and his troops in Iraq, but they are mad about the pop music, the movies, the electronic gadgets, the street fashion and the logos that emanate from that powerful country. They still believe in the glory of capitalism and the possibility of overnight fame and overwhelming wealth.

And it wasn't all that different for his own generation, André remembers. In the seventies, when he was an idealistic teenager wanting to change the world, he hated the patriotic, arrogant America of Nixon and his soldiers in Vietnam, while being mad about the music and the fashion and the high modern buildings and the whole popular capitalist culture. Or that is what he tries to remember whenever he thinks of the bruise on Aïsha's cheek. Habib isn't dangerous, he says to himself, he's just a mixed-up, searching young man. The way I also was.

One of Fauré's piano compositions is playing on the radio, a blessed, soft nocturne that, in spite of the threatening thunderclouds out there, makes him feel more at peace. He stares pensively at the double bed still shrouded in protective plastic. It stands like a museum object, an archaeological find from a bygone era.

Relic of a marriage, circa 2004, A.D.

Hester still doesn't want to sleep with him.

Earlier that week there had been a spark of hope, but it was almost instantly extinguished. That evening after they had looked at the photographs from her handbag, she was friendlier than usual and asked him if he felt like accompanying her on her nightly ramble through the sleeping village. He'd agreed eagerly and his heart had throbbed almost like an adolescent's when she allowed him to put his arm round her shoulders without her whole body stiffening. She even smiled at one of his weak jokes. After the walk he followed her to the spare room like a dejected dog, and she handed him her dream journal.

"You can read it if you want to," she said with a casual shrug. "Maybe you'll understand it better than I do."

"Can I read it here?" he asked hopefully.

"No, take it to bed with you. It's boring enough to put you to sleep."

"I haven't actually got a bed," he reminded her. "I thought I could perhaps . . . sleep in a bed for a change."

"Do you want us to switch? For me to have a turn in the living room?"

"No, Hester, I want us to sleep in the same bed for a change."

"Not on this little single bed," she said, startled. "It'll be far too uncomfortable."

"We have shared a single bed before."

"I know, but not . . . not now. I'm not ready yet, André. Please."

He pretended not to hear the pleading in her voice.

"Our bedroom will soon be done. Will you be 'ready' then?"

She looked at him for a long time, her eyes greyer and older than usual, before she answered.

"I don't know," she admitted with a sigh.

He wonders if she'll ever be ready again.

Till now, he had assumed that Hester's sorrow, her physical and emotional withdrawal from everyone round her, would be a temporary condition. The death of her daughter was a chasm that had to be bridged, carefully, step by step. He'd resolved to walk next to her, to hold her hand, encourage her – no matter how long it took to get across. A few months, he had first thought. Longer, he realised here in France, a good deal longer. Possibly even a few years. But, at some time or other, they would reach the other side together.

Now he wonders, as he looks at the double bed under plastic, if they are still on the same bridge. For all he knows, Hester's bridge leads to another destination.

Again he feels that familiar strangled sensation in his throat, but he can't evade the idea any longer. He has to ask himself, in all seriousness, whether their relationship is strong enough to survive the death of their child.

Beyond the balcony wall, the whole world has taken on an almost supernatural dark blue sheen, as when you slide a filter in front of a camera lens to get a particular effect. Even Fauré's lovely nocturne can no longer soothe him, he realises as he mounts the scaffold to carry on painting. The storm should break soon.

I was so absorbed in my ridiculous idea of following the child – ducking from wall to wall, imagine, like a detective in an old-fashioned movie! – that I truly did not notice the heavily overcast sky. Neither the flashes of lightning in the distance, nor the dull rumble of thunder. When a bolt of lightning suddenly cracked like a whip over the square, I jumped with fright, and before I knew what was happening, I felt the first plump drops splashing on my bare arms.

From behind the obelisk of the war monument, where I'm sheltering – not against the untimely rain, but so that my innocent prey won't notice me – I see her approaching from the direction of the little school. Within seconds, the square is awash with water, the sluice-gates of heaven completely opened. She has an umbrella with her, I notice with relief. (How could her mother have known this morning that it would rain? Why didn't I also give my son an umbrella to take to school?) And yet the rain is falling with such force that she runs for the shelter of the café veranda, then shuffles along cautiously right up against the wall. I retire soaking wet to the municipal building and try to shelter under a bit of an over-hang. She won't see me now, I comfort myself, her full attention is on battling the elements. If it weren't for the bright red of her umbrella, I wouldn't be able to see her either.

When the umbrella disappears round the corner, I consider for a moment dropping my pathetic plan and going to shelter in my own home. And yet it feels as if it's already too late. I can hardly get any wetter than I am. So I take a deep breath and follow the red umbrella.

I have asked Aurore where she lives, more than once, but every time she just points vaguely in the direction of the nar-row streets behind the café. And as I know, it's no good try-ing to elicit an address in a village like this. Most streets don't have official names written up on neat boards. Most people live "next to the school" or "behind the church" or "opposite the castle tower". If you want to send somebody a letter, you simply write *Le Village, Lunel*, on the envelope.

This is the frustration that has brought me this afternoon to the square, to hide like a clumsy private eye behind the war monument, waiting for school to come out. If any of the townspeople have noticed my extraordinary movements, it would only have confirmed the rumour that I'm slightly off my rocker. The foreign woman who walks the dark streets at night and never talks to anyone but herself and her cat.

Well, I have news for the suspicious townspeople. I have decided to go and talk to Aurore's adoptive mother. Not necessarily today, but some time or other.

First find out where she lives.

I try to follow the moving umbrella at a discreet distance. The pelting rain shields me by dampening my footfall on the cobbles, but it also protects my prey. She could instantly drop from sight behind this curtain of rain.

I suppose I could simply have asked the child if I could walk home with her. That would have been the polite thing to do. But what if she refused? Said, sorry, my mother wouldn't like it? No, I decided, too much at stake to be polite.

When she stops in front of a light-green door, her body half-turned in my direction, I drop my head low on my chest and shrink against the stone wall next to me. Like a foolish toddler who thinks you won't see him if he shuts his eyes tight. Luckily the umbrella obscures her view and, suspecting nothing, she slips inside. The last I see, by the light of another streak of lightning, is the tomato red of the umbrella disappearing behind the pistachio-green door.

I'm left alone in the street. Only now do I become aware of my T-shirt and jeans that are drenched and clinging to my body, my hair hanging in sodden strings over my eyes, my teeth audibly chattering. Mission accomplished. Now I know where she lives. Now I can turn round satisfied and walk home.

But I don't turn round. I walk as if in a dream to the light-green door and begin to hammer on it. Too wet and cold now to care what the child's adoptive mother might think of me.

It's an attractive woman with short, dyed blonde hair who opens the door, somewhere in her forties, dressed like me in T-shirt and jeans. Except that her clothes are of course dry. In her right hand she holds a home-rolled cigarette.

"Bonjour," I say when her mouth drops in surprise. "Sorry to trouble you, but the storm caught me unawares. May I please wait a while here with you? Just till the worst is over?"

She nods, amazed speechless that anyone could be this wet, and steps back for me to come in. Over her shoulder I see the child sitting at a kitchen table.

"Hester!" Aurore exclaims. I can't decide whether it's guilt or pleasure I hear in her voice.

"Do you know each other?" asks the blonde woman.

Aurore comes closer warily, her expression now clearly guilty, a bit of chocolate spread on her upper lip.

"Not really," I say quickly. "We have talked once or twice on the square."

"Are you the woman from Africa?"

I nod and look at the puddle of water forming on the clay tiles round my feet. The woman from Africa. I've never introduced myself like that to anyone.

"Aurore told me about you." She frowns, perplexed, looks at the child, then at me. "I thought you would be . . . darker."

"Sorry to disappoint you." I grimace at my silly remark and put out my hand. "My name is Hester. I live up near the castle tower. Temporarily. In a few months I have to go back. To Africa."

"Beatrice," she introduces herself.

"As in Dante?"

"Pardon?"

"Dante. The writer. His beloved was Beatrice."

"Oh, Dante!" She wonders if she hasn't let a mad woman into her house. I see it in the alarmed way her eyebrows lift and her smile freezes. "No, that's not why my mother called me Beatrice. She wasn't exactly a reader. I like reading, but I must admit Dante is above me," she goes on with a nervous whinnying laugh. "I prefer a good thriller. Or travel books."

"Dante's *Inferno* could be thought of as a kind of journey." I say crossing my arms over my shivering chest. "A journey through hell."

Her eyebrows go up again. Another high braying laugh.

"But look at you shivering!" she exclaims. "We must do something straight away to get you dry. Aurore, go fetch some towels from the bathroom quickly. Bring the big green ones on the middle shelf. Take off your shoes," she instructs me, "and put them over there on the heater. Come along to the kitchen."

Clearly a practical woman, I see now, someone who isn't easily unsettled. Even the unexpected appearance of a drenched foreigner wanting to talk about Dante has only disconcerted her momentarily.

"Can I lend you a hairdryer?" she offers, pulling out a chair for me next to the kitchen table.

"No, it's not necessary, thank you."

"Are you sure? I have lots of dryers in the house. I'm a hairdresser, see, I work from home. People come here or I go and cut hair at their houses. Remind me to give you my card." I wonder if it's that obvious that my hair needs professional care. But before I can say anything, she goes on. Every now and again she interrupts her words with a nervous laugh. "What about your clothes? Can't I lend you something dry to put on?"

"No, please not, I don't want to be any trouble . . . just wanted . . . want to wait for a while, please, " I stammer, suddenly on the brink of tears, touched by so much thoughtfulness.

I don't know what I expected. Surely not that she would chase me out into the rain. But definitely not that she would offer me her own clothes.

"Well, then, what about a cup of coffee? It's no trouble, it's been made," she adds and points to the coffee machine next to the microwave oven.

I nod and watch Aurore come running down the stairs with a pile of towels in her arms. Now I understand where her intricate hairstyles come from, the dozens of short pigtails with their coloured balls, the maze of little cornrow plaits, the geometric pink paths on her head. Clearly her hairdresser mother's work. Today is a cornrow day.

I take the top towel, dark green and soft as moss, and start rubbing my hair energetically. Aurore sits on the chair opposite me, her black eyes fixed on me, chewing the chocolate bread that was left forgotten on the table when I turned up so unexpectedly. I smile at her from under the towel, and feel my heart kick against my chest when she returns my smile, pleased.

"She reminds me of my daughter." The words slip from my mouth, unplanned, as I take the coffee from Beatrice.

"How old is your daughter?"

I take a deep breath, as if to plunge into cold water.

"She would have been six. She died earlier this year. In an accident in Cape Town. South Africa. Where we live."

All in the same breath, without coming up for air. My body becomes weightless. My voice – and all other sounds – comes drifting to me from incredibly far away. The clink of a teaspoon against the china cup, the scraping of wood over a tile floor when Beatrice pulls out the chair between Aurore and me, the constant swishing of rain against the kitchen window.

"Sorry to hear that." Beatrice sits down slowly, takes a plastic pouch of tobacco out of her jeans pocket and starts to roll a cigarette. "Do you have other children?"

"A boy of thirteen."

"I know what it feels like to long for a child." She keeps her eyes on her fingers that are pecking like birds at the tobacco;

211

drop, fly up and peck again. "For many years I hankered after a child. Before Aurore finally came."

I know I'll cry if I try to say another word, so I only nod and rub the moss-green towel with renewed vigour over my wet hair.

"Of course it's not the same," she says apologetically and lights the rolled cigarette. "I mean, to long for a child you've lost and to long for a child you've never had. But yearning is yearning."

I dry my hair as if I've become deaf and mute.

"Aurore, sweetheart, go and play in your room for a while. Hester and I want to chat."

"I want to hear what you talk about, "says Aurore without moving.

"Aurore . . ."

"I didn't know your child was dead," Aurore says to me, looking almost accusing.

"I will tell you about her one day," I promise.

"When?"

"Well, don't you and your mother want to come for coffee one afternoon after school?" I look at her mother, ashamed of the sudden note of pleading in my voice.

"Just say when," says Beatrice with a flash of pity in her eyes.

"Next week? Monday or Tuesday?" Too eager, I think. Much too eager. But I can't stop myself. "I'll bake us a cake."

"What kind of cake?" Aurore wants to know.

"Aurore, go to your room now," says Beatrice.

"Any kind of cake," I say. "Whatever you like."

"I'm crazy about chocolate cake," the child says as she walks away unwillingly. At the bottom of the stairs she turns. "What was your daughter's name?"

"Aurore," sighs her mother.

212

"Manon," I answer.

"It's a pretty name," says Aurore, satisfied, and goes off to her room without further demur.

"Her name was Manon," I repeat, more to myself than to Beatrice, who is looking at me with concern.

The moment the child leaves the room, her mother blows out a puff of smoke with a sigh and says: "I'm sorry that I didn't want her to go to you on her own . . ."

"No, I understand," I interrupt quickly. "A mother can never be too careful."

"I'm not sure. Maybe she can." She licks her upper lip to get rid of a speck of tobacco. "I'm inclined to be over-careful."

"When you consider how long you waited for her . . ."

"It's not only that. I'm typical Cancer, you know. Every time I hear a joke about a Jewish mama, I think she's probably also Cancer. And Aurore . . . she had so much trauma so early on in her life. Now it's as if I want to hang over her like an . . . an avenging angel to protect her for the rest of her life from any further harm."

She lifts her arms wide and high to suggest the wings of the vengeful angel, gives another whinnying laugh and stubs her cigarette.

"An avenging angel," I muse over my coffee cup. "I know what you mean."

Half an hour later, when it hasn't rained for a while, I walk home across the square, careful to avoid the shiny pools of water. Somewhere in the distance the thunder still rumbles, but on the horizon in the west, the low sun has already broken through the purplish-pink clouds again. From the vineyards around the village, the smell of the wet soil, more intoxicating than the most precious perfume, floats towards me on a breeze.

213

Then I see my son walking a little way ahead of me. He is pushing his bicycle up the steep cobbled street, his shoulders hanging, his whole demeanour dejected. Even at this distance, I can see that his pullover is drenched. It hangs on his bony body with the heaviness of a garment on a washing line, stretched down almost to his knees. My stomach knots with impotent love. Why didn't I, like Aurore's mother, see to it that my child took an umbrella to school this morning? Surely a mother who has lost a child, such a dreadful, careless thing to do, ought to take better care of the remaining child?

"Emile!" I call and run up to him with a feeling of guilt rolling round like a stone in my chest. "Didn't Dad think to fetch you from the bus stop?"

He looks askance at me: Didn't Mom think of it? Under the baseball cap, pulled on back to front as usual, his wet hair hangs over his eyes.

"I don't know." He pulls up his shoulders and pushes on. "I caught an earlier bus."

Of course. Only now it dawns on me that he isn't meant to be home yet.

"I didn't know there was an earlier bus," I mumble, walking beside him. A derisive snort from him is the only answer. "But how did you . . . did school close earlier?"

"I had the last two periods free."

He's lying. I don't know how I know it, but I know immediately that it isn't true.

"Has something happened? Are you upset about something?"

"No, Mom," he says impatiently, "nothing has happened."

"Are you okay? Emile, look at me when I speak to you."

The minute he turns his head to me, I regret my words. His dark eyes look right through me, accusatory, angry, defeated.

"Are yóu okay, Mom?" he asks sarcastically. "Is anyone in our house okay?"

"Probably not," I concede. "But some days we are, well, less okay than other days."

"Then it's probably that kind of day for me."

"Worse than usual?"

"I don't feel like talking about it."

"With me today things are a little better than usual." I wait for him to ask, but he says nothing, just pushes his bike along as if he doesn't care at all how things are with me or anyone else. "I met someone in the village."

"Good for you."

When did my child become so sarcastic?

"Seems to be a nice woman." I swallow hard before I come out with the next words. "I told her about Manon."

"A complete stranger?" He is so surprised that he forgets to be surly.

"I don't quite understand myself how it happened. I got drenched, just like you, and I knocked on the nearest door to look for shelter." Not quite true. He glares at me suspiciously. Now we're quits, my son. You lie to me and I lie to you. "And then we started talking."

"So that's why you're looking like this," he mumbles.

"I dried my hair with a towel," I explain. "Haven't looked in a mirror since. And the woman lent me this jersey. Almost as big as yours, isn't it?"

"No, I mean your face looks different." We've reached the dusty-blue garden gate. As he pushes the bike through the gate, he says over his shoulder, his tone still accusing: "I can't remember when last you went about smiling like that."

My fingers fly to my mouth. My lips are indeed distorted into something that could be called a smile.

⌒⌒

For a change I am the one who brings an edible offering to my husband. I walk into the kitchen where he is cooking in a silly floral apron, and plonk a china bowl full of fresh mushrooms down on the table.

"Present from Beatrice," I announce. "She and Aurore went mushroom-gathering yesterday in the forest."

"What forest?" He takes a plump brown mushroom out of the bowl and sniffs it appreciatively.

"They say just behind the hill."

"Now why don't I find a single edible mushroom in any forest, ever?"

"You probably don't look in the right places," I answer in the same light tone, hanging my damp raincoat on the coat rack next to the front door. "Or at the right times. They say early mornings are best. Especially if it's rained all night."

"So if this drizzle keeps up, we'll have a good chance tomorrow?"

"We?"

"How about it, Hes?" he cajoles. "Don't you feel like going mushrooming with me tomorrow morning at first light?"

"But we already have mushrooms!"

"They taste better if you've picked them yourself."

"Says who?" We're standing on either side of the round table, two opponents in a light-hearted skirmish. Amazing that we manage this, that in spite of everything we can still pretend there's nothing wrong. "If someone like Beatrice picked them, then at least we know they're edible. I'm not so sure you or I would recognise the poisonous ones."

"We'll take the field guide with us, look at the pictures!"

"Rather take Beatrice with you. She's a better guide than any book."

"I thought she was a hairdresser. What does she know about mushrooms?"

216

"A whole lot more than you or I. She grew up on a farm nearby. She knows that forest like the back of her hand."

He turns back to the saucepans on the stove and stirs the stew with a wooden spoon.

"And her husband?" he asks with his back to me.

"What about her husband?"

"You talk about Beatrice and Aurore all the time, but . . . ."

"All the time? That's a new reproach. You usually complain that I don't talk enough."

"It's not a reproach, Hester." His voice rises impatiently. "I just wondered if you'd met her husband yet."

"No, they were divorced soon after they adopted Aurore."

André looks up from the stove, frowning. After all the poor child had been through, his glance says. Couldn't the parents just have stayed together? That was my thought too, when I heard it. And yet, when I look at our own bewildered son, I sometimes wonder if we're not causing more damage by staying together.

"Does he live nearby?"

"No, somewhere in the north. He's remarried in the meantime. To a much younger woman by whom he has two children of his own. It must be difficult for Beatrice . . ."

"I can imagine. A white mother raising the only black child in town on her own."

"That wasn't what I meant." Now I'm the one to sound impatient. "I mean that she and her husband tried for about fifteen years to have a child, and then he left her, and zap, zap he had two children by another woman. And now that he has his 'own' children, he apparently doesn't bother about his adopted child."

"That's Beatrice's side of the story," says André in his rational manner, as he calmly stirs his stew. "Every divorce has two sides."

And if we were to divorce, I want to ask my reasonable husband, if things were driven to that point? I wonder involuntarily how our swan song would sound: My husband wouldn't allow me to grieve over our dead child. My wife wouldn't allow me to touch her. He didn't want to. She didn't want to. He wanted. She wanted. Etcetera, the eternal duet of all failed relationships, right down to the predictable refrain: It became impossible to live with him. It became impossible to live with her. At top volume. Clashing cymbals, sobbing violins, trills on the piano. It became impossible.

I leave my well-intentioned gift on the table and leave the kitchen with my tongue firmly clenched between my teeth.

⌒⌒

When he looks up from the *cassoulet* on the stove, his wife has vanished. Only the bowl of mushrooms remains like an accusation on the table. What has he done now, he wonders with the sort of resignation that takes hold of him these days when things between him and Hester go wrong.

And they seem to be going wrong all the time.

A few moments of superficial communication interspersed with long deep silences. The problem is that he just doesn't understand his wife's behaviour any more. This sudden intense friendship with a country hairdresser, for instance. Is it because she really likes the woman? Or is it above all because she wants to share the woman's daughter with her?

Or perhaps even wants to inveigle her away.

"What do you talk about?" he wanted to know last week in all innocence when she had been visiting Beatrice for more than an hour. "Do you have any common interests? Books, movies, politics?" Another faux pas, he realised too late. Her eyes immediately became defensive. So he pressed on, what else could he do, to a more bantering tone. "Or do you talk about hairstyles?"

"We talk about our daughters."

"Nothing else?"

"Other things also." She shrugged and avoided his eyes. "Dreams and angels and star signs and. . . "

"Star signs!" he exclaimed mockingly.

"Beatrice believes in such things. But most of the time we talk about Manon and Aurore."

He looked at her uncomprehendingly. They were on either side of the round table, as they were this afternoon. The kitchen is clearly the only neutral territory in this undeclared war, a kind of no man's land where enemy camps can at least communicate in a way. The upper floor has become André's headquarters, against his wishes, without his being able to do anything about it. The middle floor is Hester's, especially the spare room, which she absolutely refuses to call anything but "Manon's room". The living room on the ground floor is where their son withdraws himself from the battle, where he can stare sightlessly at the TV screen, the sound turned up unnecessarily high. The kitchen is where everyone feels more or less equally safe. Or equally unsafe.

"I thought it was what you wanted, André," Hester accused him that day, her voice unusually aggressive. "That I should talk to someone about Manon."

What could he say? That he more particularly wanted her to talk to him about their daughter? That she had drifted even further away from him since she befriended Beatrice?

Now that's a new reproach, she would say.

"I just wonder what you'll do when we're back in Cape Town. Will you limit your friendships to women whose daughters remind you of Manon?"

She drew her breath in sharply and quickly left the room.

219

That's what she does these days when they're skating on thin ice. Simply skates away and leaves him to fall into the hole on his own.

He replaces the lids on both saucepans, the one with beans and pork, the other with tomatoes and lamb, and turns the plates down so that the stew can simmer slowly. *Cassoulet* is a complicated affair, too many ingredients and too much cooking equipment. Two separate saucepans, his French cookbook instructs. More suitable for a feast than for a crumbling little family's silent evening meal. He can't think what possessed him to tackle this today. Something to do with the steady drizzle, the knowledge that the summer really is over, that the mild autumn days will soon turn to melancholy winter's evenings. Maybe he only wanted to welcome the winter properly.

He puts a cassette in the portable cassette player next to the fridge. When the first notes of Alban Berg's violin concerto sound in the empty kitchen, he considers for a moment lying on the floor, but the tile floor looks just too bare and cold. And also too dirty. Aïsha didn't turn up last week to help with the housework.

André removes the floral apron, pulls out a chair and sits next to the round table, drops his head in his hands to concentrate better on the music. *In memory of an angel.* Berg composed this violin concerto for the deceased daughter of the famous architect Walter Gropius and Alma Mahler, the widow of the composer Gustav.

André has always been fascinated by the relationship between music and architecture; between the aesthetics of the ear and the eye, as he thinks of it; between fleeting, transitory sounds and solid, immovable creations. That is probably one of the reasons why this concerto has always moved him deeply. Long before he himself had a deceased daughter.

220

He read somewhere that Walter and Alma's daughter was also called Manon.

It would be easy to confirm this snippet of information, but he chooses not to. It would make the concerto too personal. He'd no longer be able to lose himself in the sounds of the violin.

⌒⌒

It's the worst month of his life, decides Emile while he stands waiting dejected at the school gate, petrified that she won't see him. Even more afraid that she'll see him and pretend not to. Which would only be his just deserts.

The worst month, he decides, of the worst year of his life. And it's all entirely his own fault.

It's true that she looked past him on that first day – but it really wasn't necessary for him to make such a drama out of it. She was probably just excited at being back and keen to share her holiday adventures with her girl friends, to giggle and scream and gossip, the way girls do, with Bianca's crowd. If he'd given her the chance, she might even have walked home with him that same day. But he felt so sorry for himself that he bunked the last two periods, slunk away from school and hitch-hiked home. For the first time in his life, he thumbed a lift from a complete stranger.

It was so ridiculously easy that he wondered why he hadn't done it long ago. Instead of sitting with a lot of potato ladies in a stuffy bus. He'd barely stuck out his thumb, when the first car stopped. A fairly battered old Peugeot. Driver with grey ponytail, bushy beard and dirty fingernails. The second lift was better, in a metallic grey Mercedes with leather seats and air-conditioning, except that the driver's wife complained all the way that he was driving too fast. Only three lifts and he was back with his bike where he chains it to a lamppost on the square each morning before taking the bus.

Maybe just beginner's luck – or perhaps the people had been sorry for him as they could see there was a storm on the way – because when he tried it again the following week he had to wait far longer before someone stopped. In the end, he arrived home about an hour later than usual, afraid that his father wouldn't buy into his lie about a puncture in the bicycle tyre. But then his father hadn't even realised that he was late. And his mother, well, she doesn't notice anything anymore, does she?

The crowd round the school gate is starting to thin now and still there is no sign of Nathalie. Bianca and Lola and her other girl friends passed a while back in a giggling bunch, as usual almost walking into him without noticing him. He's starting to think that it really wasn't a good idea to hang around the gate in a sulk. Like a dog waiting for its master, that's how he will look to her.

If she ever shows up.

But some time or other she has to walk past here, unless she plans to sleep in a classroom tonight. Maybe she's watching him from behind a tree or somewhere, to see how long he's prepared to wait for her before he gives up. Something else she can snigger about with Bianca and the girls.

It doesn't feel fair. After all, he's had his punishment, that day when he hitch-hiked for the first time. The first hour everything felt like a fantastic dream, but the last stretch that he had to cycle turned into a nightmare very quickly. He'd thought he would reach Lunel before the storm broke, but he'd scarcely pedalled a quarter of the way when the clouds right above his head were struck by the most unbelievable bolt of lightning he had ever seen. The next moment it was as if buckets of water were being emptied over him. In a

222

panic he looked for shelter, but there was only a tree here and there next to the road, and he'd always heard that a tree was the last place one should shelter in a thunderstorm. So he carried on pedalling as hard as he could, as wet as a fish and blinded by the water streaming over his eyes, a bloody blind fish on a bicycle. A frightened blind fish on a bicycle. He expected to be felled by a bolt of lightning at any moment, or to be hit by a car. He couldn't see the white line in the middle of the road, couldn't even see the road surface itself under the wheels of his bike, everything was torrential and fluid.

And when to his amazement he did after all arrive home alive, he was even more the hell in with Nathalie. As if it was her fault that he'd so nearly died. The whole weekend he was in a foul mood. That Monday at school he refused to talk to her – even when she tried to talk to him. Just to show her.

Now he can't remember all that well what it was he'd wanted to show her.

And soon the whole thing was completely out of hand. She stopped greeting him and told all and sundry about this fantastic guy she'd met in Spain. Within a few days the whole school knew about her holiday romance – and that of course made Emile look like the loser who'd been dumped for the Spanish boyfriend. After that he was too proud, or just too idiotic, to try to make peace. But today he's decided enough is enough. He will talk to her, even if she laughs in his face. And now it seems he won't even have the opportunity to be laughed at. If he waits here any longer, he'll miss the bus.

The school grounds behind him are deserted, the large stone building quiet and empty, only a few staff cars still parked under the plane trees. The trees have started shedding their enormous brown leaves. Some stick to the cars like gigantic gloves, others dance slowly over the ground and flutter past the flower beds to settle at his feet. He bends absent-mindedly to pick up a leaf and starts walking towards the bus terminus.

A block further on, she is sitting unconcernedly on a low wall next to a canal, chewing on some chocolate. His heart almost leaps out of his mouth when he realises that she has been eyeing him for a while from far away. He pulls his cap lower down on his forehead, lets the rucksack dangle more casually across his shoulder and drags his trainers more deliberately over the pavement.

"Hi," she greets him as he walks towards her ever more slowly. "Want a bite?"

"Why?" he asks suspiciously.

"Why not?" She rolls her eyes and shakes her head. "I promise you it's not poisoned. Let's call it a peace offering."

When he goes to take the chocolate from her, he realises that he's still holding the large brown plane-tree leaf and presses it clumsily into her hand. "I think I also owe you a peace offering. I don't have anything else."

"A leaf."

He notices the beginning of a smile at the corners of her mouth as she studies the strange present. That gives him enough courage to start talking quickly.

"I'm sorry, really. I behaved like a baboon. I was waiting for you at the school gate to apologise."

"I know," she says, as the corners of her mouth lift a little further. "I mean I saw you waiting, but you didn't see me because your head was hanging somewhere round your knees."

"How did you know I was waiting for you?"

"Who else would you be waiting for?" He is so glad to see that wide smile trained on him like a spotlight again that he doesn't even mind that she's teasing him. "I thought it would be better not to argue there among all the schoolchildren about who actually owes who an apology. So I came to wait for you."

"How did you know I'd come this way?"

"But I know you. You always come this way."

"Except when I'm with you. Then we go a different way each time."

"See? You need someone like me to make your life more interesting."

"It looks like it," he grins. "I want to be friends with you again. I don't care about your Spanish boyfriend."

Now it's her turn to look suspicious.

"What do you know about my Spanish boyfriend?"

"The whole school knows about your Spanish boyfriend."

"Me and my big mouth."

For the first time she looks a little embarrassed while she plays with the leaf in her hands. He sits down next to her on the low wall.

"I don't mind, Nathalie, really not. It doesn't bother me if you have ten Spanish boyfriends, as long as we can be pals again."

Suddenly he also doesn't care if he misses the bus. By now he knows of more adventurous ways of getting back home.

"I don't have ten Spanish boyfriends. To tell you the truth, I don't even have one."

"Did you lie?" he asks, breathless with amazement, relief, confusion.

"No. Exaggerated a little maybe. Want more chocolate? It was just a holiday romance. You know. When the holiday is over, the romance is usually over too."

He nods as though he knows exactly what she's talking about, as if he's had dozens of holiday romances, and breaks off another row of chocolate squares.

225

"Aren't you going to see him again?" he asks, letting the chocolate melt slowly on his tongue.

"Maybe next summer. But by then he'll probably have another girl. And hopefully I'll have another guy."

He looks around like someone waking from a nightmare, indescribably relieved to feel the hard stone wall under his buttocks, hear the lapping of water behind his back, to see the few pedestrians in the quiet street. The clouds that have been hanging over the roofs all day have unexpectedly disappeared. The sky is open and blue above them, even though the sun is dipping and their shadows stretch long and thin in front of them. He will most certainly miss his bus, but he's not the least worried about it.

"But aren't you going to write or phone each other?"

"I sent him an e-mail the other day. Then I realised I had nothing really to say to him. We never really talked. You know. Not like you and I."

"Well, but, what did you do then?" He tries to tease, but his voice betrays him by skidding out of control on the last two words.

"Oh, you know, what one does when you have a holiday romance." Her long neck is bent, her eyes on the plane-tree leaf in her lap. Then she looks at him from under her eyelashes, with an unexpectedly provocative expression. "Do you want me to show you?"

He almost falls backwards into the canal. Just manages to steady himself, clears his throat desperately to get his voice deeper, and asks: "Now?"

"Well, it depends . . . " she smiles. "Remember what you said to me right in the beginning in your own language? And you promised to tell me what it means when you know me better?"

"I don't know you well enough yet," he wards her off immediately.

226

"Well, then we'll just have to wait, won't we?"

"But we are . . . I mean, we are pals again, aren't we?"

"Of course, you baboon."

He grins gratefully. Funny, he thinks, being called a baboon has never sounded like a compliment before.

8

Dear Myriam, I write on a postcard depicting three elephants, *my daughter died recently.*

It's the first time that I've written the phrase, officially and indelibly, black pen on white paper. It's taken me exactly nine months to manage it. Like a pregnancy, I realise when I notice the date above the message. Nine months to bring her into life and nine months to admit to her death in writing.

When, I wonder looking at this sentence, does 'recently' stop being recent?

After a year? In that case I'm almost at the deadline. But it isn't true that time heals all wounds. Some wounds eat at your insides until you're nothing but an empty shell. My husband is always nagging at me to come out of my shell. I don't know how to warn him that some days it feels as if there's nothing left in the shell, nothing that can crawl out, nothing that can reach out to other people. There are times when I think of myself as an egg that's been sucked dry through a minuscule hole; if you look at me, I look like any other egg, but if you touch me, you'll feel the difference right away. I've become weightless. Light and empty.

I miss her every day and every night, I write on the elephant postcard, one of a pile that we brought from Africa. Especially every night. *The sorrow and tears when the candle is snuffed. Oh the red patchwork blanket.* No, I don't write that.

It gets harder each time to choose a suitable picture for my message. Mountains and beaches won't do it for you, I've decided. Or perhaps I'm afraid of what it will do to you. To look at a photo of a wide open landscape while you're incarcerated in a cell where you can only see a little square of light. (Or maybe you can't even see a square of light, how would I know, what do I know of French prisons?) Therefore I stick to my animal theme. Feels safer that way. The first time it was a lion, last month a rhinoceros, this time three elephants, two big ones and a cute baby. Soon my pile of animal postcards will be used up.

What then?

Do I send you pictures of Provençal animals? Is there such a thing as a typical Provençal animal? All I can think of is a cicada. Weeks since I last heard one. Summer is definitely over.

No, when I don't have any more animal pictures left, I'll probably be forced to write you a real letter.

How presumptuous I sound.

Perhaps you don't even read my words. Perhaps you can't read. Perhaps you don't want to read. Maybe you'll tear the three elephants neatly in half and throw them into the wastepaper basket without even looking to see who it's from. (Would there be a wastepaper basket in your cell?) Or you think, oh please, not that pathetic woman again who tries to comfort me with pictures of wild animals! It's quite possible that you don't even like wild animals. After all, it's mostly Europeans and Americans and Japanese who romanticise the dangerous animals of Africa. The Big Five. For people who live among the Big Five, they're probably not romantic, just lethally dangerous.

For you who have lost two daughters, the deprivation must be twice as great as it is for me, I write. *And yet, in a perverse way I envy you because you are going to be locked up for many years – far from your country and your former life and every-*

thing that reminds you of your children. I have to return to my country in a few months' time. I feel like a wounded soldier being sent back to the front.

I have to return to the scene of the crime, literally and figuratively. The city, the street, the corner shop where my daughter was shot. I'd like to say I'm not ready, the wound isn't yet healed. The problem is that for ages now it hasn't felt like a wound, rather like the lack of a wound. An amputated leg that continues to throb with pain. An eternal absence.

Maybe I should do what soldiers do and simply go AWOL. That's what I write to you, just to see what the words look like on paper. Maybe I should AWOL.

As usual I don't know how to end off. *Your friend?* No, that sounds like a women's magazine. *Your admirer?* But then I'm not a teen writing to a pop star! *Your supporter?* Even worse. Sounds like vintage underwear.

No, rather just: *Regards, Hester Human.*

I'm going to pop the elephants into the yellow postbox on the square immediately, before I get cold feet, before I decide to tear up the message. I mean, before I deprive you of the chance to tear it up.

⁓

He has become accustomed to seeing his wife with her head low over the kitchen table, but this time he encounters two women with bowed heads. He stops on the bottom step, a little put out, and wipes his paint-spattered hand across his stubble while taking in the unfamiliar scene, uncertain whether this is progress or deterioration. Surely it's a good thing if Hester wants to share her pain with someone. But he really doesn't know if he can handle another grieving woman in his house.

Only then does he realise that it isn't Hester who's crying.

Hester is in the surprising role of comforter, her arm sympathetically draped around the younger woman's shaking shoulders, her fingers stroking the long black hair. André fights the almost irresistible urge to flee before he is seen, back to his son's room where he can carry on peacefully painting the walls, away from this female kitchen drama which heaven forbid he should get involved in.

But it's too late. Hester looks up, her face burning with indignation, and says: "André, you'll have to talk to Habib. It can't go on like this!"

Aïsha shakes her head and wipes her tearful face.

"What can't go on like this?" asks André.

"He's terrorising her! He pushed her around again last week and threw away some of her clothes and locked her in her room. That's why she couldn't come here."

"Habib?" asks André to gain time.

"Who else?" Hester replies impatiently.

"Family affairs, Hester. We don't have the right to interfere."

"You're his employer. And I'm her employer. That makes it a labour issue."

"What do you want me to say to him?"

"Tell him if he doesn't stop terrorising his co-worker, you'll fire him!"

"It's not that simple, Hester. I need him to . . ." The contempt on his wife's face takes his breath away.

Aïsha, who's meanwhile walked over to the sink to get a glass of water, studies them with swollen eyes. When she speaks her voice is calmer than either of theirs.

"Please, don't let Habib lose his job," she says. "It will make everything even worse."

"How can it get worse, Aïsha?" Hester cries hotly.

Something like disbelief flashes across Aïsha's troubled

231

face. Then she looks down so that her hair falls forward and hides any further emotion.

"If he no longer works here, he'll forbid me to come too. And we need the money at home."

Hester takes a breath as if to argue, but then just shakes her head at the young girl. There you have it now, André wants to say to his wife, but he decides rather to keep quiet as well. He realises only too well that Hester is on higher moral ground than he.

"Does anyone want tea?" he asks, walking to the stove to boil water.

"Please," whispers Aïsha.

"What would we do without tea?" asks Hester.

He doesn't know if she's being sarcastic. His wife has become a mystery to him, as she was in the first heady weeks of their relationship almost two decades ago. The difference is that then he looked with excitement and wonder for a key to the enigma. Now all he feels is utter exhaustion.

Back in the safety of his son's room, he turns up the volume on the radio to drown out the women's voices from the kitchen. If only it were so easy to silence his conscience. He tries to identify the trilling notes in the piano piece on the classical station. Beethoven, he suspects, but which Beethoven? *Bagatelles?*

He uses a screwdriver to lever off the lid of a tin of white paint and stirs the contents with a stick. Like thick creamy milk it looks, like the farm milk that as a child he used to drink in his grandfather's milking shed, the cow's body heat still in it. His children never knew that farm. It had been sold long before they were born. But a part of the money from the farm found its way here to France via his father's will, paying for this neglected house. He pours the creamy paint into a flat container, sits back on his haunches and stares motionlessly in front of him, listening with half an ear to the piano music.

Perhaps he should have used the money to buy a sports car instead.

Habib helped him yesterday to fill the holes in the walls of Emile's room with cement; tomorrow the patches will hopefully be dry enough to take the first coat of paint. Meanwhile he has tackled the woodwork on his own, the window frame, the doorjamb and the skirtings that all still need painting. On days like today it feels as though the work will never end. As if he'll be trapped for the rest of his life in a nightmare of paint smells and wood shavings and soul-destroying physical labour.

Habib still works only three days a week, partly because André can't afford him every day, partly because Hester doesn't want him in the house every day. Hester can't even bring herself to greet her husband's helper politely when he arrives in the mornings. But if Habib has noticed her growing antagonism, he doesn't show it. In André's presence he is his cheerful whistling self. Which, André has to admit, is probably not his real self at all.

We need the money, Aïsha said. Habib needs him just as much as he needs Habib, André tells himself, tackling the doorframe with a paintbrush. *Work for the night approacheth.* The season has turned already. He feels the autumnal bite in the air when he goes to buy fresh bread in the early morning.

Besides, Emile is anxious to have his room back. The child is grumpier than ever since he's had to sleep on the studio couch in the living room. And yet he refuses adamantly to use the spare room. Like his mother, he seems to regard it as "Manon's room". With this difference: Hester would willingly spend the rest of her life in that room, while Emile will hardly set foot in it.

233

When the work in the main bedroom was completed, Hester had to leave the spare room to share a bed once again with her lawful spouse. André suspects she did it only for Emile's sake, so that the child wouldn't realise how uncertain the future of his parents' marriage had become. As if Emile hasn't known for a long time, thinks André, painting the frame furiously, as if this uncertainty wasn't contributing to his aggressive behaviour, his moody silences, his sarcastic outbursts.

It can't go on like this.

The question is just what they can do about it. About their relationship, about their son's misery, about their employees' family discord, about this house beginning to hang like an albatross round their necks.

He tries to concentrate on Beethoven's piano composition, tries to paint with slow even strokes, but after another fifteen minutes he gives up, throws the brush down on some plastic, wipes his hands on a turpentine cloth and digs his wallet out of the pocket of his work clothes. When Hester bought the wallet years ago in Italy, the brown leather was as soft as a baby's blanket. Now it is only nostalgia that stops him from replacing it. He snaps it open and takes a photo out of one of the compartments.

His daughter in their garden in Cape Town. Running towards him, laughing, a naked baby doll in her hands, the old oak tree green in the background. He took the photo a few days before her death. Had it developed only afterwards. During the past weeks he has been studying it regularly, almost obsessively, as if he could find a shadow of impending death somewhere in the photo, if only he searched patiently enough. Perhaps behind the garden wall. In the branches of the oak tree. In the bare plastic body of the baby doll.

It seems utterly impossible that he could not somehow

sense the proximity of death that day. This is what he thinks every time he looks at the photograph. Just outside the front door, around the corner, in the nearest shop.

⁐⁐

The moment Emile gets into the bus with Nathalie, he decides it was a mistake. The eyes of his fellow passengers immediately flicker with curiosity. A few of the old ladies greet him like a long-lost grandson. *Ah, Emile! Comment vas-tu?* One of them turns right round in her seat to stare openly at him and Nathalie as they sit down in the back of the bus.

The inquisitiveness doesn't appear to bother Nathalie. Maybe she's used to people turning to stare at her. Because she's so pretty, because she's so tall, because she's so black, whatever.

"I'm crazy about buses," she says delightedly.

"I hate buses," he grumbles.

He's happier than ever that they can talk English to each other, otherwise everyone in the bus would've eavesdropped. Diagonally across the aisle one of the grinning greyhaired ladies desperately tries to catch his eye. He deliberately looks right through her while the bus slowly shudders its way out of the undercover terminus.

"Well, I suppose I wouldn't like such a long bus ride every day either," Nathalie concedes. "But I'm glad I can ride with you today."

"Me too," he says and, damn it, starts blushing again.

Life just isn't fair. It's the first time in all these months that he's seated next to someone he wants to talk to – and now it feels as if he's going to blush every time he opens his mouth.

He risks a quick look at her, but her face is turned to the window. She stares at the medieval city wall as if she's never seen anything so old and imposing, reminding him of the American tourists always meandering through town half in a swoon. Well, of course, she is sort of American; certainly speaks like one. And it's probably the first time she's seen the wall from a bus. Maybe that's enough to make one feel like a tourist.

Actually in a way he envies her. For him, the wall has long ago become just another wall, just as the wide Rhône with its strange flat barges has become just another river, and the famed Pont d'Avignon just another derelict bridge in the middle of just another river, and the world-famous vineyards of Châteauneuf-du-Pape just more bloody vineyards.

And yet, once they leave the industrial area behind, those ugly grey factories and identical hypermarkets that make his father groan as if from a stomach ache, he has to admit almost reluctantly that the vineyards look their best at this time of year. All these golden autumn colours bathed in the late afternoon light. He feels his heart welling up in the confines of his chest, almost too much to bear, as if something is going to erupt somewhere. Or maybe everything just feels so swollen up because he's sitting too close to Nathalie. Definitely a mistake to invite her.

By Monday the whole school will think they have a thing going. Only the two of them will know that there's nothing on the go – unless you can call a very good friendship "a thing". And that's just as well, he says to himself over and over, that's all he can handle at this stage.

Peet, the Dutch nerd with whom he finally made friends last month – while Nathalie wasn't talking to him – said if one were to ask him, Nathalie was looking for more than just friendship. But then how would a nerd like Peet know what girls want? He thinks because he has three sisters, he automatically knows three times more than someone like Emile who doesn't have a sister at all.

236

Emile hasn't told him about Manon. Nathalie is still the only person with whom he can talk about Manon. Maybe that's why he's so afraid of putting a foot wrong. What if he tried something hopelessly stupid, like kissing her or grabbing her or whatever one is supposed to do with thirteen-year-old girls, and she got so pissed-off that she didn't want to be friends with him any more? On the other hand, what if she really wanted him to kiss her and he was too green to realise it? Then she'd probably also end up pissed-off.

"What's wrong?" asks Nathalie.

Her face suddenly feels too close to him. Nowhere to hide from those black eyes.

"Nothing. Why?"

"Looks as if something's bothering you."

"No, it's nothing, it's only . . . Nothing."

"Are you sorry you invited me?"

"No!" His voice is far too high. "Of course not," he tries again. Now his voice sounds unnaturally deep, as if he's trying to copy the villain in an old-fashioned movie.

"But a little nervous?"

"About what?"

"I don't know," she giggles. "I'm feeling rather nervous."

He gulps down his spit.

"Well, no," he lies, "after all, there's no reason to feel nervous."

"I suppose not," she says and turns to the window again.

Yellow and orange and brown vineyards flash past the bus. Then I'll just have to wait, won't I? That wás what she said, wasn't it?

⌒⌒

237

"Do you think it's okay to leave them down there on their own?" asks André with an awkward little cough before getting into bed.

"What else can we do?" Hester is in bed already, paging through a magazine. "Sit on the stairs and eavesdrop?"

"I sound like a neurotic, suspicious father. I know."

"You are a neurotic, suspicious father," says Hester with a shadow of a smile.

André lowers himself heavily onto the bed, but doesn't actually crawl in under the duvet. Under normal circumstances Hester would be the neurotic parent. A year ago the very idea of such a scenario would have had her hyperventilating. Their almost fourteen-year-old son alone with a pretty girl in a dark living room, supposedly watching a DVD, while the parents on another floor (completely out of earshot) prepare for bed. But Hester has become so uninvolved in her son's life that she now manages to page through a magazine calmly.

"Emile says she's not his 'girlfriend'," he tries to convince himself. "They're just good friends. So it's not as if he's going to jump her the moment we leave them alone, is it?"

"Maybe she'll jump him," Hester remarks dryly.

"How lucky can a boy get?" asks André in the same dry tone, even though he instantly feels a constriction in his throat.

They are after all responsible for Nathalie while she's under their roof. He wonders what Laurent and Naomi would do under similar circumstances. He sees Laurent's massive bear body and feels those huge hands tightening round his throat.

"Get into bed, André," commands Hester. "The children haven't given us any reason to distrust them."

"They've also not given us any reason to trust them," he replies gruffly, but nevertheless gets into bed obediently.

He picks up a detective novel from the bedside table and searches perfunctorily for the place where he stopped reading last night. They're almost thirteen and almost fourteen years old, he carries on his imaginary argument with his wife, they're two ticking time bombs full of hormones. When he was fourteen, wanking was sometimes the only thing that made life worth living. Perhaps it's different for kids today. There's so little sexual mystery left for them. You see everything in movies and on TV, as Emile has pointed out. It's even possible that they'd rather play with electronic gadgets than with their private parts.

But hormones are hormones. And down there in the dark living room his son's hormones could at this very moment be losing the battle with his common sense.

"Maybe you could go and get a glass of water in the kitchen," says Hester unexpectedly, without looking up from her magazine. "Then you could check on the living room in passing. If it would make you feel any better," she adds with the same awkward clearing of the throat with which he'd opened this conversation.

"Hmm," he says as if totally absorbed in his book. "When I've finished this page."

So she isn't that uninvolved, he thinks with an emotion he last felt so long ago that he's no longer sure what to call it. Perhaps, indeed, something like hope.

☙☙

It's possible that he'll regret this for the rest of his life, Emile realises as he and Nathalie eat a late breakfast in the courtyard. Enjoy the sunshine, his father said, it's probably the last weekend we'll still be able to eat outside. Not regret that he invited her, of course not, just sorry that he let an opportunity slip through his fingers.

He lay agonising about it till deep into the night. Struggled for hours to go to sleep in his "new" room with the sky-blue walls and the new blue-and-green cover and curtains. Selected by his father and mother, of course. They know he likes blue and green. The truth is that he doesn't give a damn what this room looks like. In four months he'll be going home to his proper room and his proper bed. Meanwhile, on the other side of the wall, you could almost say right behind his back, Nathalie spent last night in Manon's bed. Or perhaps she was also lying awake for a long time, tossing and turning and worrying about things she doesn't understand.

Not that it looks as if she had a sleepless night. With a dark skin like that, shadows under the eyes and other signs of a bad night can easily be hidden. He tries to study her surreptitiously and sees a croissant crumb on her broad upper lip. He wonders if he'll ever have the courage to touch her lips, even just with his fingertips, even for something so silly as to brush a crumb from them.

"So what are we doing this morning?" she demands.

"What do you feel like doing?"

"I'm too lazy to feel like anything," she yawns and stretches her arms high above her head. Now she looks like a tree, he thinks. A long, slender poplar. "You decide."

No one has ever warned him that it's so difficult to be friends with a girl. If this had been, say, his mate Zakes sitting opposite him, he'd be able to ask him straight out what he really wanted: Do you want me to kiss you or what?

Well, of course thát wouldn't be what he'd ask Zakes.

"What's so funny?" she asks through another mouthful of croissant.

"Nothing. I'm just in a good mood." He points to his own top lip. "There's a crumb on your lip. Other side."

She licks it off, quickly, her tongue shockingly pink. Slightly disappointed, he stares at the place where the crumb

240

had been. He wonders if he'll ever again have such a good excuse to touch her face.

◠◠

I push open the iron gate to take a short cut through the cemetery, as I sometimes do when I'm feeling more melancholic than usual, and catch my breath. A yellow-and-white carpet has been unrolled here overnight. Almost every grave is abundantly bedecked with chrysanthemums. Only here and there a bare pile of earth, a particularly worn old stone cross on which the chiselled letters have become illegible. The uncared-for graves of the nameless, loveless dead.

Now I suddenly understand why the *épicerie* looked like a nursery last week. The dozens of flower pots set out on the pavement in front of the shop made me feel so unexpectedly light-hearted that I bought a tub of the brightest yellow chrysanths for our kitchen table. I thought that was the idea. To brighten up the environment with a last flash of flowering colour before the grey of winter descended on us. Only now do I realise that the flowers were meant for the dead.

I forgot that it was the first of November tomorrow, a public holiday in France, a day for honouring the dead and the spirits and the saints. I forgot that chrysanthemums are regarded as cemetery flowers here, rather like arum lilies where I come from. To be honest, I hadn't realised that death was still taken so seriously here in the heart of the super-modern continent of Europe.

For the first time in my life I wish that I also had a grave to decorate.

My daughter's ashes were scattered over the sea near Cape Point. I didn't want a grave to care for. I would never have been able to leave the country if her remains had stayed behind buried in the ground.

241

Blinded by sudden tears I stumble over the marble edge of a gravestone and graze my knee. I touch the warm blood on my knee in surprise, taste the salty tears on my lips and wonder, for the hundred thousandth time, how it is possible to continue living without my daughter. To bleed viscous red blood, shed streams of tears, to sweat and to dream and sometimes, just sometimes, even to laugh. It is such an unnatural condition, I think as I crouch weeping by the grave of the unknown family Foussier. And yet, here I sit, blood and sweat and tears and everything. Alive.

From the corner of my eye I see a family bringing flowers to one of the other graves. Husband, wife and a skipping dark-haired girl. A little further on, an elderly man stands with bent head in front of a gravestone of shiny new black marble. I didn't expect to see all these people here. Usually it's completely deserted, just me and the silence of the dead, when I use this as a short cut. When the family walks past me, the woman shoots me a sympathetic glance and quickly looks away to spare me embarrassment. Evidently wondering who the weeping stranger at the Foussier family grave is. A prodigal daughter, a cousin by marriage, a friend from afar?

An intruder, I think, someone with no right to sit here grieving amongst the chrysanthemums.

I don't belong here, not in this graveyard, probably not even in this country. I don't know the traditions of this place and I don't understand the customs of its people. I get up hastily, drop my dress over my bleeding knee, wipe my tears and walk away like a dignified prodigal daughter.

Back to the chrysanths on my kitchen table. Maybe I should take that tub to one of the nameless, neglected graves. In that way compensate for my foreignness and my ignorance.

Halfway down the hill, next to the vineyards still glowing

242

in autumn shades, I meet Beatrice and Aurore. They're also carrying a pot of chrysanthemums each.

"For the grave of my parents," says Beatrice after we've greeted with the usual kiss on the cheek.

She notices that my eyes are red with crying and looks at me with concern. I turn away and smile at Aurore. The child looks like an angel in a loose white dress; a black angel with a head full of little silver balls instead of a halo.

"You're all dressed up. Are you going to a party?"

"No," she says solemnly. "I'm going to the cemetery."

"We do this every year," explains Beatrice. "She insists on dressing up when we come to put flowers on the grave. I let her be, as long as I can wear what I like."

Beatrice is wearing faded jeans and a loose jumper, as usual.

"There's blood on your dress," Aurore indicates with her eyes since she's using both hands to hold the heavy flower pot.

"I fell. My knee is bleeding a little."

She regards me, eyes shiny black over the white chrysanthemums.

"Is that why you were crying?"

"Yes," I answer, relieved to have an excuse for my tearful condition.

"You go on ahead, my sweet," Beatrice suggests. "I'll catch up." Aurore hesitates, her curiosity truly stimulated now. "Go on, you know you like talking to your grandmother and grandfather on your own."

It takes me a moment to realise that Beatrice is referring to her daughter's dead grandparents. Aurore gives me a last searching look, almost reproving, before she carries on unwillingly. I know her well enough by now to realise that as soon as we're alone again, without her mother's discreet discipline,

243

she'll bombard me with questions: Do you always cry when you fall? What is the worst you've ever been hurt? How many times have you been in hospital? Do you have any scars on your body? It's true that she sometimes displays a macabre interest in wounds and pain – quite understandable, given her personal history – but by this time I also know that she's un-quenchably curious about anything and everything. And I don't mind at all. I thought Manon was the most inquisitive child I knew. I sometimes grew tired of her never-ending ques-tions. Now, of course, I sorely miss those questions.

"You didn't cry because you fell, did you?" says Beatrice, following her daughter with her eyes.

"No, I fell because I was crying. Didn't watch where I was going."

"In the graveyard?"

"A coincidence. I'd forgotten about *Toussaint*. When I saw all the flowers, I just broke down."

"A graveyard is a good place to cry," she says and lightly brushes my cheek.

The touch is so unexpected that I almost stagger back. I'm no longer used to people touching me. While my daughter lived, my body was like a field tilled daily by my loved ones. My daughter's sticky fingers tracing the lines round my eyes and the grey threads in my hair. My husband's loving hands framing my face. My son, even my son who has now become so untouchable, brushing my fringe away to plant a kiss on my forehead. Now the land lies fallow.

"I had my daughter cremated because I didn't want to be tied to a grave."

It sounds as if I'm apologising. I'm not sure for what or to whom.

"Sometimes one needs a place to grieve." She looks at her child's white dress getting smaller in the distance. "Her family were all thrown into a mass grave in Rwanda. I think that's why she makes such a fuss of our annual *Toussaint* visit to my parents' grave. She didn't even know them, you know. They died long before she was born. But it's terribly important to her that we bring flowers every year. The whole ritual, the solemn dressing up, coming here on foot, all of it. She tells them what has happened in the past year, she leaves little drawings and letters for them on the grave . . ."

All of a sudden I wonder what happened to Myriam's children. They must be buried somewhere in this country. Just another nameless grave that won't be adorned with chrysanthemums today, not visited today or tomorrow or any other day, by anyone.

No one will ever leave them drawings.

The idea distresses me so much that I greet Beatrice brusquely and walk away swiftly, the autumn landscape making no further impression on me. Snatches of a sad song drift through my head, something that Jacques Brel used to sing about chrysanthemums and loved ones dying. From chrysanths to chrysanths, from grave to grave, all the time closer to our own deaths. *J'arrive.* That's the chorus, as I recall: I'm coming.

Wait for me. Faster and faster down the hill. I'm coming, I'm coming, I'm coming.

9

Every morning when he goes to buy bread, the bite in the air is a little sharper. This morning there's a wind as well, which has obliged him to go digging in his suitcase in the dusty storeroom for his old leather jacket before he can set off for the bakery. On his way back over the square, the collar of his jacket turned up high against the wind, he notices that most of the large brown plane-tree leaves have by now been blown off. The feeble sun lights the pale dappled tree trunks in an unusual way, like sculptures in a museum, very different from summer when one is inclined to notice only the luxuriant green crowns. The water gushing out of the mouth of one of the stone monsters looks unpleasantly cold, gleaming like shards of ice.

Winter is definitely on its way. A hostile army advancing every day, that's how it feels to him, while he tries to secure his stronghold. His only consolation is that the attack cannot be worse than the one they survived at the end of the previous winter, during those first miserable weeks in the stone house. This time they are more prepared, better armed. Last week they lit a fire in the restored fireplace, even though it wasn't cold enough, just by way of a practice run. To his relief the cleaned-out chimney drew like a dream. No suffocating smoke in the living room, only a blessed warmth spreading through the whole of the ground floor. Now we're ready for winter, he said to Hester.

And yet he can't shake off a premonition of disaster.

At the war monument in front of the *mairie* there are three sheaves of flowers with red-white-and-blue ribbons, still fairly fresh, placed here the other day to commemorate the end of the First World War on November 11. Somewhere nearby a shrivelled old greybeard who was a young soldier in that far-away war is reputed to live – though according to the baker he has been senile for too long to remember anything of it. Soon there will be no one left to remember, not here, nor elsewhere in Europe.

Transience, thinks André, that is still the underlying theme of this year abroad. The coming and going of seasons, buildings, people. Like a melody that emerges, fades, returns again in a piece of music.

The village gets more deserted by the day. After the last flurry of activity of the *Toussaint* school break, the streets have been almost as empty this past week as they were when they first arrived nine months before. There are fewer teenagers on the square too. Jason and his cronies don't hang around the fountain any more. The cicadas stopped long ago, the birds have flown to warmer climates, even the flies have disappeared. It is so still that his footsteps sound unnaturally loud on the cobbles.

The next holidaymakers are only expected in spring. By then he and his family will no longer be here. What will become of his family, where his wife will be, whether he will still have a family by spring, all of that he doesn't dare think about. One day at a time, he reminds himself, it's the only way to survive. To jump from one moment to the next, fearless as a flea, without brooding about the past or agonising about the future.

Unfortunately you can't live only for the moment if you've taken on a restoration project such as his. Every project needs a schedule, a timetable, and that obliges you to plan ahead, to think of tomorrow and the day after and next week and next month. He has followed his schedule so faithfully that little remains to be done in the last three months – exactly as he had planned. By winter his task had to be largely accomplished, so that his overexerted body could rest and his underutilised intellect gradually get back to full function before returning to his architectural firm in Cape Town by spring. By winter, he had resolved, he would read more, spend more time with Emile, walk longer distances with Hester. Get to know his wife better, discover her anew, maybe even court her again. That's what he had resolved.

Before Manon's death.

But even after the tragedy he had hoped that things would improve by winter.

Now he no longer hopes. He only wants to get the finishing touches on the house done and return to where he belongs. In a week or two he'll no longer need Habib's help. The remaining tasks he'll tackle on his own. He suspects that he'll miss his helper's whistling presence, but Hester can't wait to be rid of him. Only last week she complained again that he was still "terrorising" his sister. André had tried as usual to remain reasonable, saying it wasn't worth making an issue of it at this stage. Only two more weeks, Hester, he'd placated her, then you need never see him again.

Hester had nearly exploded with indignation. The point isn't whether she sees Habib or not! The point is that he doesn't have the right to lock his sister up and push her around and to tell her how she should dress!

There's a thin line between reasonableness and indifference, speculates André, walking through his garden. Here too, the summer colours have disappeared, only a few tired late roses and a few faded lavender stalks remain. A sometimes invisible boundary between wise tolerance of the behaviour of others and a foolish refusal to criticise that behaviour. And he has a growing suspicion that he has landed on the wrong side of the line.

As he pushes open the front door, he finds himself facing a scene he's been fearing unconsciously for weeks. Only when he sees them standing on either side of the kitchen table – their bodies as tense as two boxers in a ring, their voices so hot and inflamed that they don't even hear him come in – he realises that this is what he's feared all along. This confrontation between Hester and Habib.

"Doesn't matter whát you believe," hisses Hester. "You don't have the right to impose your beliefs on your sister."

"And you don't have the right to tell me how I should treat my sister."

No trace of the usual easy smile on Habib's face. Nothing calm or bovine in his attitude. His eyes look blacker than usual, his face more severe, his puffy cheeks hidden under black stubble. When did he stop shaving, wonders André bemused. Is it possible to work alongside someone for days without really looking at him?

"But I have the right to report you to the police," warns Hester. "You live in a country where women have certain basic rights, the same as men, and if you don't . . ."

"Who are you to preach to me about the country I live in?" Habib interrupts her. "How long have yóu been living here?"

"Hester," says André and they both swing round to face him. Both expressions equally guilty. "What's going on here?"

"I told you I was going to talk to him if you refused to," Hester answers challengingly.

"Habib, will you please excuse us?" asks André. "You can carry on with the painting in the spare room. I'll be there in a minute."

Habib gives him a strange look, relief mixed with disdain, before marching out of the kitchen.

249

"Hester." André slams the newly bought baguette down on the table, pushes his hands into his jeans pockets. It's at such times he wishes he still smoked. Something to control this unwelcome tremor in his hands. Habib's aggressiveness has shocked him more than he'd like to admit. "You only have to put up with him in the house for two more weeks. Can't we spend the last fortnight in peace?"

"There hasn't been peace between him and me for a long time, André. Only difference is that we've now openly declared war."

"But is it really necessary? If he'll soon not be working here any more?"

"It's necessary exactly because he'll soon not be working here any more. If he doesn't work here any more, if he needn't be afraid he's going to lose the job, he can do as he likes to his sister. That's what I'd like to prevent. I want him to know that I know. That I won't let him get away with it."

"And when we go home in three months? How are you going to protect Aïsha from her brother then? Closed circuit TV? Interpol?"

"I can't believe what I'm hearing!" Hester exclaims. "Are you telling me I don't have the right to help someone in need, because I won't be nearby for the rest of my life to help her? And if I were to see someone drowning? Should I avert my face and walk on? Because I won't be there next time to jump into the water again?"

"Hester, you know that's not what I . . ."

"What's become of you, André? The good Samaritan who'd take off his shirt for a shivering stranger. That's the man I got to know, the man I grew to love, not this . . . this . . . cynical bastard in front of me."

"What's become of you, Hester?" As he says it, he knows he'll regret it, but he can no longer stop himself. "You're also

250

not the woman that I grew to love. You interfere in other people's lives because you can't sort out the mess in your own. Open your eyes, look around you, here in your own house. Save your own child if you're looking for someone to save!"

"I couldn't save my child! My child is dead!"

"One child is dead." André takes a deep breath and wonders what Habib in the spare room must think of this yelling altercation. It's as if, suddenly, after months of unspoken accusations, they've crossed a dangerous boundary. Unexpectedly landed in a minefield of wounding words. He tries to keep his voice even as he goes on, but the words come out unsure, shaky and pleading. "The other one is still alive. Your husband is still alive. Even if it's not the man you grew to love. We can learn again how to love each other."

She looks at him for a long time with tears streaming down her face. Her mouth opens and closes without any sound coming out. It's too late, he thinks. That's what she's trying to say, but can't. Not yet.

At last: "Do you think so?" she asks, before turning to go out of the front door.

He feels bone weary, right to his marrow. He drags his body up the stairs like a heavy suitcase, groaning, to the spare room. Habib is sitting in the corner, his back to the room like a naughty child, painting the skirting. André decides to say nothing more about the argument and starts stirring paint with a stick in another container.

"Women," mumbles Habib. "They're like bitches. If they don't get disciplined properly, they'll one day bite the hand that feeds them."

"*What are you saying?*"

Habib looks round quickly and grins conspiratorially at him. "Just a joke."

"I've had it to here with your jokes, Habib," he says in Afrikaans, suddenly so infuriated that he could shove the paint-covered stick down the young man's throat.

Because of this sexist little shithead, he thinks, angrily churning up the paint, he and his wife have just had an argument during which all kinds of unforgivable and unforgettable accusations were hurled around.

Habib gives a forced laugh and paints on, whistling.

Only a few more days, André says to himself, then he'll never again have to listen to this whistling.

⌒⌒

His arm is getting tired but he keeps his thumb extended hopefully. The first car stopped within five minutes and dropped him on the other side of Orange. Well begun is halfway won, his father likes to say. He's come more than halfway, now it just needs patience. Hitch-hiking is like gambling, says Peet the Hollander, you can't always win, and sometimes you have to lose for a long time before you can win.

Peet has never hitch-hiked and probably never gambled either, but Peet is the sort of guy who's always making smart-arsed remarks about things he knows fuck-all about. A know-it-all rabbit, that's how Emile thinks of his new pal, a sort of Bugs Bunny with long legs and two massive front teeth and eyebrows so blonde that they're almost invisible. But then, Emile says to himself, better to have a rabbit for a mate than to have no mate at all.

Three more cars flash by. The drivers don't even look in his direction. Then two heavy trucks follow, much more slowly, thundering up the incline, and for a moment it looks as if the last one is going to stop. He grabs his rucksack to run up to it, but no, just his imagination. He stares at the truck accus-

252

ingly till it disappears over the rise, and pulls the collar of his anorak up high against the icy wind.

When he tells Nathalie or Peet about his unauthorised hitch-hiking, he makes it sound like an exciting adventure – as if he's an explorer like Marco Polo, or a space traveller like Mark Shuttleworth – just to see the admiration and the envy in their eyes. Concern also from Nathalie, which makes him feel pretty good. But the truth is that hitch-hiking is mostly bloody boring. Maybe that's how exploring and space trips are too. Other people see only the glamour, not the boredom. The frustration and the aloneness. And the fear always lying just underneath the surface. He thinks of it as a crocodile whose jaws can suddenly open wide and wipe you out in one bite. Fear that you might get into the "wrong" car, that something could happen to you, that someone might do something to you.

The next car is upon him before he has put his thumb out, a white Renault without any passengers that flashes past as fast as all the others. But then, amazingly enough, the red brake lights go on and the car pulls off the road about a hundred meters further on. Dangerously sharp, he'd say, perhaps not a good idea to get in with such a reckless driver. The straps of his heavy rucksack hurt as he jogs closer. To hell with being careful.

Only when he reaches the car out of breath, it hits him. It's his father's white Renault Clio. It's his father at the wheel, with a pile of timber that he has just bought on the back seat, his face frighteningly calm as he leans over to open the passenger door for Emile.

"Get in," he orders, his voice a few degrees below freezing. "I can't wait to hear your explanation."

His father doesn't drive on immediately, just sits there, looks at him, his eyes so cold that Emile thinks of a lizard. No, not a lizard. The crocodile that's been waiting under the surface all the time.

"I missed the bus, so I thought I'd try . . ."

"I said I want to hear an explanation, not a lie."

"I missed the bus, Dad," Emile lies on blindly. "I know it's no reason to . . ."

"If you ever miss the bus, then you wait for the next one an hour later. That's what we agreed. Or you phone home so that we can make another plan." The wind plucks at the car. Emile is fighting with all his might against the tears that burn behind his eyelids and wishes his father would rather shout at him. Or drive on, please just drive on so that he'll have to turn that crocodile face away from his paralysed victim. "But that isn't what happened today. Look at your watch. What time is it?"

"Twenty past five."

"The bus leaves between five and ten past. If you only started hitch-hiking after that time, you couldn't possibly have got this far."

"I was excused the last class of the day, Dad. I didn't want . . ."

"You mean you bunked the last class of the day. The last two to be precise. You slunk away from school and started thumbing without waiting for the bus and it clearly isn't the first time this has happened."

"That what has happened?"

Now he is so apprehensive that his voice sounds high and tearful. A silver-grey Peugeot races past them and the driver hoots a long and pissed-off blast at the white Clio illegally parked on the shoulder of the road. No reaction from his father.

"I waited for you at the school gate, Emile. I had to buy the shelves and stuff, and then thought it would perhaps be a good idea to go and surprise you. Then, of course, I was the idiot who got the surprise. I hear you weren't at school for the last two periods."

"Where'd you hear that, Dad?"

"I cornered Nathalie. Of course she tried to cover for you, said you'd complained of a stomach ache or something, but she's not as accomplished a liar as you."

"I did have a stomach ache, Dad!" It's simply a reflex action that still keeps him arguing, a chicken running around with its head chopped off. "I didn't know what to . . ."

"Shut up, Emile." For the first time his father's voice rises sharply. "Now I'm going to talk and you're going to listen – and when I've finished with you, it's not going to be only your stomach that will ache. Comfort yourself that it could have been far worse if someone else had stopped to pick you up. A paedophile or a drunkard or a sadist or just an ordinary criminal wanting some sport with a thirteen-year-old schoolboy. Do you realise what you're doing?"

It probably wouldn't help to tell his father that he'd thumbed his way home a few times and hadn't yet been picked up by any sort of pervert.

"Fasten your seat belt," orders his father as he puts the car into gear and swings back onto the road. "It was a double period of French that you bunked, wasn't it? I went to speak to your French teacher."

Not that too. He wishes he could press a button to make his seat shoot through the roof of the car like James Bond or one of those cool movie dudes, and then one of those cute little parachutes will open over his head to deposit him gently in a vineyard way over there. He'd even be prepared to do it without the parachute. Anything rather than sitting here trapped next to his father, listening to a litany of his sins.

"She was in a hurry, so it wasn't a long conversation, but

255

I didn't need a long one to get the drift. According to her you've absented yourself at least four times in the last two months during the double period on a Friday afternoon. And you definitely can't afford it, she believes. Your marks in French are the lowest in the class."

"She's an absolute dragon! She picks on me all the time because my French isn't good enough! I don't understand anything about French grammar, and the more she rants, the less I understand."

"And according to you, that's an excuse to take French leave," says his father with snide sarcasm. "As if your French is going to improve magically if you don't pollute your brain with any of the rules of grammar."

"I don't care if my French never improves. I don't care a damn for French or France or anything in this bloody country."

Now he's bawling like a baby, but even that he doesn't care about. Just another transgression that his father can add to his long list: Bunks classes. Slinks out of school. Hitch-hikes without permission. Doesn't understand French grammar. Lies to his father when caught out. Cries when frightened. And then his father doesn't know the half of it. Like that he's learned to forge his mother's signature. That more than once he's taken a note to the French teacher, apparently from his mother, to excuse his absence. To one or two of the other teachers also.

"I was so upset and angry that I decided not to go and fetch you from the bus terminus. I didn't want to swear at you in front of a lot of strangers. Thought it would be better to drive home and wait for you there. And then I got another unpleasant surprise when I saw you in the road with your thumb in the air. I feel such a fool, Emile. A naive, unsuspecting bloody fool of a father who is deceived and lied to by his only son.

256

I'm afraid to ask what else you do that your mother and I don't know about."

Now for the fireworks. His father is gesticulating so wildly with one hand that the Clio accidentally swings over to the fast lane, in front of a metallic-coloured sports car. The sports car grazes past them while the driver hoots and swears, his gestures even wilder than André's. Emile is so shocked that his tears dry up immediately. For the rest of the ride, while his father's furious reproaches explode like crackers around his head, he sits rigid with fear, his eyes fixed on the road.

If they were to have an accident now, it would be yet another sin in his never-ending catalogue: Pisses his father off so much that he writes off his car. Causes his father to land in hospital. Or worse.

Another member of the family dying in front of his eyes.

It feels as if it's never going to end. The nightmare ride, his father's volcanic anger, the suspicion that everything that will now happen to him, everything that has ever happened to him, is his own fault. That he's going to be punished for the rest of his life because that day in the corner shop he didn't jump in front of his sister. Because he didn't shield her body from the bullets. Because he didn't die in her place.

☙❧

"We were in an elevator. When we got in, we knew it would fall. We just didn't know how far it would fall. But there was no other way of getting down, no stairs or anything else, so we had no choice. All we could do was to hope that we'd only drop one or two floors. That we'd get hurt, but not die."

I watch Beatrice in a frameless full-length mirror leaning against the wall in front of me. I sit on an upright wooden chair in her untidy living room, a black plastic cape draped over my shoulders with her standing behind me, cutting my hair. Every now and again, our eyes meet in the mirror.

"We huddled close to each other on the floor," I continue. "Probably because we thought two bodies together wouldn't break as easily as one on its own. I don't know. And then we began falling, faster and faster. And then we realised that it would be much further than two floors. That we wouldn't survive the impact. And then I woke up."

The small silver scissors in her right hand flash like lightning round my head. My hair rains down about me, forms a dun brown pool on the tiled floor round my feet. I wonder if all these meteorological metaphors have something to do with the fact that my first impressions of this blonde woman and her modest house were formed during an unforgettable thunderstorm.

"Such falling dreams – falling down a precipice or from a great height – are usually to do with the end of things," says Beatrice and fixes my gaze for a moment in the mirror, before giving her attention again to my hair. "Or with our fear for the end of things."

"What sort of things?"

"Pfft," blowing through her lips. "Anything. The end of a life, as in death, or the end of a relationship or even just a specific time of your life. Any farewell, parting, you know, from a specific place or person or thing."

Soon I have to take leave of her and her adopted daughter, go back to where I apparently belong, to Africa, where fresh miseries are produced non-stop. The next destructive famine, I heard this week on the radio, is threatening the Republic of Niger. Where is the Republic of Niger, I wondered when I heard that. Why does it sound like a swear word? Niger is just north of Nigeria, I see on the map on my son's bedroom wall, and it does indeed sound like a cursed country. About 85% of the population is illiterate and the average birth statistic is something like eight children per woman. Where are you, God? No answer, just the scissors whistling whish whish whish above my head. Another cloud of hair falling to the floor.

"Not too short," I warn, suddenly anxious.

"It can also be something as simple as a farewell to your hair," Beatrice remarks, amused. "We're all afraid of change. Any change. But I promise you this head of hair needs a change. Don't worry. You won't know yourself when I've finished with you."

That's exactly what worries me. I've got used to myself, I want to tell her, with untidy hair and all.

"But I don't think your dream has anything to do with your hair," Beatrice continues and snips recklessly on. "Do you want to know what I think?"

She's clearly going to tell me anyway. Beatrice considers herself an interpreter of dreams, a sort of soothsayer of the subconscious, a medium between the rational and the irrational. She also believes in ghosts and guardian angels and reincarnation and all sorts of inexplicable phenomena that I've never really been able to get into. The better I get to know her, the better I understand why my husband finds our friendship so strange. And yet, the better I get to know her, the greater my need for her comforting, tolerant, female presence.

"You and your husband trapped together in a falling elevator. It's fairly obvious, isn't it? You feel trapped in your relationship. You see no way out. You know the end is coming, but you don't know how long it will take or how bad it will be. You cling to each other for self-preservation. Not to try to protect each other."

I shake my head alarmed, almost a little panicky. I've never talked to her or anyone else about the worsening state of my marriage. The sudden movement of my head causes her

259

to take a bigger cut out of my hair than she meant to. She draws in her breath sharply and clicks her tongue. Now there's nothing for it. The rest will have to be shorter as well, otherwise I'll have an unattractive chunk out on one side of my head.

"Or perhaps it's just a situation that you fear," she adds apologetically, avoiding my eyes in the mirror. "Maybe you're just afraid you'll feel caught in your relationship one day."

"You know I don't really believe in the interpretation of dreams, don't you?" I sigh after watching her in silence for a while. "But in this case . . ."

"Keep that dream journal of yours," she instructs. I have told her that I sometimes – far less often these days – write my dreams down in a book that my husband gave me. The elevator dream is just another one that I chose not to write down. It was too unsettling, I was too lazy, I didn't want to brood on it any more. Maybe I just shrank from the perfectly apparent "explanation" that my friend has just rubbed under my nose. "If you read it again in a few years, you'll find patterns and paths that you can't see now."

"What good will that do me? It's now that I've lost my way. I need a road map now, Beatrice, not in a few years' time."

She puts the scissors down and rubs her open fingers through my hair. Then she switches on a dryer that makes such a high-pitched whine that I have to strain to hear her when she continues.

"One day it may become a Guide for you."

That's something else Beatrice believes in, Guides, along with ghosts and angels and stars that control our lives. Guides are living creatures or inanimate things or anything in between that helps our souls to find a path through life. I decide to steer the conversation back to a more rational shore.

"At the moment the worst relationship in our home is in

any case not that between husband and wife, but between father and son," I confess.

André and I have after all been drifting apart for months in such a listless, half-hearted way, we have sort of become used to it. It's the sudden distance between André and Emile that's caught us all on the wrong foot. It's a violent, aggressive thing. A male, testosterone-driven thing, my instinct tells me. Something that makes me feel clumsy and superfluous and pathetically passive.

"Is André still cross about the hitch-hiking?" asks Beatrice, while she does something with the dryer that makes my hair look thicker and heavier, almost as if I have more hair after she's just snipped off half of it.

"The hitch-hiking, bunking classes, the fact that he falsified my signature . . . André feels the child made fools of us, for weeks, maybe even for months, so he'll never again trust him. And Emile's attitude is, well, if my father isn't going to trust me ever again, why should I even try to regain his trust?"

"And you, Hester?" Estegh. That's how she pronounces my name. Aurore and Aïsha as well. Without the first letter and with a soft rolled 'r' at the end. "Where do you stand?"

"I think they're both overreacting. But I also think it wasn't necessary for André to punish the child quite so severely. He's withdrawn his pocket money and forbidden him to watch TV or play any electronic games for three weeks, which is a terrible punishment for a lonely child who spends all his free time in front of the TV or Gameboy. But that isn't the worst of it. He also wants to forbid him to go to Nathalie's birthday party next month. It's the first time that Emile's been invited to an evening party, a *boum*, as you call it, with music and dancing and so on. And it isn't just any *boum*, it's Nathalie who invited him, so you can imagine what a catastrophe it will be for him if he isn't allowed to go."

261

"The poor thing!" cries Beatrice, shocked. "Can't you twist your husband's arm?"

I can only shake my head. I surely needn't tell her that these days I don't touch my husband's arm too much. Or any other part of his body.

"It's not easy bringing up children, is it?" Beatrice sighs and stands back to admire her handiwork. "What do you think?"

"About bringing up children?" I look at myself in the mirror slightly flabbergasted. "Or of the miracle that you've perpetrated on my hair?"

Her whinnying laugh sounds almost excessively loud in the sudden silence after the hairdryer is switched off.

"Glad you like it. And talking of children . . ."

The front door has just clicked open and Aurore comes into the living room with her red rucksack. She gives Beatrice a hug and turns to me in surprise.

"Ooh, la, la! I didn't know you were so pretty!" she exclaims before kissing me on the cheek as well.

"Don't listen to her," teases Beatrice. "I pay her to flatter my clients."

I hold the thin little body tight for a moment and breathe in her little-girl fragrance. Like wet earth after a long drought it smells to me, like freshly ground Kenyan coffee on a Sunday morning in bed, like figs and strawberries and asparagus and coriander, like all my favourite smells and flavours. Like my own daughter. Then I open my arms and let her go before she takes fright, before she retreats, before she senses the consuming hunger in my body.

A few days later I flee from the house. Out there the mistral seems to be building up into a hurricane. But that is nothing in comparison with the emotional storm raging under our roof. The battle between my husband and my son, by this time mostly wordless, hangs like a suffocating cloud between the four walls of our house. The minute I close the garden gate behind me, I gulp thankfully at the air, even though I have to keep my head low so that the breath isn't immediately blown out of my mouth.

The first weeks after Manon's death, I recall as I take the winding path to the graveyard, we three survivors were too shocked and too sorrowful to comfort one another – but also to reproach or accuse or scold. Like wild animals, we kept each to his own corner, each licking his own wounds or chewing his own limbs. After that the early hardship and hard physical labour in our French house kept us away from one another's bodies for months. And now that the house is at last habitable, now that we should be moving nearer to one another, now we are starting to tear each other apart. The senseless arguments between André and me. What's become of you? What's become of yóu? The unbearable antagonism between André and Emile. What's become of us?

We remain wild, inconsolably wild. France hasn't broken us in. Nine months in Europe hasn't been long enough to tame us.

Beyond the graveyard I change my route. The wind is raging too hard up there high on the hill, my ears have already started hurting from the onslaught, I don't think I'll manage to walk up to the cherry orchard or to the cross at the top. On a day like today it's better to keep your body low against the ground, slither like a snake underneath the wind. So I swerve to the left onto a dirt track that will lead me in a wide arc back to the village.

Now the wind is buffeting me from behind like a bumptious goat, but for the first time I can lift my head to look at my surroundings. Everything is growing browner by the day, the flaming autumn colours almost extinguished, the grey village crouching in the crook of the hill. My eyes automatically look for the familiar beacons. The round castle tower; the rectangular church tower; the row of almost bare plane trees on the square. The clay tile roof of the stone house I've just fled from; the roof of Aïsha's house on the outskirts of the town with something red fluttering on the washline, shocking like a bloodstain against the grey-brown landscape; the roofs of the narrow lane to the right of the square where Aurore and her mother live.

These past days I've been longing for Aurore's embrace as I sometimes long for coffee in the mornings.

My husband is right. I like Beatrice, but the most important reason I seek out her company is still her child. My husband is always right. That little stick-figure child with the penetrating gaze and the inquisitive questions can make my own child live for me again. Each time it feels like a miracle, even if only for a moment, the way a butterfly sometimes comes to land on your body unexpectedly. And because I know that my husband is right yet again, I've stayed away from the house with the pistachio-green door, away from the child with the red rucksack and the marbles in her hair. *This isn't mine, this isn't yours, it's another man's thing that you can't have.* Another of my daughter's favourite folk rhymes.

The narrow dirt track is even more deserted than my usual route. On the way to the cherry orchard I still encounter the odd car or another walker. Where I'm walking now, there's no fresh sign of man or machine. The route drops slowly to a fairly thick forest next to a narrow stream, where the only regular visitors would seem to be a few wild boars. Beatrice taught me to recognise the signs: ground that's been dug up by long tusks, shrubs that have been flattened by heavy bodies, and of

264

course, the characteristic piles of dung. Beatrice has also assured me that there's little chance that I'll encounter a wild boar in the middle of the day, but I look round carefully all the same and tread harder than necessary on the dry leaves and broken branches under my feet. Better to warn an animal that you're entering his territory so that he can get away in time. That's what my father taught me as a child in the veldt of Africa.

The more melancholy he got, the more he rambled. In the veldt or in the mountains if it were at all possible, otherwise in suburban neighbourhoods and busy streets, wherever. I'm aware that in the last few months I've also started to walk almost compulsively.

When I hear the sudden crack of a large branch breaking and notice a movement among the trees out of the corner of my eye, my heart convulses with fright. I wheel round, but instead of a bad-tempered boar with long lethal tusks, I see a stocky male figure with a rifle in his hand. A hunter, I realise, deeply relieved. Then I recognise the hunter, standing rigid about thirty meters from me, and the relief turns into a more complicated emotion.

It is Habib.

We stare at each other wordlessly. No hypocritical polite greeting between us. We have long since passed politeness. A derisive expression flashes over his unshaven face and he takes the rifle in both hands. And all at once I'm terrified, far more frightened than of a wild boar.

Even in my anxiety, the irony of the situation strikes me. In the surrounds of Cape Town, I would never venture woman-alone on such a remote path. Overcareful perhaps, but in that country one can't be too careful. Danger lurks around every deserted corner, in parks and station toilets, in dark streets and unlit buildings. Even in the light of day, in the shop on the corner. The most dangerous animal on the wild continent of Africa is man. My daughter's death confirmed this. But here in the safe European countryside I have started to shake off my neurotic carefulness. The people are as meek as lambs, the snakes and spiders are not poisonous, even the ugly black scorpion we often find in the house is apparently not deadly. What is there to fear here? Poisonous mushrooms?

Now a man stands in front of me with a rifle in his hands and contempt in his whole bearing. The beginnings of a beard darken the lower half of his face. His eyes look black with resentment or rage or something worse that I would rather not identify.

No one would hear if I screamed.

I try to convince myself that this paralysing fear is exaggerated. Surely he isn't going to lift the rifle and shoot me! Or rush at me and rape me. Even if he despises me, even if he hates me, that doesn't mean he'll do me bodily harm. No, he wants to threaten me, that's all. Show who is master. See fear flicker in my eyes.

Bully with a gun.

If I go on looking him straight in the eye, the way you're supposed to do with a fierce dog, I can possibly hide my fear. And yet I can't stay motionless like this for much longer. I know I have to get away, but my legs won't obey my brain.

Then he takes a step forward and my brain sends enough adrenaline to the rest of my body to get my limbs moving again. I turn my back on him and do my best to walk away quickly but with dignity. When I hear the shot, I wonder if this is what my daughter felt in that last fraction of a second before the pain exploded in her chest. Unbelieving. Uninvolved. As if it all just had to be a game.

Then it strikes me that I've not been hit.

I cast a bewildered look over my shoulder as my steps

gather speed to a jog, and see that he aimed the rifle in the air as if to shoot a bird. But the grin on his face leaves no doubt about his intention. He has shown me who is master.

The last shreds of my dignity are blown away right there. I run the rest of the way home, but it's only when I burst panting into the kitchen and my husband looks up in concern from the stove and asks what is the matter, that I start to cry. In a very different way from the past months. It's not loss or anguish that sends the tears coursing over my cheeks. It is humiliation and rage and maybe even hate that makes me sob for minutes in my husband's arms.

And yet, when I'm able to speak again, I do not tell my husband what happened. He won't understand, I tell myself, he'll say I brought it on myself. And maybe I have.

"I don't want to be here any more." That's all I mumble as I dry my tearful face. Over and over. "I don't want to be here any more."

"Never mind, it's all right," my husband comforts me, clicks his tongue and pats my back awkwardly. "Not long to go."

I have been put in my place. That's how it feels. I still haven't worked out where that place is supposed to be – surely not the half-life that I'm living here, even less my former life in Cape Town – but I feel that I have once and for all been put in my place.

WOUNDS

10

The first Christmas without her. Sounds like the title of a poem.

If I could, I'd write a poem. Or compose a piece of music. Like Alban Berg's violin concerto that my husband was listening to again last night on the couch with his eyes closed. *In memory of an angel.* If I could – if only I could! – I would turn to music to drive the silence from me. Or create a painting. Or a sculpture. Create sómething.

But I'm not an artist. I'm someone who doesn't know what to do with the burden of sorrow that I've been dragging about for months now. My only remaining talent, it feels, is to grieve. Maybe after all also a form of art. *I do it exceptionally well. I do it so well it seems like hell.* With apologies to Sylvia Plath.

I stand in front of the large new French window in the bedroom with the cat in my arms. The landscape out there is as bare as my heart. No colour remaining, no purple irises, red poppies, yellow sunflowers along my walks, all cold and bleak now. I don't even feel like walking any more, my chest hurts when I breathe, as if the freezing air is shrinking and drying out my lungs. Or that's what I tell myself, that it's the foul weather that's keeping me confined to the house, not the irrational fear that grips me every time I consider taking one of the paths circling the village.

Habib's rifle shot really did put me in my place. For the last week I have stayed indoors, as befits a respectable woman, or a frightened woman. Show me a respectable woman who isn't frightened.

271

We light a fire every night. We leave the coals smouldering in the grate all night, and the next morning we kindle the ash patiently until a little flame flares up. Rather a calming effect, such a primitive daily task. Because the house is meant to be a holiday home, a summer retreat rather than a winter stronghold, my husband decided not to install central heating. The other reason is that his inheritance has been spent. But at least we're not dependent solely on fire-generated heat like earlier generations. We sleep snugly with an electric heater next to the bed. We also involuntarily sleep closer to each other, my husband and I, to share our body heat. Those are the physical consequences so far of the winter in our house. There will no doubt be emotional ones as well.

I've become involved in the protracted battle between my husband and my son, against my will, as is the way of wars. Collateral damage. All I wanted to do was to persuade André to let Emile attend Nathalie's birthday party. Before long, André and I were yelling at each other, dreadful reproaches that can never be retracted. What a terrible mother I've been the whole year to Emile. What a horrible trial my marriage has become for me. How sick and tired we all are of one another.

What's been said, is said.

And after all those dreadful words, while we were still staring at each other in shock, he said he was in any case intending to allow Emile to go to the party. Just wanted the child to suffer a bit. Which made me explode all over again.

Suffer a bit?

"Suffering is all the child has done this year! First his sister is shot in front of his eyes! Then he gets dragged off to a country where he doesn't want to be! Forced to learn a language that he doesn't want to speak! Don't you think that's enough?"

"That's no excuse for lying and deceiving his parents. He had to be punished."

"He has been punished, André. Now he must start living again."

"You too."

"We're not talking about me now."

"It's high time we talked about you again," he said holding his hand up to his eyes as if to ward off a harsh light.

I turned and left the kitchen. I don't want to talk about me, nor about anyone else for that matter, I want to surround myself with silence. It's the only way I can sometimes – if I listen very carefully – still hear my daughter's voice.

On the other side of the wall.

Christmas without her.

I suppose I should really be grateful that we're spending this Christmas in strange surroundings. In Cape Town everything, absolutely everything, would have been a reminder of former happier Christmas times. The muggy heat, the south-easter draping that white tablecloth of clouds over the mountain, the thousands of tourists taking over the city, the crowded beaches and lack of parking space, "Jingle Bells" and "Silent Night" played to death in glittering shopping centres.

Here it's winter, the wind blows from another direction, it's not the tourist season, there are no beaches around us, not many glittering shopping centres either, and in the shops we do get to, the traditional Anglo-Saxon carols are, thank heaven, not so tastelessly overdone. You could almost forget it's Christmas. Almost.

A single string of coloured lights is festooned across Lunel's main street. *Joyeuses Fêtes,* spelt out in little red and green bulbs. Happy festivals. No reference to specific festivals, probably so as not to offend religious minorities, or perhaps so that the same lights can also be used for the Bastille Day festivities in summer. The window of the bakery is decorated with golden angel's hair and red ribbons, draped around an enormous round loaf of bread, and in the little supermarket there is a plastic knee-high Father Christmas that roars ho-ho-ho! every few minutes. Enough to drive any customer screaming out of the shop within fifteen minutes.

That's all. The sum total of the "Christmas spirit" in Lunel. Quite manageable for a family that recently discovered that all three of its members suffer from Christmas phobia.

And then I think again of Myriam and wonder how she will see this Christmas through. For her also the first without her children, as well as her first behind bars. Think of Myriam Soro, I reproach myself as I did in those first alienating weeks in this house, and count your blessings, Hester Human.

It doesn't always work.

$$\backsim\!\!\backsim$$

"No, it's okay, you needn't come in with me," Emile says and scrambles out of the car quickly.

Don't even think of coming with me. He tries to seem in command of the situation, but it's not easy to seem in command of anything when your teeth are chattering with cold. Maybe also with nervousness. Oh, come on, he remonstrates with himself, it's not that bad. It's only a party. With a few girls and music.

"You're sure?" says his father behind the wheel.

"You have the present?" his mother asks from the passenger seat.

"Yep. You can go now. See you later."

His words come out in a cloud of vapour on the icy air. It's his first evening party, but definitely also his last if his mother or his father were to accompany him to the front door. Deliver

274

him like a pizza or a parcel from the post office. It cost him a hell of a battle with his father just to stand here shivering in the cold dark street in front of Nathalie's apartment building. He hasn't won the battle by a long chalk, only a skirmish (with a lot of help from his mother, admittedly) so he can't afford to lower his defences. He pulls the hood of his tracksuit top over his head, drags his baggy jeans lower down over his hips and looks anxiously at his new Nike sports shoes. He's been kicking at all the stones in his path for days, but they still look conspicuously new. A peace offering from his mother. Or a bribe? She bought them because she wanted him to make peace with his father. He accepted the shoes and pretended to make peace. It was the only way to get to Nathalie's *boum*.

"Midnight," his father reminds him. "See that you're waiting down here at twelve o'clock."

Like bloody Cinderella who had to leave the ball just as it was warming up.

"But not out here in the cold," his mother warns. "Stay in the entrance hall."

"But make sure you're next to the door so that you can see the street," his father adds. "I don't want to have to get out to come and look for you."

Emile sighs – another cloud of steam escaping from his mouth – and wishes they would clear off.

"Enjoy it," says his mother, her voice pleading.

"Behave yourself," orders his father.

Fuck off, thinks Emile with a false smile and turns away before they can offer any more platitudes. Where could the other guests be, he wonders in the hush of the bright but empty entrance to the apartment building while waiting for the lift. He glances at his watch and sees it's exactly seven thirty, which means he is punctual, but it doesn't make him feel any better. You're probably not supposed to turn up on time at your first evening party. When he gets into the cramped old lift, it feels as if he's dreaming, one of those dreams in which you're playing a new sport without knowing the rules. He swallows his panic and forces his index finger to press the button for the top floor. Here we go, he says to himself as the lift shudders and creaks its way upwards. It's only a party. With a few girls and music.

An hour later he's standing a little to one side against a wall with a glass of warm Coke in his sweaty hand, looking furtively at the huddle of giggling girls in the middle of the room. He can't get over how óld they all look tonight, with glossy lips and glitter on their eyelids and long earrings and pendants round their necks and wild hairstyles. And sexy clothes, totally different from the gear they wear at school, very tight jeans and bare tummies and tits wherever you look. Bianca's breasts are just about erupting out of the top of her blouse. They look sort of overinflated, rather like those pale pink bubblegum bubbles that sometimes hover for several seconds in front of her mouth. He's heard the comments of the older boys. A girl who can blow like thát . . . Bianca Blow Job, they call her behind her back. Only because of the bubblegum bubbles, as far as he knows.

"How're things?" It's Peet, the Dutch guy, coming to lean against the wall next to him, an attempt at a tough grin on his face. "Are you going to ask Nathalie to dance?"

"Not yet," squeaks Emile like a cornered mouse. He takes a gulp of Coke to oil his vocal chords before continuing. Keep it low, he says to himself, growl like a lion. "Maybe later tonight."

"Surely you're not going to let this chance slip through your fingers?"

"Later," Emile growls.

"If later won't be too late," Peet warns and lifts his eyebrows in the direction of a circle of older boys smoking out on the balcony. "By that time one of them may well have grabbed her."

Emile deliberately looks away from the balcony, taking another gulp of Coke while his eyes search the large living room that Nathalie and her girl friends have transformed into a rather bare, candlelit dance floor. Her father's life-size sculptures of steel and wood have been carried out and the expensive carpets rolled up and the soft furniture covered with sheets. Luckily he doesn't have to look for long. It's impossible to miss her, in the first place because she towers above the other girls with her long legs and long neck, in the second because she has the darkest skin in the room, and in the third because she's undoubtedly the prettiest girl present. This last thought is probably not what his father would call "objective judgement", but he doesn't want to spoil his mood by thinking about his father. If hé were ever to have a *boum,* his father would definitely not keep to the furthest end of a long passage in another room, watching TV, like Nathalie's parents. No, the bugger would find an excuse to look in on them every five minutes. Like a dark cloud moving in front of the sun. And then there's his mother. One look at her funeral face would be enough to drive away all the guests. No, there's no way a *boum* would work in his house.

"It's still too early to think of dancing," he growls.

"It's all I can think of," confesses Peet. " I've decided to ask Bianca for a dance."

Emile gapes at him.

"What can I lose?" asks Peet with a nervous snigger that makes his front teeth look even bigger than usual. "The worst that can happen is that she'll say no. But just suppose she says yes, and I can get my hands close to those . . ."

The excitement takes his breath away and he has to gesticulate. He looks as if he's trying to pluck two massive apples from a tree. Pathetic, thinks Emile. That such a clever guy can carry on like that about a pair of tits.

And yet he has to admit he's glad that Nathalie isn't prancing around with a pair of protruding tits like Bianca, or exhibiting such a large expanse of bare belly as Lola, because then he definitely wouldn't have the courage to dance with her. Where do you put your hands, where do you rest your eyes, what do you do with your feet – and other body parts – when such large stretches of bare female flesh suddenly come so very close? The way he feels now, the dancing isn't going to work in any case. She's hardly spoken to him since he walked in this evening. Not that she's unfriendly, of course not, it's just that she isn't any friendlier towards him than towards any other guy at the party. Except maybe for Alain, one of the hard-arses standing out there smoking in the freezing wind. Him she'd graced with a wider than usual smile. And he can't blame her, decides Emile. Like all the other girls, she looks closer to twenty than to thirteen tonight. Of course an older guy, a smoker, a drinker and a swearer like Alain, would be more attractive to her than a thirteen-year-old baby face with a few pimples.

And an unreliable voice.

He thought that when your voice broke it would be more or less like a glass breaking. Splat, there it is on the floor, all in bits and pieces, end of story. *All the king's horses and all the king's men couldn't put Humpty together again.* The next day you'd be speaking in a nice deep man's voice. But no, he's discovering it's more like a car slowly giving up the ghost. One day you can't get it started, the next it's okay again. It's been going on like this for weeks. One moment he's speaking with his ordinary rather silly boy's voice, the next moment he sounds like a fat lady singing opera.

It's just not fair.

Nothing seems fair tonight. For instance girls only have to paint their faces to look seven years older. If he painted his face he wouldn't look any older, he'd simply look like a thirteen-year-old poofter instead of a thirteen-year-old nerd. Nothing he can do to disguise his age, except to put a paper bag on his head and shut his trap so that his voice won't embarrass him.

He hears her laugh again and unexpectedly catches her eye over the bobbing heads around them. There are advantages to being tall, he decides while they look into each other's eyes for a fraction of a second. Then she looks away and the moment is lost, but something must have happened, some or other message sent and received, because he feels less lonely and unwanted and unhappy than a few moments ago.

He walks over to the nearest table to pour another Coke. Peet is still leaning helplessly against the wall, his eyes never leaving Bianca's bouncing breasts, like a rabbit caught in the headlights of a car.

"Won't you pour me one too?" says Nathalie unexpectedly next to him, holding her glass out to him. "Are you okay?"

"Why do you ask?"

"I don't know, you look sort of . . . like you're not totally here." Her eyelids and lips are glistening in various shades of gold. Her nails too, he notices on the hand holding her glass. He is so fascinated by the golden nails that he doesn't stop pouring before the cold drink starts foaming over the edge. She pulls her hand away laughing. "See what I mean?"

"*Putain,* sorry, man. No, of course I'm here, where else could I be?"

She considers him with her head at an angle. Tonight it's not only her smile that blinds him, it's this whole golden shimmer about her. Like a goddess she seems to him, something that you can't look at full-on.

279

"Hmm," she says. "As long as you don't plan to slink away. Remember, if you leave before dancing with me, I'll never speak to you again."

And then she glides away and he's left there with an idiotic grin. Only about a minute later it strikes him that he must look as ridiculous as Peet who is still staring at Bianca Blow Job's breasts like a hypnotised hare. But, unlike Peet, at least he knows he'll have his dance before the end of the evening.

They go to a movie, *Lost in Translation*, which leaves them both feeling slightly sad. A story full of silence and yearning and unspoken solitude. Afterwards they have a light late-night meal in an empty restaurant, not because they're hungry, only to fill the time till midnight when they have to fetch Emile from his party.

The choice on the tourist menu is predictably boring: onion soup, goose liver paté, snails in garlic sauce. But that's all right, thinks André, he's in no mood for adventure or surprises tonight. And as for Hester, well, it's been months since it mattered to her what you put on her plate. He chooses the onion soup for himself and the snails for her.

As he watches her hold the snail shell with the pincers and scrape out the flesh with the long pointed fork, he remembers how she giggled many years before, the first time they ordered this exotic dish in a French restaurant. She couldn't get a proper grip on the shells with the pincers; one of them catapulted in a wide arc over the table, landing in André's glass of red wine. "Do you think I should tell the waiter there's a snail in my wine?" he asked snorting with laughter.

But now he just sighs and asks whether she liked the movie. She nods without looking up from her operation with the pin-

280

cers and fork. It makes him feel like a pathetic lover trying to find out from his partner if it was okay for her as well. If you have to ask, Hester once remarked, it's usually a sign that it was nót okay for the partner. They don't speak again till the waiter removes their plates.

Then André asks if she's thought about what she wants for their Christmas meal.

Whatever he wants, she answers.

"What about oysters?" he prods. "Apparently it's a traditional Christmas dish over here. After all, you like oysters."

"If you want to."

"And *foie gras?*"

"Can we afford it?"

"It's Christmas, Hester," he says with a flash of irritation in his voice. Which makes her drift even further away from him and this meal in an empty restaurant. By now she's floating somewhere high above the tables with their starched white linen cloths. Soothingly he adds: "I know you don't feel like the fuss and the effort, but we must think of Emile. He's a child. He needs Christmas."

"Does he?" Without sarcasm, simply a pensive question. "Why don't you ask him what he'd like to eat?"

"Because I'm afraid he'll say hamburgers and *frites*. Or suggest that we have our Christmas meal at McDonalds."

"Maybe not such a bad idea," she says with a lopsided smile. "I'm not sure that he's still enough of a child to enjoy Christmas. Do you remember how he spent the whole of last year working on his gift list? First he wanted a magician set, then a telescope, then a new Playstation – or a Game Cube? – at any rate every month it was something else. Then he had to scrap something else from the list because it was getting too long. And now he's asking for nothing. Not of me, anyway. Has he asked you?"

281

André shakes his head and watches the waiter bringing the coffee cups.

"It's as if he's become too scared to ask for anything," says Hester .

"We've all become too scared to expect much from life," says André. "But he's still a child . . . "

It sounds as if he's trying to convince himself, he realises.

"Open your eyes, André," sighs Hester. "We haven't had a child in the house for a very long time."

⌒⌒

"So how was it then?" I ask in the kitchen without really expecting a detailed answer. "Your first *boum?*"

"Not bad," mumbles my son, half asleep over his breakfast cereal.

That's as far as we got the night before as well. Not bad, he mumbled, in the car on the way back from Nathalie's party. And what the devil could I really expect? You can't exactly live with a teenager for months on end with a shut mouth and a heavy tongue and then one fine morning expect him to open his heart to you! You'll reap what you've sown. It's I, after all, who sowed the silence in this house.

"Did you dance with anyone?"

I'm leaning against a kitchen cupboard next to him, looking at his hunched shoulders under the worn old T-shirt that he sleeps in. So fragile, I think, so little flesh between the skin and the bone.

"Uh-huh," he answers and stoops even lower over his cereal, pulls his neck even further in between his shoulder blades.

"With Nathalie?"

My voice is so artificially sweet that my tongue feels sticky.

"Uh-huh."

282

"And with any other girls?"

"No, only with a few of the boys."

I take a quick sip of coffee to hide my surprise.

"Do boys dance with each other at parties these days?"

"No, Mom, I'm not a bloody poofter. I just said it so you'd stop asking these stupid questions!"

"Is that a way to talk to your mother?" asks André, who has just appeared in the front door with a baguette under his arm.

"I wasn't rude," Emile protests without looking at his father. "I just wanted her to leave me alone."

"That's true," I say hurriedly because I can see another confrontation looming. "He wasn't impolite, André, he just wasn't in the mood . . ."

"These days he can't open his mouth without being rude," André interrupts and plonks the bread on the cupboard next to me. "It's not what he says, its hów he says it."

"And he can't open his mouth these days without picking on me," mumbles Emile and holds his open palms like blinkers on either side of his face. "Nothing I do is good enough for him."

Why do we so constantly use the third person when we're arguing, I ask myself in panic. Why have we become too afraid to look each other in the eye and to say "you"? It's as if "you" sounds too personal, too familiar, for three strangers like us who happen to live under the same roof.

"Please, you two," I plead and put my hand out involuntarily to touch Emile's shoulder, to stop him from jumping up and storming out of the room and slamming his bedroom door behind him with a bang like a pistol shot. "It's too early in the morning to be arguing."

"It's not all that early," says André curtly. "I'm going to drill those holes in the wall of the spare room."

"Why?"

"For the bookshelf that you want there."

"No, I mean why drill holes on a Sunday morning?"

"Why not?" mutters André on his way out of the kitchen. "It has to be done sooner or later."

Perhaps that's why he's so crabby. He hates doing anything in that spare room. Of all the rooms in the house, that's the one he's altered least, where he worked fastest on the little that had to be done. These days there are two small single beds with new spreads in the room, new white cotton mats on the floor, white cotton curtains in front of the window, but it just won't turn into a spare room. It will always be Manon's room.

Emile lifts his head and listens to his father's footsteps fading up the stairs, his expression simultaneously relieved and regretful.

"What would you like for Christmas?" I ask and pull out a chair next to him.

Not that I'm trying to make up to him. It's probably too late for that, I've just realised yet again. Simply because my legs suddenly feel too weak to carry my weight.

"Oh, I don't know, a game for my Gameboy or the computer, whatever. I don't really care."

My eyes fill with tears as I watch him lift the breakfast bowl to his mouth to lap up the last of the milk. Overcome with love for this child with his clumsy skinny body and his bad temper and his shame and his guilt. And yet, how difficult it has become to show this love. Harder and harder by the day.

Then he surprises me by looking unexpectedly at me – staring straight into my eyes instead of somewhere past one of my ears as usual – and asking with a frown: "And you, Mom? What do you want for Christmas?"

My children. I want my children back. The daughter who's dead and the son who's become so remote that it sometimes feels as if he too is dead.

"That you and Dad should make your peace," I say when I can trust my voice again.

"Mom, I must have apologised ten times by now, for bunking classes and hitch-hiking and lying and for everything else that I've ever done wrong in my life. And every time Dad just says uh-huh, apologies mean nothing, I have to shów that I'm sorry. I mean what more does he want me to do? Crawl around on my knees and whip myself?"

"He wants you to lóók sorry, Emile. He says you always apologise from a great height. As if you're doing him a favour by talking to him."

"But he's totally f . . . He's not right in his head, Mom! I don't know what's got into him! I think he wánts to stay cross with me, no matter what I do. So why should I do ánything to please him?"

"Do it to please me," I beg.

Why should I do anything to please yóú? I read the question in his challenging look, before he drops his eyes to the empty bowl.

"Emile, I know we don't exactly live in a cheerful house," I press on.

"Understatement," he snorts.

"But if you and he are always . . . at loggerheads, it makes everything even worse."

"So now that's also my fault!" he exclaims and gets up so brusquely that he almost knocks the chair over. "Mom, are you going to tell me it's because Dad and I are fighting that you've been moping around with that miserable mug for months now?"

"No, that's not what I wanted to say, Emile, I only meant . . ."

But he charges out of the kitchen without listening any further. I've lost him as well.

⤚⤙

285

"Do you still write down your dreams?" asks Beatrice a week later at the same kitchen table.

I shake my head and stare out of the window. The little lemon tree's leaves definitely look shinier and healthier than a year ago. Some small comfort, at least. It's weeks since I wrote anything in my dream journal. Since I've been sharing my husband's bed again I just haven't been able to do it. She doesn't enquire further, just looks at me with concern.

"The so-called festive season has always made me melancholy," I admit after we've been drinking our tea in silence for a while. "This year is worse than ever."

"You need to get out of the house." She pushes her blonde hair off her face, takes her little tobacco pouch out of her jeans pocket and starts rolling a cigarette. "It's not good for you to be in here brooding all day long."

"What else can I do? It's too cold to brood outside."

"Wrap up warmly, Hester." Estegh. Suppressed impatience in her tone, like a rumble of thunder in the distance. By now I know the signs. Everyone who cares about me eventually gets tired of this ceaseless grieving. "You can't spend the whole winter in the house!"

Why not, I wonder. It's not only the low temperature and the icy north wind that keep me at home. It's also the growing fear that somewhere in a secluded street or on an isolated footpath I might encounter Habib. I haven't seen him since the day he scared me with the rifle. But I stay afraid all the time. I simply can't shake off the feeling that he's watching me. That he's waiting for an opportunity.

To do I don't know what.

It's a different feeling, completely different, from when my husband used to watch me so incessantly. I knew André was doing it out of love, even though his surveillance sometimes irritated me immensely. These last weeks André has turned his

286

all-seeing eyes from me. As if he no longer cares. Or maybe he just got tired. After all, even God must tire of being eternally watchful. And I must admit that I feel lost. Like a long-term prisoner released without any preparation. Nothing to stop me from doing something really stupid.

I'm convinced that it will be better for everyone if I stayed behind in France. But I lack the courage to tell them, to read the shock and disappointment and incomprehension and accusation in their so-similar dark eyes. My dearest husband, my dearest son. Rather say nothing, I think, rather just at the last minute – do what? Refuse to get onto the plane? Secretly slip away from the airport? Leave a farewell letter begging for their forgiveness?

Myriam, I wish you could give me advice. Is muteness the inevitable price for betraying your dearest and nearest?

"Look here, *maman*!" Aurore runs into the kitchen waving a drawing triumphantly in the air. "For the first time in my life I've managed to draw a house that doesn't look like a shoe box!"

Today it's plaits again. Dozens of narrow plaits flat against her head in complicated geometric patterns. Her black eyes are as big and bright as always in her slender face, reminding one of a little Japanese animation character.

"I only gave her a few basic guidelines," says André from behind her. Now that his Project is more or less finished, he at last has the time to give her the long-promised drawing lesson. "She caught on immediately. She's quick."

"Quick as a rocket," Beatrice says proudly, admiring the drawing.

"Next time we'll draw outside! André says the only way to learn how to draw a house is to sit outside and draw a real one."

"In this freezing weather?" asks Beatrice alarmed.

"True artists don't worry about the weather," announces André loftily, before winking at Aurore and saying to her out

287

of the corner of his mouth: "We'll wait until the wind has died down, won't we?"

I am amazed at my husband, at the good-natured teasing and the grin that suddenly splits open across his face. He was worried that I would try to steal this little girl away from her mother. Now it seems he is enticing her away from her mother ánd from me.

"Don't you want some cool drink, Aurore?" I ask. "I bought the green kind that you like best."

"But it's much too cold for cooldrink!" exclaims André. "Let's rather make you some hot chocolate."

She follows him eagerly to the fridge and watches him pour the milk into a saucepan. I wonder if it's envy, this heaviness in my mouth, this leaden tongue.

Then she turns unexpectedly back to me and asks: "Why don't you have a Christmas tree in the house?"

"Aurore . . ." chides her mother.

I catch my husband's eye, at the stove where he's heating the milk, and read a complicated message in it. Sympathy, reproof, maybe even something malicious. I told you so.

"Well, this isn't our real home, after all," I make excuses. "We didn't bring our Christmas decorations with us."

"But I'll make decorations for you!"

"Good idea," says André with his back turned to me. "You make us some decorations and I'll go and saw off a branch in the forest. If we can't have a Christmas tree, we can at least have a Christmas branch."

I don't want a tree in the house. I don't even want a branch. No shining and sparkly decorations, no gifts, no joy. Not without my daughter.

But it looks as if I'm going to lose this battle too.

⌒⌒

He suddenly remembers that it was on this very park bench that he first admired her legs. A sultry day in summer when she was watching a bunch of toddlers clambering on the jungle gym. Her denim skirt was unbuttoned in front and he could see her bare knees and sleek brown thighs. After that she bought them ice cream. Her licking tongue reminded him of a pink lizard scurrying out of a crack and slipping back in.

Now it's winter: low pale sky, only one child on the jungle gym – dressed so warmly that he looks like the little Michelin man with tyres round his body – and not a glimpse of Nathalie's legs. No skin showing anywhere. She's wearing jeans and flat boots lined with wool and at least three layers of sweaters and a coat over all three, thick gloves and a woollen cap pulled low over her forehead and a knitted scarf covering her mouth. It's actually only her nose that's still visible.

"Snow time, folks," she announced earlier. "When the sky goes pale like that, there's always snow on the way, hey?"

He wouldn't know, he said, and reminded her that he'd spent his entire life in a country where snow was rather scarce. Oh yes, she said and shook her head wonderingly. She kept forgetting he was from Africa.

It is actually far too cold to hang around in a park, but they were unexpectedly given a free period and they didn't have money on them to go and drink something hot in a café. And they wanted a last chance to talk before school closes tomorrow for the short Christmas break. At least, hé wanted to talk. What shé wants, is as usual a mystery to him.

"You found quite a few admirers at my *boum*, you know?" From the way the knitted scarf stretches across her cheeks, he can tell that she's grinning from ear to ear. "At least three girls told me they can't believe how well you dance."

"Stop making fun of me." Now he's going to blush again and his voice is going to scale the heights, he realises in a resigned sort of way.

"No, I'm not teasing. I told them but of course, what do you know, in Africa even the white boys can dance." He gives her a mock indignant dig in the ribs. She leans forward laughing, her breath forming a cloud of white vapour above the scarf. Then she shakes her head and says more seriously: "There's óne girl who's especially impressed with you."

He gives her a covert glance, afraid that she'll hear how wildly his heart has started hammering. A fat dark-grey pigeon with a damaged wing is strutting right in front of his feet, so near that he notices the greenish tinge of the bird's breast feathers.

"And who would that be?"

"Can't you guess?"

This time his unreliable voice doesn't even manage to emerge from his mouth. He clears his throat anxiously and keeps his eyes on the fat pigeon with the wing dragging on the ground. The bird isn't injured, he suddenly realises. This is just courting behaviour. Like humans make advances, make eyes, check out, chaff. Which might be regarded as a sort of injury, after all.

"What colour hair does she have?"

"Black."

"And what colour eyes?"

"Black."

He draws a deep breath.

"I think I may have an idea," he grins.

"She wanted to know if I'd mind if she asked you to go to movies with her."

He looks at her totally nonplussed.

"And what did you say?

"What do you think? Don't touch him, he's mine," she growls in a deep voice before roaring with laughter again. "No, man, I said she can ask you whatever she wants, it's not as if I've taken out a patent on you!"

He takes a deep gulp to hide his disappointment. "Who are you talking about?"

"About Lee of course!" She throws open her arms dramatically. "Don't tell me you haven't noticed how she's been looking at you these past few days?"

Lee. The emaciated little Asian girl. Black hair and black eyes, that's true. And a silver ring in her eyebrow. He heard somewhere that she shoves her finger down her throat after every meal.

"That's ridiculous. She can't stand me."

"Oh yes, after dancing with you she can." Her eyes sparkle merrily under the woollen cap. "Way to go, brother."

She holds out her hand for a high five, but the thick fabric of her gloves smothers the sound and spoils the effect.

"Hey." She looks at him enquiringly. "I thought you'd be pleased."

"It's cool." The wing-displaying pigeon has disappeared. The little grey one that has replaced it has the dirty crumpled appearance of a bundle of laundry. Not much chance of impressing a female pigeon if you look like that, thinks Emile with pity and gets up so suddenly that the whole flock of pigeons near them fly off. "Come, our bums are going to freeze if we stay out here any longer."

He holds out his hand to help her up off the bench. Those are the only times he dares to touch her, helping her out of a chair or off the floor or so. And today her gloves are so thick that he can't even say he's actually touched her.

That's why that single close dance at her party was so unforgettable. Why he can't even remember that he danced

291

with Lee and who knows who else. All he can remember is the weight of Nathalie's head against his shoulder.

Thát he will remember for the rest of his life.

11

In the deepest darkest part of the night there is a hammering on their front door. At first he thinks it's part of his nightmare: his son playing an African drum with a bone through his nose, as in a colonial cartoon of a cannibal; his wife who's been asleep for a century in an impenetrable jungle. He knows he has to wake her, but he can't clear a path through the dense vegetation with his bare hands, and his son's drumming tum-tum-tums ever more urgently in his ears. Then he starts awake and realises that the tum-tum-tumming is coming from some-where in the house.

He shivers with cold once he's out from under his down duvet, feels around with his bare feet on the floor until he steps on an old jersey, pulls it on quickly over his pyjamas, and stumbles to the door without switching on the light. Rather let Sleeping Beauty sleep on. But she rolls over and her lazy tongue forms something like: "Whe'ya going?"

Then she also hears the wild hammering and sits up star-tled.

"Someone at the front door?"

"I'm going to look," he whispers. "You stay in bed."

Halfway down the steep stairs – as fast as he can descend without breaking his neck in the dark – he hears her footsteps shuffling behind him.

"You don't have to get up as well," he assures her over his shoulder.

She says nothing, just carries on walking behind him. And

293

for some reason it makes him feel grateful. Past Emile's room, at least it sounds as if hé hasn't woken up yet, down further by the wider staircase, through the kitchen where a pool of moonlight lies like spilt milk on the terracotta floor, all the way to the front door. Which he's once again forgotten to lock, he realises as he feels the doorknob shockingly cold under his fingers. Anyone could have walked in here and murdered them all. No, he stops himself. He isn't in his native land now.

"Who is it?" he asks in a subdued voice.

"Aïsha. Can I come in!"

It sounds like a command rather than a request. Her voice isn't as breathy and uncertain as usual. He hears Hester's intake of breath behind him as he opens the door.

"Aïsha!" exclaims Hester and opens her arms wide for the young girl.

André looks at the purplish-blue bruise round Aïsha's right eye and the bloodied swollen lip, and his head begins to spin with rage.

"Was it your brother again?"

"Can I stay here tonight?" she asks with her hand in front of her bruised mouth. She's having trouble talking, as if her tongue is swollen as well. "I'm too frightened to go home."

"Of course," says Hester. "Let's go to the bathroom so that we can doctor your face."

"Shouldn't we rather take you to hospital?" asks André.

"No!" She is so distraught that she forgets to hold her hand in front of her mouth. Now André sees that she has lost one of her front teeth. This upsets him even more than the swollen lips and the bruised eye socket. "Not the hospital. They'll ask questions and I don't want . . . I can't tell them . . ."

In spite of everything she actually still feels obliged to protect her brother.

"But, Aïsha, sooner or later you're going to have to . . ."

"Leave it for now, André." Hester silences him, leading the girl to the bathroom. "We can talk about revenge and justice later. What she needs now is comfort and rest."

An hour later André and Hester are sitting at the kitchen table, each with a mug of hot chocolate. They look like two middle-aged tramps: he with a paint-bespattered old jersey over his washed-out flannel pyjamas, she with a man's dressing gown in checks, its cord long lost, tied at the waist with a floral scarf. Their hair is standing up unkempt, their faces are puffy and creased from too little sleep, his with grey stubble round the mouth as well. Not so long ago they were part of the cream of society in Cape Town, André thinks almost abstractedly, a professional couple with two lovely children in a designer home on the slopes of the mountain. In the blink of an eye everything started slipping, the crack of a firearm causing a sort of domino effect, and look where they are now.

"Perhaps I should go and make sure she's asleep," says Hester.

"No, if she's just fallen asleep, you might wake her," André stops her. "Wait a little longer."

"I'm just afraid I might have doped her. I gave her two pain pills *and* two sedatives."

"I didn't even know we had sedatives in the house."

"Oh, they're pills left over from . . . the funeral week. Pills that the doctor prescribed for me. You remember, they kept me pretty well doped most of the time."

"Already a year ago, can you believe it?" sighs André.

The first anniversary of their daughter's death is around the corner. Yet another trial they have to get through together before they can go back home. He puts his hand out instinctively to take hers lying inert on the table next to the mug of hot chocolate. To his surprise, she doesn't pull it back, doesn't shy away, but lets him be. He folds his hand over hers.

"I told her she could lie low here for a few days." Hester looks at him anxiously. "At any rate until her face looks better, till she can go out in public again."

"And if her brother comes looking for her here?"

"Then we tell him to leave her alone."

"And if he gets violent?"

"Then we phone the police. We can't refuse, André. She has nowhere else to go."

"What about her mother and father? Can't they protect her against her brother?" But he knows it's a rhetorical question. Clearly Habib is master of that house. He drinks his hot chocolate pensively. If he'd talked to Habib seriously months before, as Hester had begged him to, then it mightn't have been necessary for Aïsha to come hammering on their door tonight with a black eye, a bruised mouth and a lost tooth. Of course, it's more than likely that a confrontation with Habib would have achieved nothing – except that he might have lost his handyman. But he should have tried. Even if he hadn't managed to bring Habib around, he would at least have retained his wife's respect.

"Of course we can't refuse," he sighs.

"Thank you," whispers Hester, leaning back in her chair with relief.

He looks at their hands, his right hand round hers, on the grainy wooden table top. Like a sculpture, he thinks, lit with almost unnatural brightness by the bulb directly above the round table. He can't remember when last she allowed him to hold her hand for this long.

"I suppose we'd better get some sleep as well," she suggests.

They climb the stairs side by side and stand together in the open door of the spare room. In the dim light from the passage, the curled up figure on the bed looks smaller than she really is. The way she's lying, with her face turned to the door and the blanket pulled up high over her head, reminds André of the child in whose room she is now sheltering. Just as well it's too dark to make out the expression on Hester's face. He takes her hand again and leads her further up the steep stairs to their double bed.

When he lies behind her back and slides his hand under her nightdress, she doesn't strain away as usual. For the first time in weeks – months? – he falls asleep with his wife's bare breast like a fruit in the palm of his hand.

⁖

It feels almost like the time before, when there were four of them in the house. Only quieter than then. He and his father have less and less to say to each other, and his mother has for ages now not exactly been a chatterbox. And the injured Moroccan girl sitting in the fourth place, where his sister would have sat if his sister were still here, is apparently also not in a mood to chat. Not with a mouth punched up like that.

"*Bon appétit,*" says his father to the subdued table as they all start eating.

Well, not quite all. Aïsha twirls her fork gloomily in her plate of pasta. Emile watches her discreetly. Difficult not to stare. A pretty girl with the face of a boxer after a bad bout – one eye purplish and almost swollen shut, a hideous scab on her lips daubed with mercurochrome, probably all that his mother had to hand, and that black hole in her mouth where her tooth should be. He was almost frightened out of his wits this morning when he walked out of the bathroom straight into this apparition. No one had thought to warn him that she'd come to sleep in Manon's room in the middle of the

297

night. And why she looks as she does, they still haven't explained to him. Apparently her brother had got at her, that's all he can make out.

"You must try to eat something, Aïsha," his mother says softly. "Even if you aren't hungry."

"I can't," mutters Aïsha through her puffy lips.

"Too sore?"

"No. There's ham in the pasta. It's not halaal," she adds, seeing Hester's puzzled frown.

"*Merde*," says André slapping his open hand against his head. When did his father learn to swear in French, wonders Emile, quite impressed. "Where was my mind? I just didn't think about what I was doing."

"It's my fault as well," says Hester. "I saw you making pasta alfredo. I could have warned you that Aïsha isn't allowed to eat it."

"No, it's nobody's fault," says Aïsha "That's just . . . how it is."

"There's cold chicken in the fridge," suggests Hester. "Or otherwise we can quickly do some scrambled eggs. What do you feel like?"

"No, don't go to any trouble, I'll have some bread," says Aïsha. "I'm not really hungry anyway."

"Are you sure?" asks André. "Sorry, it really was stupid of us."

"Forget it," says Aïsha, breaking off a piece of the baguette. "I'm just sorry that the pasta will go to waste."

"That's something you don't have to worry about," says Emile, who as usual has eaten faster than anyone else at the table and now has an empty plate in front of him. "I'll do what's expected of me."

This makes the other three smile – Aïsha's fingers quickly flying up to cover her mouth – and suddenly the atmosphere isn't so very heavy any more.

"I'm used to it," he explains, taking Aïsha's plate. "My friend Zakes in Cape Town is also Muslim. Every time we're in a place where there's ham or bacon or something like that in the food, he gives me his plate. Sometimes we swop, then I give him my pudding. He has more of a sweet tooth than me."

"It's not even that I'm all that religious," says Aïsha embarrassed. "I mean, I've tasted alcohol and done other things that good Muslim girls aren't supposed to do. It's just . . . as if my brain tells me don't be stupid, what can a little piece of ham do to you . . . but I'm afraid my stomach will protest. That I'll get nauseous or get cramps or whatever. I mean, sometimes the body is more powerful than the head, isn't it?"

"Most of the time," Hester agrees.

What's his mother talking about now? wonders Emile. Why are there always so many layers of hidden meaning underneath the words of grown-ups? This business with Aïsha's face for example. No one's prepared to tell him exactly what happened, or why. As if he's a little boy who knows nothing about violence, as if they've conveniently forgotten what he experienced a year ago in a corner shop in Cape Town.

☙

Dear Myriam. Today I sent you the last of the African animals. A row of giraffe walking across a road, disciplined and graceful as ballet dancers, long necks swaying, loping along on their thin legs. My son recently remarked that his best friend reminds him of a giraffe. And it's true, you know, she and her mother both have that height and lithe grace that make some women from East Africa so exotically irresistible to us who are paler and smaller.

You're from Central Africa, you're shorter and more com-

pact, your features broader – but you're still a beautiful woman. Or you were when I last saw you in the newspaper. Even
that appalling emptiness in your eyes couldn't quite erase
your beauty. I wonder if there will be the faintest spark of that
beauty left when you walk out of prison ten, fifteen, twenty
years from now.

Speaking of beauty: I wonder if you received my Christmas
parcel. A round pink soap and body lotion smelling of roses
and a box of chocolates. I don't know if you're allowed to
receive edibles. I don't know if you're allowed any presents
from outside at all. But after all these days there are machines
that can see right through gift wrap and chocolate boxes,
metal detectors and such things, all kinds of ways to ensure
that the present hasn't been tampered with. That I haven't hidden any pills or razor blades in the soap or chocolate.

I posted the parcel in secret because I didn't want my husband or my son to know about it. They'd think it ridiculous to
send a parcel to someone who'll probably never open it. And
they'd be right, of course.

And yet I've always been taught that it isn't the gift that
counts, it's the thought behind the gift. I thought of you, Myriam. That's what's important.

I thought of you over these so-called festive days, I wrote
this morning on the postcard. *It must have been a difficult
Christmas.*

I'm standing in front of the French window of my bedroom
with my forehead pressed to the cold glass. Outside fine white
specks eddy around, something like snow, but as soon as they
hit the ground they melt. My breath fogs up the glass under
my face, a spot of vapour that gradually grows bigger until
the whole pane is misted over and I can't see out anymore. I'll
go mad if I can't get out of this house. And yet I'm more
frightened than ever to venture out.

300

Since Aïsha has been sheltering under my roof, I'm more afraid than ever that I'll meet her brother somewhere out there.

But some good things have also happened since Aïsha came hammering on our front door the other night. It's as if someone has opened a shutter to let light stream through a dark room. Or a window to let in fresh air. The tension has lessened. Emile talks more and is laughing more. At this very moment I can hear him laughing in his room where he's showing Aïsha how to play a game on the laptop computer.

No, Myriam, she hasn't taken my daughter's place, that's not what I'm saying. Her presence has just altered the relationships in the house in subtle ways. Emile is in a better mood, so he sounds less rude when he talks to his father. André doesn't want to lose his temper in front of an outsider, therefore he's more patient with his son. And I want to nurse and comfort and care for her, which means that I have less time to lie in a dispirited heap on my bed or hang glumly over the kitchen table.

All the same, there's still enough happening in the world to depress anyone for good. And now I'm not even talking about Africa's everlasting miseries, I'm talking about the everyday horror of life here in Europe. So safe on the surface: high income, high literacy, high life expectancy. But as soon as you scratch a little below the surface, if you look for what we'd like to call the soul, then nothing looks safe any more.

Within two weeks two mothers here in the peaceful French countryside have murdered their children. Two respectable middle-class women, married to decent men, living in nice houses in lovely little Provençal towns. One, who is described as "gentle and shy", took a butcher's knife one morning and cut the throats of her two infant children, then drove with bloody hands to the vineyard where her winemaker husband was working, to tell him what she'd done. The other one, "a dedicated nurse", had access by virtue of her job to less primitive murder weapons. She first gave her children sleeping pills, then mixed a deadly potion which she fed them by means of an intravenous drip. Then she lay down between the two dead children on her marriage bed and waited for her husband to come home.

I can't get over it. I'm still staring at the flurry of specks outside the window. Now it is undeniably snow, fine and feathery, a white blanket spread out on the balcony wall. Are there by chance more mothers murdering their children of late – or am I simply noticing newspaper reports that I would formerly have overlooked?

You have opened my eyes to many things, Myriam.

"It's snowing!" yells Emile from his room, his voice hoarse with excitement. "Mom! Dad! It's snowing! I'm going outside!"

"Wait, I'm coming too!" calls André from the ground floor where he's been lying on the couch listening to music.

"Wrap up warmly," I call, but Emile's footsteps thump so loudly down the stairs that no one hears me.

By the time I reach the kitchen, they are both outside. Aïsha stands longingly by the window. Her eye is less swollen today. Her mouth also looks better, but she still refuses to see a dentist, still wants to wait a few more days. Too afraid of questions she doesn't want to answer. Too afraid to go out, afraid that someone in the village will realise that her brother assaulted her, afraid her brother will find out that she's sheltering with us.

You've grown up, I want to say to her. You've become a frightened woman.

What were the names of your daughters? That's what I wanted to know from you this morning, Myriam. *Can't recall that I ever read it anywhere – and it suddenly feels like vital*

302

*information to me. Mine was called Manon. This week it is
exactly a year since she was murdered. Oh, Myriam, will the
sorrow never end?*

The most despondent postcard I've ever sent you. Sorry, it's
too late to do anything about it, I can only hope you don't
read it. Maybe you haven't read anything at all that I've written. We all know that most messages in bottles never actually reach anybody. Most of them are carried along for years,
decades, even centuries, by sea currents, till one day the bottle
breaks against a rock or a huge ship and the letter gets swal-
lowed up by the water.

⌒⌒

And suddenly he's there, with a wild beard and a feverish look
in his eyes, in the kitchen where Aïsha is helping me pack the
clean dishes away. Aïsha draws a deep gasping breath and
steps back. I also involuntarily retreat with a large glass bowl
and a cloth in my hands. It's no use trying to reason with him,
I realise immediately. And yet I know that I have no other
weapon but words.

"Habib. Is there anything I can do for you?"

"You can keep your nose out of other people's business," he
snarls at me.

"If you'll keep your feet out of other people's houses. You
don't have the right to barge in here. Do you realise that
you're committing an offence?"

"Shut your mouth, *salope*. I've come to fetch my sister."

The violence of his words makes me stagger another step
back. No one has ever sworn at me with such contempt. For a
second I think of bluffing, calling to my husband just to put
the wind up him, but then it strikes me that he must know that
André isn't at home. He probably watched the house – maybe

303

even for days – to be sure that he wouldn't be chased away by André. Emile is in his room doing homework – with his earphones plugged deep into his ears, if I know him, and rap rhythms pounding through his head. He won't even realise there's an intruder in the house. And it's better that way, I decide. This is a matter for adults.

"I don't believe your sister wants to be fetched." I hear my voice shake. I feel Aïsha's hand trembling against my arm. He steps closer and she and I both step back. We can't retreat much further, he's driving us into a corner. The kitchen table is all that separates us.

"Tell him, Aïsha."

Aïsha makes a smothered sound and tightens her grip on my arm.

"Say something, Aïsha," I hiss.

"If she doesn't come willingly," Habib threatens, "I'll have to drag her out."

"If you come one step closer I'm calling the police."

A laughable threat, because he's closer to us than we are to the telephone, but I'm desperate enough to try anything. I register the scornful smile flashing through his beard. And then, to my amazement, Aïsha pulls a cellphone out of her jeans pocket and thrusts it into my hand.

"Ring 18," she mutters.

In a single movement Habib jumps over the kitchen table and kicks the telephone out of my hand. I groan with shock and pain, my fingers numb, as Aïsha screams, high and panicked. Out of the corner of my eye I see that Emile has appeared behind Habib, in the doorway leading to the stair, while Habib is trying to grab his sister's arm.

"No! You can't do that!" I yell and jump in front of her.

His fist hits my face from the side, with such force that I fall over and land flat on my haunches on the floor. The glass

bowl slips from my left hand and smashes to pieces on the terracotta tiles. It's the first time I've ever been hit in the face
with a fist, another ghastly first, but I'm so shocked that initially I feel no pain. Aïsha screams again, hysterically, drawn
out, unceasingly, and behind her screaming I hear my son's
roar of rage.

"Leave them alone!" shouts Emile while going for Habib
with his fists. "Leave them alone! Leave them alone!"

And Habib, caught by surprise by this attack from behind,
staggers back and loses his balance and also lands on the floor –
I've by now jumped up to try and protect Emile – and grabs a
large shard of the broken salad bowl and gets back onto his
feet holding the shard in front of him like a knife. But Emile
is past feeling fear, it's as if he doesn't even see the weapon in
his opponent's hand, he just charges on to get in another blow
with his fist. Then suddenly everyone is screaming at one
another and Aïsha jumps onto her brother's back from behind
and clutches his neck in a stranglehold and I grab my son's
shoulder to pull him away.

But it's too late.

The rest happens in slow motion. Every action unbearably
drawn out and also without sound. I realise that everyone is
still screaming, because I see the gaping mouths, but I hear
nothing any more. I see Habib's hand flying up to Emile's face.
I see how the razor-edged shard cuts across his cheek. I see the
disbelief flash in my son's eyes as he lifts his palm to his face
and feels the sticky blood under his fingers. I see, I see, I see,
it feels like for ever and ever, the desperate expression on
Habib's face as he raises his knee between my son's legs. Emile
gasping and crumpling forward in agony. Habib shaking off
his sister like a shabby coat, his fist shooting upwards to
deliver the final blow to my son's chin. Emile's head snapping
back. His body falling backwards. I put out my arms in a futile

305

attempt to break his fall. But it makes no difference. Once again it's too late.

The next moment everything returns to normal speed. Emile's head hits the terracotta tiles with a loud crack that makes me realise that my hearing has also returned, and he lies there with his eyes closed, motionless, lifeless, and I hear someone wailing unceasingly. It takes a few seconds before it hits me that it's my own voice wailing.

Everyone around me has become still.

My son is lying still and stretched out on the floor. Aïsha is staring at me with her hand in front of her mouth, her tearful eyes wide with shock. Habib is looking around dazed, as if he's wondering how he got here. Then he swings around without another word, hurries from the kitchen and slams the front door behind him.

I want to yell something at him, something that will wound him for the rest of his life, but I'm on my knees next to my son who thank God, thank God, thank God, is still breathing, and that is suddenly all that matters.

"Ring that emergency number," I say to Aïsha, my voice inexplicably calm, far calmer than I'm feeling. "We need an ambulance."

෴

The bed is hard and high, the walls white and cold like the previous time, but the nurses are talking a different language. Last time they spoke three languages, Afrikaans, English and Xhosa. Now he only hears French. He's in France, he remembers, in a French hospital. A large dressing on his cheek and a bandage round his head.

Alone. Just like last time. Terribly alone, waiting for his father or mother or any familiar face, any reassuring voice.

306

Someone who will tell him that it was all just a nightmare. The heat, the shop, the ice creams that he and his sister took from the self-help freezer in the corner. The two men with balaclavas over their faces who suddenly jumped yelling from behind a shelf waving revolvers around and shouting at the customers to lie down on the floor. No, not a nightmare, a movie. He'd seen the scene so many times in American movies that it felt as though it was not happening to him, as though he was only a spectator. He was frightened of course, his heart was thumping against his breastbone. But his disbelief was greater than his fear. It can't be. That's what he thought.

It can't be!

He can't be in hospital again, lying here wondering if anyone still remembers that he's alive. If anyone cares that he's still alive?

He turns his head on the pillow towards the window, carefully, because every movement makes him clench his teeth in pain, and sees that it is dark already. Which doesn't tell him much, doesn't help him to calculate how long he's been lying here, because this deep into the European winter it's dark almost all day long. At least that's what it feels like when he gets into the bus in the dark every morning and comes home in the dark every afternoon. But today is Wednesday – if it's still today – which means there was no school this afternoon. It was still light when he walked into the kitchen – he can't remember why he went there in the first place – and saw Habib strike his mother.

Something inside him suddenly snapped, something that had been wound up far too tight for far too long, and all his fear evaporated. He wouldn't be cowardly *again*.

He doesn't recall much after that, a hurricane of kicking and hitting and shouting and hurting, blood on his hands, screaming women's voices – and then he woke up in an ambulance racing to the hospital with wailing sirens. His mother's concerned face leaning over him. Like last time. No. Last time he was awake when they lifted him in. Awake but hysterical, apparently, so they gave him an injection to calm him down. Last time his mother wasn't with him, that's one of the reasons he fell apart, because he didn't know if his father and mother would ever forgive him. Or if he could ever forgive himself. Much harder, the latter, that's something he knows nowadays. Last time, he fell asleep in the ambulance with the wailing sirens, against his will, while two emergency workers kept muttering over the stretcher next to him. "We're losing her . . . we're losing her . . . we're losing her."

And when he woke up in the hospital bed, she was gone.

They'd lost her.

He shuts his eyes so tightly that it hurts because he doesn't want to remember that day, he would give anything on earth to never again think about that day, but now it all comes back. Unasked, unwelcome, unstoppable. The entire movie. No, more than a movie, because he feels the sticky sweat in the crook of his legs, the stuffy heat of that day, he smells the ice cream that they took from the freezer, strawberry for her and caramel for him, he relives it with all his senses. Every unforgettable moment.

They're walking barefoot to the corner shop, but it's so un-usually hot that some patches on the pavement feel like stove plates. Manon begins to skip on the spot in panic and reach-es her arms out for him to pick her up, but he doesn't feel like walking through the streets with his little sister in his arms. Just think what it will look like if one of the older boys in the neighbourhood should see him.

"You're a real baby, you know?" He quickly jumps to the next patch of shade under one of the large old oak trees and teases her from there. "You'd swear your little feet are going to melt."

"I'm not a baby!" she shouts, her face pink with heat and anger. "My feet are hurting and if you don't want to pick me up, I'll go back to fetch my slip-ons at home!"

"Jeez, okay," he grumbles, because if she arrives home on her own, crying, he'll be the one to be scolded. Look after your sister, he hears every single day. You're bigger and stronger and more sensible. You must look out for her. "I'll piggy-back you. *Baby.*"

She runs thankfully to where he's standing in the shady spot.

"And what will I get for my trouble?" he demands.

"A bite of my ice cream," she promises, scrambling up on his back as agile as a monkey, putting her arms round his neck.

"Three bites," he decides. "Hey, how many times have I told you not to hold so tight? You're throttling me!"

"What do I get if I stop throttling you?" she giggles.

He plays at trying to shake her off, but she clings to him like a rodeo rider. Her breath is warm against his ear and her curly hair tickles his cheek.

"Okay, a bite of my ice cream," he promises.

"Three bites!" A little burst of laughter and she clasps his throat a little tighter.

"Two," he says and gurgles melodramatically and staggers this way and that across the pavement as if in the throes of dying.

"No, you get three of mine and I get three of yours, otherwise it's not fair."

"Why don't we just swop ice creams? I'll eat yours and you eat mine?"

"No, stupid, it's nicer to taste two kinds."

"Who's your 'stupid'?" he asks and tickles her, which makes her go limp with laughter and slide off his back.

And if he'd known it would be the last time he'd piggy-back her, the last time he'd hear her laugh? Would he have held her closer? Made her laugh even more? Or would everything have happened exactly as it did, because people are the way they are and things happen the way they happen?

There aren't many people in the shop. The fat man behind the counter, his swarthy face glistening with sweat, large patches of perspiration under his arms on the shiny red fabric of his open-neck shirt. A youngish woman in a very short skirt paying for a packet of cigarettes, an older woman in a pink domestic worker's uniform moving slowly between the shelves, two young black men at the magazine rack in the corner, and Emile and Manon at the ice cream freezer in the opposite corner. As usual Manon can't make up her mind – strawberry or chocolate? – and uses a counting-out rhyme to decide the issue. "Eeny, meeny, miny, mo," she recites while Emile rolls his eyes impatiently. The chocolate ice cream wins – and then at the last minute she takes the strawberry after all.

They have just turned to pay at the counter when the two men at the magazine rack pull the balaclavas down over their faces, pluck out pistols and start screaming at everyone. One runs to the entrance to prevent more people from entering, the other one orders the customers to fall down on the floor and the man behind the counter to open the cash register. Emile dives to the floor immediately. He wants to pull his sister down with him, but she's skipped a few steps ahead and is now standing petrified in the middle of the aisle. The nearest robber swings his pistol towards her and shouts: "Flat on your fucking face! Now!"

310

Is it possible that she didn't understand what he was saying to her? Because English wasn't her home language, because she was only five years old, because the balaclava in front of his mouth muffled his words, because he spoke with a strange accent? Or perhaps simply because she had never seen a scene like this in a movie. Her father and mother had always tried to protect her from any form of violence – in films, on the computer, even on the TV news. Now she was standing in a shop in the street where she lived, staring uncomprehendingly at two screaming masked men brandishing pistols. Did she think it was a *game*? Some or other prank? A dream?

Before she can react, the man behind the counter also pulls out a pistol and fires a shot, which makes the robber nearest the entrance flee immediately. The other one realises he's cornered. Emile looks up from where he's trying to leopard crawl to his sister and sees the whites of the man's wide open eyes, the only visible part of his face, and hears Manon starting to cry aloud. (Is this when she realises it's not a game?) And then it seems as if she's getting down onto the floor after all, terrible relief washing over Emile, until he realises that a second shot has been fired. That the robber has shot at Manon, or worse, that the man behind the counter has aimed at the robber and hit Manon.

The robber is now trying to shoot his way out toward the door. He ducks from shelf to shelf while the man behind the counter also fires a few more shots and someone on the floor, possibly the woman in the short dress, makes the most awful whimpering sounds, almost like a little puppy. Emile crawls on his stomach to his sister. He sees the blood on her chest and the disbelief in her flickering eyes and the strawberry ice cream melting in a pink puddle on the floor. Then the robber falls over backwards, just a few steps away from him, with a bloody hole in his throat, his eyes dead. Suddenly it's terribly

311

quiet in the shop. Probably barely a second of complete silence, no one stirring, but after all the shouted commands and the wild shooting and the general panic, it seems endless.

Emile breaks the silence with a scream that rises uncontrollably in his throat, a scream that's never ever going to end, a scream that he will carry with him for the rest of his life, while he holds the hand of his dying sister.

Look after your little sister, he hears every day. You must take care of her. You must look out for her.

"Don't cry, son," he hears his mother whisper as she wipes the damp skin under his eyes with her fingertips.

"Aren't you angry with me?"

"Why would we be angry?"

She leans across the hospital bed, her face very close to his. Her cheek looks swollen and sore.

"She's dead, isn't she?"

Her grey eyes blink rapidly several times.

"Shh. You have to get some rest. You're still a little confused."

"I should have looked after her better."

"Emile . . ."

"I'm sorry, Mom."

"She's been dead for a while," his mother whispers while she wipes away more tears next to his nose. "A year already, to be precise."

As long as that? He frowns and feels the bandage on his head. He looks through the window at the darkness outside. It's as if someone has shot holes in his memory. For the first time in a year he can remember clearly what happened that summer's day in the corner shop, second for second, utterly and unbearably clearly. But a sort of mist hangs over the last three hours.

"Were you with me in the ambulance?"

"I was with you all the time."

He shakes his head. "When I woke up just now . . ."

"I was out in the corridor talking to the doctor. They're going to put the stitches in tomorrow. We've asked for a plastic surgeon to do it, to make sure you won't have an ugly scar. And you can choose whether you want local or general anaesthetic."

"Don't leave me alone, Mom," he begs.

"I won't, son."

"When Manon died, I was alone in the hospital for hours."

She shuts her eyes and shakes her head, brushes tiredly over her painful cheek.

"We were in a state of shock. They gave me a lot of pills to calm me down before we took you home. And your father was like the living dead . . . he just sat there, on one of those ugly plastic hospital chairs, tears streaming down his face . . . "

He has often wondered what happened in those first few hours, how they received the news, whether they were terribly cross with him. Whether they hadn't deliberately stayed away from him. He has never dared to ask them about it.

Now he says without looking at his mother: "Please don't leave me alone again."

"I'm going to sleep in the chair next to you," she assures him. "I'm not going to leave you alone again."

"Not even when we go back to the Cape?"

He sees the sudden alarm in her eyes.

"What do you mean, my love?"

"I want you to stay with us. With me and Dad."

She doesn't answer right away. She looks at him in a strange way, as if there's something she doesn't understand but is too afraid to ask.

"I'll stay with you both as long as you need me," she promises and leans forward to plant a kiss on his forehead.

☙❧

They are sitting on either side of their sleeping son's hospital bed, each holding one of his hands. It is quiet in the room and pitch dark outside the window on the fourth floor, not even a glimmer of a star in the black sky. Without having to discuss it, they decided they would both spend the night with their child. They haven't spoken much since André arrived, in any event not a conversation that could be followed by anyone else. Every now and again their eyes meet over the child's body and then they carry on with their wordless communication; each one's gaze full of self-reproach and guilt and remorse.

"When I think that I brought that bastard into the house!" André suddenly bursts out. "He could have killed all of you!"

"Shh." Hester points to the sleeping child. "That's not what he wanted to do. He wanted to give us all a fright – hurt us – not kill us."

"It could have turned out differently. We know how easily things can turn out differently from what one wants, don't we? If Emile's head had hit that floor any harder, he could have been dead. Or suffered brain damage. If that shard of glass had nicked his eye, he could have been blinded. It's bad enough that he'll have a scar for the rest of his life, but it could have been so much worse!"

"The plastic surgeon says he shouldn't be left with too much of a lesion," Hester tries to console. "After a few years it will hopefully be just a faint little line on his cheek."

"What is it with us, Hester?" André drops his head into his hands, his elbows resting on his knees. "Why can't we protect our children against injury? Why can't it be us who get shot at and hit and cut?"

"André. He was trying to protect me today. That's why he got injured."

"I know," sighs André. "I know."

314

A few minutes tick by before Hester asks: "Do you know what tomorrow's date is?"

He lifts his head and looks at her in surprise.

"I thought about it the whole week," he admits, "but with all that's happened in the last few hours . . ."

Aïsha had been waiting for him at the house, trembling and tearful, and told him how her brother had stormed in, that Hester had tried to protect her, that Emile in turn had tried to protect Hester. Emile was the one most seriously injured, she told him crying, his cheek gashed, the back of his head split open, unconscious. André jumped into his car and drove like a man possessed to the hospital. An hour later he couldn't recall a single second of the journey. One moment he was standing in his kitchen listening with rising panic to Aïsha, the next he was here in the hospital with his wife and son.

The doctor explained that he would stitch the cut and do a brain scan and keep the patient there for a few days to make sure there wasn't more serious damage.

"Like what?" André whispered, speechless from shock and fright.

"At this stage there are no signs of further problems," the fatherly grey-haired doctor soothed his fears. "But with head injuries one can't be too careful. We want to be absolutely sure he's all right before we send him home. And the rest will probably do him good. According to your wife he's come through a traumatic year."

So have all of us, André wanted to exclaim and lean his head on that fatherly shoulder and weep his heart out.

And the nightmare seems to be never-ending. Here we bloody-well are, in a hospital *again*. Exactly a year after our daughter died.

He just nodded and went to sit opposite his wife, as he is sitting now, with their son's body a bridge between them.

"It couldn't have happened on a worse day, could it?" he mumbles with his head again in his hands.

"I don't know. I've been wondering about that for hours. Beatrice would probably say it was destined to be so. That it should have happened today of all days."

"Ah," sighs André, *"The Hairdresser's Guide to the Universe."* She doesn't react to his mocking tone.

"Some or other Guide who wants to teach us a lesson?" she muses.

"As if we haven't learnt enough in the past year."

"Have we though?" she asks, staring unseeing in front of her.

"We should probably try to sleep for an hour or two," he says after they've sat in silence opposite one another for a while. "Shall we switch off the light?"

Half an hour later he knows that he won't get any sleep tonight, not in this armchair, more uncomfortable than a tourist-class airplane seat, not with all the awful memories that have been churned up by this visit to the hospital. Yet he keeps his eyes closed – too tired to force them open – and tries to replay the scenes in his head as a spectator rather than a participant. The only way, he has learned, to keep the pain at bay.

That afternoon he arrived home earlier because it was the last week of the children's school summer holiday, because Hester constantly hinted that he wasn't spending enough time with them, and because it was in any case too hot to work. The children had been hanging listlessly round the house, complaining about not having a swimming pool. "Everyone has a pool," Emile had grumbled, "except us." André laughed at him and said he would take him to the nearest township so that he could see how many children there knew the luxury of a private pool. Hester could see another argument brewing be-

316

tween father and son, so she suggested that the children go to the corner shop to buy ice cream while André got changed.

"We can drive to the beach as soon as you get back. For a sunset picnic. How does that sound?"

They were all instantly enthusiastic about the idea.

"Well then, here's money for the ice cream. I'll be packing the coolbox."

The children set off laughing and arguing while André went to the room to take off his long trousers, socks and shoes and jump into the shower eagerly. No question of a last good-bye. No premonition of danger or disaster.

Nothing.

Even half an hour later when Hester had finished packing the coolbox and the children weren't back yet, they weren't worried. (Why not, André wonders now. How is it possible that they could have been so carefree, so unsuspecting, so fearless?) Emile had probably met a friend along the way, they might have stopped at someone's house, after all it had happened before that they would "quickly" slip out of the house and only return about an hour later. They knew everyone in the street. It was a secure, prosperous neighbourhood. They weren't even alarmed when they heard the wailing sirens. They lived in a big city with a high crime rate. The shrill sound of police sirens and ambulance sirens, car alarms and burglar alarms in homes, the barking of fierce dogs and the shouting of fierce security guards, all these ominous sounds had long become background noise. Even in a safe, prosperous neighbourhood like theirs. (Unbelievable, André now thinks. Where he's living now, he would be startled out of his wits if he were to hear a siren or an alarm.) It was only when the doorbell rang and he saw two sombre policemen on his doorstep, that his heart was crushed by an invisible hand.

"Mister Human?" the older, bigger man said. About his own age. Probably also a father of half-grown children. These

317

thoughts flashed through his mind before the man's words sank in. "I'm afraid we have bad news . . ."

After that he was so shocked that he has no clear memory of the next few hours. Just a jumble of emotions. The spark of hope that the child was perhaps still alive as they raced to the hospital. The suffocating fear that she was no longer alive. The uncertainty, the incredulity, the dazedness. And then, in the hospital, the lifeless five-year-old body. The red-blonde curls damp against her forehead. The plump bottom lip, the dirty fingernails, the graze on her knee where she'd fallen the week before. All these insignificant details he noticed, drank in, just to keep the overall image of his dead five-year-old daughter from settling in his thoughts.

André gets up quickly, forces his eyes open, waits for his heartbeat to subside while looking round the dark hospital room. His mind still refuses to connect when it comes to that image. No parent can look at his dead child without damaging his eyes, he sometimes thinks. It's like staring straight into the sun, something that gets burned into your eye tissue, and thereafter nothing is ever quite as clear again.

It is the most extreme loss of innocence.

Emile mumbles something: restless, anxious, indistinct sounds. Hester immediately leans over him and strokes his forehead. André watches his wife in the weak light filtering in from the passage. The child gives a smothered cry and rolls his head on the pillow. André grips his son's hand securely.

This is what remains, he thinks, this ordinary trinity. Father, mother, son.

"Shh," whispers Hester. "We're here, love. We'll stay with you."

Perhaps it's true, thinks André. He's become too afraid to hope. But perhaps Hester has at last come back to them.

❦

318

To think there are parents who never see any of their children lying helpless in a hospital bed. Is it worse when it happens for the first time, when you still have your parental innocence, the illusion that your children will be an endless source of joy and fulfilment? Or is it worse when you've been there already? There, as far as any parent can go, to hell and back.

If you've seen one of your children lying lifeless in a hospital.

I wander through the long, bleak corridors of the hospital trying to swallow the awful coffee I've just bought from a vending machine. I need the caffeine to stay awake. The restless night in the armchair next to my son's bed has begun to take its toll. The doctors all seem impatient and unfriendly, the nurses like enormous white bats, nowhere a comforting face. Maybe I'm just so tired that I'm hallucinating. I want to go home, shower and wash my hair, get into clean clothes. And sleep for at least twelve hours on end. But home feels so far away I don't know if I'll ever get there again.

The cut on Emile's cheek has just been stitched under local anaesthetic, with me holding his hand. He was pale with fear – like many males he has a phobia of needles; even the most insignificant prick to draw a drop of blood for a medical test terrifies him – but he stared fixedly in front of him and didn't once complain. It is months since I've sat so close to him for so long, both of us unable to escape. And because the spotlight above the operation table shone blindingly bright on his face, I noticed for the first time the dark down on his still childish upper lip.

My son is becoming a man. Probably has been doing so for a while, but I didn't want to see it, for months I've deliberately been looking past him to protect myself. He had to come and lie in a hospital, with a cut on his cheek and his dark eyes full of fear and a bandage round his head, for me really to see him

319

again, at last. The surly young man with the downy upper lip who still needs me.

Who would have thought that?

I make a face involuntarily as I force down the last sip of coffee, throw the plastic cup into a garbage can and walk back to my post next to my child's bed. Only yesterday I still thought I would be able to turn from him and his father. Not get on the plane at the last moment. Let them go their own ways. Without me, for the time being.

Now everything has changed.

⤚⤙

"Aïsha!" I call as I open the front door. "We were worried about you!"

The swelling round her eye has subsided, just a yellowish tinge that she hides under make-up. The scab on her lip looks dry and healthy, but the tooth still hasn't been replaced. We greet in the French manner, kiss on cheek, making me grimace when my sore cheek brushes against hers.

"With all our swellings and bruises we probably look like two old ladies who've had plastic surgery," I try to joke. "Take off your coat, come and have some tea."

"How is Emile?"

"Much better than when you last saw him. And you?"

"Also better than when you last saw me."

When I returned home from the hospital on the day of the attack, she was no longer in the house. Just left a note on the kitchen table saying how sorry she was about everything, that she didn't want to inconvenience us any longer, that she was going back to her parents.

"I came twice yesterday too," she says, lifting the cat onto her lap in her customary way, "but there was no one home."

"We were at the hospital most of the time. But it's going well. The doctor says we can bring him home tomorrow."

"I wanted to go and visit him."

"It's not too late."

"Won't he mind?"

"On the contrary. He'll be delighted. You can imagine how bored he is by now. Only his mother and father hanging round all day. Oh yes, and Nathalie was there yesterday. That made his day."

"What does it look like, the . . ." She struggles to find the right word, points uncomfortably at her cheek and drops her eyes quickly to the cat in her lap. "The cut on his face?"

"The stitches aren't out yet. There's a large plaster on it, so for the present one can't see anything. But hopefully it won't be an ugly scar. On the other hand, Nathalie said yesterday that her knees go weak at the sight of a guy with a 'pirate scar'. So I suppose now he hopes that *something* will still show."

"I'm really deeply sorry about what happened."

Suddenly she looks close to tears. I pull up a chair next to her and take her hand.

"It isn't your fault, Aïsha."

"If I hadn't come to shelter here . . ."

"Listen to me, Aïsha. If you knew how many times I've said to myself: If I hadn't on that day, at exactly that moment, told the children to go and buy ice cream . . . Would my daughter still be alive? I don't know. No one knows. I just know that you can drive yourself insane if you start thinking like that."

She looks at me silently. I have never spoken to her about my daughter's death. I get up to take the whistling kettle off the stove.

"My brother has disappeared," she says while I pour boiling water into the lavender blue teapot. Her voice is even softer than usual. "The night after . . . what happened here. He hasn't been home since."

"Do you have any idea where he might have gone?" I ask carefully.

She shakes her head and scratches the purring cat behind its ears.

"I think he's gone far from here. To make sure the police don't pick him up."

"Did you lay a charge against him?"

She glances up at me swiftly. Confusion flickering like candlelight in her dark eyes. "But didn't you?"

"We were dealing with more important matters. If my husband had seen him on Wednesday, he wouldn't only have charged him, he would surely have assaulted him too. He was quite beside himself with rage. But now . . . I don't know . . . what do you think?"

"It doesn't matter what I think. It's your son lying there in hospital."

"You could also have ended up in hospital, Aïsha. You know that. But you still didn't want to lay a charge."

She sits with her elbow on the table and holds her hand like a shield in front of her eyes while she slowly stirs her tea.

"He's my brother," she says at last, too uncomfortable to look at me. "I don't want him to have a criminal record."

"You'd prefer him to go on assaulting you?"

"I don't think he will hit me again any time soon. He's had a big fright. And as long as you're here he won't venture near the village."

"And when we leave in a month's time?"

"I don't know," she admits with a shrug and slowly sips her tea. "I think it will be okay. I think he's learned his lesson. He isn't a fanatic Muslim, Hester, he's just . . . a lost Frenchman. I should know him by now."

"And suppose he comes back, Aïsha, and again tries to force you to cover your head and prevent you from wearing the clothes you want to wear?"

"Then I'll probably have to marry a creepy old widower as soon as possible," she says mockingly. "Once I'm married my brother won't have any say over me any more."

"No, then it's your husband who has the say, isn't it?"

She gives me that wise old woman look of hers and for a long time says nothing, then decides to change the subject.

"What's going to become of the cat when you go?"

"Do you have any suggestions?" I ask hopefully.

"I can adopt him if you'd like that."

That's what Manon would have liked, I nearly say.

"Won't it be a problem for the rest of your family?"

"Habib doesn't exactly like cats," she says and strokes Fantôme's back absent-mindedly. "But then Habib isn't there any more."

I nod, grateful. For the time being Habib isn't there any more.

"I'm going to miss you, you know You were my first French friend."

"I'm not French," she reminds me. "I'm Moroccan."

We smile complicitly.

"No wonder it was so easy."

12

Transience, says my husband, is what this year abroad has taught him. Transience – and how to lay floor tiles, he adds with a laconic smile. He's already using the perfect tense, I notice. We're only leaving in three weeks' time, but he has already started pulling up the tent pegs. The work on the house is done, his Project completed, his sabbatical expired. His body is still here but his head is in Cape Town already, in his architect's office with the view over the sea, engrossed in the next challenging project.

His office has always reminded me of a cathedral, the fantastic light falling through the large windows, the almost devotional space, the creative gravity and the enthusiasm bordering on worship. I don't have any such salvation. Religion, job satisfaction, creativity, call it what you will, I have no raft to jump onto, no plank to grab hold of, nothing to get me from here to there. From here where I can survive in safety, protected and sedated and half dead, to there where everything will be dug up and torn open, glistening and dangerous, immediate and overwhelming. Nothing to stop me from sinking.

What do I have to look forward to? Forcing bored schoolchildren to conjugate French verbs? Listening to the predictable complaints of my colleagues in the staffroom at every break? I wasn't always so cynical about my work. There was a time when I was a good and enthusiastic teacher. But I've spent a year in the land of loss. It's a place that changes one.

I don't know if I'd still describe myself as a "francophile".

I'm disillusioned with France, actually with the whole of Europe, with the potential for violence always lurking just underneath the top layer of civilisation.

I'm sitting in the kitchen with a cup of cold coffee and a clean sheet of paper in front of me, listening to the lament of the wind around the house. *Oh the flock of white geese.* A last letter to Myriam, I decided. *The closer to the mountain, the cooler the breeze.* But the paper is still clean, a beach without footprints, and my coffee is getting colder.

This morning I went for a long walk in spite of the wind. Now that Habib has apparently fled, I can walk again without fear. All the familiar paths I want to explore one last time.

In and out of the narrow alleys of the village, diagonally across the square where a layer of ice covers the fountain water on some mornings and where the circle of teenage smokers has for quite some time not been seen, under the bare plane trees and past the deserted veranda of the café, past the double-storey stone school building where the little crowd of pupils scream and yell at break like a great multitude. My eyes always involuntarily look for Aurore – impossible to miss her among the pale winter faces – and my wistfulness lifts a little if she sees me and waves enthusiastically.

Or towards the other side, past the bakery and the super-market, in the direction of the sunflower fields, now of course just bare stretches of earth, and the wild hedges where in summer I ate the sweetest blackberries of my life.

Or up the hill, with the winding road past the graveyard and the olive grove and the high vineyards right up to the cherry orchard where I lay grieving in spring.

Or once again to the other side, down to the thick undergrowth near the river, to the forest where wild boar and pheasant are hunted and where shots frequently ring out in winter. Where Habib taught me a lesson. These days I make sure

I wear the reddest of red scarves when I go that way so that no hunter can mistake me for his prey.

And wherever I tramp, I'm filled with wonder at how still everything has become, how stark and colourless and bare, all except the shiny red berries clustering in some of the hedges like Christmas decorations. I thought the landscape was empty, minimal like a Japanese water-colour painting, when we arrived here a year ago. Now I see that it can become even emptier. The vineyards have recently been pruned, the long swaying shoots cut, leaving only the truncated stumps in the stony soil like bodies with amputated limbs.

I won't be here when those stumps produce leaves again.

My husband still likes to believe that he's rebuilt this house so that our family may one day holiday in it, but he has already decided we won't be able to afford an overseas holiday next year. We'll have to let the house to get an income from it. A material reward for his sweat and labour, for the pain and suffering and hardship of the past year, that may be how he regards it. I wonder if we'll ever holiday here. It just doesn't feel like a holiday home. Too many tears have been shed under its roof. Too many reproaches hurled against these walls. Too many wounds nursed here.

And I've still not written a word to Myriam. I stare at the blank sheet with a growing feeling of betrayal. I take a sip of coffee, now so cold I spit it out and empty the rest into the sink. As if I'm betraying her by returning to my country. Such foolishness!

∽∽

Last. Strange that a word can lurk in the head like that and consume all other words and thoughts. At this moment Emile would like to look at Nathalie, really look openly, instead of stealing glances, so that for the rest of his life he'll be able to recall the exact shade of her skin in the late afternoon light of the weak winter sunshine. Not black, not brown, not caramel, not a single colour that he can place or name, maybe a combination of all the colours that he knows. But every time he turns towards her, the monster in his head roars: Last. Last. Last.

The last time he'll walk with her through the streets of Avignon. The last time they'll eat together at McDonald's. (Also, as it happens, the first, but that just makes that "last time" bite even deeper.) The last chance to say what he's been trying to say for months.

She walks with long legs and graceful strides next to him, all giraffe, as always. The only coherent idea still in his head, besides the knowledge that something is over for ever, is the hope that he will see her again one day. Otherwise he won't be able to walk away from here today and fly off home in a few days' time.

Home.

That's the only word that can drive out the monster in his head. Home, home, home, it beats in his blood. He invited her for a hamburger at McDonald's, a sort of farewell present after school closed today for the winter vacation. When school reopens two weeks from now, he'll be far from here. At home.

"I'll come with you," she agreed, "if we promise each other we won't get sad."

"Deal," he said immediately. "I don't feel like a sob story either."

"And the one who breaks the promise, pays for both," she suggested laughing.

Now she grins nervously and says they should perhaps have invited some other friends along too. Like who, Emile wants to know. Like Peet, she says. And what about Winston?

"Winston is a drip," grumbles Emile. "He's not my friend."

"He likes you!"

"So what? You don't have to be friends with everyone who likes you, do you?"

"I suppose not, but . . ." she says and looks away.

If someone has as few friends as you, he can't be too choosy, can he? He wonders if that is what she was about to say.

When she looks at him again, her expression has changed, her smile now teasing. "And what about Lee?"

"What about her?" he wants to know.

"Maybe we should have invited her as well? And Bianca – to keep Peet company?"

"It's not company that Peet wants from Bianca. If he had to sit opposite her at a table, he'd get all tongue-tied and his eyes would pop and his brain would fly out of his ears. It's gross, enough to put anyone off their food, I promise you."

"Okay, forget about Bianca," she giggles. "But you could have given Lee a last chance."

"A last chance to do what?"

"Well, like asking for your address in Cape Town or giving you a kiss or whatever. You know?"

No, thinks Emile, how would I know? A little way ahead in Avenue de la République, he sees the giant yellow M of the fast food restaurant and involuntarily lengthens his strides.

"If she'd really wanted to do something," he says, "she could have done it by now."

"You didn't exactly make it easy for her, you know!" Nathalie stops with her hands indignantly at her sides. "Ever since I told you that she likes you, you've been looking right through her!"

"I've always looked right through her. She's so skinny I can't help it."

"Another reason we could have invited her!" Nathalie exclaims laughing. "Don't you think she could do with a hamburger?"

"Listen, please stop trying to lumber me with your friend," he requests in mock irritation when they get to the glass door of the restaurant. "It's too late. I'm off in a few days. And anyway, I like someone else."

Her head turns towards him in surprise, but he looks straight in front of him – blushing, of course, he can feel the burning sensation under his new scar – and she says nothing more.

As usual there's a crowd in the restaurant and they have to wait in line a long time to order their food, but they entertain each other with silly remarks about other customers and laugh loudly every so often. Anything to avoid a sob story, says Emile to himself. And yet, halfway through his hamburger and an enormous helping of fries, he perceives a change in her face. She's still smiling, but there's a seriousness there.

"There's one thing you have to do before you leave," she says.

There are many things I should have done, he wants to say.

"You have to translate a sentence for me," she says. "You know what I'm talking about, don't you?"

Not immediately.

"Something you said to me in your own language," she reminds him.

He should have known that she wouldn't let him get away with it.

"*Jy is baie mooi,*" he says in Afrikaans, before translating the words. "You are very pretty."

"Thank you." She smiles almost incredulously, as if no one has ever told her that she's pretty. "You aren't too bad looking yourself, you know? Especially since getting that pirate scar on your cheek."

329

If this had been a movie, it would have been the perfect moment to lean across the table and take her hand. But this isn't a movie, so all he takes is another bite of his hamburger. He chews as slowly as he can, waiting for the embarrassment to subside.

"And the girl you like so much?" she asks with a forced laugh.

He is astonished. For the first time since he's known her, he has the impression that she's feeling just as insecure as he does.

"You know who it is."

She nods, her eyes now pitch black with seriousness. He almost stops breathing. His life, it seems, depends on what she will say to him next. Then she claps her hand over her mouth and opens her eyes comically wide.

"Oops! We said we weren't going to get serious."

"We said we weren't going to get sad. That's not quite the same."

"We said we'd be cheerful. Doesn't matter if we're serious or sad, the point is we're not being cheerful. Don't worry, it's my fault, I'll pay for the hamburgers."

"No ways," he immediately protests, his male ego bruised. "I'm the one who invited you."

"A deal is a deal," she silences him. "I'm not as hungry as I thought. Do you want the rest of my *frites*?"

And with that, the moment has passed. His opportunity for a romantic farewell gone for ever. And maybe better so, he tries to convince himself while watching her lick a splash of ketchup from her plump upper lip. Now he needn't even tell Zakes and Pietman and Dylan about her. He needn't share her with anyone else.

She can remain what she was from the beginning: a possibility rather than a certainty. Something that might even entice him back to this country one day.

"You're very pretty," he says once again.

Perhaps that's all he's been trying to say for months.

⁓⁓

Late at night André heats a mug of milk in the microwave oven, stirs in a drop of honey and a good shot of whisky, and drinks it slowly, standing in front of the kitchen window staring out. Almost full moon, no clouds, stars like splinters of ice in the black sky. *As wide as the Lord's mercy, the fields lie in starlight and shade.* He's a little surprised at a well-known Afrikaans poem popping up in his head so unexpectedly; when last did that happen? Hester is supposed to be the poetic one in this relationship – although it's been many months since Hester has said anything poetic.

Except perhaps for the promise that she whispered to her son in hospital the other night.

A week from now they all fly home. He doesn't know how long his wife's promise will hold if her previous life starts to overwhelm her. And that's not the only reason he can't sleep tonight. He's been struggling with something he's keeping from her. He wonders what her reaction would be if she were to know. Would she feel betrayed? No, he decides, wandering through the living room with his mug of milk – closing an open magazine here, picking a cushion up off the floor there – betrayal sounds far too dramatic. Protection, is how he'd like to think of it.

He sinks down onto the couch, sips his spiked milk. Stares absently at the last coals glowing in the grate. The stone frames round the doors glimmer palely in the moonlight. He looks round with a feeling of modest gratification: not as an architect proud of his creation, simply as a labourer satisfied with his handiwork. He rubs his hands, feels the calluses on

331

his palms and the hard skin on his fingertips. Strange to think that he'll soon be sitting in an office again, wearing neat clothes, having clean nails, working more with his imagination than with his calloused hands.

He switches on the TV with the remote and shakes his head at the tattooed female singer on his son's favourite music channel. The sound is turned off, which makes the vulgar dance movements and sentimental expressions look all the more absurd. If the warm milk and whisky don't work, he'll have to take a tablet. Hester has mentioned those tranquillisers somewhere in the house. If the expiry date hasn't passed by now. They were after all prescribed more than a year ago.

Difficult to believe. Some days it feels like yesterday.

Other days like something that happened in a former life.

Impatiently he presses the remote to eliminate the tattooed teenager and walks back into the kitchen to leave the empty mug in the sink. This is the room that probably gave him most trouble: the floor tiles, the wall tiles, all the electrical equipment that needed to be installed, the wooden cupboards that had to fit exactly, all his own handiwork. Habib's also, of course, but he still prefers not to think of Habib. He still can't forgive himself for bringing such danger into the house. Working unsuspectingly alongside Habib during all those months. Refusing to listen when Hester tried to warn him. Allowing his wife and son to be assaulted in their own house.

He's failed miserably, he thinks, going slowly up the stairs, careful not to stumble and wake his wife or son. He's failed, once again, in any family man's most important duty. Once again he hasn't been able to protect his family.

In the bathroom with the womb-like walls – another room that cost him a lot of sweat and sore muscles and quite a few calluses – he rummages in the second-hand cupboard under the basin where their basic first aid kit is kept. Plasters, antiseptic ointment, aspirin. No sign of Hester's sedatives. He sits on the edge of the Victorian bath and tries to figure out where she would have hidden the packet. In the smaller bathroom on the top floor?

On the way up he quietly pushes open his son's bedroom door. In the moonlight streaming through the open shutters, the child's body is a motionless lump in the bed. He goes forward until he can hear the even breathing, a faint snoring sound in the nose that's still slightly blocked from a head cold, and looks at his son's sleeping face. The scar on the left cheek is still pink and a little raised. Not a large cut, but even in the moonlight it can't be missed. An unwelcome souvenir of this year in France that the child will carry for the rest of his life.

The empty room next door is kept closed to conserve heat and maintain an even temperature in the house, but as on so many other nights André can't resist opening it. That ritual of look-how-peacefully-the-children-are-sleeping has over the years become a compulsion. First looking into one child's room, then the other. Even if the other child's bed has been empty for a long time, the room cold as the grave. A ritual is a ritual. Something you can't just shake off. He opens the door just a crack and stares with dull disbelief at the empty bed.

Then he takes the narrower steeper stairs to the top floor, sneaks past his sleeping wife in the double bed, and closes the door of the small bathroom behind him before switching on the light. Here too he finds no trace of the tranquillisers. He looks through all the little bottles on the shelves, opens all the drawers making much more noise than he realises, until Hester suddenly appears in the doorway, her face creased with sleep and her eyes not properly open.

"Wha' ya looking for?" she mumbles.

"What became of those tranquillisers of yours?"

333

"Why?"

He looks at her uncomprehendingly for a moment, as if he can't really remember what he wanted the tablets for. She gives a long yawn and goes to sit on the toilet with her pyjama trousers pulled down to her knees and urinates in a thin whistling stream. He'll never tire of looking at her, it dawns on him, even in such an undignified position on the toilet.

"I can't get to sleep."

"Is it because we're . . . on the way home that you're so stressed?"

"I suppose so," he answers and evades her eyes. "Everything that has to be arranged at the last minute. Everything still to be packed and put away . . ."

"Beatrice is coming to help all day tomorrow," she reminds him and yawns again.

"I know. You go back to bed. We needn't both stay awake."

"Have you looked in my handbag?" she asks over her shoulder as she leaves the bathroom. "For the tablets?"

"Where's your handbag?"

"Down where our coats and jackets hang," she answers from the bed, her voice already dull with sleep.

He quickly slips down the stairs – this time with the light on – and finds her worn black handbag on the coat rack near the front door. He puts his hand in without looking and feels around in its depths as you would search in dirty dishwater for a knife or a fork. Women's handbags have always made him inexplicably nervous. He finds something rectangular. Not a flat box of pills, he sees as he lifts out an envelope with photographs.

That envelope, he recalls, with thóse photographs.

The moonlight is bright enough to look at the photos next to the window. In the top one, all four of them are sitting on an armchair with a Christmas tree behind them, he and his son with silly faces balancing on the armrests, his smiling wife between them, his daughter safely in her lap. Safely.

He pushes the envelope back into the bag without looking at the rest of the photos and climbs the stairs to his room again.

Sooner or later tonight he'll surely fall asleep, he consoles himself. Meanwhile he has enough to think about. The almost six years that his daughter spent with them, instead of the many years ahead that they'll have to live without her. The thankfulness he felt the other night in the hospital when he heard that his son wasn't seriously injured. And his inexplicable love for his wife. Indestructible too, he's beginning to suspect, after all they've lived through this year.

Love at a distance, he thinks in the doorway of his room as he admires his wife's sleeping form in the double bed, that's what he'll have to get used to. Sometimes she'll allow him to caress her, sometimes even to make love to her, he hopes. But mostly they'll live on two islands with an immeasurable stretch of ocean between them. And that's not so bad, he tries to convince himself, that's probably how most relationships work anyway. He just knows he has lost too much. All he wants now, is to keep what he still has.

She's lying on her side as always, with one leg stretched out and one knee bent up, her hand protectively in front of her mouth. Protective, apologetic, defensive, how would he know? All his former certainties have fallen away.

He gets into bed and carefully slips in behind her back, as close as possible without waking her. For a long time he lies listening to her breathing before he risks sliding his arm round her waist. She groans and stirs restlessly, but she doesn't roll away from him.

All his certainties have vanished, except the love he feels for her.

"I have something to tell you," he whispers into her neck.

"I didn't want to tell you, I wanted to wait for you to discover it for yourself, in the hope, of course, that you never would. But it feels deceitful to keep quiet."

She sighs and mumbles something like 'whassit'.

"That woman in the prison is dead," he whispers. "Myriam Soro?"

She arches her back and pulls up her legs into a foetal position. No, not deceit. Definitely not betrayal. It's just a question of protection.

"I saw it in the newspaper this morning. A small item. Easy to miss. Looks like suicide. An overdose of pills. It's a mystery how she got her hands on the pills."

She shakes her shoulders and moves away from him, out from under his arm. Not deceiving, he says over and over to himself, just protecting.

"I threw the newspaper away and decided not to tell you. If it had happened at any other time, I would have acted differently. But we leave in two days' time. You needn't know, Hes, it would just upset you. And if you heard it in some other way, well, I suppose I could always pretend I hadn't known either."

No further movement from his wife or sounds out of her mouth. All he hears, is her steady breathing. And his heart hammering in his chest like a hand against a door.

⮞⮜

Last night I woke from a terribly strange dream and noticed that the moonlight outside was casting an extraordinary sheen over everything. It drew me from my warm bed to stumble sleepily to the window. A thick layer of fresh snow on the balcony and the surrounding roofs reflected the moonlight like a mirror. A magical scene for which I had to wait until my last night in this house. The snow appearing so silently while we slept unsuspectingly. To wake and find everything different, unrecognisably different, from a few hours before when we went to bed

Unreal. That's the word that came to mind.

In my dream Myriam also looked unrecognisably different from the newspaper photograph that I hid for weeks in the kitchen drawer. She was smiling, a wide wonderful smile, and her eyes were gleaming. But she didn't speak, even in my dream she was still mute, just pointed to two little girls walking below us on a dirt road. We were sitting on a roof, a clay tile roof like here in France, but the two children below us were somewhere in Africa, of that I'm sure: the uneven dirt road, the dust hanging in the dry air, the thorn trees in the background, everything pointed to that. "What are their names?" I wanted to know. She showed me that they were wearing cardboard signs around their necks. *Tempête* was written on one and *Tonnère* on the other. "Are these the names you chose for your children?" I wanted to know. "Storm and Thunder?" She just nodded with that wide, wide smile.

I think about this strange dream while walking up the hill for the last time, slowly and laboriously because with each step I sink to my ankles in the fresh snow. Apparently more snow is not predicted – for which I'm thankful because we have to leave for the airport in a few hours and neither I nor my husband is used to driving in snow. Yesterday the house was cleaned from top to bottom – Aïsha and Beatrice both came to help – and our suitcases are packed and all our baggage ready to be loaded in the car. Just this last walk, not really for sentimental reasons, more to fill the time till we leave.

I have to stop every few steps to catch my breath. Every time I look back, I see my winding footprints following me like a guilty conscience. In front of me the snow is foam-white

337

and pristine, no other tracks, no one having gone up the hill before me today. After all my wandering of the past year, I ought to know this landscape like my own face in the mirror, but the snow makes everything look different. The knobbly black vine stumps, rough grey trunks of the olive trees, the stone wall curving round the graveyard, every bit of flat surface is covered with a layer of snow as thick as a mattress. The long weeping branches of a willow look indescribably fragile, a creation of handblown glass, gleaming in the white light.

I wish my daughter could see this!

I wonder if for the rest of my life I will feel this yearning every time I see something that somehow moves me.

I walk past the gate of the graveyard, where she persuaded me to adopt the black kitten, many months before, when she was still near me all day long. Yesterday Aïsha carried the cat home with her. And what if her brother returns, Emile asked worriedly, and kicks Fantôme out? If her brother returns, I thought, it won't be only the cat that's in danger. But I said nothing because Aïsha so badly wants to believe that her brother has learned his lesson, that he has had a big enough fright, that he will treat her better in future. I can only hope that, contrary to my disillusionment and pessimism, she's right. Or else that she'll find a husband who'll treat her better than her brother. That the proverbial creepy old widower won't be too old or too creepy.

I held her tight, her and the cat in her arms, and then opened my arms to let them go. That's all I've been doing this past year, I realised at that moment. Opening my arms – at first they had to be forced open, but by now I've learned to open them with a kind of acquiescence – and letting go.

Aïsha's eyes filled with tears and she looked down to whisper something to the cat. Fantôme regarded me with large

338

yellow eyes, a little reproachful because I'm going away, but also rather pleased with his new caretaker. My eyes remained dry.

I did say, didn't I, that I've learnt to let go.

Every so often a pile of melted snow falls from the branches of a tree, a soundless white flurry that frightens me and a few times narrowly misses me. Three quarters of the way up I have to stop again, gasping for breath. I look out over the town, finding it difficult to discern the landmarks: the round castle tower, the rectangular church tower, the roof of our house halfway between the castle tower and the single tall cypress tree. Everything looks the same under the snow, like bodies under white sheets, vague shapes in the distance.

A crowd of yelling children playing on the square – amazing how far their voices carry on the floccose white silence – helps me to find my bearings. If that is the square, then the church tower must be a little higher up to the left . . . and the castle tower closer to me . . . and the cypress in a straight line to the right of the round tower. Yes, I see it, there's our house. Where my husband will now be walking tensely back and forth and compulsively looking under beds and on top of cupboards to make sure that we haven't forgotten anything important. Where my son will be sitting moodily on the couch watching MTV because we've forbidden him to hang around in his room after it was cleaned and tidied yesterday. How well I know them. How much I love them.

How nearly I let them go too.

My son will have a scar on his face for the rest of his life because he wanted to defend me. Maybe it isn't even love, maybe only instinct. This same instinct that now makes me stay with him and his father.

Perhaps this is the famous instinct for optimism that my mother believes comes with the motherly instinct.

Then again, maybe this is exactly what love is? Love that refuses to go away, never will, in spite of everything?

My eyes rove back to the square where the children are running and stopping and yelling and ducking, having a snow-ball fight, I would guess. I imagine that I recognise Aurore's bright pink anorak amongst the moving flashes of colour. It was difficult to take leave of her and her mother yesterday, even more difficult than of Aïsha and the cat, but now that's done too. The slight and tentative little body in the bright pink anorak, the questions in those black eyes, the fragrance of her forehead. *Mother's child, Mother's tousle-haired child.*

I turn away from the village to walk the last stretch up to the cherry orchard. Still no other tracks, no sounds besides the cawing of two crows in an uncultivated field higher up the hill. Small black specks in the wide open white landscape, the only movement, now that I can't see the children on the square any more. No, I notice when I look back to measure the depth of my footprints in the snow, quite a way lower down the hill another lone walker has appeared.

The cherry orchard looks almost as breathtakingly vaporous and floating white as it did in spring. One can almost imagine that it's blossom and not snow clinging like foam to the branches, at any rate until you realise that everything around the orchard is also white, winter white instead of spring green. I make my way past the orchard, taking the winding footpath to the top, so that I can take a last look at the whole valley. Maybe I have after all become sentimental about my farewell, because suddenly my eyes are stinging with tears. Or it could also be simply because my feet are aching with cold.

Panting now, I stumble up the steep path to the top, lean for a while against the iron cross to get my breath back and wonder, suddenly disenchanted again, what I actually wanted to see from up here. Everything is white, boringly and endlessly white. And my feet are aching and my fingers feel frozen. But I've gone to the trouble of getting here, so I compel myself to take the time to look out over the valley. And for the umpteenth time I wonder what Beatrice would have made of last night's dream.

Or you, Myriam. You were, after all, the one playing the leading role.

I dreamt that while we were still sitting on that clay tile roof – you still mute, with that beatific smile – you pointed to something behind me. On turning round, I saw that a piece of white cloth had caught in a TV antenna, a little white blanket that I'd knitted before Manon was born. And there it was now, hanging in tatters, flapping in the wind, like the sail of an old-fashioned ship that has come through a terrible storm at sea. A pirate ship, that was the image that came to mind.

And when I looked back, Myriam, you had vanished. Not fallen off the roof, because then I'd surely have got a fright, and there was nothing frightening about your disappearance. You were suddenly just not there. Like a rainbow. Gone.

And then I woke and noticed the unearthly moonlight and walked to the window and saw the fresh snow outside. This part, when I was already awake, felt more unreal than the dream. Inexplicable, isn't it?

My eyes sweep over the white valley far below me one last time and I turn round, suddenly colder than I can bear and in a hurry to get away from here. When I pass the cherry orchard again, I see that the other walker has progressed to the near side of the cemetery. The black speck has become larger, taken shape, grown arms and legs, acquired a head and my husband's long body.

341

Truly. It's my husband who has come looking for me. *Come in out of the cold, my love.* He walks with his hands deep in the pockets of his old black leather jacket, one of our son's dark woollen caps pulled low over his forehead, my reddest scarf round his neck. So that I wouldn't miss him? Head bent low, eyes on the ground, deep in thought, following my winding footprints in the snow. *I will show you where to step.*

I raise my arm to wave at him. He looks up and stops a moment and waves back. It looks as though he's smiling, but it's too far away to be sure.

We walk slowly towards each other, careful not to slide in the snow.

ENTERTAINING ANGELS

'A real rarity ... funny, wry ... hard to resist.' *New York Times Book Review*

'Sharp, intelligent, provocative and honest, it's also very, very funny.' *Mail on Sunday*

'Heartbreaking enough to matter and risqué enough to make you laugh, shudder, or maybe both.' *Milwaukee Journal*

'One of the discoveries of the year. A magical tale, beautifully written and humorous. You'll be glued to every word.' *Company*

'For those who've encountered romantic travails, the kind of good company misery loves.' *The New Yorker*

'*Bridget Jones* with more brain cells and much more style ... real emotion and real humour ... a real book, for that matter.' *Cosmopolitan (France)*

'Unlike any fairy tales you've ever read ... funnier and more varied than Angela Carter's Freudian rewrites and subtler than Fay Weldon's wish-fulfillment fantasies ... A beguilingly fresh and optimistic look at life after marital breakdown.' *London Time Out*

'Funny, intelligent , and inventive ... A modern-day fairy tale with an irreverent feminist twist.' *Kirkus Reviews*

'Inventive ... puts a witty feminist spin on the brothers Grimm.' *Ms. Magazine*

'Delightfully loony.' *Booklist*

CHILDISH THINGS

'Van der Vyver writes perceptively about the delights and agonies of growing up.' *The Times*

'As complex as anything Margaret Atwood has written ... finely shaped, deliciously bitter-sweet novel.' *Mail and Guardian*

'Marita van der Vyver's exuberant, compassionate meditation on growing up is funny and occasionally heartbreaking.' *Mail on Sunday*

'Evocative, nostalgic portrait of the mid-seventies ... sometimes agonizing, sometimes hilarious, often profound.' *The Argus*

'A book to think about and read again.' *Brigitte (Germany)*

BREATHING SPACE

'Van der Vyver's compelling novel ... covers ten years in the lives of a group of ten friends ... counterpointing accounts of births, marriages, adulterous liaisons and deaths with the turbulent events taking place in the world outside. It all makes for an absolutely gripping read.' *The Times*

'Van der Vyver has written yet another important part of the documenting of our history and she has done it with grace and humanity.' *Cape Times*

'Marita van der Vyver is one of South Africa's greatest literary assets: she is able to create the atmosphere of a country in turmoil yet deal so skilfully with the characters involved that you could actually be in any country in the world.' *The Argus*

'A gripping encounter ... Van der Vyver's sensual style colours and crafts the novel.' *Pretoria News*

'A rich book, a multi-layered book, like a thickly-applied oil painting, where each stroke of viscous paint offers a different nuance and under-standing.' *The Argus*

'Another winner from a fine South African author.' *Cape Times*

'Breathing life into Afrikaans literature'. *South Africa Times UK*

'Engaging and authentic.' *Mail and Guardian*

TRAVELLING LIGHT

'Though it is written with a light and rapid touch, often irreverent and very funny, it is a profoundly satisfying read.' *Mail and Guardian*

'Van der Vyver writes with a light touch, amusing even when the subject matter is serious, and the peripheral characters are all beautifully drawn and make for a satisfying read.' *Natal Witness*

'It's a blast from beginning to end ... She writes well, has a wonderful sense of humour and tells a story of friends, family and lovers that's quite endearing.' *Pretoria News*

'Van der Vyver knows how to entertain. She also knows how to give real-life drama a magical twist.' *Femina*

'She examines the question of cross-cultural relationships and the chang-ing nature of South African society ... a wonderful read, arguably better than any of her previous novels.' *Mail and Guardian*